Booku

ALSO BY CHRISTOPHER NUTTALL

The Royal Sorceress

Bookworm

Christopher Nuttall

Elsewhen Press

Bookworm
First published in Great Britain by Elsewhen Press, 2013
An imprint of Alnpete Limited

Elsewhen Press, PO Box 757, Dartford, Kent DA2 7TQ
www.elsewhen.co.uk
British Library Cataloguing in Publication Data.
A catalogue record for this book is available from the British Library.
ISBN 978-1-908168-22-1 Print edition
ISBN 978-1-908168-32-0 eBook edition

Printed and bound by CPI Group (UK) Ltd, Croydon, CR0 4YY

To my wife Aisha, in love and gratitude

Prologue

Alone in the darkness, he waited.

He had long since become accustomed to the gloom, even though he cursed it with every breath he took through his ravaged throat. The power that had once raised him high – which had made him among the strongest of sorcerers, the masters of the world – was all that kept him alive. It was a bitter irony that all of his power, all of the secrets he had won through dangerous research into the limits of magic, could no longer be used for anything else. The final curse from his enemy or an unexpected gift from his own patrons, there was no way to know. All that mattered was that he could not die.

Time moved quickly in the unchanging darkness. It had been years as mortals reckoned time since his final, catastrophic defeat, yet he could not help playing and replaying the struggle for power over and over again in his mind. If he'd done this, if he'd done that...but the one thought he never allowed himself to have was what would have happened if he'd chosen to avoid the temptations magic promised. To be someone happy, but small; never to have involved himself with the destiny of the entire world...it was a fate worse than death, worse than facing the ten million devils baying for his soul. He could not have avoided his reach for power, even knowing his possible fate. Power was all that had driven him for a very long time.

It had driven him to ruin. He had long since overcome the pangs of hunger or thirst; his magic kept him alive, against all reason. His soul remained chained in a body permanently on the verge of death. Madness had threatened more than once, assailing his mind and offering permanent release from torment, yet he refused to take the final step and plunge into the abyss. He didn't want to die, or to lose himself. It was all that kept him together.

And there was the plan.

It had started life as a fantasy, one of many of the dreams of revenge that tormented him as he lay still and unmoving in the dark hall. He had returned to it again and again, until it had finally penetrated his mind that the plan was no fantasy. His power to influence the outside world was limited, subtle rather than the vast magical acts he had performed before his fall from grace, but it existed. Slowly, wary of signs that his enemies were waiting for him to reveal himself before destroying him, he reached out with his mind. Putting the pieces into play had required great care and the plan had come close to disaster more than once, but he was patient. His immortality, once a curse, allowed him to work slowly where mortal minds would have demanded speed.

A seed, planted in fertile soil. Promises made to those unable to see the long game. The slow corruption of those who believed themselves immune to vice. A hint of power here, an offer of wealth there...piece by piece, the tools came together. His influence reached back towards the home of his enemies and slowly intruded into their sphere. No one saw his hand behind a series of coincidences. They would never have believed in his existence without conclusive proof, and no one had laid eyes on him for hundreds of years.

And slowly, but surely, the endgame came into view.

It was time to knock over the first domino...

And then a mighty empire would come tumbling down.

Chapter One

The sun rose above the Watchtower, scattering rays of light down towards the Golden City below. As the light glittered off the shining temples, the voices of the priests rose in greeting to the morning light. The bells, each one a representation of a different god, rang out, sending a glistening crescendo across the city. It seemed to hang in the air, echoing off the five mountains that surrounded the metropolis, before slowly fading away into a deafening silence. In its wake, the sound of the city coming to life seemed dull and faded. Nothing could compete with the morning chorus.

Elaine No-Kin cursed the morning as she tried to close her eyes and go back to sleep. The tiny apartment seemed too warm, even in the mornings, but it was all that they were able to afford. She tossed and turned as she pulled the blanket back over her head, knowing that it was futile. It was already too late to go back to sleep. The sound of Daria getting up and coming into Elaine's room only reminded her that she had to get up herself.

"Get up, you lazy thing," Daria called, as she tugged at Elaine's blanket. "I don't think you dare be late again, do you?"

"No," Elaine said. She'd been reprimanded twice for being late, even though it hadn't really been her fault. But no one was interested in excuses, not in the Golden City. There was no shortage of trained, but untalented magicians to do the work their betters chose to ignore. "I don't want to be late at all."

Daria snorted as Elaine released the blankets. She was already standing in front of the mirror, studying her reflection as she donned her enchanted earrings and necklace. Elaine felt a hot flash of envy – her friend's redheaded looks brought no shortage of admirers – before swinging her legs off the bed and standing up. There was no time to waste admiring Daria, or cursing her own mundane appearance. She walked out of the bedroom and into the bathroom, splashing cold water on her face to wash away the last traces of drowsiness. There were spells to wake oneself up, without ill effects, but she'd never been able to master them.

And besides, the voice of one of her tutors whispered in her ear, *magic has a price...*

Elaine shrugged off the memory as she walked back and stood in front of the mirror, glaring at herself. She saw a mousy girl with light brown hair, dark eyes and a slightly oversized nose, one large enough to suggest that one of her parents – whoever they'd been – had been an aristocrat. It had certainly been suggested by the other children at the orphanage, and later by her classmates at the Peerless School. They'd taunted her for being motherless since the day they'd realised that no one was interested in adopting her. In truth, Elaine wasn't entirely sure why she'd been accepted into the Peerless School. Her magical talent was very limited, barely more than any hedge witch. A hedge witch would probably be more useful than her to anyone who needed genuine magic.

She pulled off her nightdress and reached for her tunic and shirt. As a graduate of the Peerless School, she was entitled to wear black, but she'd never felt the urge to show off her very limited talent. Instead, she wore subdued brown that matched her hair. It was strictly functional. She didn't have the money to waste on adorning herself.

"I may be home late tonight," Daria said. "Jade was talking about going to the Arena, and then to one of his favourite eateries. And after that...who knows?"

Elaine felt herself flush. An upbringing in the orphanage hadn't prepared her for the life of a free woman in the Golden City, although she didn't really want to go out dancing and enjoying herself with young men. Or so she told herself; in truth, part of her would have loved to go out and just lose all of her inhibitions. She looked over at Daria, who was donning a red dress that showed off enough of her legs and chest to make Elaine blush. Her friend seemed to have a knack for meeting people and making friends that Elaine lacked.

"Have fun," she said, automatically. Daria didn't notice, but then she never did. She was a good friend, perhaps the best friend Elaine had, yet she never seemed to notice when anything was wrong. "Try not to catch anything you don't want to catch."

Daria chuckled as she headed into the small kitchen. "I'll keep myself safe," she promised. "And you'd better be off. Miss Prim will have you transfigured into something more useful if you're late again."

Elaine nodded, picking up her wand and placing it into the small holster hidden within her sleeve. Most magicians hid their wands in dimensional pockets, where they could be retrieved at a moment's notice, but Elaine had never had the skill or patience for such complex spells. Besides, it sometimes came in handy not to have to cast a spell to recover her wand. Without it, she was barely capable of any magic at all.

"Have fun," she said, again. Daria *was* her friend, after all. "I'll try not to wait up for you."

The hex on the door hissed at her as she placed her hand on the knob, reluctantly recognising her signature and allowing her to exit. Even combining their resources, they hadn't been able to afford an apartment in the better parts of the city, not when the entire population of the Empire seemed determined to move to the Golden City. The landlord charged incredibly high rates, too high for her to afford if she were to lose her job. She silently cursed him as she walked down the stairs and out onto the streets. Whatever he did with the money he collected from his tenants, it didn't include renovating the apartments. There was no security hex on the outer door.

As always, the streets were crowded with people trying to get to their workplaces or merely wandering the city, enjoying their chance to see the Empire's capital. Elaine had to smile at the expressions on some of their faces as they gawked around, looking up at the Watchtower or down towards the Imperial Palace. History had been made in the Golden City, from the First Necromantic War to the disappearance of the Lost Prince. On every corner, a statue of some nobleman from the wars or particularly legendary wizard seemed to gaze down disapprovingly at the tourists infesting the streets. In their days, Elaine was certain, the Golden City had been truly golden.

She walked along the streets, careful to ignore the horses and carts as the aristocracy headed towards the Imperial Palace to start playing politics with the Regency Council and the Grand Sorcerer. There had been a time when she'd wondered if her magical talent would be enough to win her a place among the rich and powerful, but like all of her dreams it had come crashing down into dust. She simply didn't have the talent to serve as a Court Wizard, helping to maintain the fragile peace in the Empire, or as an Alchemist working to push back the boundaries of magical knowledge. All she was...was a librarian.

It wasn't a bad job, really. Books had always fascinated her, even as a child. The orphanage had had quite a few books and her guardians had insisted that she learn to read, believing that it would be easier for her to attract a family who might adopt her. That had never happened, even as she grew older, but she'd never lost the fascination for books. And if she couldn't afford her own collection – even the new-fangled printed books were expensive – at least she could work with them in the Great Library. It was a position of great responsibility. Miss Prim had told her so time and time again.

"Read all about it!" one of the broadsheet criers shouted, breaking into her thoughts. "Duke of Tara to visit the Golden City! May be engaged to Princess Lorraine! Read all about it!"

Elaine ignored the proffered paper and strode past the crier. She wasn't entirely sure that she approved of demeaning the printing press by publishing stories about the rich and famous, but she had to admit that it was encouraging people to read. Not that they always printed the truth, of course. Even in her position, she knew the underlying reason why the Duke of Tara would be visiting the Golden City – and it didn't have anything to do with asking the Regency Council's permission to wed anyone. The Grand Sorcerer, the supreme authority in the Empire, was dying. And if the

Duke happened to be in the Golden City when the Grand Sorcerer died, he'd be in a position to influence the outcome of the contest to select the next Grand Sorcerer.

The thought made her look up towards the Imperial Palace, a dark building of towering, brooding stone. No Emperor resided there now, not after the Second Necromantic War. Officially, the royal bloodline had died out when the Witch-King made his desperate grab for supreme power before unleashing a nightmare across the entire world. Unofficially, there was supposed to be a missing heir – but no one had come forward and successfully claimed the Throne. A vast number of pretenders had certainly *tried* over the years, but they'd sat on the Golden Throne and had never been seen again. The Throne, it was said, knew the true royal bloodline. No substitutions were accepted.

She halted as she turned the corner, just long enough for a line of soldiers to march past and down towards the Watchtower, positioned on the North Peak. Elaine had read enough history to know that the Watchtower had saved the city during the First Necromantic War, but had been destroyed and rebuilt during the Second War – after which it had been maintained by the Regency Council. There was no threat to the Empire, at least as far as she knew, but doubtless they had their reasons. It was also a none-too-subtle reminder of their power, of the mailed fist within the velvet glove. The Golden City was the Empire's capital. No disturbance could be tolerated within its walls.

The last of the soldiers tramped off into the distance, followed by a small number of young boys with dreams of becoming soldiers themselves. Elaine shook her head in wry amusement at their antics, before glancing up at the position of the sun. She was running late and she really needed to move more quickly. Miss Prim would definitely not be happy if she were late. Thanking the gods for her decision to wear her tunic, rather than a long skirt, she started to move as quickly as she dared. The crowds pressed in around her, seeming to grow thicker as she approached the centre of the city. They'd been joined by small children on their way to school, escorted by their mothers or, in some cases, the family slaves. Elaine shivered when she saw them, remembering her tutors at the orphanage. They'd threatened to sell her into slavery if she didn't behave herself.

She allowed herself a small pause for breath as the Great Library came into view. It was a towering building, although not as tall as the Imperial Palace, surrounded by statues of famous Alchemists. The statues remained still as long as people were watching them, but they seemed to move slightly when they were unobserved. They were part of the Great Library's defences against unwanted intruders, but they had always given her the creeps. The statues seemed to hate her somehow, even though she couldn't have explained why. It was probably a reflection of her own limited sensitivity to magic.

The massive stone doors opened for her as she approached, recognising her magical signature as one who was allowed access. Successive Grand Sorcerers hadn't been inclined to place all their faith in the statues, no matter how many enchantments had been used to make them obedient and invincible guardians. The Great Library was protected with layer after layer of defensive spells, some bluntly obvious to even the merest of magicians, some so subtle and deadly that any would-be thief would have no opportunity to realise that they were there until it was far too late. Even the Peerless School, a building designed to contain magical accidents caused by trainee sorcerers, was less well defended than the Library. But then, the magical knowledge stored within the stone walls was the source of the Empire's power. It could not be allowed to fall into the wrong hands.

Inside, the cool dry air left her feeling uncomfortably sweaty as she ran through the corridors, feeling them twisting and turning around her. The interior of the building lay within a pocket dimension, making it literally bigger on the inside than on the outside. Elaine had been told that the Great Library was actually *alive*, at least on some level, but she'd never been able to sense any governing presence. Perhaps it was just too subtle for her senses to detect, or perhaps it didn't talk to mere humans. The Great Library had outlasted both of the Necromantic Wars and many other conflicts besides.

The corridors straightened out suddenly and she found

herself in the foyer. It was a luxuriously decorated room, covered with paintings of librarians through the ages, but there was no mistaking its purpose. Not *everyone* could be allowed access to the Great Library, or all of the collections housed within its walls. Students from the Peerless School, Senior Wizards, the Regency Council...they had access. Everyone else had to apply to the Head Librarian and convince her that they deserved to enter the Great Library. One day, Elaine told herself, she'd be in that position of power. It was an oddly cheerless thought.

"Elaine," a stern voice said. Elaine froze, and then tried to calm herself. "What have I told you about being late?"

Elaine held back several different answers and did her best to look contrite. "I'm sorry, Miss Prim," she said. "The roads were crowded today."

Miss Prim glowered at her. She was a tall woman, old enough to be Elaine's grandmother – and a slave, bound to the Great Library. From the rumours Elaine had heard, Miss Prim – not her real name, but one foisted on her by the Grand Sorcerer – had been one of the more successful would-be thieves who tried to steal books from the Library. After she'd been caught red-handed, she'd been enslaved – and, as punishment, assigned to the Library she'd tried to rob. The spell binding her wouldn't allow her to leave, or to do a bad job.

"We are going to have to do something about your lateness, my girl," Miss Prim said, severely. Her voice had a knack for cutting through to the heart of any issue. "It really is quite unacceptable. The demand on our services has been rising over the last few months..."

As the Grand Sorcerer prepares to meet the gods, Elaine thought, sourly. Every Senior Wizard in the world would be considering their own bid to become Grand Sorcerer. They'd be studying, brushing up on their spells – and making contacts with other wizards and even the mundane community. Power was a drug to many wizards and the position of Grand Sorcerer was the most powerful position in the world.

"...And so I expect better from you," Miss Prim concluded. "Consider yourself lucky that we are no longer in the habit of beating our inferiors. I suggest that you go get yourself suitably presentable for doing your job. You're going to be assisting some of the very best wizards in the city."

Elaine nodded as she walked through the foyer and into the small office behind the desk. The Great Library had a dozen reading rooms and a hundred different open collections, but few of the visitors would be interested in books they could buy for themselves. No, they'd be interested in the restricted volumes, the ones kept firmly under lock and key. Some of them would even try to convince her to retrieve books from the Black Vault, despite the Grand Sorcerer's edict forbidding access without permission from the Regency Council. Elaine found herself silently praying that none of them would be foolish enough to turn nasty if she had to refuse their demands. The Great Library itself took care of any troublemakers, but the effects had an unpleasant tendency to spill over onto unsuspecting bystanders.

She donned the grey smock worn by library staff and took a moment to check her hair. There were a dozen other assistants in the Library at any one time, scattered through the reading rooms and at helpdesks. Despite herself, Elaine knew that the job was important – and it required a special class of person, someone who could be trusted not to abuse the access granted to them by the Library. In her case, it hardly mattered how many forbidden tomes she read, whatever the rules said. She simply didn't have the power to utilise many of the spells other wizards used daily, let alone dark spells that hadn't been used since the Necromantic Wars.

"Room Thirteen," Miss Prim said, when Elaine emerged from the office. "Daphne's on the desk, but she needs help finding material. Too many wizards up there and they're getting impatient."

"Yes, Miss Prim," Elaine said. She turned and walked down the corridor. Sometimes, the corridors shifted, seemingly at random, but this time the Library seemed inclined to remain still. Room Thirteen was larger than the foyer, with a handful of desks manned by grumpy wizards reading older books and making notes. A small line of wizards stood in front of the main desk, waiting impatiently for their turn. Elaine walked around the desk and looked up at the first in line – and realised, too late, that it was someone she already knew.

"Frogeye," a delighted voice said. "How nice to see you again."

Elaine wanted to sink into the floor. Of all the people who had to visit the Great Library – and who she had to serve personally – it just had to be Millicent. The one person she'd met whom she never wanted to see again.

Wonderful, she thought, bitterly. *This day just keeps getting better and better.*

Chapter Two

"Millicent," Elaine said. "I..."

"I am absolutely *delighted* to see you, Frogeye," Millicent said. She ran one hand through her long blonde hair, calling attention to the shamefully tight white shirt she was wearing. "This...*girl* wasn't going to give me what I wanted."

Elaine winced, inwardly. Millicent, blonde, beautiful and with a magical pedigree as long as her arm, had decided to hate her from the day that Elaine had been accepted to the Peerless School. A young orphan girl couldn't help Millicent with her carefully-planned career, so Millicent had felt free to pick on Elaine for five years of hell. Elaine remembered – she couldn't forget – days when she'd discovered that someone had stolen her supplies, trapped her wand and scribbled on her books. And the week she'd spent as a frog after Millicent had decided to practice her transfiguration on an unsuspecting victim. No wonder Daphne had been uncooperative. Millicent had a remarkable talent for irritating people.

"Here," Millicent said, thrusting a sheet of paper at Elaine. "I want these books, *now*."

Elaine scanned the list, wishing that she was strong enough to stand up to Millicent. But Millicent only respected magical power and good breeding and Elaine had neither. No one knew who her parents had been, or why they'd chosen to abandon their daughter, but Millicent hadn't hesitated to draw a possible conclusion. Illegitimate children were still regarded as shameful, even ones who showed signs of magical power. And Elaine's power had never been significant enough to convince her unknown parents to change their minds.

"You want *all* of these books?" Elaine asked, in surprise. None of them were on the prohibited list for a fully-qualified sorceress, but they were all alarmingly close to the line.

Some of them had only been one vote from being added to the Black Vault. "Do you have...?"

Millicent grinned as she produced a scroll and passed it over to Elaine. "My aunt, Lady Light Spinner, the *next* Grand Sorcerer, was kind enough to grant me permission to study how I liked," she said. "Now hop to it, Frogeye, or you'll be hopping around for the rest of the day."

Elaine rebelled the only way she could, by studying the parchment carefully. Lady Light Spinner *was* known to her, although she hadn't realised that Millicent was actually her niece – but then, the family ties between the senior wizards were often confusing. And she *did* have the authority to permit Millicent to study any tome outside the Black Vault itself. Elaine checked the magical seal, doing her best to ignore Millicent's twitching wand arm, and then passed it back to her tormentor. Maybe she could take longer than she would normally have done to locate all the books.

"It seems to be in order," she said, blandly. "Why don't you take a seat and wait while I go find the books?"

"I'm in Room Fourteen," Millicent said, flatly. "Bring them to me there. I shall have others ready for you to find by then."

She swept out of the reading room, leaving Elaine staring after her in helpless rage. Millicent had always been a bitch, but then she'd had the breeding and magical power to back it up. She hadn't even been significantly punished after the frog incident, even though the Administrator himself had lectured her in front of the entire school. A less well-connected girl might well have been expelled, or forced to serve as the test subject for junior potions. Shaking her head, she picked up the list and skimmed through it again. Some of the items on the list were definitely not books she wanted Millicent to read.

But there was no choice. Leaving Daphne behind in the reading room, she stepped into the office and through the hanging mirror on the wall. Like most magical buildings, the Great Library had a reflection within the mirrors, an alternate dimension that could only be accessed by its staff. Elaine felt her head swim as she entered the mirror world and looked around. Great stacks of books lay everywhere, some covered with dust that suggested they hadn't been touched for a thousand years. There were some books, Elaine knew, that hadn't been opened even during the worst days of the Necromantic Wars. Miss Prim had told her that the sorcerers of those days had feared the secrets within the books far more than they'd feared the Witch-King and his armies of undead servants.

Where the mundane world had the reading rooms and other compartments for the staff, the mirrored world had endless rooms of books. Elaine picked up the list, selected the first title, and concentrated, allowing the magic in the Great Library to guide her to the book. It had been stuffed into a nearby room and buried under a pile of other dusty tomes, as if the last user had taken care to hide it from casual view. Only the staff – and the senior wizards – were permitted access to the mirrored dimension, and the magic in the Library made it impossible to hide anything permanently, but someone had definitely tried to conceal it. Elaine glanced at the title as she pulled it out from its hiding place, shaking her head. A tome on ways to boost one's own power reserves by uniting with other magicians was the last thing Millicent should have needed. Elaine knew, to her everlasting regret, that Millicent had power to spare. And why would her aunt have given her permission to read the books anyway?

She mulled over the question as she found the other books on the list. One of them was on transfiguration, ways to maintain a change long enough for reality to catch up with the spell, while another was on ways to brew complicated potions. Two of the books were written in a language that had been dead and gone for a thousand years, although a simple translation spell would allow Millicent to read them. And one of them talked about bargains that could be made with the gods. Elaine smiled savagely as she added that one to the growing pile of books. There were enough cautionary tales about magicians who tried to bargain with the gods to make her hope that was what Millicent had in mind. But then, Millicent was good at avoiding blame for her actions. Maybe she'd manage to charm the gods too.

One of the books was out already, according to the Library. It was a strange book, one that discussed ways to tame magical creatures like werewolves and mermaids, at least according to Millicent's notes. Elaine suspected that it was actually something far darker. They'd learned about potions that could be made by someone with access to werewolf fur, or mermaid scales, potions that were quite definitely on the forbidden list. But Millicent would have to wait for it, she told herself as she walked back towards the mirror. There were strict rules against disturbing one patron because another wanted a book.

The mirror flickered around her as she stepped back into the normal world, carrying the books with her. Millicent had said that she would be in Room Fourteen, naturally. Room Fourteen was normally reserved for senior wizards and while Millicent didn't count as a senior wizard, no one was likely to argue with Lady Light Spinner's favourite niece. The door opened as Elaine approached, spying Millicent seated on one of the comfortable chairs and reading through one of the older catalogues. They dated back to the time before one of the first librarians had designed the spells that automatically updated the catalogues when a book was added to the Library's stock. No book was ever allowed to *leave* the Great Library, even one that had been thoroughly disproved by later research. The very thought was blasphemous.

"There's an article in *Alchemical Monthly* about a new version of Luminous Potion," Millicent said, in an almost friendly tone. And then she reverted to form. "But you wouldn't care about that, would you? Your potion skills were non-existent."

Elaine ignored her as best she could. Millicent was right, of course. Elaine hadn't had great success with potions, although surprisingly few students became Potion Masters. It required skill, patience and innate talent, all traits that Elaine lacked. But she'd managed to master enough potions to pass her exams, even if she hadn't made any of them since she'd left the Peerless School. Even the potions designed to help with female issues were easier – and safer – to buy from a local apothecary.

But she *was* a good librarian. "Your books," she said, shortly. "I'm afraid that one of them is currently out on loan to one of the other readers, but I'll pick it up for you when it is returned."

Surprisingly, Millicent didn't choose to make an issue of it. "Leave them here, Frogeye," she said, taking the first book from the stack and blowing off the dust. "And here's the next list."

Elaine sighed. "I'll go find them for you," she said, wearily.

"Hop to it," Millicent said. She chuckled, as if she hadn't been making the same joke for three years. "I'll let you know when I need you."

She kept Elaine busy for nearly an hour before Miss Prim finally arrived and ordered Elaine to deal with someone else. Elaine, relieved, spent the rest of the morning in a different part of the Library, dealing with customers who all seemed to want to brush up on their spells and studies of ancient magic. Maybe it did make a certain kind of sense, she resolved, after finding yet another pile of books. The Grand Sorcerer was dying, after all. Millicent had mentioned that her aunt would be the next Grand Sorceress, suggesting that Lady Light Spinner definitely intended to try to compete herself. Elaine couldn't think of that as anything other than bad news. If Millicent was unbearable now, what would she be like if her aunt became the Grand Sorceress?

The question nagged at her mind as she took a break and then walked down to the workroom below the main Library. Miss Prim kept her staff moving from position to position, ensuring that they had the experience to take on any role at a moment's notice. Elaine had been told to start examining a new consignment of books that had been left to the Library, but she hadn't had time to start on it for several days. It was a relief to finally have a chance to get to work on the boxes. This was *real* librarianship.

Every magician in the world – and everyone who fancied themselves a magician – collected books on magic. There were thousands of copies of some common spellbooks, along with books on theory and books on creatures that had been touched by magic. None of *them* were on the prohibited index, although it wasn't unknown for a long-lost copy of a prohibited book to emerge when a dead would-be magician's collection was examined. Some of the books had been very dangerous, only prevented from causing harm by the fact that their owner barely had enough magic to light a candle. According to Miss Prim, several copies of *Shade's Darkest Shadow* had only been found when the boxes of books had been opened in the Great Library. Elaine knew better than to doubt her.

She'd run through the standard curse and hex detection spells when the boxes had arrived in the Great Library, but she ran through them again before she picked up the first box and deposited it on her worktable. Nothing showed up as dangerous, which didn't mean anything; it was easy enough to conceal a hex from most of the detection spells. Elaine braced herself and muttered an incantation under her breath. The spells that bound the box together came apart, allowing her to remove the wood and stack it up neatly in one corner. Inside, a small pile of books awaited her attention. She paused, long enough to enjoy the thrill of not knowing what she'd find inside the box, and then picked up the first book. It was disappointing. *Common Magic* was a standard reference work for students, but even Elaine had long since surpassed it.

Shaking her head, she reached for the notes that recorded where the books had come from and skimmed through them. Duke Gama, the younger brother of King Hildebrand, had fancied himself a magician, like many of the younger nobility. No real power, according to the notes, but that hadn't stopped him buying up every magical book he could lay his hands on. Some of the less scrupulous traders had probably enriched themselves at his expense, Elaine realised, as she pulled up a pair of books that were known hoaxes. Duke Gama hadn't had the experience or magic to tell when someone was trying to con him into buying worthless parchment. Elaine put the two books to one side, marked for disposal. The Great Library's laws against not throwing out books didn't apply to books of false spells and non-existent powers. No wonder Duke Gama hadn't achieved anything when he'd tried to work magic.

The next book was much more interesting – and, like Millicent's reading list, one step short of prohibited. *Naming of Demons* should have been on the prohibited list, but there were so many copies out in the world that even the Inquisition regarded attempting to track them all down as futile. There were no instructions on how one could *summon* demons, yet merely knowing their names and natures could give a lucky amateur a chance at calling them up from the darkness. Elaine glanced at two of the pages, shook her head at some of the illustrations, and then placed it on the trolley. Miss Prim would have to inspect the copy, determine if it was identical to the others stored within the Great Library, and then decide what to do with it. She'd undoubtedly end up adding it to the Library's collection. Duke Gama's ghost would probably be pleased at the thought.

The next five books were cheap trash from a basement printer, a series of hopelessly unrealistic novels about a wizard who seemed to have so much power that it was hard to see how he ever had any problems at all. Elaine remembered reading a couple of them while she'd been in school, only to marvel at how many inaccuracies the unknown writer had managed to stuff into a handful of slim volumes. Even the Grand Sorcerer would have had problems matching the hero's spell-casting ability, although maybe he would have had as many girls throwing themselves at him as the hero. Magical talents bred true; everyone knew that. She felt herself flush as she recalled an offer made to her by one of Millicent's peers, a magician with more magic in his little finger than Elaine had in her entire body. He'd thought that she would jump at the chance to have his baby.

She added the novels to the pile for disposal and then picked up the next book – and found herself flushing again. *A Guide To Sex Magic* wasn't anywhere near the prohibited list, even though it was one of the more dangerous books ever written – if used by someone who didn't know what they were doing. It was possible to use sex to generate magical power – the illustrations left absolutely nothing to the imagination – but it required intense concentration and a dedication that surpassed even the most sour-faced of Potion Masters. Her generation of magical students had preferred to pass dog-eared copies around and use them as props when trying to pick up the opposite sex. Memories of the days when some of the boys had discovered copies and tried to talk the girls into bed – for research purposes, naturally – left her flushing darker. Why did some people, like Millicent, manage to glide their way through life when others, like Elaine, just kept stumbling?

The final book caught her eye and she picked it up, puzzled. There was no title on the front, not even one of the glyphs that some wizards used to represent their names. It was a small book, almost the size of the diary she'd tried to keep at the orphanage before two of the older girls had stolen it and put it down the toilet. She turned it over and over in her hand, trying to see how to release the pages from the spell holding them together. Had Duke Gama stumbled upon one of the spells that writers used to keep their works secure? Or had someone else done the spell for him? Every kingdom was supposed to have a Court Wizard representing the Grand Sorcerer – and making sure that none of the local rulers harboured dreams of rebelling against the magical order. Surely Duke Gama could have convinced the Court Wizard to cast the spell for him.

She muttered an incantation under her breath and was surprised when the book refused to open. A second spell produced no other effect, nor did a third. That *was* a surprise; it suggested that the spell on the book was personalised, perhaps complex enough to be the work of a senior wizard. Elaine knew that some wizards used similar spells to keep their work from being read by their peers, but she'd never heard of a non-wizard being able to use such a spell. Surely...

The book seemed to flicker with magic. Elaine felt it, a sudden sense of something *uncurling* from within the book. She wanted to drop it as the magic field suddenly spiked, but her hand refused to let go of the pages. There was a brilliant flash of light, a sense that something was being pushed into her head, and then she crashed down into darkness.

Chapter Three

...There was fire...and ice...and someone was calling her name...and she wanted to call back, but her voice was tiny against the roaring that filled the air...and strange memories that weren't hers were raging through her mind...and...and...and...

"Elaine!"

Elaine's eyes snapped open. She was lying in bed, her head spinning as if someone had slapped her several times. Her mind felt thick and congested, her thoughts moving slowly through her brain. It took her what felt like hours to recognise the face bending over her and then it seemed to take hours more before she could reply.

"Dar...Daria?"

"You're awake," Daria said. Her friend leaned down and gave her a hug. "What happened to you?"

Elaine found herself struggling to recall. She'd been at the Library, she'd served Millicent and a dozen others, and then she'd opened Duke Gama's box...and then nothing. But her mind felt as if she'd spent years cramming for a single exam, yet could no longer remember even what she'd been cramming for. She felt faint, even as she struggled to sit upright. Where was she? And what had happened to her?

"I...I don't know," she said, struggling to look around. She wasn't at home, wherever she was. The bed was in a small room, illuminated only by a single glowing bulb of light. A hospital, perhaps, except she could hardly afford to pay for treatment. What had happened to her in the Library? "What happened to me?"

Daria looked down at her, her large eyes worried. "They found you in your workroom, slumped over the table," she said. "Something sounded the alarm and called them to help you. But you were completely stunned, so they brought you to the Merciful Rest. I hear that Miss Prim is going to be picking up the bill for your stay."

Elaine stared at her. "How long...how long have I been out?"

"Four days," another voice said, from behind her. Elaine looked up to see a tall thin man, wearing a long white robe. A druid, she realised; a sorcerer who specialised in medical treatment. "Whatever hit you hit you very hard. It must have been a very powerful curse bound into that volume."

A memory flashed into Elaine's mind. There had been a sealed book, held closed by a charm...and she'd tried to open it. And then...nothing.

"I thought we were going to lose you that first day," the druid added. "None of our treatments seemed to work, but thankfully you started to come out of it on your own. Is there a god of librarians who might have protected you?"

"I don't know," Elaine admitted. There was a god for just about everything, but she couldn't recall one specifically for librarians. Her head was refusing to clear. She hated having headaches at the best of times, yet this was far worse than anything she had ever experienced. "But if there is, I will light a candle in thanks."

"That would be a good idea," the druid agreed, dryly. He produced a wand from his sleeve and started to run it up and down her body. "Most of the curse seems to have dissipated on its own, but I'd recommend a few more days of rest. Stay away from magic too – this curse seemed to have tried to hijack your own magic and galvanise it into attacking you. You *were* very lucky. Something of that power should have killed."

"I don't understand," Elaine said, slowly. "I *checked* for deadly spells."

"Some of the black magicians who create new curses are very good at hiding them from our detection spells," the druid said. There was an odd note in his voice, one that promised blood and pain for any dark magician he caught. "I'd give a great deal to meet the bastard who invented this one. My best guess is that it was really nothing more than a standard compulsion spell, but with enough power to slip right into your mind and try to force you to commit suicide. Now, I'm going to put you back to sleep and..."

Elaine opened her mouth, but it was too late. His wand touched her forehead and she was out like a light.

***

The next time she opened her eyes, it was daylight. Bright sunlight was streaming in through a window she hadn't noticed the last time she'd been awake. Her head felt better, although it still seemed as though there was something jammed inside her mind. Elaine sat up in bed and looked around, half-hoping that Daria was sitting next to her bedside. But there was no sign of her friend. Instead, there was a jug of orange-flavoured juice and a small gourd of potion for her to drink.

She looked over at the door as another druid stepped inside. He was older than the first druid, with a long white beard that hung down to his legs, but his eyes were kind and Elaine liked him on sight. One hand held another gourd of potion, which he passed over to her and motioned for her to drink it. It tasted foul, but somehow she found herself thirsty enough to swallow it all down. He picked up a glass of juice and passed it to her. Elaine swallowed gratefully. It tasted far better than the potion.

"I should hope so," he said, when she pointed that out. "I don't want people drinking more of my potion than they need. It can be addictive to those with weak minds."

He sat down beside the bed and looked at her. "How are you feeling now?"

"Strange," Elaine admitted. "What...what happened to me?"

"Someone cursed you, as far as we can tell," the druid said. He seemed unaware that the other druid had told her the same thing. "We had to feed you ourselves over the past few days, before you finally recovered enough for us to risk allowing you to awaken. I'm afraid that you're going to have a few more rough days ahead of you."

He shrugged. "And there's an Inquisitor who wants to have a few words with you," he added. "Do you feel well enough to talk to him?"

Elaine stared at the druid. "An Inquisitor?"

"I don't think that you're in any trouble," the druid said,

hastily. Very few people ever wanted to meet an Inquisitor, let alone find themselves on the receiving end of an Inquisition. The Inquisitors answered to the Grand Sorcerer alone and had wide powers to investigate suspected breaches of the Mage's Code. "The curse was powerful enough to warrant immediate investigation. Whoever set that trap might be setting other traps for unwary mages."

Elaine remembered the boxes from Duke Gama she hadn't opened and shivered. "I understand," she said. She doubted that she'd ever feel well enough to talk to an Inquisitor, but it was something she had to do. "Tell him...tell him that I'm ready to talk to him."

"I have told him that your condition may still be serious," the druid said. "If you feel distressed, just tell him to leave. Even an Inquisitor has limited power in my building."

He stood up and walked to the door. "I can call your friend," he added. "If you should happen to want company...?"

"Yes, please," Elaine said, quickly. Daria had been with her, hadn't she? And she was the only friend Elaine had in the Golden City. "When can I go home?"

"Maybe in a few more days," the druid said, as he opened the door. "I'd prefer to keep you under observation for a while. Whatever hit you was *new* and we had to guess at the correct way to treat you. The next person might not be so lucky."

He left the room. A moment later, the door opened again and the Inquisitor stepped into the room. Like all sorcerers who wished to advertise their nature, he wore long black robes and carried a wand at his belt, but unlike most magicians he wore a single ring on his ring hand, a silver skull. His face was stony, half-hidden behind a charm that prevented his features from being clearly seen. Elaine had never been so close to an Inquisitor and had to fight the urge to back away as he sat down beside her bed. His unseen eyes seemed to be staring right into her soul.

"You are not in any trouble," he said, in a surprisingly gentle voice, "but we do need to know what happened to you. I am Inquisitor Dread."

He paused, as if he expected her to recognise the name. All

Inquisitors abandoned their birth names when they graduated and put on the silver skull that marked their rank, although very little was known about how they were trained by their superiors. There had been any number of rumours, including some that suggested that demons were involved somewhere, but Elaine knew nothing for sure. Dread didn't seem to want anything from her in return, even her name. But then he probably knew everything about her already.

His voice darkened, slightly. "How much do you remember?"

Elaine had to think back carefully. All of her memories appeared to be slippery, sliding away from her the moment she tried to recall them. "I...I was opening a box from Duke Gama," she said, finally. Had Duke Gama been a real magician? She couldn't imagine anyone wanting to use a curse to seal up a book unless it was their own curse. "There was an unmarked book in the box..."

The Inquisitor reached into his robes and produced a book. "This book?"

"Yes," Elaine said, staring. How had he managed to take it out of the Library? Miss Prim would have had quite a few things to say about it...but he *was* an Inquisitor. And he worked for the Grand Sorcerer himself. "I...I tried to open it and then..."

Her mind refused to recall anything past that point. There had been something, but what?

"There was a curse of some kind woven into the book's pages," Dread said. He seemed more interested in the curse than the effect it had had on her, but Elaine supposed she couldn't blame him for that. "Most of it had dispelled itself by the time I examined it carefully. I think it must have been intended to murder whoever opened it without permission."

Elaine shivered. Just how close had she come to death? "But...but Duke Gama wasn't a real magician," she said, finally. "How did he make the curse?"

"A very good question," Dread agreed, gravely. He peered down at the book, flipping through an endless series of blank pages. "It is possible that the Duke received tutoring from a rogue magician instead of the Peerless School. Given his rank, it is unlikely that he would have been accepted at the school even if he had applied. But it is equally possible that a black magician cast the spell for him and he trusted in his own precautions to prevent the book falling into the wrong hands. His decision to send the books to the Great Library after his death might have been intended to prevent his brother or nephew from trying to open the book."

Elaine nodded, slowly.

"But we will be following up on this as a matter of urgency," Dread added, before Elaine could speak. "If someone else produced the curse for him, who knows what *else* he may have done in the years between his work for the Duke and the Duke's death?"

His lips twitched into a humourless smile. "Do you have any idea what the curse was intended to do?"

"Not really," Elaine said. "I thought that it was nothing more than a lock to keep unwanted people from reading his private thoughts."

Dread looked at her for a long moment. "Perhaps I misspoke," he said. There was an odd note of puzzlement in his voice. "Do you know what the curse was intended to do?"

Elaine felt her mouth opening before she quite realised what was happening. There were whispered stories about Inquisitors, about how they possessed voices that could command obedience from anyone, no matter how powerful they were. He could have ordered Elaine to throw herself at his feet and do anything and she would have obeyed. She couldn't have lied to him, even if she had *wanted* to lie to him. Elaine had experienced compulsion spells before – Millicent and her cronies had thought them a terrific joke – but this was different, far more powerful than anything she'd ever known.

"No, sir," she said, quietly. "I don't know what it was intended to do."

"I had to be sure," Dread said. There was no apology in his voice, even though she felt violated on a level that no one, not even Millicent, could have matched. He might have thought that it was justified and maybe he was right, but Elaine disagreed. How *dare* he do that to anyone? "The druids inform me that you will recover in the next few days.

I have spoken to your superior and convinced her to allow you two weeks to recuperate from your ordeal. Should you learn anything else about the curse that struck you, you will of course contact the Inquisition at once."

There was no compulsion in his voice this time, but it was an order. "Yes, sir," she said, as he stood up. "Will you be sending someone to visit King Hildebrand?"

"There *will* be an investigation," Dread assured her. He walked over to the door and then stopped. "I suggest that you spend the next two weeks in bed. It will improve your chances of making a full recovery."

Elaine hesitated, and then decided to gamble. "Inquisitor," she said, slowly, "they say that the Inquisition knows everything."

"We certainly like to give that impression," Dread agreed. "But you must realise that our knowledge is not to be shared."

"I just wanted to ask," Elaine said, hating just how vulnerable she sounded. "Do you know who my parents were?"

Dread, for a moment, looked almost kindly. "I'm afraid that that piece of knowledge isn't known to the Inquisition," he said. "If there had been something...scandalous about your birth, we might have had a record, but there was nothing that my predecessors knew about when you were born."

Elaine flushed. Of course there hadn't been. It wasn't as if she was the secret love child of the Grand Sorcerer and the Dark Witch. Her magical talent was so weak that it was quite likely that her parents had had no magical talent of their own. And if she'd been born to a prostitute in the Golden City, her mother might have believed that she would have a better life in the orphanage than on the streets. But that wouldn't have attracted the Inquisition's attention. Why should it have?

"Thank you," she said, and sank back into the covers.

The next thing she realised was that Daria was standing beside her bed. "You look much better," her friend said. "The druids said that you could go home in a day or two. I've missed you dreadfully..."

"You missed having me to help clean up after your latest boyfriend," Elaine said, and tried to tell herself that she wasn't bitter. She could have had a boy of her own, if it wasn't so completely inconceivable that a boy would be interested in her. "You should get him to help with the cleaning."

"You can't ever trust a guy to do the cleaning," Daria said, dryly. "Besides, he only wanted one thing and didn't even bother to attend to *my* needs, so I dumped him. I should have taken him shopping first before inviting him to bed."

"I didn't think that you had the money to go shopping," Elaine said, trying to sit up. Her head was threatening to split open again. "Or did you happen to find something so interesting that they gave you a bonus?"

"I can still go look," Daria said. "You should try looking at clothes instead of those books you love to read. Clothes make the woman, don't you know?"

She shrugged. "Anyway...what happened to you?"

Elaine opened her mouth to say what little she knew, just before she felt something unlocking itself in her mind. She let out a yelp as new knowledge flooded her brain, leaving her feeling as if she'd finally understood something she should have realised all along. The curse that had been used to secure the book...hadn't been *intended* to secure the book. It had been waiting for someone to pick up the book in the right place...

...Each of the steps involved with crafting the curse flooded into her mind. A simple spell to deflect anyone without enough magic to energise the rest of the curse, followed by a series of complicated incantations that seemed to have been designed for the Great Library. As if the first realisation had been enough to unlock the second, she realised that the curse had somehow reached out, using *her* magic, to absorb the entire collected knowledge of the Great Library. Millions of books, hundreds of thousands of spells...all crammed within her skull. She screamed out loud as the knowledge blazed through her mind, knowledge that the senior wizards had locked away long ago. Spells so dangerous that even the Witch-King would have blanched at the mere thought of using them floated inside her mind...

...Knowledge that was forbidden on pain of death.

"Elaine," Daria said. Her voice seemed to come from a

very far distance. "Elaine!"

"I'm...I'm all right," Elaine lied. The druids hadn't known how to deal with her, if only because they hadn't realised that the curse had been far more than just a simple murderous incantation. She knew now how it had worked, and what would transpire if Dread realised what had happened to her. "I think I'm all right."

"I think you need more potion," Daria said. "I'm calling the druid."

"*No*," Elaine said, panicking. What would happen if they realised the truth? "I'm all right, really. Just let me sleep."

Chapter Four

Elaine lay in bed, thinking hard.

Her old tutors used to say that the difference between a magician and a non-magician was that a magician would remember every spell perfectly, as soon as they learned them. Even Elaine, with her limited magical talent, had the perfect memory of a magician, even though some of the spells she'd learned were beyond her ability to actually cast. Now...now every spell known to the world floated through her mind, including some forgotten and some long prohibited on pain of death.

The necromancers who had started the First Necromantic War had known how to raise the dead. Their grimoires had been recovered after the war and stored in the Black Vault, just in case they were needed by some future Grand Sorcerer. All of the spells they had used to create vast armies of the undead were floating through Elaine's mind, waiting to be used. It would be easy to reanimate a soulless corpse and send it out charged to kill the living, infecting their dying bodies with the curse that would see them rise again. She had wondered, when she'd started to study magic, precisely how the Witch-King had solved the problem of keeping the curse going over such vast periods of time, but now she understood. His spells had fed on its victims and just kept going.

And there were other secrets within the Black Vault. Truth spells that were impossible to resist, far beyond the voices used by the Inquisitors. And she knew how those worked too now. Spells that could turn someone into a frog, or a cat, or a slug, or an inanimate object permanently, warping reality far beyond anything Millicent had ever done to her. Names and rituals that could be used to summon demons from the darkness, or call down the gods to the mortal plane, or recall the souls of the dead to the world of the living. Spells that could boil a person's blood in their veins, or make them a devoted slave, or any number of atrocities that could be carried out by someone with enough magic and ruthlessness to make it work. The tales stored within the Black Vault shocked her. Who would have known that the Witch-King had once been a Grand Sorcerer? That had *never* been included in her History of Magic classes.

Some of the other spells made little sense to her, until she started combining the spells with the knowledge that had been dumped into her head. One spell stripped a person of their magic permanently, something that she had always been led to believe was impossible. Why would the Grand Sorcerer have bothered to enslave Miss Prim if there had been another way to render her harmless? But how badly would knowledge of such a spell shake up the established order? Maybe the Grand Sorcerer kept it to himself for a reason, or maybe he didn't even know it existed. He might never have bothered to search the Black Vault himself, even though he was the one person with unquestioned right of access.

Her mind started to spin as darker spells assailed her. She could create a disease that would send an entire population to sleep, only for them to awaken as her creatures, body and soul. Or she could call down lightning from high above and strike down Millicent, or create a volcano right in the heart of the Golden City. She found herself staring temptation right in the face and shuddered at what she'd learned about herself. Maybe there *was* a good reason why the Grand Sorcerer was the only person permitted access to the Black Vault. He *already* ruled the world and didn't need such powers to enforce his rule.

Restlessly, she pulled herself to her feet and stared out of the window over the city. As always, it was illuminated by countless magical lights, lights she now understood how to create for herself. The Watchtower, positioned on the mountain, seemed to her eyes to glow, marking the presence of sensitive magicians watching for any sign of a necromancer like those who had started the war. All of the knowledge flowing through her head seemed to confirm one thing she had been taught in school; the defeat of the Witch-

King had been a very near thing. The Necromantic Wars could have ended with the Lords of the Dead ruling over an undead world for the rest of time.

She looked over into the mirror, seeing her haunted eyes and tired expression. It was a surprise that all the new knowledge hadn't changed her, but perhaps it had in some ways beyond her ken. There were spells that could have made her as beautiful as Millicent, reshaping her body until she had the charm and sex appeal of a succubus. And yet, there were less dangerous ways to use magic for cosmetic purposes, but they wouldn't have changed who she was. Even if she had been far better looking that Millicent, she would still have been the same Elaine underneath. She couldn't have hoped to compete with her.

There was a click as the door opened, revealing one of the druids. "You should be in bed," he said, reproachfully. "You're not ready to get up without supervision."

Elaine hesitated. There were spells that could make him forget what he'd seen, even though he would be protected against accidental magical discharges from his patients. Or there were spells that could convince him to let her go now and then forget that she'd ever existed. But using them would be wrong. She'd hated it when Millicent had made her run through the corridors naked or humiliate herself in front of the other girls. It would be wrong to use her new knowledge to do the same to others.

"I just wanted to stand up," she said, as she walked back towards the bed. Whatever else could be said for the foul-tasting slop the druids fed her, it did give her remarkable levels of energy. But then, most of it was meant for recovering from the curse that had hit her. "Do you have something else to drink?"

"You should be eating properly now," the druid said. "I'll have something brought in for you. Eat it – and if it stays down, you can probably consider leaving tomorrow."

Elaine watched him leave, shaking her head. Now that she knew what the curse had done, she felt much better, at least physically. But mentally...? She knew what the Inquisitors would say if they discovered what had happened to her, even if it hadn't been her fault. There were some magical curses that meant that their victims had to remain segregated from normal society for the rest of their lives, or transfigured into stone to ensure that they could no longer threaten anyone else. And *her* curse was knowledge...knowledge she hadn't intended to acquire, but still made her an incredible danger to the *status quo*. The Inquisition would try to wipe her mind and, if that failed, kill her. They wouldn't have any choice.

She looked up as one of the nurses entered, carrying a small tray of stew. The smell reminded her of how hungry she was, even though she had been fed a number of potions over the last few hours. It suddenly seemed the hardest thing in the world to take small bites and nibble the food, hoping that it wouldn't start forcing its way out of her stomach again. Some of the potions the druids had given her didn't seem to like competing with proper food.

But this time it all stayed down, thankfully. She closed her eyes and went to sleep, praying to the gods that Inquisitor Dread wouldn't return to ask more questions with his voice of compulsion. She'd have to answer...and that would be the end of her. They'd kill her if they couldn't cure her and she knew, somehow, that there would be no cure. Whoever had designed the curse hidden in Duke Gama's book had meant it to stick.

***

"You're much better," the druid said, the following morning. "I think you can probably go home, but remember to take it easy for the next two weeks. Do not use magic unless you absolutely need to. And come back here for a check-up before you go back to work."

Elaine nodded, not trusting herself to speak. Druidical healing didn't come cheap, but Miss Prim had clearly picked up the bill, just as the druids had promised. Maybe the Inquisitor had had a word with her, or perhaps her Guardian had spoken to one of his contacts in the establishment...or maybe she was nicer than she chose to act. If it had been a normal illness, she would have preferred to stay in the hospital, particularly if someone else had been paying for her treatment. But this was different. She didn't dare attract more attention.

"I'm glad you're feeling better," Daria said, as they left the building. "I've missed you."

"I'm glad you managed to come pick me up," Elaine said, only partly truthfully. Daria was a comforting presence, but she was also alarmingly cheerful when Elaine wanted to get home and hide under the bed. "Didn't your work have something to say about it?"

"I just happened to mention that there was an Inquisitor involved," Daria said, with a wink. "They couldn't fall over themselves fast enough to give me a couple of days of leave to be with you. I'll have to go back tomorrow, but by then you should be settled into bed. I don't like seeing you ill."

"I don't like being ill," Elaine said, ruefully. "Did you hear anything from Miss Prim?"

"Not a word," Daria said. "But you know how the senior wizards feel about my sort. They don't want to commit themselves to anything they don't have to."

Elaine stumbled as new knowledge flooded into her mind. Daria had come from a travelling family, one of the Traveller sects. The Travellers had some strange magic of their own, magic that wasn't well understood by the establishment, perhaps even by the Grand Sorcerer himself. They shunned the Travellers, even the ones who had left the road and taken up permanent residence in a city. But they didn't seem to put any blocks in their path. The Travellers were allowed to move from state to state as they pleased.

And there was something else, something so important that no one had written it down.

"But don't worry about a thing," Daria continued. She hadn't noticed Elaine's sudden distraction. "Miss Prim didn't notice the curse that zapped you, did she? She's really not in a good place to complain about you taking a few weeks off to recuperate."

Of course she didn't, Elaine thought, coldly. Her new knowledge illustrated exactly what had happened to her, and why the curse hadn't triggered any of the wards that were supposed to protect the Library. Someone with a fantastic level of skill and patience had built it up, and then compressed it down into something that had needed her magical field to fuel its transformation into a deadly spell.

By the time the wards had registered that there was a problem it had already been too late.

"I suppose not," she said, finally. "But you know what people can be like."

She leaned on Daria's arm as they walked down the street. It seemed busier than she remembered – had it really been six days ago? Thousands of newcomers thronged through the streets, from high-born aristocrats to low-born magicians considering their chances of becoming Grand Sorcerer. Elaine could understand exactly how they felt; she'd been treated as a low-born herself, if only because no one knew who her parents had been. It bred an icy cold determination to succeed in those who had the talents to carve out a magical career.

"I hear that the Empress of the South is on her way to the Golden City," Daria said, cheerfully. She'd always paid more attention to rumour and gossip than Elaine. "I don't think that she's a magician herself, but she probably wants a chance to try to seduce the next Grand Sorcerer. Rumour has it that they had to send her a female Court Wizard to try to stop her seducing her minder...and she still slept with her. Not that anyone dares say so outright, of course."

"Of course," Elaine agreed. The Empress of the South controlled vast territories that had barely been touched by the Necromantic Wars. It had given her a degree of independence from the Empire that wasn't shared by most other states – and their rulers. She also had a reputation for ruthlessness that matched most of the senior wizards. Being appointed to keep her ambitions under control couldn't have been the easiest post in the world, even if the Empress' seductive talents had been nothing more than rumour. "Or maybe they just wanted to try to weaken her position."

"I don't think it worked," Daria said, after a moment. "The Empress doesn't have the sort of kingdom that we can meddle with openly, not without risking too many consequences."

She shrugged as they reached the apartment block, glancing at the landlord's private apartment. It was warded, unlike the rest of the stairwell, and clearly marked as such. Even without her new knowledge, Elaine had known that it was weak...but now she knew how to unlock the ward without actually breaking it, leaving the occupants unaware that anyone had entered their apartments without permission. The small letterbox at the bottom of the stairs included a small amount of junk mail, an invitation to renew her subscription to a broadsheet that covered magical books and a demand from their landlord that they pay their rent or face eviction. Elaine felt the old flicker of helplessness, matched with the sudden awareness that she *did* have the power to punish him for taking liberties with a pair of magicians. Some of the spells she now knew were well within her capabilities.

"Nothing important, of course," Daria said, as they walked up the stairs and into the apartment. Elaine was surprised at how much she'd missed it. "I think that they never actually send us anything important. We'd probably fall down dead from shock if they did."

Elaine glanced at one of the pieces of junk mail – an advertisement for an eatery that offered food at all hours of the day – and then threw it towards the bin. Miss Prim had been known to rage that the printing press hadn't really been a benefit to librarianship, even though it made it easier for printers to produce thousands of books. Whatever had been published back before the printing press had *needed* to be published, but now *anyone* could publish a book, from a genuine magical textbook to a trashy romantic novel. There were other libraries in the city that catered for people who wanted to read fiction. It didn't have to be based on reality.

"I was expecting something from my Guardian," Elaine said. She didn't want to admit how much not receiving something hurt, even though she had little reason to expect it. He'd certainly made his feelings clear the last time they'd spoken, four years ago. "You'd think he would have cared enough to ensure that I was well."

"What do you expect from a man so inbred that his ears stick out?" Daria demanded. "You know that he never really cared for the duties forced on him by his rank. And it isn't as if you became anything important to him. Forget him and concentrate on getting better."

She grinned, suddenly. "Do you want to come out tonight

with me? I could take you to the dance hall and find you a nice attractive man to dance with..."

"I couldn't," Elaine said, softly. And she couldn't. If she were to go, she'd be nothing more than a wallflower, watching helplessly as others, more confident than herself, danced the night away. And the thought of a man dancing with her...she wanted it, but how could she work up the nerve? "You go and have fun. I'll be here when you get back."

A thought crossed her mind. There were spells in her mind now that could change how a person thought. Perhaps, with a little rewriting, she could use one on herself. If she made herself more confident, she could go dancing and enjoy herself the way that other girls enjoyed themselves. But she knew how dangerous such spells could be. She might rewrite her personality permanently. Or maybe even have the spell wearing off after she had started, but before she was finished.

She looked over at her roommate and felt the old flash of envy. Daria was kind and caring, but she had the kind of life that Elaine wanted. And that hurt more than she wanted to admit.

"I should stay with you," Daria said. "You shouldn't be alone for the first night...and druids don't count. Do you know that they swear vows of chastity that are bound into the magic? They can't even get hard..."

Elaine flushed. "Shame really," Daria added, mischievously. "I thought that that younger druid was right up your street. Young, educated, bookish...he was lovely. Shame about the vows he took..."

"But he worked with female patients," Elaine pointed out. There were female druids, but not that many of them. "Without the oaths, who knows what he might do when he was alone..."

"But men aren't *animals*," Daria said. She paused in mock consideration. "Actually, they *are* animals. I misspoke..."

She broke off as the magic field surrounding the Golden City suddenly twisted, snapping into a new configuration. Elaine felt the sense of loss running through the city, feeling tears prickling at the corner of her eyes as she looked up at her friend. Daria, irrepressible Daria, looked as if she were about to cry. They both knew what had happened. The Grand Sorcerer was dead.

Chapter Five

Only the very wealthy, or those belonging to an incredibly old bloodline, enjoyed large gardens in the Golden City. The city had always been confined by the Five Peaks, for reasons that had probably made sense long before the rise of the Empire. Some of the knowledge in Elaine's mind whispered that the city's founders had tapped vast levels of natural magic below the mountains, using it to protect the heart of their vast empire. Maybe it was nothing more than tradition these days, but it was still forbidden to build outside the mountains, even away from the Blight.

Maxim, Lord Howarth, had never lacked for money and breeding. From what Elaine had heard during her long stay at the orphanage, Lord Howarth was merely the latest in a long line of inbred aristocrats piling up debts on the gaming tables while protecting his aristocratic rights with a single-minded determination that would have taken him far, had he applied it to anything else. Even the Golden City's notoriously unmerciful creditors preferred to wait and bide their time rather than try to collect from one of the city's foremost bloodlines, knowing that attempting to bully him into paying up might earn them the wrath of the entire aristocracy. Elaine found it hard to understand why anyone would choose to squander so much wealth and status on gambling and whoring, not when his name could get him into any establishment in the land. He was little more than a waste of life.

She halted outside the gates and hesitated. By law, each orphan who remained in the orphanage when they entered their teenage years had to have a guardian from among the aristocracy. It was one reason why the orphanage worked hard to have each child placed in a good home – or at least somewhere away from the orphanage – before they grew up, if only because the aristocrat might have resented the demands on his time. There were stories of some orphans who had been adopted into wealthy families and given a chance to succeed, but as far as Elaine knew they were only stories. Adopted children couldn't compete with bloodline in the aristocratic world. It was more likely that an illegitimate son would be retrospectively legitimised than an orphan would be brought into the family.

Lord Howarth had been appointed Elaine's Guardian when she'd turned thirteen and grown into a woman. She wasn't sure why Lord Howarth had accepted the position in the first place – given his breeding and general reputation, he could probably have avoided the responsibility – nor why he'd never severed ties between them once Elaine had graduated from the Peerless School. Not that he'd ever done much for her, she had to admit. He gave her one interview per year, asked her a handful of questions that sounded as if he didn't care...and nothing else. He hadn't even bothered to mark her graduation with a party, let alone see her after she'd graduated. Elaine had honestly never expected to see him again.

Bracing herself, she walked up to the gate and pressed her hand against the seal. A man like Lord Howarth had little trouble in purchasing the most secure wards in the empire, even though he was no magician himself. Rumour had it that he kept a small army on the grounds to protect his privacy, including a pair of combat magicians. Elaine should have found out, but didn't. She cursed her own oversight as the gates slowly hissed open, revealing a long pathway leading up towards the mansion. The grassy field surrounding the building would have been fun to run on as a child, if she'd ever been allowed. Lord Howarth had no children of his own. His line might end with him.

Knowledge whispered in the back of her mind as she walked up the pathway towards the house. Someone in the Howarth line had played a vitally important role in founding the Empire, and in fighting and winning the First Necromantic War. Elaine pressed one hand to her head as the knowledge refused to congeal into specifics; whoever had written the sealed histories had refused to be too clear on what had actually happened. It was strange – surely they should have expected the records to be sealed until long after their death – but there was nothing she could do about it. Perhaps the writer had had reason to believe that the wards surrounding the Great Library weren't as impenetrable as everyone had thought.

The steps leading up to the house were surrounded by statues, strange demonic creatures cast in stone and empowered by magic. Elaine had known, even before running afoul of the curse in Duke Gama's book, that they were the house's first line of defence, but now she knew how to create them for herself, if she wanted unstoppable defenders. They weren't the most dangerous known to magicians, yet they were almost impossible to defeat by anything less than a sorcerer with a great deal of power to spare. A footpad with a sword wouldn't be able to hold one off for a second. Very few would dare to slip into Lord Howarth's territory uninvited and only a handful would have survived the experience.

She put one foot on the steps and felt magic crackling around her, before it slowly faded away into nothingness. The wooden door at the top of the steps – strengthened by magic – opened, revealing a hulking monstrosity of a man. Judd, Lord Howarth's butler, had given her nightmares from the first day she'd visited his mansion to have her Guardianship formally confirmed, even though he'd never been anything other than polite to her. The knowledge bubbling through her mind confirmed that there had been good reason to fear. Judd was very far from human, a rocky statue granted human seeming and powered by a spellbound demon. Elaine had heard that Judd had been around for centuries – something that should have been impossible, even with the strongest magic – and now she knew why. Her Guardian's long-distant ancestor had created a servant for his family who would be loyal, obedient – and utterly unstoppable. Destroying the fleshy form wouldn't release the demon from the spells binding it to the mortal plane, merely allow it to bring more of its power to bear against the imprudent trespasser.

Elaine shrank back, feeling her mind desperately scrabbling for the handful of rites they'd been taught to banish demons – and the far deadlier rituals stuffed into her mind by the mysterious curse. Judd waited, as always giving the impression of endless patience combined with a certain disdain for her presence. Daria had once commented that servants were, if anything, even more snobbish than their masters. Judd certainly seemed to actively disapprove of Elaine's presence. But then, who was she really? Nothing more than an orphan girl whose parents were mysteries and whose magical talent was hardly worth considering. If Lord Howarth had hoped that she would grow into something useful, he'd been bitterly disappointed.

"I've come to see my Guardian," Elaine said, fighting to keep her voice steady. The same laws that insisted orphans had to have protectors from among the aristocracy also insisted that the orphan had the right to see her Guardian whenever she chose, but Lord Howarth had never considered himself bound by the rules. "I trust that he will see me?"

Judd seemed to consider, and then he bowed, using one great hand to invite her into the mansion. Elaine felt a trickle running down her back as she stepped inside, leaving Judd behind her to close the door, before he walked past her and down the long corridor. The first time she'd visited the mansion, Judd had given her a lecture on how everything in the building was charmed to prevent anyone from taking it off the premises – as if he'd expected her to be a thief! Now, with adult eyes, Elaine could see just how tacky most of the assembled valuables actually were, although that wouldn't stop them from being worth more than her entire yearly salary. Lord Howarth's family had been determined to acquire more material goods than anyone else and never give anything up. She paused to study a tiny golden statue of one of the gods, before a cough from Judd drew her back down the corridor. Lord Howarth had never been particularly religious. Elaine couldn't remember ever having seen him entering a temple.

The butler paused outside a heavy stone door and knocked once. It swung open, revealing a study that had been designed for Lord Howarth's father, a man who had been genuinely interested in the books he collected before his untimely death. Elaine had wanted to read some of the volumes on the shelves, but naturally she'd never been allowed to soil them with her grubby orphan hands. They weren't books on magic, or they would have been examined by the Great Library after the Lord's death. He'd been more interested in genealogy than magic. But all of his breeding hadn't stopped him from drinking himself to death.

"Elaine," a voice said. Lord Maxim Howarth was sprawled over one of his father's couches, studying a leaflet from the racing tracks. There were all kinds of magical safeguards built into the fields to prevent cheating, all of which could be subverted with the correct spell. Elaine wondered just what her Guardian would say if he knew that she could ensure that his chosen horses always won, before pushing the thought aside. She'd never been *that* desperate for his approval. "I was...relieved to hear of your recovery."

Tradition dictated that Elaine should go down on her knees before him, but a strength she didn't know she had kept her upright. Lord Maxim Howarth wasn't more than ten years older than her, yet he looked almost old enough to be her father. He'd been slim when she'd first seen him, but now even the most expert tailoring in the world couldn't disguise his growing paunch or the lines on his face. His dark hair was thinning out and his eyes were too bright, a mark of some of the more complex – and illegal – potions he took to entertain himself. Some of them were banned even to people of his rank, which was probably why he wanted them. He'd always considered himself above the law.

"I am glad to hear it," Elaine said, with equal insincerity. The law stated that her Guardian should continue to interest himself in her well-being until she married or reached a social position where she could be reasonably assured of a long and happy life, but Lord Howarth had never bothered to show any interest in her ever since she had graduated. She was surprised that he'd even heard that she'd been ill. "It was a most unpleasant experience."

Lord Howarth shrugged. He'd probably felt worse after the first drink of narcotic potion. "But you recovered and your medical bills were met by the Great Library," he said. He'd probably been worried that she'd try to make him pay for it, even though he could have afforded to finance hospital treatment for the entire city without even noticing the cost.

"I fail to see what that has to do with me."

Elaine felt a flash of hot anger, tempered by a dull helplessness that had been part of her ever since she'd realised that she would always be a victim. "I need to ask you some questions," she said. Spells danced through her mind, spells that could compel him to tell her the truth – or give her half of his inheritance. Judd's looming presence behind her wasn't as much a deterrent as he might have hoped. There were words that banished even the most persistent and deadly of demons in her mind. "Why did you become my Guardian?"

Lord Howarth shrugged, languidly. "There are...duties that come with one's birth," he said. Elaine felt her eyes narrow in disbelief. Since when had he even considered the possibility that his birth brought responsibilities as well as the freedom to enjoy himself into an early grave? "I merely felt that such duties had to be honoured."

Something snapped inside Elaine's mind. "You never showed any concern for such duties before," she said. "Why now? Why *then*?"

"Have a care," Lord Howarth said, coldly. And yet there was something else hidden under his voice. "I can have Judd take you outside and thrash you for imprudence."

Once, that threat would have stopped Elaine from pressing the matter any further. She'd known that Lord Howarth had ordered several of his servants whipped over the years, once for a crime as petty as having his bath water slightly too cool for his enjoyment. And technically he *was* her Guardian, with almost paternal power over her.

"Of course you could," she said, keeping her voice calm, "but that won't stop me asking the question. Why did you become my Guardian?"

She heard Judd's hulking form rustle behind her, but kept her eyes on her Guardian. "Why did you decide to take on my Guardianship?"

Lord Howarth met her eyes, but looked away first. "It was...pointed out to me that I had a duty to uphold," he said, finally. "My father had promised to serve as a Guardian when the next child required a Guardian. He was one of the patrons of your orphanage and I believe that he took it seriously. When he died...I was in the position of choosing to renounce his word or taking up the position myself. You were the child in need of a Guardian."

Elaine wasn't sure that she believed him. It was true that an aristocratic family passed clients, favours and debts down the line from father to son, but becoming a Guardian was something different from calling in favours incurred by the previous generation. Perhaps it was why he'd never shown any real interest in her, even after she'd been accepted into the Peerless School, and yet...something about it didn't quite ring true.

"Right," she said. Judd's presence seemed to loom closer, but she refused to look away from his face. "Who pointed it out to you?"

"Councillor Travis," Lord Howarth said, finally. "He said that I should honour my father's wishes or no one would ever take me seriously again."

Elaine felt her knees buckle as she fought to prevent herself from laughing out loud. The thought was absurd! Councillor Travis had made his money in trade, not something that a respectable older family like the Howarth Family would consider respectable. Travis would have gone to Howarth to beg favours, not the other way around. He certainly wouldn't have had the influence to make a noble lord assume a responsibility he didn't wish to assume.

And yet she had the strange feeling that Lord Howarth was telling the truth.

"That was good of him," she said. Part of her was astonished that she'd pushed it so far, but there was one more question to ask. "I assume you read my file at the orphanage?"

"Well, of course," Lord Howarth said. He seemed to be relieved that they'd moved away from Councillor Travis. Elaine made a mental note to go back to that issue at a later date. Even if her Guardian was telling the truth, there was something about it that didn't make sense. "I had to be sure that I wasn't assuming the Guardianship of a thief."

"Of course not," Elaine muttered. Never mind the fact that an orphan would have better reason than most to steal. She cleared her throat. "Do you know who my parents were?"

"I was told that you'd been passed to the orphanage as a baby," Lord Howarth said. He shrugged. "The orphanage never bothered to investigate your parentage. You could be the last surviving heir to the Empire for all I know, or the daughter of a scullery maid and a noble-born son. The gods know that such births are rarely treated as important to the families..."

Elaine nodded. Bastard children were a problem for any noble family, particularly when their sons were raised in a world where lower-class female servants literally couldn't say no. Very few families would consider such a child an equal, no matter the circumstances of his – or her – birth. Farming the child out to an orphanage was one of the kinder ways to deal with the situation. Elaine had always considered such families to be heartless. She wondered, absently, if she was actually *related* to Lord Howarth, before dismissing the thought. If that were true, she would have preferred to forever remain Elaine No-Kin.

"I suppose they do," Elaine said. Lord Howarth shrugged, again. He really didn't care very much about her, she realised, but *that* was no surprise. She'd never been given any reason to assume he cared. "Could you ask if they kept some records they never showed you...?"

"They would have shown me everything," Lord Howarth said. He looked up at her, sharply. "Why do you care, all of a sudden? You might not like what you find out."

"I don't know," Elaine admitted. She honestly didn't know where the desire to know the truth behind her birth had come from. It had always been part of her, but it hadn't been important...not until she'd been hit by a powerful curse. And then she'd dared to ask an Inquisitor about her birth. There had been a time when she would have preferred to die rather than speak to one of the Inquisitors. "I think..."

Something clicked in her mind. "You don't have any money left, do you?" she asked. It seemed impossible, and yet Councillor Travis had been in a position to influence her Guardian. And he'd seemed to worry about the cost of her medical treatment. "You've finally spent your inheritance..."

"Throw her out," Lord Howarth ordered, so sharply that she knew that she was right. "Now."

Judd grabbed Elaine's arm and dragged her out of the room, back down the corridor towards the door. A dozen spells rose up in Elaine's mind for breaking his grip and freeing herself, or banishing the demon back to hell, but she pushed them down. There was no need.

She was still chuckling when Judd threw her out of the gate and onto the street.

Chapter Six

"He's got no money left?"

Daria started to chuckle. "No money...and he owes money to every loan shark in the city!"

"I don't think it's quite so funny for him," Elaine said, before she started giggling herself. It *was* funny, damn it. "He might have to start watching what he spends money on now."

"Drink and whores," Daria said, tartly. She shook her head in disbelief. "I wonder how long it will be before he has to sell his grand house."

"Maybe he can't," Elaine said. The orphanage hadn't been a proper school, but they had battered reading, writing and basic maths into her head. She might have become an accountant – or a housewife – if she hadn't had a talent for magic. "The house could already be used to back a debt. Someone might be intent on claiming it even now."

She grinned at Daria. "Maybe he'll have to sell some of the tacky ornaments his family has been collecting for a thousand years," she added. "And what will happen when people realise that he's selling them off?"

The great houses in the Golden City seemed strong and untouchable, which was probably why Lord Howarth had got away with his gambling debts for so long. But if the loan sharks scented weakness, they would probably start demanding more and more guarantees from her Guardian before they agreed to hand over further cash. How long would it be before one of them decided to call in the debts and demand the mansion in payment? And what would happen when they tried? The aristocracy might close ranks behind Lord Howarth, or they might throw him to the wolves for fear of provoking their own creditors to demand immediate payment. It would take the Grand Sorcerer to sort out the mess – and the Grand Sorcerer was dead.

"Well, he deserves it," Daria said, unsympathetically.

"How exactly has he treated you over the last eight years? The best that can be said of it is that he largely ignored you."

She paused. "You're not his adopted daughter, are you? You can't get any of this muck on you?"

Elaine snorted. "I'm not even a ward to him," she said, dryly. "I don't think they can demand that *I* pay his debts, or anything that I might have to do if I *was* his daughter."

"Perhaps you *are* his daughter," Daria said, mischievously. "Would you inherit his debts if he spent your entire life ignoring you?"

"He would have to have started having kids when he was seven," Elaine said. She had wondered, back when she'd hoped that Lord Howarth would be more than a distant presence in her life, but the timing didn't work out. It was possible, she supposed, that she was his half-sister, yet that wouldn't force her to pay any of his debts. "Besides, he spends more money each day at the tracks than I earn in a year. His creditors aren't going to get money out of me that I don't have, are they?"

She chuckled as she walked back into her room. "I think we'd better get dressed," she added. "It won't be long until the funeral begins."

It had been nearly two years since she'd worn sorcerer's black. The robes had been given to her after her graduation by the staff, a tradition that Millicent and her cronies hadn't hesitated to use to make fun of the younger Elaine. Only *poor* graduates were allowed to keep their robes. Richer graduates tended to purchase their own tailored robes after their graduation and exchange them regularly, in keeping with the dictates of fashion. Elaine had had to let out the hem herself over the last few days, using half-remembered sewing lessons from the orphanage. Neither of them could have afforded a tailor, or even one of the seamstresses from the poorer parts of the city.

She pulled the robe on and looked at herself in the mirror. Graduate or not, she just didn't *look* very impressive. She bit her lip as she picked up her wand and stowed it away in her sleeve, wondering if she should even go to the funeral. Everyone who was anyone would be there, attempting to make deals and political alliances even during the funeral itself, but *she* wasn't anyone. The Grand Sorcerer hadn't even been a nodding acquaintance. She'd only ever seen him once, at a dinner hosted by the Peerless School. And she couldn't even remember what he'd looked like.

There had been a faint note of unease hanging in the air as she walked back to the apartment after Judd had tossed her out of the mansion's gates. The Grand Sorcerer was dead...and everyone knew that that meant the competitions to select his successor were about to begin. Once he was decently buried, the competition would start in earnest. Elaine half-wondered what would happen if she'd been born with enough talent to make her own bid for supreme power, before pushing the thought aside. Even with the spells floating within her mind, including ones that would see her put to death if anyone realised she knew them, she was no match for a more talented sorcerer. Anyone who thought they could be the next Grand Sorcerer would have power to spare.

"Come on out," Daria called. "What do you think?"

Elaine stuck her head out of her room and smiled at her friend. Daria wore black, setting off her long red hair nicely, with her robes pulled tightly around her body. She looked spectacular, even though she was going to a funeral. Elaine made a mental bet with herself that there would be no shortage of sorcerers trying to ask Daria to come out with them. The normal rules about how unmarried females should behave didn't apply to female magicians.

"Striking," she said, resignedly. The spells that would have made her just as stunning floated up to the surface of her mind again, tempting her. Each time she pushed them back down, it got a little harder. "You'll bring the dead back to life."

"Let's hope not," Daria said. "The last thing I need is to be branded a necromancer and chased out of the city by a horde of angry sorcerers."

Elaine shrugged. "I suppose not," she said. She checked her wand out of habit, before heading over to the door. "Shall we go?"

The streets were buzzing with people as they walked towards the Parade of the Endless, the massive arena at the heart of the city. Elaine saw hundreds of guards and soldiers trying to keep order and failing miserably, if only because thousands of magicians and sorcerers had descended on the Golden City, intent on networking while they buried their former master. Every year, there was a magical convention – and every year, families were dispatched out of the city by everyone who could afford to send them away to safety. Magicians loved to show off, or play practical jokes on the defenceless commoners...and there was no longer a single authority who could provide a final sanction for misbehaviour. The streets wouldn't be safe until the new Grand Sorcerer was established and had a chance to impose his authority. Still, she doubted that any of them would try to pick a fight with two graduates in black robes. It was very hard to gauge a magician's power until it was too late.

"Over there," Daria said. "That's Hanson – I used to date him before I graduated. Nice guy, but a little grabby in bed. Watch yourself."

She pulled Elaine over towards the young man and his cronies before Elaine could object. Hanson *was* fairly handsome, in a bland way that suggested he used glamours to improve his looks. Hardly uncommon among sorcerers, male or female, but something Elaine had always considered rather dishonest. He smiled brightly when he saw Daria and gave her a hug, before looking over at Elaine and dismissing her a moment later. Elaine rolled her eyes, even as she felt the old stab in her heart. She would have loved to have a guy chasing her, just once.

And there were spells in her mind now that could turn Hanson, for all his magical talent, into her devoted lover...

The crowd pressed closer as they approached the gates. Elaine had only been to the Parade of the Endless once before, but in its own way it was as magical as the Great Library. No matter how many people crammed into it, it would always be large enough for more – and all of the spectators could see perfectly. The knowledge in Elaine's head provided a precise description of the spells used by the city's founders to warp space around the Parade of the Endless, hollowing out the interior to allow it to become bigger on the inside than on the outside. In some ways, it was rather like the mirrored alternate dimension that made up so much of the Great Library. Mirror magic was complicated and very unstable, at least under normal circumstances. The sheer level of talent that had gone into producing the Great Library stunned her. Even knowing how it had been done, she doubted that any of the magicians of her era could have duplicated the feat...

"But I'm telling you, this is my wife," a man was saying. Elaine felt a shiver as she recognised the man he was trying to speak to as Inquisitor Dread. Who governed the Inquisitors when their only master was dead and his successor not yet selected? The Inquisitor looked tired, even behind the glamour hiding his face. "One of those bastards did *this* to her!"

He was holding onto a pig's neck, despite its struggles. "You have to do something," he insisted. "She can't remain like this forever!"

The press of the crowd pushed Elaine and Daria away before she could hear Dread's response. With so many sorcerers around, it was unlikely that the Inquisitor would be able to catch up with the culprit before he managed to escape into the crowd. The gods alone knew what the poor woman had done, if anything. Perhaps she'd been rude to the magician, or perhaps she'd refused a crude attempt at getting her into bed, or perhaps she'd just been a convenient victim. Dread could probably break the spell once the man had stopped begging for assistance and let the Inquisitor do his job.

Daria grabbed her arm as the magic caught at them, allowing the crowd to see the small party gathered at the bottom of the arena. "Look," she hissed. "See anyone you recognise?"

Elaine sucked in her breath. Millicent was standing with some of the senior wizards, right next to a woman wearing a black garment that covered everything but her eyes. The woman was holding Millicent's arm tightly, as if she didn't quite trust the young sorceress to behave herself. Beside her, there were several wizards she recognised from the Peerless School, tutors in everything from potions to advanced spell-binding. She'd never liked the spell-binding teacher, she recalled, not least because of his thoroughly unpleasant branch of magic. He'd always given her the impression that he would have preferred to have *everyone* wearing one of his collars, with him in firm command of them all. The potions master beside him, by contrast, was fat and always friendly, even to a girl with strictly limited talents for producing potions to order. Elaine had some good memories of his patient tutoring and how he'd helped her get a passing grade.

"That's Millicent," she said, sourly. At least *something* had managed to distract her nemesis from her studies. "Who's the woman who's hiding her face?"

"Lady Light Spinner," Hanson supplied. Elaine was surprised he'd lowered himself to answer her question. Perhaps he was just trying to impress Daria. "She is the Court Wizard to the Empress of the South."

Elaine remembered what Millicent had said and shivered. If Millicent had been telling the truth, Lady Light Spinner intended to try to become the next Grand Sorcerer. A Court Wizard in such an important post would be incredibly powerful – and whatever else could be said about Millicent, she didn't lack talent or power. If her relative became Grand Sorcerer – Grand Sorceress – Millicent would be even more unbearable.

"And maybe she *was* seduced by the Empress of the South," Daria added, with a wink. "You think that she might be a man under that veil?"

Elaine started to giggle, only to force it down as silence rolled out from the centre of the arena. The Caretaker, the current head of the Regency Council in the absence of a Grand Sorcerer, stepped forward. He was an old man, a distant relative of Lord Howarth if Elaine recalled correctly, although there were few formal ties between their families. She wondered absently if the old man knew about his relative's spending problem and what, if anything, he intended to do about it. Letting a noble family fall into wrack and ruin wouldn't make him popular, but failing to force his relative to pay his debts could unleash unpleasant consequences. It hadn't been *that* long ago since the wealthy merchants had successfully pressed for their own representation on the city's council.

And without a Grand Sorcerer, whose decision would be unchallengeable, who knew who would still be standing when the dust settled?

She smiled as she caught sight of another man standing to one side with his fellow commoners. Councillor Travis was a dour-faced man, with a pleasant-looking wife and a pretty daughter. Still not a social equal to Lord Howarth and the rest of the aristocracy, he was probably richer than any of them – or maybe all of them put together. His family had been among the first to take advantage of the iron dragons built by the technicians to bring the Empire closer together and it had given them an unbeatable edge. Perhaps his daughter could marry Lord Howarth and bring her dowry to the aide of the Lord's finances. But would she ever be accepted by High Society?

"Thirty-seven years ago," the Caretaker said, his voice easily audible throughout the arena, "a sorcerer stood before the Regency Council and was elevated to the position of Grand Sorcerer. He ruled firmly, but fairly, striking a balance between the different poles of our society. It was our dearest wish that he would continue to rule for many years to come."

And that, Elaine knew, was nothing less than the truth. It was humbling to realise that the Grand Sorcerer – the *late* Grand Sorcerer – had ruled for longer than Elaine had been alive, but the time between Grand Sorcerers was always uneasy for everyone. The knowledge in her mind whispered a single question; what was worse than a single all-powerful sorcerer ruling the world? *Two* all-powerful sorcerers, fighting.

"But the gods have chosen to take him from us to their realm," the Caretaker continued. "It is fitting that we now consider the position he held – and the responsibilities he discharged so capably. The Grand Sorcerer serves as the ultimate bulwark of our society. To rule is also to serve – and he understood that better than many other rulers. We will miss him now that he is gone."

He stepped forward to the black casket positioned in the exact centre of the arena. "I charge you all to remember what he did for us," he said, softly. His voice was still easy to hear. "And to remember that power alone is nothing without responsibility. May his successor be so wise."

"May his successor be so wise," the crowd echoed.

Elaine caught sight of Millicent and saw her staring soberly at the casket where the Grand Sorcerer lay. Millicent was part of the established order in a way that Elaine could never be, but the established order had been badly shaken the moment the Grand Sorcerer passed away. She understood, better than Elaine would have done without the new knowledge in her head, just what it meant to lose the centre of their world. All of the old certainties had died with the Grand Sorcerer.

"The Grand Sorcerer was a great man," Administrator Mentor said. The master of the Peerless School looked grim, despite his youthful looks. Elaine remembered a very unpleasant interview with him after Millicent had successfully framed her for theft and shivered inwardly. She had managed to prove her innocence eventually, but it had come at a cost she hadn't been entirely willing to pay. "He knew what he could do – and what he should not do, even though it was within his power. We will not see his like again."

Daria nudged her. "Wasn't he the one who had you caned?"

"Yes," Elaine said, shortly. *Millicent* wouldn't have been punished like that. But Millicent had powerful relatives and Elaine had no relatives at all. "Do you think that he wants to become Grand Sorcerer himself?"

"He has the power and connections," Daria muttered back. "And he has been master of the Peerless School long enough to grow bored. He might want to grasp the highest position in the world."

Elaine shrugged and turned back to watch the funeral. Each of the tutors and councillors had a chance to speak. Councillor Travis spoke briefly, but fittingly, commending the Grand Sorcerer for his services to the city. Millicent's aunt didn't speak at all.

Finally, the Caretaker stepped forward again. "We shall not see his like again," he said, softly. "And now we bid him farewell."

The casket blazed with a brilliant white light, so bright that Elaine had to cover her eyes from the glare. A faint afterimage seemed to hang in the air for a long moment, and then it was gone, reducing the Grand Sorcerer's body to dust. His soul was long gone. And yet there were spells in Elaine's mind that would have allowed her to call him back to the world...

"Goodbye," the Caretaker said.

Elaine saw the expression on the Administrator's face and shivered. The senior wizards were sharing the same thought. Their master was dead...

...And the contest to select the next master was about to begin.

Chapter Seven

"Put a smile on your face," Daria urged. "This is supposed to be a party."

Elaine looked up at her. After the funeral, Hanson had invited Daria to a party in honour of the Grand Sorcerer – and Daria, ignoring Elaine's protests, had insisted on dragging her along. Elaine felt terribly out of place; the singing, the dancing, the couples kissing in the rear of the vast hall...it all felt alien to her. How could *she* join the couples on the dance floor...even though part of her *wanted* to join them and dance the night away?

"I should go home," she said, shaking her head. "I don't belong here."

"Oh yes you do," Daria said. "You deserve a chance to have some fun, you know? Come and dance."

"I can't dance with you," Elaine protested. "That's...that's not decent."

"I think no one bothered to tell those two that it isn't decent," Daria said, nodding towards two boys who were dancing together. "Which one of them is the girl, do you think?"

Elaine flushed as Daria pulled her to her feet. "But I wasn't going to dance with you," Daria added. "You! Come over here."

One of Hanson's friends came over, staring blankly at Daria. "You two are going to dance," Daria said, firmly. She leaned closer to the boy's ear and whispered something in it that made him flush. "And if he lets you down, I'll cut off his..."

The boy pulled Elaine's stumbling form onto the dance floor before Daria had a chance to finish her threat. He clearly didn't doubt that Daria's wrath would be terrible if he messed up with Elaine. It felt harder to dance than Elaine had expected, even with a surprisingly patient tutor who didn't seem to mind if she trod on his foot. The beat of the music was difficult to follow and she kept placing her feet wrongly, until she finally realised how to dance. And then the dance came to an end.

"You just need practice," the boy said, as the dancers filed off the floor. "And now..."

Elaine watched him go and sighed inwardly. Of course he hadn't wanted to dance with her. Daria had bribed or threatened him into cooperating and he was now off to collect his prize. The gods alone knew what Daria had offered him...but Elaine could guess. A dance, a kiss...or something more intimate. She didn't really want to know.

"That's enough of feeling sorry for yourself," Daria said, firmly, as Elaine appeared next to her. "I saw you smiling on the dance floor. Get back out there and get another guy."

Elaine flushed bright red at the very thought. "Come on," Daria said, seriously. "This dance needs two couples."

She waved to a pair of strange boys and invited them to join the two girls. Elaine had barely any time to think before the bandleader started calling out instructions, ordering the partners to take hands and start moving through the steps. This dance was more complicated than the last one...she looked up and saw her partner smiling nervously at her. He was just as worried as she was...oddly, that made her feel better about herself. The music started and they fell into the steps, moving slowly through the first two circles. And then the music started to speed up...

Elaine was laughing as the dance came to an end. Daria smiled at her, gave the boy she'd been dancing with a kiss on the cheek, and then winked at Elaine. Elaine's partner didn't look as if he expected a kiss, thankfully, but just as Elaine was about to head back to the tables he caught her arm and awkwardly pulled her back into position for the next dance. Elaine opened her mouth to object, saw Daria's firm stare from the side of the room, and allowed him to lead her without further objection. The next dance went well, but the one after it was too complex for her to follow easily. It was a relief to note that several other dancers had had to leave at the same time.

"Want to join me for a drink?" The boy asked. He hesitated, and then flushed. "I'm sorry. I sound like an idiot."

Elaine knew exactly how that felt. "I'd love to," she said. "Just...juice, please. Nothing alcoholic."

The boy nodded and headed over to the bar, where a pair of half-naked girls were serving drinks. Elaine watched him taking the drinks and heading back to the table, astonished at her own daring. There was a time when she would have fled rather than face a reasonably handsome guy. Maybe Daria had slipped her something to make her less inhibited, a simple charm or limited potion. Or maybe whatever had happened to her in the Great Library had given her more confidence than she had possessed beforehand.

"I...I don't even know your name," the boy confessed.

"I'm Bee. Blame my mother; she always loved bees as a child."

Elaine smiled. "Elaine," she said. She wasn't going to mention that she was an orphan, at least not yet. The last thing she wanted was sympathy. "You're not trying to hide your face."

"I could never get the glamour to work right," he admitted. His face was pleasant enough, although his blonde hair was cut too close to the scalp for Elaine's liking. No doubt he thought she should be wearing a dress like Daria's, one that left absolutely nothing to the imagination. "And besides, I always felt a little dishonest pretending to be something I'm not."

"I know the feeling," Elaine said. Besides, she hadn't really been able to use a glamour herself, at least before her accident. Now...a thousand different spells for creating a glamour floated through her mind, tempting her with the chance to present herself as whatever Bee wanted in a girl. But he seemed to want her for herself. Or maybe...no, she told herself firmly. She would at least try to enjoy herself. "What brings you to the Golden City?"

"My patron has plans to expand her holdings in this city once a new Grand Sorcerer gets selected," Bee explained. "I'm here to help with the work she can't dish out to the slaves. They complain too loudly."

Elaine smiled at the weak joke. "What sort of holdings does he want?"

"Political patronage, really," Bee explained. "It's really rather boring if you're not able to play the game for your own sake. And what are you doing in this city?"

"I...I was raised here," Elaine said. She had been about to say that she was born in the Golden City, but the truth was that she could have been born anywhere. Magic could easily be used to move from state to state; her parents could have lived on the southern continent and used a teleporting mage to transport their daughter to the orphanage. "I've never really been outside the city."

"They told me that the streets here were paved with gold," Bee said. "I was *most* disappointed."

They shared a laugh. "I was told that there's a land where dragons still fly through the skies," Elaine said, ruefully. "It wasn't until I was an adult that I realised that no one has seen a dragon for hundreds of years."

"Mages hunting them down for their skins," Bee said. "I heard that a coat made out of dragon skin can repel any charm or curse."

"It can," Elaine said. And they were incredibly rare now that there were no longer any dragons to hunt down and skin. The Grand Sorcerer had had one in his small arsenal of magical tools and weapons, but she didn't know of any other sorcerer who possessed one in this day and age. It was tempting to think that there might be more dragons out there, somewhere, yet if there were they were keeping a very low profile...

She staggered as a series of memories suddenly roared into her head. Not dragons, not really, but something close enough to a dragon raised by the necromancers from the pits of hell. They'd sacrificed countless lives for each fire-drake, knowing that the sorcerers desperately scrambling to stop them would have no way to counter the monsters...unless they used necromancy themselves. And necromancy corrupted far faster than any other kind of magic.

Each memory seemed to trap her within an eternity. The monsters devastating entire armies with their fiery breath, leaving their charred corpses behind on the battlefields...where the necromancers had raised them once again in their service. Each magician, battling to stop the undead hordes, dying in fire as the monsters hunted them down and killed them. Children, barely old enough to walk, being herded into death camps to have their life energies drained away by the necromancers, who were already becoming bloated with the power they'd stolen from the act of murder...

...And the Witch-King, a dark figure towering over the battlefield, acknowledged by all of the necromancers as their master...

Bee touched her shoulder and Elaine snapped out of it, breathing hard. "Are you all right?"

"I...I think so," Elaine said, quickly. She didn't know what to say to him. Bee wasn't a sorcerer in his own right; she doubted that he had any magical talent at all. How could he understand what she was going through? And if she told any magician, they'd be obliged to call the Inquisitors and tell them what had happened to Elaine. "I think the air just got to me, for a second."

"That's not good," Bee agreed, gravely. Elaine cursed herself for her timidity. The closest she'd gotten to a likeable guy and she just *had* to scare him away. "Would you like to go outside for a few moments?"

Elaine flushed. She knew what Daria did with some of the boys *she* picked up at parties...

"I didn't mean like that," Bee assured her, hastily. "I just thought you might like some air."

"I think I'd like to dance again," Elaine said, surprising herself. "Let's go back onto the dance floor."

The music had changed again, becoming a style that was surprisingly less formal than the earlier dances. Elaine found it harder to follow, if only because there was *nothing* real to follow at all. The dancers seemed to be inventing their own steps, some managing to look good, others managing to look like idiots. Elaine wished, for the first time, that she had worn a shorter skirt. Daria *had* tried to talk her into borrowing one of her dresses, but Elaine hadn't been able to bear the thought of revealing too much of her legs. Besides, if she'd fallen down, the guys would have all been able to look up at her undergarments.

She looked over and saw Daria holding a guy she didn't

recognise, kissing him with a desperation that seemed oddly out of place. Her friend had always been more sociable than Elaine, with an entire string of boyfriends, yet...could she be worried about the future too? Elaine had known what was likely to happen even before all of the forbidden knowledge was dumped into her head. The next Grand Sorcerer was likely to turn everything upside down just to stamp his own authority onto the world.

Bee looked down at her. "Are you sure you're all right?"

It would have been easy to kiss him. Perhaps that was why she didn't. "I think so," she assured him. "In fact..."

Someone slammed into her back, knocking her to her knees. Bee caught her and helped her to her feet, just in time to avoid a second blow that nearly clipped the side of her head. Elaine knew who was standing there before she saw her; Millicent and her cronies had arrived. She hadn't even considered the possibility of running into her old enemy at the dance club. Daria had certainly never mentioned her.

"Well, well, well," Millicent said. The other dancers were giving them a wide berth, knowing that Millicent wasn't someone to challenge unless their magical powers were great enough not to have to care about her – or her relatives. "Look who decided to get above herself and come join us tonight."

She looked over at Bee. "And couldn't you find someone better to dance with?"

Bee met her gaze evenly. Elaine would have been impressed, if she hadn't realised that Bee simply didn't know who Millicent was. "I do not need...you to tell me who to dance with," he said, coldly. "I suggest that you leave. Now."

Millicent stared at him as if she hadn't been able to imagine that anyone, apart perhaps from an Inquisitor, would stand up to her. And then she smiled in cold delight.

"This girl shamed herself before the whole school," she said, with an unpleasant smile. "And I think that you won't be defending her any longer."

She clicked her fingers, casting a spell with casual ease. Blue light washed over Bee and he froze in place. The charm was a simple one for a magician to deflect, so simple that a standard magical protection amulet infused with magical power could protect a mundane non-magician, but Bee had no protections at all. He would be rooted to the spot until someone cast the counter-charm or it wore off on its own. Given Millicent's power, she'd probably intended the spell to last for days.

Elaine stared at her, unable to move. She had been afraid of Millicent since the day they'd first met, since Millicent had decided to hate her. The mere thought of meeting Millicent was enough to keep her rooted to the spot, without any freezing charm. Millicent knew it too. There was no need to use magic to bind her feet to the floor when fear did it far more effectively.

"And I think it's time to show you why you will never amount to anything," Millicent said, lifting one hand languidly. "You will not show your face here again..."

There was a scuffle as three of Millicent's friends caught Daria, fighting her with magic and their bare hands. Daria was stronger than Elaine, perhaps the strongest girl Elaine had met, but Millicent's friends seemed to share some of her power. Elaine saw one of them stumble backwards as Daria's fist met her face, but the other two caught her and held her firmly. They'd pushed something against Daria's throat...

"You don't even know her secret, do you?" Millicent observed. "Maybe you should find out, but not now."

Her hand shaped into a casting posture and she tossed a spell at Elaine. A transfiguration spell, just like the one she'd used years ago, keyed to her own magic. Even a trained wizard would have difficulty undoing it without Millicent's help. Elaine felt the spell touch her, its perverse nature grappling with her body and altering it against her will...

...And then time seemed to slow down. The spell broke apart into its component pieces, each one instantly recognisable to her. Elaine felt one of the spells that had been forced into her mind rising up inside her, shaping a thought that required little power to turn into a spell. Her magic flared around her and Millicent's spell shattered as casually as if it had been nothing more than a gossamer thought. Other spells, some far darker than anything

77

Millicent had ever unleashed on her as a joke, rose up to match it. Elaine realised that her entire skin was buzzing with magic, not the magic forced upon her by Millicent, but something that rose from deep inside her. She might have had limited power, far less than Millicent had on her worst day, yet she did understand spell-casting on a level she couldn't have put into words. And Millicent couldn't have hoped to match...

...The spell, driven by hatred and rage and a burning lust for revenge, flared into existence within her mind. In some ways, it was even related to the spell she'd triggered when she'd opened Duke Gama's book. It would feed on Millicent's power rather than being dependent upon Elaine's own limited talent.

Her hand snapped out before she had quite realised what she was doing. Millicent was staring at her, shocked beyond words. She'd *known* that Elaine didn't have the power to throw off her spell so casually. Elaine didn't let her have a chance to react as power throbbed through her mind, magic feeding upon magic until it was beyond her ability to contain. The spell flashed from her power to Millicent and overwhelmed her. Any sorceress knew how to counter spells, but this was different. Her desperate attempt to counter what Elaine had unleashed was too late to save herself.

Millicent let out a yell as she shrank, shrinking so rapidly that she made a whirring sound. Her hands went up in a desperate attempt to strike back, but they turned to stone before she could do anything more than shape the first part of the thought that might have saved her. Before Elaine's astonished eyes, not quite believing what she had done, Millicent became a tiny statuette of herself. Power danced in front of her eyes, sending her staggering forward almost as if she were drunk, forcing Millicent's friends to step back in horror. They'd joined her because she was a bully, because it was safer to be one of her cronies than feel her wrath – and become the butt of her jokes. And now their patron had been transfigured against her will by someone she had always despised...

And even her aunt might be unable to restore her to human

form.

Elaine had no time to think. Her head buzzing, her thoughts feeling as if they were on fire, she stumbled forward and ran into the night.

Chapter Eight

The darkness seemed to reach out for her like a living thing as Elaine ran, barely aware of the crowds of people wandering the streets. Few of them showed any sign of concern, but why should they? The Golden City was not always kind to those caught up in conflicts between magicians, or those who served as the butt of magical jokes. Elaine finally slowed to a stop, panting desperately, to find herself in a darkened alleyway. There was no one else around as far as she could tell.

Her skin hurt, as if she'd been sunburned and it was only just starting to ache. She'd felt something like it before as a student, when her magical abilities were being studied and gauged by her tutors, but this was different. Even she had gained the control and discipline to keep a single spell from rebounding on her...yet she hadn't unleashed a single spell. She'd unleashed hundreds, perhaps thousands, of tiny spells that had worked in unison to produce an effect she didn't have the talent to create with a single spell. No wonder Millicent had been taken so badly by surprise. All of her countering charms had been used on the assumption that there was only one spell that needed to be deflected. She could have countered half of the spells Elaine had unleashed and still not saved herself from an unwanted transfiguration.

There *would* be consequences, Elaine knew. She wasn't a well-connected magician, or a student out on the town who knew that her idea of fun would be indulged, but someone without power and connections. Maybe the Inquisitors would have let it pass if she'd worked her spell on a mundane, without power or connections, but Millicent was connected to the very highest levels of society. And yet...the thought of seeing her most hated enemy so savagely and suddenly reduced was satisfying on a level Elaine couldn't begin to comprehend. Power, the kind of power she'd never had, tempted her. All the knowledge that had been poured into her head offered ways to enhance her magic, or to use it more efficiently than she'd ever learned in the Peerless School. But there would be a price...

She looked up sharply as she heard a snuffle, as if there was a dog sniffing its way towards her, but saw nothing in the semi-darkness. There were thousands of spells that could produce light, but somehow casting even one of them seemed beyond her power. She lifted a hand, peering into the gloom, yet there was still nothing. She wasn't even sure where she was...

...And then Daria stepped out of the darkness towards her. "Elaine," she called. Her dress was torn, leaving her forced to use one of her hands to hold it together or lose whatever remained of her modesty. "Elaine...are you all right?"

Elaine stared at her. "How did you find me?"

"Carefully," Daria said. She winked at Elaine, who could only stare back at her. "I decided to leave the chaos behind and come after you before they recovered from their shock."

Elaine fought down the urge to giggle. All of Millicent's cronies followed her because they had thought – had *known* – that she was an incredibly powerful and well-connected young woman. Better to laugh at her jokes and indulge her sense of humour than to be on the receiving end of her torments, better to watch someone else suffer than suffer themselves. But they would just have seen their leader transfigured against her will, forced into a form that would make being a frog seem comfortable and familiar...and transformed by someone they had believed to be barely strong enough to light a fire. Their world had just turned upside down.

She winced, remembering Bee. "And Bee?"

"I saw a pair of Inquisitors on their way to the club," Daria said. "I think they'll take care of him. He may not be very important in himself, but his patron is important enough to command attention even from the skulls. I wonder what they will make of Millicent."

Elaine shuddered. Inquisitor Dread had terrified her even when she hadn't been the target of his investigation, only the unwilling victim. What would he say to her if he had to hunt her down for breaking the rules? And yet she hadn't really broken any of the rules, not when Millicent had done the same to her in the past. But convention, the same convention that gave magicians free reign to wreak havoc as they experimented with their powers, probably didn't apply when the victim's family was so powerful.

"I should run," Elaine said. Millicent would surely tell the Inquisitors what had happened to her – and who had done it. She'd lose a great deal of her reputation – and maybe many of her cronies – but that would be no consolation for Elaine. "But where can I go?"

"Home," Daria said, firmly. "You need a rest and a chance to eat something. I don't think they're going to waste too much time trying to catch you."

"Not if I go home," Elaine said, through a sudden wave of dizziness. Magic had a price...and she'd never worked such a complex series of spells before. "It will be the first place they look."

"If they bother to look at all," Daria pointed out. "Do you really think that Millicent is going to be honest with them about what happened to her? The entire city would hear about it by the morning...and they'd all be laughing at her. I dread to imagine what her aunt would say to her after she recovers from being a tiny statue."

"There were hundreds of witnesses," Elaine said, with some irritation. "They could tell..."

"They won't want to get caught up in a feud between magicians," Daria said. "I think they'll suffer the kind of memory loss that even the most complex of memory charms couldn't produce. And besides...what are they going to charge you with in the absence of a Grand Sorcerer?"

She reached out and took Elaine's arm. "Besides, you don't want to stay here," she added. "Do you realise how close you came to the Blight?"

Elaine shivered. If she hadn't been so tired, she would have sensed the wild magic floating through the air, mocking her with its promise of power unleashed by the wizards who had called the Blight into existence. And yet she knew better than to go anywhere near the Blight. Wild magic could inflict changes in a victim that no amount of controlled magic could repair. There were no warning signs warning people to stay out of the Blight. The Golden City's council felt that anyone stupid enough to go into the most dangerous place in the world, short of the scorched continents that had once played host to the Witch-King's armies, deserved everything that happened to them.

Centuries ago, a cabal of wizards had experimented with a branch of necromancy that wasn't – technically – forbidden. Murder offered vast magical power to the necromancer willing to take it; they'd reasoned that trapping a victim in an endless death would offer a bottomless supply of power, even though it wouldn't have the same charge as a true murder. The Inquisitors had moved to stop the cabal and they'd fought back, unleashing all of their magic in one final cataclysmic burst. They'd contaminated the entire area with wild magic.

And wild magic was difficult, almost impossible, to control. It surged through the Blight like waves crashing over a beach, threatening random transformations – or death – to anyone caught up inside the field. No one lived in the Blight, not even the lowest of the low. With space in the Golden City so limited, the council had offered a vast reward for anyone who cleaned up the wild magic and opened the Blight to habitation again. So far, no one had succeeded.

Spells floated through her mind as Daria pulled her away from the alley and back onto the streets. Wild magic couldn't be dispersed; it had to go somewhere. There were spells that would tap the wild magic and use it up slowly, but surely – spells that no one knew even existed, perhaps not even the Grand Sorcerer. Elaine had known how many books of secrets were stored in the Great Library long before they'd all been jammed into her skull. One man, even the Grand Sorcerer himself, could not have read them all. And he could never have seen how to take some of the more complex spells apart and reassemble them in a form that might have served to drain the Blight.

Elaine had never been ambitious – but then, she'd known she had neither the talent nor breeding to be ambitious. What if *she* cleared the Blight? The Council had offered thousands of Crowns to the sorcerer who succeeded – and with that sort of money, who knew what she could do? Millicent would certainly never try to hurt her again...

...And yet it would attract attention. The Inquisition would start asking questions until they worked out what had happened, and then they would execute her for being in possession of forbidden knowledge. It didn't seem fair at all, but they would have no choice. The secrets within her mind whispered that there was a price to pay for greatly expanding one's power, a price that was most often paid in sanity. There were ways to make oneself more powerful than the Grand Sorcerer, capable of working enough magic to destroy the entire city, but if she tried she would go insane. They claimed that that was what had happened to the Witch-King...

History, the history she'd never been taught in the Peerless School, started to drift through her mind. The first necromancers had been evil; they'd wanted power and hadn't cared how many thousands they'd had to butcher to gain enough power to turn the world into a living nightmare. They'd had to be stopped – and it had taken six bloody years of fighting in the First Necromantic War to stop them. But that victory had come at a price. The Sorcerer Valiant, a name even the most uneducated knew from legends passed down from the wars, had absorbed the collected knowledge of the necromancers directly, using it to defeat them at the end of the war.

And then he'd become the Witch-King and unleashed a necromantic conflict more horrific than the first. Power had driven him mad. Dark knowledge had fuelled a quest for power that had threatened the fragile peace he'd helped create. And when the conflict finally came, there had been little left of the sorcerer who had saved the world. He'd become the maddened Witch-King.

No one knew that, outside the senior wizards. No one knew that the heroic Valiant and the dreaded Witch-King were one and the same. But Elaine knew...

...And in a moment of insight, she wondered if the spell that had been worked on her, that had jammed all of the Library's knowledge into her head, was related to the spell that had started the long process of turning Valiant into the Witch-King.

She stopped dead, staring at the stone beneath her feet. It was so hard to focus, but most of her tutors had been very capable at imparting knowledge to young minds and she remembered most of what she'd been taught. Many compulsion and enslavement spells worked by placing irrepressible thoughts into helpless minds, commands that the victim couldn't even begin to disobey. Could it be possible that placing vast amounts of knowledge into a mind would start corrupting the mind and eventually driving the victim mad? The thought was terrifying. Could *she* become a new Witch-King herself? And yet Valiant had been an incredibly powerful sorcerer even before he'd started to tap the secrets of becoming a necromancer. Elaine had far less power to use as a base for becoming a monster.

Maybe she *should* go to the Inquisition. They would kill her and end whatever threat she posed long before she went mad.

"Come on," Daria said, encouragingly. Her friend sounded remarkably composed for someone who looked to be on the verge of exposing her breasts to the crowds around them. "We're nearly there. Or maybe..."

She let go of Elaine's hand and walked over to one of the roadside stalls. Elaine had never fully trusted the meals one could buy on the streets, even the ones cooked by people who understood the concept of basic hygiene. Daria seemed to eat far more meat than was good for her and never seemed to get ill, while Elaine had learned the hard way not to eat more from the street eateries than she needed to barely satisfy her hunger. Elaine watched as Daria haggled briefly with an older woman standing behind the portable stove and eventually purchased two wrapped parcels of meat. Her mouth started to water as she smelled the cooked chicken and bread inside the packets. Daria opened one, sniffed it quickly, and then passed it to her.

"I had all the toppings on mine," she said, by way of explanation. Elaine nodded in understanding. Daria seemed capable of drinking spicy sauces that set Elaine's mouth on fire. "That one should be fairly sedate."

"I wonder if it's edible," Elaine muttered, as she picked up the first piece of chicken. Her stomach growled and she swallowed it without hesitation. It tasted surprisingly good, although there was a faint aftertaste of cooking fat. "What about yours?"

Daria held up a piece of chicken covered in bright red sauce. "I've had hotter meals," she said. Elaine caught a whiff of the sauce and shuddered. How anyone could eat it was beyond her. "Did I tell you that I once dated a guy from Cinnabar? Now *he* knew how to cook the hottest of meals."

Elaine remembered Bee...and shuddered. "Do you think he's ever going to want to see me again?"

Daria seemed to understand. "I think that he's a nice guy," she said, seriously. "And he seemed to like you. Perhaps he'll want to go out somewhere a little quieter in the future."

"If he ever wants to see me again," Elaine repeated. Just once – just *once* – she would have liked to meet a guy and indulge herself without any fears for the future. "He'll probably hate me for the rest of time."

"Maybe he'll find it exciting," Daria said, and winked. "There are some guys who just *love* the thought of being enchanted by a woman."

Elaine flushed. She'd never been part of the inner circles when she'd been a teenager, but she'd heard rumours. Some of them had been so absurd she'd been sure that her peers were trying to trick her into believing their lies. And yet some of the knowledge forced into her head left her wondering if the rumours were actually true. How could anyone get addicted to the sensation of being enchanted against one's will?

"Then surely he'd want Millicent, not me," Elaine said, bitterly. Millicent enjoyed men, particularly the men who wanted to form an alliance with Millicent's family. The gods alone knew if she'd ever seal with a particular man, although some of the higher families pushed their daughters into marriages for dynastic purposes. Whoever ended up unwillingly sealed to Millicent would be entering hell itself. "*She* wouldn't hesitate to turn him into a frog for looking at her sideways."

"I don't know," Daria said. She patted Elaine on the shoulder as they reached their apartment. "Listen to the voice of experience for a moment. You've enjoyed your first taste of male company and there's no need to ruin it by pressing ahead too fast." She leered cheerfully at her. "Take it from me – men like doing the chasing, not being chased. The secret is to run away slowly enough to be caught."

"That makes no sense," Elaine protested.

"Just you wait until you have more experience," Daria said, as her leer became a grin. "Like I said, don't try to move ahead too fast. Men always value what they have to fight for more highly than what they get for free. Maybe on your next date you can kiss him a little, leave the passionate embrace for the third date and..."

Elaine felt herself flush, again. "You're disgraceful," she protested. "I can't do that."

"You said you couldn't dance either," Daria said, not in the least bit offended. "And yet tonight you were dancing as if you'd been dancing for years."

They reached their apartment, dumped the remains of the paper wrapping in the bin and headed to their rooms. "Get some sleep," Daria advised. "Tomorrow you can start thinking about what you're going to wear on your next date."

Elaine hesitated. "Daria," she said, slowly, "why did Millicent say that you had a secret?"

"Everyone has secrets," Daria said. "I have secrets that belong to my folk – I bet you that Millicent has secrets of her own. She probably thinks that the Travellers had other ideas than just making sure that one of their people got a proper education when they left me here."

Elaine shrugged. "Do you think that the Travellers would take me in?"

"Only if you married one of my brothers," Daria said. Elaine blinked. Daria had never *mentioned* brothers before, let alone the rest of her family. "Take it from me, you don't want to do that. They're dreadfully...traditionalist, set in their ways. And besides, your children would be accepted, but you'd never be fully one of us."

"I see," Elaine said. "That doesn't sound very nice."

"They're not very nice people," Daria admitted. "You know how most people treat Travellers, even ones who are harmless. They're never convinced that they should be nicer to people because no one is nice to them."

Elaine could understand that, all right. "I'll get some rest," she said, "and I know what I'm doing in the morning."

"Looking up protection spells, just in case?" Daria hazarded.

"Research," Elaine said, firmly. It was time that she started to try to figure out what had happened to her, preferably before the next surprise caught up with her. "Maybe I'll even go back to the Library."

Daria grinned, unpleasantly. "Sweetheart, I have *never* heard it called *that* before."

Chapter Nine

Duke Gama had been the younger brother of King Hildebrand. Elaine had known that from the notes attached to the crates of books she'd opened when she'd been hit by the curse, but according to the writers of *Peers of the Empire* it was the single most important fact about the dead Duke. The writers waxed endlessly on the subject of how worthy his bloodline was of the highest positions in the Empire, but they were remarkably short of actual details that might be of some use to her. King Hildebrand was the ruler of Ida, a small state only a few hundred miles from the Golden City, whose son had been angling for a marriage alliance that would tie them to the strongest magical families in the world. It took seventeen pages to tell Elaine something that could have been said in a few sentences.

But maybe it wasn't too surprising, Elaine told herself. Ever since the last Emperor had died, killed in the Necromantic Wars, the Grand Sorcerers had worked hard to keep the nobility from having any real power. They'd helped *start* the First Necromantic War because they'd feared that the magical bloodlines – and magic's seemingly random choice of new magicians – would eventually swamp the non-magical bloodlines. Now, after the wars, the kings and dukes and even empresses were subordinate to the wizards. The whole system of Court Wizards was intended to keep them in their place. There would be no repeat of the Necromantic Wars.

Some of it she'd known from reading between the lines back at the Peerless School, but other details only made sense when viewed through the prism of the new knowledge that had been poured into her head. Magicians were intensively competitive; the first necromancers had worked their dark deeds intending to make themselves supremely powerful, rather than unleashing hell purely for fun. Now, magicians had an opportunity to develop their magic and climb the ladder towards Grand Sorcerer, something that required them to uphold a system that limited their freedom of action. And the Peerless School steered its students towards developing what talent they had rather than attempting to gain new power. There would be no more necromancers.

But perhaps there would be. Elaine shivered as the spells started to jostle their way through her head. She could raise the dead and set them out upon the land to consume their way through the living, or summon a dead person's shade back to the world to answer questions, or...her sleep hadn't been peaceful at all. All of the images of the past, of the hero who'd become the Witch-King, had marched through her dreams, warning her of what she might become. And the potion she'd taken to ensure a dreamless sleep had failed badly. She couldn't understand why.

She flicked through the book again and shook her head. Ida might have had one of the oldest noble families in the Empire, but it was a tiny state, barely fifty miles across from one end to the other. Only bad terrain and a certain ruthlessness had stopped her neighbours from conquering her centuries before the Necromantic Wars. They'd even held out against swarms of flesh-eating undead unleashed by the necromancers, although the undead had had problems operating in the extreme cold. Elaine had heard reports that melting glaciers had released hundreds of undead from their frozen sleep, whereupon they'd set out to continue their quest for human flesh. At least they were less dangerous without the necromancers guiding their actions. A small troop of soldiers and a wizard or two could have dealt with them before they became a major threat.

Duke Gama had had magic listed as one of his interests, but he'd never studied in the Peerless School or even been tutored by hedge witches from the surrounding countryside. There was more magic in the world than that controlled by the Peerless School, and it *was* possible that Duke Gama had somehow avoided being noticed by the Grand Sorcerer, but if he'd had real power surely he would have used it to enhance his chances on the marriage market. Instead, he'd collected books and a handful of artefacts that had been forwarded to the Great Library upon his death...

...Unless he wasn't dead at all. There were spells that were meant to confirm that an aristocrat had passed into the realm of the gods, but they could be tricked by a clever magician or subverted by someone with enough power to simply override them. What if Duke Gama had *intended* his books, including the cursed volume, to go to the Great Library? It would have only been a matter of time before Elaine – or one of her fellows – opened the book and was struck by the curse. Maybe he'd found a way to do the impossible and burgle the Great Library. Who needed the books when all of their knowledge was inside a hapless human head?

And yet...it seemed a risky plan, one rife with uncertainties. What if the Inquisitors had realised what had happened before Elaine left the hospital? Or what if she'd gone to them and confessed to what had happened? Or what if the curse had killed her outright? The druids had said that Elaine had come *very* close to death. Someone with more power might have been killed as their magic was tapped to fuel the curse.

She closed the book with some irritation and looked over at the next one. Somehow, Ida had escaped having the normal thousands of volumes of books written on her history. But then, Ida had simply never been very important. Apart from the Court Wizard – a fellow named Trebuchet, according to the latest guide to magicians and their families – there seemed to be no magicians of note living within the mountainous kingdom. Ida seemed to like to keep herself to herself, although perhaps *that* wasn't so surprising. The advantages that had kept the kingdom as free as any other state in the Empire wouldn't allow it to build an empire of its own. On the great plains below the mountains, Ida's soldiers would be cut to ribbons by the armoured troops of the nearby states. They could raid, but little else...

...and none of that now that the magicians ruled the world.

A crash from below, followed by footsteps coming up the stairs, announced Daria's arrival in the apartment building. She came in through the door, holding a set of papers, and smiled cheerfully at Elaine, before taking the seat opposite her and picking up one of the books.

"This doesn't look like a guide to protection spells," she observed. "What do you think you are doing?"

"Researching," Elaine said, crossly. She'd borrowed the books from one of the smaller libraries, borrowing everything she could find on Ida and its ruling family, which hadn't really been very much. "I don't have time to think about guys."

"There's never a better time to think about guys," Daria said, putting down the book. "I thought you liked Bee."

Elaine snorted. "Do you think about anything else?"

Daria smirked. "By the gods, I do believe I don't," she said, deadpan. "Naughty Daria. Very naughty Daria."

"I'm thinking about paying Ida a visit," Elaine said. "You want to come with me?"

"I thought of a way we could make money," Daria said. "You know that there are thousands of touts in the city, right?" Elaine nodded. "So why don't we join them in betting on who will be the next Grand Sorcerer?"

"It's only been a day since the funeral," Elaine said. It was strange how it felt much longer, but then the funeral had been a minor event compared to accidentally turning Millicent into a statue. Had she even been transformed back into a bitch yet? "Don't they have any decency at all?"

"They have a week to register before they actually begin the competition," Daria said. "Rumour has it that some of the senior wizards actually dropped *out* of the contest before their names were even listed. Do you think that that is remotely likely to be true?"

"I don't know," Elaine said. Putting one's name forward as a possible candidate meant accepting the rules of the contest, as laid down by the first Grand Sorcerer. He'd been the most powerful survivor of the Second Necromantic War and no one had dared to dispute too openly with him. And yet, there *was* no rule against withdrawing from the contest. "Maybe someone is just trying to fiddle the odds."

"No doubt," Daria agreed. She picked up a sheet of paper and glanced at it. "Ready?"

Elaine blinked. "For what?"

"First on the list of declared candidates is Administrator Mentor, our old master from the Peerless School," Daria said.

"The touts like his chances; he was the old Grand Sorcerer's friend and he has access to all the books stored within the Peerless School. And don't forget that he played a role in directly shaping the last few generations of magicians. And if he wasn't powerful, he would never have been able to hold his post..."

Elaine, whose only close contact with Administrator Mentor had been when she'd been punished for one of Millicent's pranks, shrugged. "He didn't really shape me, did he?"

"He certainly helped shape Millicent and the others like her," Daria pointed out. "They probably owe him a few favours, if only for covering things up and even protecting them from the wrath of their families. Millicent's family might not care what she does outside of their houses, but others would certainly be very angry with their children if they knew the half of it. The Administrator certainly has a very good chance."

She smiled. "The next person on the list is Count Lucas, who is supposed to be the illegitimate son of the Duke of Randor," she continued. "Unlike most of the parents of bastards, the Duke of Randor saw to it that his son got a good education and eventually went to the Peerless School. He graduated with high honours two years before we went into the school and...since then, he doesn't seem to have done much. But he could have been doing anything even if he didn't build a proper reputation."

"The name is familiar," Elaine said. She grinned as she put it together. "He used to go to the Great Library – probably still *is* going to the Great Library while I've been off work. I think he was studying rare magical hybrids from the outer continents."

"Or maybe he thinks he has the power to defeat all comers in the arena," Daria agreed. "The touts aren't sure what to make of him. He doesn't have the reputation of the Administrator or most of the other senior wizards, but surely he wouldn't put his name forward unless he was fairly sure that he could back it up. Or maybe he'll just back out before the contest actually starts."

She leant forward. "I don't suppose his recent fields of

interest taught you anything about his aims?"

"Nothing," Elaine said. Despite herself, she *was* getting interested. "Who's next?"

"Millicent's auntie, Lady Light Spinner," Daria said. "She's supposed to be an initiate into the Elysium Mysteries as well as one of the Peerless School's most powerful graduates in the last thirty years. Unsealed, which is interesting given her breeding. Maybe she couldn't have children or maybe she just had the power to tell her family to go to hell. She served in a couple of minor roles before becoming Court Wizard to the Empress of the South after the scandal broke about how the last wizard had been seduced by the Empress. And apparently she hasn't even resigned from that post even though she's competing in the arena."

Elaine snorted. Senior wizards loved their status. "She'd have to resign if she became Grand Sorceress," she pointed out. "And what do the touts say about her chances?"

"Second, under the Administrator," Daria said. "It doesn't hurt that her family is connected to many of the more powerful magical bloodlines. I have no doubt that they will bring pressure to bear on her opponents if necessary. But there's only ever been one other female Grand Sorcerer and that wasn't the best experience the Empire ever had."

She smiled, humourlessly. "Countering her is Vlad Deferens, one of the more...politically outspoken sorcerers in recent years," she added. "You've probably heard of him."

"Yeah," Elaine muttered. "The one who keeps claiming that female magicians are unnatural and should be allowed to serve as nothing more than breeding stock."

"What do you expect from someone who grew up in Gor?" Daria asked, wryly. "Half of their magic – and their culture – is based around keeping their females properly respectful to the males. Even ten years in the Peerless School and then the Golden City hasn't convinced him that women are more than baby-factories on legs. Let him have the power of the Grand Sorcerer and there will be riots in the streets. Every female magician in the world will stand against him."

She shrugged. "But he has power and one hell of a reputation for squashing magicians who break the rules," she added. "Rumour has it that he was the one who suggested that your boss should be enslaved rather than killed outright. The touts think that he has a good chance, unless some kindly magician kills him before the contest begins. Or maybe he will be killed in the contest. Deferens isn't the kind of person to back down if challenged."

"The gods help us if he does get into power," Elaine said. "Who else is there?"

"Wizard Kane has decided to join the contest, but he's not a particularly well-known candidate," Daria said, checking her list. "No great achievements, no great political relationships...he may decide to back out quietly rather than go into the arena as a contestant. And then there's the final contestant, the really strange one. Prince Hilarion of Ida."

Elaine stared at her. "Of *Ida*?"

"Of Ida," Daria confirmed. "Do you know him?"

"Only through reputation," Elaine said, picking up one of the books. Prince Hilarion was, if she recalled correctly, the heir to the throne. What was *he* doing serving as a magician? Come to think of it...*was* he even a magician? "How...how did *he* get in?"

"Turned up at the arena, demonstrated his magic and then put his name into the pile of candidates," Daria said. "The touts don't know what to make of him either. He never even went to the Peerless School. As far as anyone can tell, he never had any formal training at all. And yet he thinks he can become Grand Sorcerer."

Elaine frowned, puzzled. It wasn't impossible to get a magical education outside the Peerless School, but anyone who wanted real power should definitely have gone to the Golden City. And yet...if Prince Hilarion was the heir to Ida, maybe his father had hired a wizard to train his son rather than have him go to the Peerless School and end up sucked into the political struggles that ranged through the Golden City. But how could he feel that he could compete with the mighty magicians who were going to face one another for the greatest prize of all? Unless he thought that he might have an ace in the hole...

The thought struck her like a blow between the eyes. Maybe he *did* have an ace in the hole, Elaine herself. What could someone who hadn't sworn the Mage's Oath do with the knowledge loaded into Elaine's head? The thought was terrifying. He could boost his power, push himself into a position that matched the Witch-King himself...and then win the contest. But the Inquisitors would act, wouldn't they? Unless they couldn't – how could they when they were sworn to uphold the orders of the Grand Sorcerer?

Daria leaned forward. "Are you all right?" she asked. "Does he sound familiar to you?"

"I was reading about Ida," Elaine said. Daria had provided the piece that linked the puzzle together. Duke Gama might not have been a magician, but his nephew definitely was. He could have enchanted the book Elaine had opened and then waited for her to emerge from hospital...complete with the knowledge he needed to make himself the most powerful sorcerer in the world. "I think I definitely need to go visit the kingdom."

"But the action is *here*," Daria protested. "Think about our chances of winning money..."

I could clean up the Blight and win money, Elaine thought, sourly. *If I dared risk exposing myself like that...*

"I have to go," she said. "*Someone* needs to follow up on what Duke Gama did to the book that stunned me – and besides, I don't want to be anywhere near Millicent when she returns to normal."

"I suppose there is that," Daria said, reluctantly. "You go if you want. I have to stay here and try to make money." She grinned. "Do you want to place a bet? If Prince Hilarion does become Grand Sorcerer, anyone who bids a hundred Crowns will win a million from the touts."

"If I had a hundred Crowns, I'd find something better to do than place bets," Elaine said. "I'd prefer to bet on the Administrator myself..."

She broke off as there was a furious knocking on the door. Daria walked over and opened the door while Elaine cringed, certain that it was an Inquisitor intent on asking her precisely what had happened to Millicent. Instead, it was a tall footman wearing a bright red uniform that made him look faintly absurd. No one would have risked laughing openly at him, not with the gold braid that denoted his mistress.

"Magician Elaine No-Kin," he said, as he marched into the

room. His voice boomed through the tiny apartment, the voice of a man who was used to getting his way. "You are commanded to present yourself before the Lady Light Spinner. Attend on her or face the consequences."

Elaine and Daria shared a look. "Maybe," Elaine said, finally. "And maybe not."

Chapter Ten

The footman stared at them. Whatever he'd expected, it hadn't included open defiance.

"My mistress summons you," he said, returning to his instructions. Elaine caught sight of the jewelled collar around his neck and shuddered. He wouldn't have any choice but to do exactly as he was told. The enslavement charms worked into the collar would see to that. "She insists that you attend upon her..."

"Very well," Elaine said, tiredly. There would *definitely* be consequences for what she'd done to Millicent, no matter how much the bully had deserved a nasty shock. "I will come with you."

Daria caught her arm. "Do you want me to come with you?"

The honest answer to that was *yes*, but Elaine shook her head. If Lady Light Spinner had decided to punish her personally, Daria would just be caught up in the crossfire. "I'll be fine," she said, slowly. "You stay here and I will be back soon enough."

She allowed the footman to lead her down the stairs and into a gaudy carriage that was waiting outside the door. The two horses in front of the vehicle snorted as Elaine climbed into the cabin, and then started to pull the carriage down the street. They didn't have to worry about the crowds on the roads, not with the sigils on the carriage marking it as belonging to one of the most powerful women in the world. And besides, anyone who tried to block its path would probably wind up tasting the coachman's whip.

Elaine tried to calm herself as the coach rattled its way through the streets, concentrating on exercises she'd learned at the Peerless School. They didn't really help, not when she knew that a very unpleasant interview awaited her. Who knew how Millicent's aunt would react to what had happened to the bully? Even if she disliked Millicent and everything she did, she would certainly not take her forced transformation into a statue very lightly. It would only give her enemies ideas. She caught sight of a pair of gates outside the carriage before it rattled to a stop in front of one of the oldest mansions in High Tory. At least Lady Light Spinner couldn't afford a garden of her own. Perhaps she'd buy Lord Howarth's when it became clear that he needed a large infusion of cash. If she waited long enough, she'd probably get it very cheaply.

The door opened and the footman helped her down onto the pavement. A pair of dark-skinned maids awaited her, wearing fancy uniforms – and collars around their necks. Absurdly, Elaine found herself wishing that she'd worn something a little more formal than her dark shirt and second-hand trousers. If she'd known that Lady Light Spinner wanted her to call on her...of course, if she'd known, she would have taken more care to hide herself. The Inquisitors weren't the only ones who'd want answers from her.

She smiled as she was led into the building and up a long flight of stairs that seemed to stretch upwards into infinity. Like the Great Library, and the Parade of the Endless, the building had been tied to a pocket dimension that allowed it to be far larger on the inside than on the outside. It was a testament to the power and wealth of the bloodline that had produced Millicent – and Lady Light Spinner. What they couldn't do for themselves they could buy on the open market.

A long corridor, decorated with paintings that seemed almost alive, opened up in front of her. Elaine was impressed, despite herself. It took serious magic to create soul figments that would live on after the person in the painting was dead. Lady Light Spinner could call upon all the knowledge and wisdom of her ancestors, something that reminded Elaine that *she* had no ancestors. Her family was still as much a mystery as ever. The maids escorted her into a small sitting room and pointed to a chair. Lady Light Spinner entered a moment later, still wearing the black garment that hid everything but her eyes. It was difficult even to get a sense of the outline of her body.

Something crashed down beside her and Elaine jumped. The statuette lay on the table, with Millicent's stunned and frozen eyes staring at her. Elaine felt herself shiver again as she saw her rival's helpless form. Lady Light Spinner and all the other magicians in Millicent's family had clearly been unable to reverse what Elaine had done...

...If it were *possible* to reverse it. There were spells in her mind that touched on wild – and chaotic – magic, using it to cause permanent transformation. She *thought* that she hadn't done that to Millicent, but she'd been so dazed that it was impossible to say for sure what she'd done that night. Had it really only been yesterday that she'd faced and beaten Millicent for the first time? Whatever happened to her, it was difficult not to feel a certain pride in what she'd done. Millicent would never think of her so lightly ever again.

"You transformed my niece into a statue," Lady Light Spinner said. Her voice was cold, almost emotionless. "You will undo the transformation. Now."

The old Elaine would probably have done as she was ordered, at once. But the new Elaine had different ideas.

"Millicent treated me badly ever since we first met," she said, trying hard to keep the pain out of her voice. But what had she done to deserve such a powerful tormentor? "Why did you allow her to treat anyone like that?"

"Millicent needs to learn certain lessons for herself," Lady Light Spinner said. "You will undo the transformation now."

Elaine felt cold rage bubbling up within her. How *dare* the woman lecture her like that, or try to force her into doing anything against her will? "She turned me into a frog for a week," she said, remembering all the humiliations that Millicent had forced upon her. "Why shouldn't I leave her like that forever?"

"Because if you do, I will be forced to deal with you," Lady Light Spinner said. She held up a single gloved hand and clicked her fingers. Elaine felt her body suddenly frozen helplessly, just as Millicent had done to Bee. The charms she'd used to shield herself had failed completely. "And you will not enjoy that experience."

She waved a hand dismissively and Elaine found that she

could move again. "At least you're not trying to pretend that Millicent is somehow a good person," she said, after a moment. She wanted to yell and scream, but she had the feeling that that would be pointless, perhaps worse than pointless. "Why did you allow her such freedom of action?"

"You know as well as I do that it is power that determines a person's place in society," Lady Light Spinner said. It was hard to be sure, but she sounded reluctant to talk openly. "Millicent will discover that even her power has limits – and on that day, she will discover her true place in society. Those who are weak are the servants of the strong."

And *that*, Elaine knew, probably explained why Prince Hilarion had been so desperate to learn magic. As a King, even of an isolated state like Ida, he would still have had to defer to the magicians. His Court Wizard wasn't just the power behind the throne, but the person who would stop him if he tried to get above himself. And if he'd managed to gain a proper education without ever having to swear the Mage's Oath, who knew what he might be capable of doing? Maybe he'd already enchanted and enslaved his Court Wizard, who should have warned the Grand Sorcerer if his charge was developing formidable abilities.

"Millicent is a bitch, plain and simple," Elaine said. It felt *good* to finally let it all out, all the hatred and resentment she'd been forced to feel over the years. "Why should I do *anything* for her?"

They stared at each other for a long moment. "I can offer you power and wealth beyond anything you could obtain for yourself," Lady Light Spinner said, finally. It was clear that she had limits on how far she could push Elaine. But then, magical compulsions worked poorly on magicians, at least if their mistresses wanted them to perform actual magic. "Or I can ensure that Millicent never bothers you again."

It was a tempting offer. "Very well," Elaine said, finally. "If I can free her, you will have to swear an oath that you will keep her away from me – and that you will pay me one thousand Crowns in payment for helping her return to normal."

She'd expected Lady Light Spinner to haggle and was disappointed when she merely nodded slowly. "Very well," she said. "I *swear* that I will keep Millicent away from you and that I will pay you for your services, once she is free of your spell."

Elaine nodded. She knew that most magicians who swore oaths *had* to keep them, if only for fear that their magic would rebound upon them. Lady Light Spinner wouldn't have become so powerful without swearing the Mage's Oath, would she? But Prince Hilarion clearly thought that he could gain power without attending to any of the obligations, such as they were.

She reached over and picked up Millicent's stony form. It had been years since she'd studied transfiguration – and enchantment – at the Peerless School, but the knowledge forced into her head told her that this wasn't an ordinary statue. What would happen when the magic finally faded away? Millicent should have returned to normal, yet whatever Elaine had done hadn't been a remotely normal spell. Maybe her awareness would just drift away into nothingness, like some of the unluckier victims of the Blight.

Magic crackled along her fingertips, yet it seemed curiously reluctant to slide into Millicent's form. Elaine closed her eyes and concentrated, dragging up spells she'd never used outside the Peerless School, but nothing happened. Had she *killed* Millicent outright when she'd transfigured her? It was possible.

"Undo the spell," Lady Light Spinner said, remorselessly. "Now."

"I don't know *how*," Elaine burst out, in frustration. "I don't..."

As if her outburst had triggered a thought in her mind, she felt new spells coming to the forefront of her awareness. She hadn't really used a single spell on Millicent, but hundreds of tiny spells...all of which were now rebelling against her conventional attempt to free Millicent from her bondage. It would need something similar to undo the spell...she kept her eyes firmly closed and concentrated, muttering the words under her breath as they came into her mind. And Millicent's form started to shift...

Elaine threw her away and watched as she hit the floor. The statue was vibrating, stretching in and out of conventional reality as magic contested with the counter-magic she'd shaped in her mind. And then there was a loud *bang* and Millicent lay on the floor in front of them, breathing heavily. Her clothes were all torn and bedraggled by the magic that had warped her form into a tiny statue. "You're free," Elaine said. The look of absolute fear on Millicent's face felt surprisingly good after the years of torment, though part of her was appalled at what she had done, even to a girl who had treated her terribly. "Welcome back to flesh and blood."

Millicent seemed to find it hard to talk. "You...you..."

"You will say no more," Lady Light Spinner said, cutting off her niece before Millicent could say anything that might have gotten her into real trouble again. "You will report to the druids for a full examination and then we will...discuss your future. Go."

Millicent threw one more half-scared look at Elaine and stumbled out of the room. Elaine felt tired and dizzy, almost as if she was on the verge of being sick. Using magic like that should have been impossible, surely. And yet she'd done it twice. Lady Light Spinner looked up at her, her blue eyes expressionless, her face invisible behind the veil.

"You will receive your money," Lady Light Spinner said. "I thank you for your service."

"You're welcome," Elaine said, tartly. She already regretted what she'd done. "Give me the money and then I will take my leave."

"I have an offer to make to you," Lady Light Spinner said. "I need powerful young magicians to assist me in my work. Join me; work with me."

Elaine shook her head, quickly. "I'm really not that powerful," she said, truthfully. Millicent could have beaten her effortlessly if they'd matched talent against talent. "All I did was..."

"Something new," Lady Light Spinner said. "I could use you. Do you really wish to see Sorcerer Deferens wearing the robes of the Grand Sorcerer?"

"I don't think I could tip the balance," Elaine said. Surely the contest was between the candidates themselves, not their clients. But very little was known about the contest the first

Grand Sorcerer had devised. If more had been known, the touts would probably have been happier – and it would have been easier for them to start placing their bets. "I just want to get on with my life."

"Your former boss has left the Great Library," Lady Light Spinner informed her. Elaine's eyes opened wide. Miss Prim couldn't leave the Great Library...but it had been the Grand Sorcerer who had bound her to serve in the Library until his death. The charm holding her there would have died along with the sorcerer who'd cast it. "My patronage could ensure that you get her post as Head Librarian."

That was tempting, Elaine had to admit. Some of her co-workers hadn't wanted to stay in the Library for their entire careers, but Elaine would have been quite happy if she'd slowly risen up in the ranks until she became the supervisor of the entire building. It had always felt warm and friendly to her.

But she didn't want to owe anything to Lady Light Spinner.

"No," she said, finally. "I will work my way to the top on my own."

"Then go," Lady Light Spinner said. "Collect your money from the men downstairs and then walk home."

Forcing her to walk home had probably been intended as a slap across the face, but Elaine was silently grateful. She needed time to think.

***

"You turned her back to normal?"

Elaine nodded. "I don't think I had much choice," she said. "What would have happened if she'd gotten the Inquisition involved?"

"They would probably have been impressed that you managed to do it in the first place," Daria said. "But never mind...guess who came calling while you were out?"

Elaine was too tired for guessing games. "Tell me."

"Bee," Daria said, with a grin. "I took the liberty of assuring him that you'd be more than happy to go out with him tomorrow night. I think he plans to take you somewhere *very* fancy."

Elaine flushed. "I have to go to Ida the day afterwards,"

she said. It would have been simple to use one of the teleport stations constructed by various magicians, but it would have drained even the money she'd been given by Lady Light Spinner. Besides, she'd never travelled outside the Golden City before and she was curious to see the countryside. An iron dragon would take her all the way to Ida – and the station built below the mountain peaks. "I suppose dinner would be nice..."

"Just don't let him go too far," Daria advised. "Men simply cannot be trusted to know what's best for them, or for the girl. Don't let him do anything that makes you feel uncomfortable."

"I'll do my best," Elaine promised her. She glanced at the calendar on the wall while she considered. She had ten days of leave left before she had to return to the Great Library, unless she was called in early to help prepare the groundwork for Miss Prim's successor. It was possible that they would call her in, but she *was* ill. The druids would probably have told them not to bother Elaine unless it was vitally important. "Are you going to be coming?"

Daria gave her a look that suggested that she might have gone insane. "It's a chance for *you* to be with him, twit," she said. "Now why don't we go shopping. You'll want to look your best..."

She made a show of considering Elaine's face. "White is really too bright for your hair, but green or red wouldn't set it off well," she said. "Black might be good for you..."

"I am not going to buy a new outfit just for one date," Elaine said, firmly.

"Of course you are," Daria said. "This isn't just the first date, my dear; it could be the start of a whole new life for you. Just think about all the men who will be asking you out in the future." She paused in thought. "Maybe gold cloth – it should set your hair off nicely and will make you look like a lady who's worth a few thousand Crowns..."

Elaine put her hands on her hips and prepared to be stubborn. But Daria – of course – just kept going.

And she might be right. It might be fun.

Chapter Eleven

"Well, how do you feel?"

Elaine scowled at her friend. "Exposed," she said, finally. "I can't wear this in public."

She gazed at the mirror and saw her own reflection looking back. Daria had found her a gold-tinted dress from somewhere, which she had to admit looked nice with her hair, but it showed off more of her chest than she found comfortable. She had always been a little self-conscious about her chest – both Daria and Millicent had far larger breasts – and showing it off to a guy she barely knew was too much. At least on the first date.

"Then pull it up," Daria said. She reached for the dress, pulled it up to Elaine's neck and muttered a spell to keep it in place. "That should hold long enough to keep you covered – just use a standard countering spell if you happen to want to get rid of it quickly."

"As if," Elaine said, crossly. She hadn't even *been* on the date yet and she already wished that it was over. "I'm not going to take it off until I get back home." She paused, suspiciously. "The spell isn't going to wear off halfway through the dinner, is it?"

"I don't think so," Daria assured her. She'd heard the rumours about fashion disasters too, caused by spells wearing off at the wrong time. Some unlucky girls had been revealed to be wearing nothing more than charmed rags in the finest restaurants in the city. "It's tied in with the cloth – it won't fade unless you deliberately banish it. And it has protection wards to prevent someone else from making the spells fail."

Elaine snorted. She didn't need the knowledge from the Great Library to know that such spells always had their limits. If she was particularly unlucky, she might even discover that her dress fell to pieces when one of Millicent's cronies set out to embarrass her, although maybe *that* wouldn't happen in a hurry. Lady Light Spinner had sworn her oath to keep Millicent from bothering Elaine any longer.

...Although Elaine wasn't sure how far she could trust Millicent to do as her aunt commanded. The girl was a bully, someone who considered herself superior to everyone else – particularly Elaine. She'd be more likely to believe that her transfiguration was an unlucky accident rather than Elaine suddenly developing the power to make her pay for years of torment and humiliation. And that might lead her to believe that she could win a second magical duel.

"I'm dressed," she announced, pushing the thought aside. She was going to have a good time tonight, damn it. Even if she had to kiss Bee...the funny thing was that that thought wasn't even remotely repellent. "Now should I undress and wait for this evening?"

Daria blinked at her, owlishly. "Of course not," she said. "We have to do your make up and brush your hair...you should be ready just in time for when he arrives."

"But..." Elaine began. She'd never taken much time over her appearance. Getting dressed only took a few minutes, even when she'd had to wear her graduation robes for the funeral. And there were still three *hours* before Bee was due to arrive. "I can't wear this until then."

"Of course you can," Daria said. "I've known girls at the parlour who have worn their dresses for hours rather than go to all the trouble of getting undressed and then redressing later. You're lucky you don't have to go in for semi-permanent beauty transfigurations. Some of the girls I know would probably be in real trouble if their magic ran out suddenly and their faces tried to snap back to normal."

She chuckled, mischievously. Elaine shivered at the thought. Transfiguring a person – or even part of a person – placed a strain on reality. Repeated transfigurations made someone or something flexible, capable of changing its form without needing the massive level of magic needed to overwrite reality, but it also made their form somewhat fluid, without even a clear idea of what it should be. Losing the spells that pinned the new form in place might leave the victim nothing more than a fleshy mass, struggling to breathe – or kill them outright if they became stuck between transfigurations.

"Anyway, hold still," Daria added. "It's time for the next part of the program."

She pushed Elaine gently back onto a stool and started to work on her face with a tiny pair of charmed brushes. Elaine almost giggled as the brushes tickled her, just before Daria held up a mirror in front of her face, showing how her skin had paled under her touch. The porcelain doll look was popular right now, but Daria had pointed out that it wouldn't really suit Elaine at all and what she really needed was a minimal effect that showed up her eyes and hair. Elaine had found it hard to follow the technical terms and had resigned herself to doing as Daria said, and hoping. She could have changed herself using one of the new spells if necessary...

She sighed as Daria prodded at her cheekbones, thinking about the Blight. If she *could* do something about it, maybe she could claim to have been testing something new when Millicent had had her little accident. There was no reason why long-lost magical knowledge couldn't be rediscovered, even the darkest secrets of necromancy. But she'd never had a reputation as a researcher into magical techniques and someone would probably start asking questions until they got to the truth, whereupon they would execute whatever was left of her for possessing illicit knowledge. It was a shame, she told herself. The reward for cleansing the Blight would have given her enough money to build a proper life for herself.

"Not too bad," Daria said, critically. "You know how much some of the girls at the parlour would give for looks like yours?"

"Nothing," Elaine said. She had never thought of herself as precisely ugly, but it seemed obvious that men preferred large breasts and a certain lack of brains. "I don't look anything like as pretty as Millicent."

"Millicent the statue or Millicent the bitch?" Daria asked. "But you're really too old to be a blunt instrument in the wars between the sexes. You have a more subtle beauty that comes out as you grow older."

Elaine laughed. "And how much would I have to pay for compliments like that at the parlour?"

"We don't *lie* to our customers," Daria assured her, in

mock horror. "That would be *bad*. We just tell them the better news and gloss over the worse news, like the fact that showing off too much of one's chest makes it easy for the boys to see everything they want to see."

Elaine narrowed her eyes. "But you wanted me to show off most of *my* chest," she pointed out. "Even Bee would be too busy staring at my dress to look into my eyes."

"It's different for you," Daria said. "I have to make sure that you look striking, but not too striking...because too striking would be bad for you and Bee. You just want to look spectacular without giving too much away." She winked. "Men value things they actually have to fight for more than things that are given away for free."

Elaine blushed. "You keep telling me that," she said.

"And it never stops being true," Daria agreed. She stood up and peered down at Elaine. "You look good, so...why don't you wait here while I go and get you a snack? I'll have to make sure you know how to eat properly before you go – food on the dress isn't good."

"So much trouble for a date," Elaine said. "Maybe next time I should just go naked. It would save a great deal of trouble."

"Only in one of the weird sex clubs," Daria said, firmly. "Everywhere else...it would just make you look like a prostitute. There used to be an entire series of prostitutes who went naked around the city, I never found out why. Maybe they thought that it would save time too."

Elaine blushed. "I don't think I could eat anything," she said, changing the subject quickly. "I feel too nervous."

"That's why you have to eat something," Daria said. "You can't rely on a guy to know what's good for a girl to eat. Some guys took me to places that served fatty meat and little else, others took me to vegetarian places that bored me to tears. Eat something now and then you will be covered even if Bee only takes you for finger-food."

"All right," Elaine said, too tired to argue. "I'll wait here while you're getting the food."

"I'll expect you to do the same for me the next time I have a date," Daria called, as she headed towards the door. "Once you get back from Ida, you can help me get ready for my date with Tudor. He isn't much to look at, but he's great in the sack."

Elaine blushed as Daria left the room, and then looked around. She'd been in Daria's room before, but she'd never actually spent hours in it getting ready for a date. Going out with Bee would be the first real date of her life. Now...she found herself looking at the racks of clothes with new interest, wondering how many of them Daria intended to try out on her at a later date. Daria would probably have earned enough money on her own to take them to a far better part of town if she hadn't kept spending her money on clothes.

Daria's small desk was littered with cosmetic equipment, some bought from her workplace and others created by herself. She *did* have skills that Elaine lacked, particularly when it came to producing potions like the Modest Maiden and the Centaur's Friend. The former was used to prevent unwanted pregnancy while the latter prolonged orgasm in men, making it the most popular potion in the world. And yet Elaine had never been able to brew it properly herself. Maybe she should try using her newly acquired knowledge. Potion-making was as much a magical art as transfiguration and teleport gems, but it needed patience and skill rather more than anything else. Elaine had had neither.

She glanced over towards the window and blushed again when she saw Daria's collection of underwear. How anyone could wear so many different designs was beyond her, although she had to admit that it made sense when someone was intent on losing the outer layer of clothing as quickly as possible. Daria *had* offered her some of the finest underwear in her collection, but Elaine had drawn the line at silken wraps no one else would be able to see. Her friend had pointed out that having hidden secrets could be quite entertaining, but Elaine had thought that that was a step too far. Besides, no one would *know* what she was wearing under her dress.

Shaking her head, she looked down and saw a sealed chest poking out from under the racks of clothing. She hadn't known that Daria had such a chest; she certainly hadn't seen it when they'd moved into the apartment together. But then, she spent so much time at the Great Library that Daria could have moved almost anything in without Elaine realising what had happened. The chests had a reputation for being almost impregnable, unless one was powerful enough to break the seals directly...which would make it obvious that someone *had* managed to break into the chest. And yet the reputation was rather undeserved. A spell floating at the top of Elaine's mind promised her the ability to open and close the chest without being detected.

She knelt down, touched the jewelled clasp holding the chest closed, and muttered the spell, not quite sure of what she was doing. It opened automatically, revealing a pair of books in a language Elaine didn't understand – it looked to be the language of the Travellers – and a single silver amulet. Elaine stared at it in disbelief. The amulet had been created for one purpose and one purpose only. It allowed a werewolf to control the transformation from man to beast without being overruled by the animal instincts of the werewolf mind.

Elaine reached out for it and caught herself just before she touched the cursed object. No one knew exactly where the werewolf curse had begun, but it had been devastating before counter-potions and wards designed to keep out werewolves had been developed and rushed into mass production by the Grand Sorcerer. Werewolves had little place in human society; some served as bodyguards or criminals, but most of them preferred to remain in the forests and slip back down into animal habits. A bite from a werewolf, if not treated rapidly, would turn the victim into a werewolf himself. Or herself...

She remembered the growl she'd heard just after she'd fled the scene of Millicent's transformation and cursed under her breath. Millicent had hinted at Daria having a secret, a secret her friend had been reluctant to talk about. But she'd tracked Elaine down even against the distorting magic of the Blight, moving with a speed that should have been impossible for a human female. A werewolf, on the other hand, could have tracked someone right across the city in wolf form. And provided that no one saw her transform, no one would realise that the massive black dog running down the streets was anything other than a stray from the great houses.

Elaine found herself shaking as she closed the chest and sat back down on the stool. She'd never been scared of Daria, but then she'd never realised that her best friend was a werewolf. And Daria would know that Elaine had figured out her secret the moment she smelled Elaine's scent on the chest. At least she hadn't touched the amulet directly...working quickly, she pulled the chest out and stood on it to examine the clothes on the rack. There would be an excuse, of sorts, for her scent on the box.

The door opened and Daria came back into the room. "Are you all right?" she asked, seriously. Of course...a werewolf in human form would still have a far more developed sense of smell than any normal human, no matter how magically enhanced. Daria could pick up on her mood with a quick sniff. "You look a little flushed. And I told you to sit down."

"I had my doubts about the dress," Elaine said, finally. It was partly true, after all. "Maybe I should wear something in black after all."

"This isn't a funeral and you're not going to show off your powers," Daria said, dryly. "You should wear something striking...don't worry, I was nervous with my first guy too. And that...well, it didn't turn out to be as good as I might have hoped."

Elaine laughed, despite herself. "What happened?"

"He was too nervous himself," Daria said. "You want to hear a secret?" Elaine nodded, thoughtfully. "Guys are just as nervous as girls when it comes to dating and having sex; they can make a mess of it just as easily as a girl can. And yet very few of them will ever admit it. It's all about being the seductive charmer, the rogue who makes girls blush and grow horny and come out to play with them...they always lie to each other about the girls they've had and the girls they intend to have in the future. You can never believe anything a guy tells you about his past experience with girls. I've seen guys who were complete virgins boasting about the girls he's enjoyed back home."

Elaine nodded, slowly. Daria would know, of course, if a guy was trying to lie to her. She could smell him and know when he was being untruthful, or at least when he *knew* he was being untruthful. Most girls didn't really have that advantage...she looked over at Daria, remembering what she'd said about the Travelling Folk. Were they all werewolves, forced to wander from state to state because few places would take them in permanently? Or was Daria merely the victim of another werewolf during a brief stop in a forest? There was no way to know, short of asking her, and it was the one question she couldn't ask her friend.

"This may not work out," Daria said, more seriously. "Some guys who are nice are also complete bores. But consider it experience...and you never know. Bee might be your one true love, if you're willing to go back to the Southern Continent with him."

Elaine flushed. It hadn't occurred to her, but Daria was right. If she did become Bee's girlfriend, as strange as the whole idea felt to her, what would happen when he wanted to go home? Would she follow him, or would she break off their relationship because she didn't want to leave the Great Library. Except there was something to be said for going away from the Library now. The longer she remained in the Golden City, the greater the chance that someone would work out what had happened to her and drag her before the Inquisitors.

"On the other hand, you *could* use it as a chance to experiment without consequences," Daria added. She picked up the bottle of Modest Maiden and passed it over to her. "Take one sip now and another afterwards if you actually do decide to go all the way with him. And relax! This is meant to be a fun evening out for you!"

"Yes, boss," Elaine said. Daria laughed at her. "I'll do my best."

"And just relax," Daria insisted. "Nerves will ruin this evening far more than anything else, my dear. Relax!"

Chapter Twelve

"I reserved a table for us at the Darlington," Bee said, as they walked down the streets. Elaine wasn't too surprised that he hadn't bought a carriage. Outside the nobility, few people could use one to get from place to place quickly through the crowded streets. "I hope that that meets with your approval?"

Elaine hesitated, and then nodded. The Darlington was *expensive*, suggesting that Bee had plenty of money – or a complete lack of concern about where the next few hundred Crowns were going to come from. But she'd never been on a real date before, so she wouldn't have minded if it had been a simple eatery and maybe some dancing afterwards. Daria's only word of caution had been not to go back to the guy's apartment – or hotel room – unless she really did want to go all the way. Guys couldn't be relied upon to be sensible when sex was concerned.

"I've never been before," she said, truthfully. "Do you know what they're showing tonight?"

"Apparently a set of tribal dancers from the western islands," Bee said, as they turned the corner and walked up into the outskirts of High Tory. Elaine had thought that Daria had overdressed her, but judging from some of the women walking beside their men it was clear that she was actually rather underdressed for the night. There was a woman wearing a garment made of magic alone, clinging to her curves and revealing just enough to make the men stare in the hope that it would reveal more. "I've never been there before either."

The Darlington was a large blocky building on the edge of High Tory, where the nobility blurred into the wealthy merchants who paid most of the city's taxes. Elaine had heard, from Daria, that some of the Councillors were actually pressing for a greater share in the city's affairs seeing that they paid for most of them, something that the next Grand Sorcerer would have to resolve somehow. Ruling in favour of one side would only irritate the other, who might then start trying to find a way to roll back the decision. It was a responsibility she was glad she didn't have to endure.

A small crew of security personnel, wearing the formal outfits handed out by the club's owners, were checking tickets as the crowds walked into the building. Elaine's unwanted knowledge pointed out that there were a dozen ways to subvert the system and avoid the embarrassment of being asked to leave, but she did her best to ignore it as Bee produced a pair of golden tickets from his pocket. She was tempted to ask just how much he'd spent on the tickets, but she couldn't find the words to ask. He might find the question offensive.

The guard took the tickets, passed his wand over them and then handed them back to Bee. "You're on the ground floor," he grunted. "Walk inside and down the stairs."

"Thank you," Bee said, politely. Elaine clung onto his arm as they stepped inside. She'd never really liked crowds and the Darlington was heaving with the great and the good – and the wealthy. She caught sight of a Councillor she vaguely recognised with his hand around the shoulder of a girl who was wearing a white dress that left little to the imagination, before the press of the crowds separated them. Down the stairs, the confined corridor suddenly opened up into a vast arena built under the city. At least this one didn't feel to be a pocket dimension held open by formidable spells.

The vast floor was littered with tables, each one illuminated by a set of burning candles and marked with a single golden number. Bee glanced at the tickets and then started to push his way towards a table at the rear, half-hidden in shadow as some of the light orbs hovering high overhead started to go out. Their table was set up for only two people, much to Elaine's relief; the moment they sat down, the golden number winked out of existence. She had expected to discover that the candles were magical too, but they were real. The Darlington spared no expense to create a luxurious welcome for its guests.

A young woman wearing a simple black dress passed them

the menus and vanished into the crowd. Elaine looked down at it, flicking through the different pages and rolling her eyes at the cost. The meals produced by the Darlington could be had cheaper almost anywhere else, even though Bee had probably already paid for their meals. Bee pulled a strip of paper out from under the candles and started to make notes on it, trying to decide what to order. Some of the food would probably be unfamiliar to him if he'd spent all of his life in the Southern Continent, even though the Empire had worked hard to spread its ideals across the world.

Bee looked up at her. "Do you want me to order for you?"

"I'd like the steak," Elaine said. Daria would have *loved* the steak. Werewolves ate more meat than any normal human...how had she missed *that* little clue? In hindsight, it should have been obvious. "And what should we drink?"

Daria had advised her to stay away from alcohol. "Maybe an iced lime water," Bee said, seriously. Perhaps he'd had the same advice from someone else. "Do you want the carrot soup first, or just the steak? It's all already paid for."

He was so earnest that Elaine found herself flushing. "The soup first, then," she said, as the lights started to go out completely. The stage was illuminated by a glow that seemed to come from all around it. "And then the steak."

The waitress came back and collected the sheet of paper as the dancers came out onto the stage. Elaine stared with genuine interest; the men wore nothing more than loincloths, while the women wore short traditional dresses covered in sequins. It would have embarrassed Elaine to show off so much of her legs in public, but the dancers didn't seem to mind. They bowed to the audience and then started to move in time to a drumbeat that also seemed to come out of nowhere. It wasn't the kind of dancing Elaine had enjoyed herself, before Millicent had suffered her little accident, but something more complex and elegant. The male and female dancers never seemed to touch one another as they moved around the stage in a stately dance.

Elaine clapped as loudly as anyone else as the first dance came to an end, followed by a second dance performed by the men only. It was a strange dance, showing off their finely-toned bodies and the primitive weapons they carried in their hands, but Elaine found it almost impossible to take her eyes off them. The knowledge in her mind whispered that the tribes on the western islands hadn't been discovered until after the end of the Second Necromantic War and their magic had never been as formal, or precisely delineated, as the magic controlled by the Grand Sorcerer. They'd considered themselves to live in harmony with the surrounding region, sharing themselves with the wild magic of nature. Whatever the truth behind it, Elaine was surprised to find herself reacting in a very primal manner to the dance. She had to swallow hard to cover her distraction, or the sensations as her nipples hardened and pressed against the dress.

There was a brief pause as the waitresses came around, serving the soup to the guests who had ordered it. Some of the female guests had had to leave the room to go to the washroom, Elaine realised; they'd been just as strongly affected by the dance as she had, perhaps even more so. The knowledge in her head suggested that the dance was primarily a mating ritual for warriors from one tribe as they visited another tribe to ensure that they found women who weren't related to them. There was a lesson in that somewhere.

The soup tasted surprisingly good and the splash of cream set it off nicely. Once she'd eaten enough to satisfy her, Elaine glanced around to see that some of the lights had come back on, revealing who some of the other guests were. She half-wondered if she would run into her Guardian at the Darlington – it was just the sort of place he would have enjoyed – before deciding that he was unlikely to attend if he didn't have any money left. The Darlington insisted on cash in advance, apparently. It saved embarrassment later on.

"Ladies and Gentlemen," a voice boomed, from out of the darkness. "Would you all care to rise for the honourable Prince Hilarion of Ida and his companions."

Elaine glanced at Bee, and then rose to her feet. About half of the crowd had joined her, while others were choosing to shun the newcomers openly. Prince Hilarion himself was a handsome man, with long dark hair and a smile that was utterly devastating; his escorts were almost identical, save for the colour of their hair. One had bright orange hair, a colour that couldn't be natural, while the other was blonde enough to be mistaken for Millicent. All three of them carried swords as well as wands, something that struck Elaine as odd. A sorcerer who needed a sword for his own personal protection was no sorcerer at all.

Prince Hilarion gazed around the room, his bright eyes moving from person to person, as the usher escorted him to the royal box at the front of the stage. For a moment, Elaine was convinced that he was looking directly at her before he looked away, clearly counting the number who had stood up and comparing it to the number who had remained seated. Few people would dare to alienate a contestant for the post of Grand Sorcerer, but not everyone took the Prince seriously. What could one expect from a man who had never studied in the Peerless School. The odds the touts were offering would be enough to make someone rich for life if they gambled – and won – on Prince Hilarion.

He seemed odd to her eyes as he sat down, his companions taking the seats beside him. A thought nagged at the back of her mind until she remembered the work of the great Sorcerer Niven. It was simple for a magician to use a sword as a cure for impotence, provided that one took the blade to bed with oneself! Any sorcerer who carried a sword was almost certainly impotent, but would Prince Hilarion know that? He hadn't had a formal education in magic as far as anyone had been able to find out, just tutors. And those tutors had apparently refused to be interviewed.

Bee caught her sleeve as the lights dimmed again and the female dancers came back out into the stage. "Does his sword mean that he's impotent or merely doesn't have enough faith in his magic to defend himself?"

"I don't know," Elaine admitted. Trust a guy to remember what use a sword had for a magician. "He could be hoping that people will underestimate him by wearing the sword."

She shrugged as the dancers came into view. They'd changed, removing their traditional dresses for loincloths that covered their thighs – and placing shells on their nipples. Elaine glanced over at Bee and saw him staring in awe as the dancers started to move, using their arms to call attention to their breasts and thighs. If the dance the males had performed was intended for the women, this one was intended for the men...even with wards surrounding the stage, its effects were spectacular. Who knew what it would be like for a tribal boy, barely on the verge of manhood, to be confronted with such powerful evidence of feminine sexuality? Or for the girls when they saw the men.

The dancers finally bowed, the shells covering their nipples dropping off as they turned and retreated from the stage. A long series of sighs ran through the room as the men were released from their hypnotic trance, staring around at their wives and partners. Bee at least had the grace to look embarrassed, although he'd probably seen her staring at the men with just as much interest and enthusiasm. Some of the men also had to leave the room as the waitresses started serving the main course. Elaine smiled at Bee, who'd ordered a complex dish of chicken and beef, before she started to dig into her steak. The meat was surprisingly tasty and tender, although given the cost it had better be good. Most of the Darlington's customers wouldn't have hesitated to complain if they felt that they hadn't had their money's worth.

Prince Hilarion didn't seem to be eating, Elaine noticed. Instead, he was sitting in his seat watching the other guests with undisguised interest. There was something oddly composed about his expression, as if he wasn't particularly interested in anything apart from the guests, some of whom would be trying to work against him when the contest began. He should be trying to win their favour, or at least neutrality, but instead he was just watching them as though they were not important to him. None of the guests were going to like *that* kind of attitude from someone who hadn't even been through the Peerless School.

Elaine puzzled over it as she devoured the last of her steak. Prince Hilarion had to know that he didn't have the connections to make a proper bid to become Grand Sorcerer, yet he didn't seem to be interested in attempting to make those connections. And there was the fact that he was related to the man who'd sent Elaine the charmed book. The Peerless School had taught that there were more coincidences in the magical world than anyone really understood, or recognised, but Elaine was convinced that that was too unlikely a coincidence for it to be possible. There *had* to be a connection somewhere.

She was tempted to walk over to Prince Hilarion and ask him directly, but she knew she couldn't take the chance. If he'd wanted the knowledge from the Great Library, he had to be looking for her...and he presumably didn't know who'd picked up the book. Or perhaps he would have tried to convince her to join him by now, or had her kidnapped...one advantage about going to Ida was that it would be the last place anyone would expect to find her. Or so she hoped.

Bee smiled as the waitress started to take away the dishes. "Do you want to watch the rest of the dancing or go walking?"

Elaine hesitated. She would have liked to see the rest of the dancing, but she didn't really want to be near Prince Hilarion any longer than strictly necessary.

"Walking," she said, finally. "Do you want to go to the Park?"

Bee grinned. "Why not?"

The Park was the only open space in the Golden City that was accessible to anyone who wanted to stride in through the gates. According to history, the first Grand Sorcerer had planted it himself and then left it to the entire city in his will. The terms of the will had stipulated that anyone who wanted to enter had to be allowed to enter, while the Council would have ultimate responsibility for maintaining it and protecting the plants from vandals. Elaine wasn't sure how much of the story she believed – the knowledge in her head hinted at a very different story – but it was a 'night' place to go. Illuminated by moonlight, and the faint glow of the Watchtower on the North Peak, it was remarkably romantic. The shadows provided concealment for any number of activities.

Bee took her arm as they walked past a tiny set of graves buried under statues of weeping angels. The graves themselves were unusual; most bodies were cremated and then their ashes scattered on the soil outside the city. It was a tradition that dated back to the first clumsy experiments with necromancy, before the necromancers had started bringing entire graveyards to life. No one knew why the bodies in the Park had been buried instead of cremated and scattered. Some people commented that they were probably older than the Park itself and the Grand Sorcerer had hesitated to remove or defile the bodies. Elaine wasn't sure that she believed that at all.

"Thank you for this evening," she said, as they halted under a tree that draped a concealing shadow over them. There was magic in the Park, old magic; magic that might have more in common with the Blight than anyone cared to think. "I'm sorry about the last time we met..."

"It wasn't your fault," Bee assured her. He took her in his arms and it dawned on Elaine that he was about to kiss her. "Your friend was very clear on that point. It definitely wasn't your fault."

Elaine flushed. Daria had stood up for her, believed in her...and Elaine had rewarded her by peeking into a locked chest and discovering a horrible truth about her friend. "She's a good person," she said. All of the stories about wild werewolves didn't seem to apply to the one werewolf she'd actually met. "And I..."

Bee's lips descended and touched hers, gently. Elaine felt her heartbeat starting to race as long-suppressed desires came to life in her mind. She kissed him back, feeling his lips steadily increasing the pressure on her body. It was suddenly very hard to breathe as his hand touched her breast and started to stroke it through the dress. Part of her wanted to tear off the dress and make love to him right now, even though they were in the Park. And part of her knew that that would be a very bad idea.

"I can't go too far," she said, between kisses. Her hand had somehow found its way to his crotch. "I can't..."

"Hush," Bee said, very gently. "I do understand."

Chapter Thirteen

"Well, *someone* had a good night," Daria said, the following morning. "How far did you go with him?"

Elaine flushed. "How can you tell?"

Daria chuckled. "Did you look in the mirror when you woke up this morning?"

Elaine turned and glanced into Daria's mirror. She saw a girl with smeared makeup staring back at her, with faint traces of male lips on her cheek and neck. Her face was almost unrecognisable...and she had only an hour before her iron dragon was scheduled to leave for the north. She let out a yelp and ran into the washroom, splashing water on her face and trying to wash off most of the smeared material. Some of it refused to come off until she muttered a simple charm to cancel the magic binding it to her skin.

"So," Daria said, following her in, "how far *did* you go last night?"

"We kissed," Elaine said. She could still feel his fingers stroking her breast, sending strange yet remarkably pleasant sensations running down her body. Who knew what she would have done if he'd pressed the issue? "And we touched...and we didn't do anything else."

"Good for you," Daria said. She winked and passed Elaine a towel as she removed the remains of her underclothes and splashed water all over her body. "Did you decide you liked the experience after all?"

Elaine flushed, again. "Yes," she admitted. "I enjoyed myself."

"Welcome to your first step into womanhood," Daria said. She assumed a posture Elaine remembered from some of her more boring tutors. "Now, the next step is going down on him, which means taking his cock into your mouth..."

"Not for a while yet," Elaine said. Part of her, remembering the feel of his hardness against her hand, seemed to think that it would be a fantastic experience. The rest of her found the whole idea disgusting. He used his penis to go to the toilet as well as everything else. "I...do people really do that?"

"Of course," Daria said. "And just you wait until you get a guy who's willing to go down on you and use his tongue to lick you out. You'll find it absolutely wonderful." She shrugged. "Of course, guys are more reluctant to go down on girls than have the girls go down on them..."

"Let's talk about something else," Elaine said, quickly. Her ears were glowing bright red with embarrassment. And yet she'd had strange and erotic dreams when she'd closed her eyes and gone to sleep, dreams that had pushed aside the nightmares that seemed to have come with the knowledge from the Great Library. "Will you be all right here for a couple of days?"

"I owe Marla a shift or two at the parlour," Daria said. "I dare say I will be able to keep myself amused while you're gone. I just wish I could come with you."

Elaine wanted her to come too, but some instinct seemed to be insisting that it was better to go alone. She didn't want to risk exposing her friend to danger, particularly when she hadn't been able to tell her about what had happened in the Great Library, or what she'd done with Daria's chest of secrets. How could she even begin to tell her the truth?

"I'll be back in a couple of days," she assured her. At least she wouldn't have any trouble finding a place to sleep. Lady Light Spinner's gift of cash had solved more than a few problems for her. "Who knows? By then, they might even have found the final list of candidates for the Grand Sorcerer's position."

"I wouldn't count on it," Daria said. "I think they'll be counting down right until they reach the last few seconds and *then* start jumping into the contest. Too many of them will be watching to see who else is interested before they commit themselves to the struggle."

She shrugged. "But don't worry about it," she added. "Unless Deferens wins, of course. But I don't think he has much of a chance if he alienates half of the wizards in the world just by being who and what he is. Someone else will have to deal with him, of course. I wish we had the power to do that, you know."

Elaine shivered. She *did* have the knowledge, if not the power, to do something about Deferens and his views on what women should do with their lives. But anything she did would expose what had happened to her to the Inquisition. She was still astonished that Lady Light Spinner – or Millicent – hadn't reported what had happened to the Inquisitors. Perhaps they'd feared how the Inquisitors would react to Millicent's idea of fun and games, although *that* had never been a problem before. They'd had the connections to avoid the skull-wearing magicians unless they *really* stepped out of line.

"Me too," she said, finally. "Me too."

***

The Iron Dragons weren't really magical, although they did have binding spells on their boilers to prevent them exploding and wrecking the entire series of carriages hooked to the steam-powered monster. Some of the boys in the orphanage had dreamed of driving an iron dragon across the land, blowing the whistles as they roared under the bridges and carried people from one end of the Empire to the other. The network had been partly destroyed by the Second Necromantic War and the Grand Sorcerers had actually attempted to restrict the redevelopment of the damaged tracks, but money talked louder than magic in some parts of the world. Elaine could see why they might have had their concerns about the iron dragons. Anything that lessened the world's dependence on magic would have been a danger to the status quo.

Elaine took a moment to study the hulking monstrosity as she walked up towards the coaches. Memories that weren't hers rose up inside her mind, images of real dragons – or the monsters raised by the necromancers – chasing and destroying iron dragons in the opening days of the second war. The Witch-King had known just how important the iron dragons had been for transporting and concentrating troops in the right positions and knew that every destroyed section of the network could impede reinforcements from the Emperor, before the last of the Emperors had been killed in the war. It was easy to see why some people believed them to be magical, even though they were really powered by steam. Nothing that size, surely, could move under its own power.

"All aboard who's going aboard," the conductor shouted, ringing his bell. The puffs of steam from the iron dragon grew louder as the driver started to shovel coal into the engine. Elaine ran forwards, silently grateful that she'd worn something more practical than the dress she'd worn for the Darlington, and found her way into her coach. Inside, it was surprisingly cool, with long rows of seats stretching away towards the end of the carriage. Elaine hadn't been able to afford the luxurious accommodation in the first class sections, but she had managed to reserve a table and a comfortable chair. She put her bag under the seat and settled down with a book in her hand. It was several hours to Ida and she had to pass that time somehow. Two young girls, barely old enough to attend the Peerless School, sat opposite her, smiling. They looked excited to be on their way again.

The coach lurched as the iron dragon started to move, heading across the city and up towards the tunnel that led through the mountains and out into the countryside. She caught sight of strange magical energies moving through the Blight as they passed near it, before the coach plunged into darkness as they entered the tunnel. There was no light outside at all, something that left her feeling creepy before the coach finally burst back outside into the warm sunlight and headed northwards. On the other side of the mountains, there were a handful of small towns and little else. The battles that had decided the Second Necromantic War had burned away most of the settlements and, even now, few chose to live there willingly. At least it wasn't as bad as the Blight.

She smiled as the iron dragon picked up speed, heading onwards into the distance. The conductor came into the coach and moved from person to person, checking tickets with an expression that suggested he'd done it a thousand times before and had long since grown bored with the whole affair. Elaine wondered, absently, if he'd been one of the boys from the orphanage who'd dreamed of driving iron dragons across the world. But he didn't look familiar and he certainly didn't seem to recognise her. He merely took her ticket, checked it, and then passed it back. It took longer to do the girls, for some reason; their parents had decided to travel later for whatever motive of their own. Elaine had honestly never realised that there might be problems with having children travelling without their parents. It was probably something one learned from actually *having* parents.

The girls continued to chatter amongst themselves as Elaine yawned and tried to return to her book. She really hadn't slept much last night and she knew that she should be trying to catch up before she reached Ida, but she didn't want to take the risk of falling asleep on the iron dragon. What would happen if she woke up to discover that she'd been taken all the way to the far side of the empire? It wasn't very likely, but what if...?

"Hey," one of the girls said. "What's your story?"

Elaine blinked. "I beg your pardon?"

"Pretty girl travelling alone...it doesn't happen very often," the girl said. Her twin smiled encouragingly. "Why are you travelling without a man?"

"I have no husband," Elaine said. She wasn't sure if Bee counted as a boyfriend or not by now. Yes, they'd kissed...but Daria had gone further than that with boys she'd never wanted to see again. "Why are *you* travelling alone without a man?"

"Too young to get married," the girl said. She held out a hand. "I'm Sandy and that's Sandra. Don't get us mixed up or we'll get cross."

Elaine had to smile. They had the same faces, the same clothes and even the same voices, it seemed. Telling them apart would be difficult for anyone, particularly when they started using their magic as twins. Twins had great magical power, but it came at a price; they'd start blurring together into one person. But at least they'd have each other. Elaine would have given anything for a sister when she'd been a child.

"Would you like to play cards?" Sandra asked. "We really need a threesome to play properly."

Elaine smiled again and put away her book. "Why not?" she asked. "What sort of cards do you play?"

She listened carefully to the rules of the game, which seemed rather complex to her – but then, she'd never played cards in her entire life. The girls didn't seem to want to bet money, which was something of a relief, but they did want to bet sweets. Elaine lost the first four games before realising that they were cheating shamelessly, either comparing their own cards to work out what Elaine had to hold or somehow reading the back of her cards. Once she'd realised what they were doing, it was still hard to decide how to counter it. In the end, she merely decided to abandon the game and surrender some of her sweets. There was no point in picking a fight over it.

The countryside was changing as the iron dragon raced northwards. Flat plains where farmers pulled a living from the ground were steadily replaced by mountains which marked the rough edge of Ida's territory. The ruling king had apparently ordered a station built at the bottom of the mountains rather than have a tunnel constructed under the mountain or have the iron dragon network extended up the mountains. Elaine's history books hadn't been able to provide a proper explanation, although it could just be nothing more than paranoia. Anyone whose independence depended on mountains blocking the path of conquering armies would have to be leery about accidentally weakening the natural defences. But none of those mountains would deter the Grand Sorcerer if he wanted to make an example of Ida. There wasn't enough iron in the mountains to neutralise the sort of magic the Grand Sorcerer could unleash if he wanted to punish the tiny state.

"We're going all the way to Pendle," Sandy – or maybe it was Sandra – said. "Where are you going?"

"Ida," Elaine said. Had it really been over four hours since she'd boarded the iron dragon? But the vehicle was starting to slow as it approached the station and finally came to a halt, giving Elaine barely enough time to grab her bag and books before the doors opened. "I hope that you enjoy the rest of your journey."

Outside, the air was cooler and sweeter than in the Golden

City. King Hildebrand had established a small hamlet at the bottom of the mountains for the station, including a pair of inns and a set of horses and carts offering rides up to Ida itself. Elaine walked out of the station and found a driver, paying him a handful of silver coins for a ride up to the city. The driver took the coins, bit them, and then motioned for her to get into the carriage. No one else joined them as they started the long climb up towards Ida.

The experience was alarming to someone who had never been up a mountain in her life, unless one counted the brief walk up to the Watchtower when she'd been at the Peerless School and that hadn't been anything like as terrifying as the ride up towards Ida. The wind pushed and pulled at the coach, threatening to send it tumbling over the side and down towards the ground far below. The handful of habitations actually cut *into* the mountain caught her attention and she winced. How could anyone live in such conditions?

She stared around as they finally inched past a pair of forts and into the road leading to the city itself. Ida was very different from the Golden City. Like the habitations below, half of it seemed to be cut into the rock itself, while everything outside the rocky mountains was made of the same grey stone. Even the royal palace, a towering fortress on the top of one of the mountains, was the same colour as the rest of the city. There was none of the variety in the population either, Elaine realised in shock. They all wore the same drab clothes and rarely looked up as they moved from place to place. How many people even lived in the city? Maybe there were so many people that they had to ignore one another just to get some space between them. The toilets at the Peerless School had followed the same basic idea.

The coach drew to a halt and Elaine made her somewhat unstable way off the vehicle. She had planned to visit the Court Wizard at once, but her legs were arguing strongly that it might be a better idea to find a place to sleep first and go to see him in the morning. She asked the coach driver where she could find a place to stay and followed his directions to the nearest inn. It cost more than she expected, but she was almost past caring. All she really wanted to do was to sleep. The room had nothing more than a bed and a glass of water for her to drink, but she lay down and went to sleep anyway. In the morning, she told herself, she could carry out her plan.

***

She was awoken several hours later by the sound of bells ringing to greet the new dawn, just like in the Golden City. It seemed that Ida honoured the gods in the same way, although there was no way to tell if they had the same gods or worshipped others of their own. The Grand Sorcerer had never attempted to discourage anyone from worshipping any or all gods if they saw fit, apart from the gods who were little more than actual demons. Not that it mattered. Those who claimed to have messages from the gods invariably discovered that the messages weren't quite what they'd expected them to be.

Dressing quickly, she walked down to the eatery – and stopped dead. Seated on the opposite side of the room was a man she recognised, a man she'd never wanted to see again.

Inquisitor Dread.

Chapter Fourteen

The Inquisitor wore the same black robes as she remembered from earlier, his face distorted behind a glamour that she now understood perfectly. It wasn't something that shaped his appearance in his own eyes, but something that shaped his appearance in the eyes of the beholder, giving him an impression of relentless determination to see criminals brought to justice. Elaine started to step backwards when he looked up at her and waved with a single hand, inviting her over to his table. It was very definitely not a request.

"Inquisitor," she said, as she reached his table. Up close, he didn't even seem to have a smell – and his black robes seemed to fade into the shadows. "Welcome to Ida."

Dread looked up at her, his half-concealed eyes locked on her face. "What are you doing here?"

It honestly hadn't occurred to Elaine that she would run into an Inquisitor, let alone one she recognised – even though hindsight told her that the Inquisition would have dispatched someone to make enquires about what Duke Gama had been doing before his untimely death. She would have thought that the Grand Sorcerer's death would have distracted the Inquisitors, but they *did* have a reputation for never forsaking their goals for anything. Try to bribe an Inquisitor and you'd spend the rest of your life in the salt mines.

"I came to investigate Duke Gama," she said, finally. It was true enough – and besides, she couldn't think of a lie that Dread might accept without question, or without trying to compel her to tell him the truth. "I wanted to know what had happened to me."

"Looking into the question of just what happened to you is the task of the Inquisition," Dread said, flatly. "You shouldn't have come all this way to investigate yourself."

Elaine gathered herself and stared back at him, willing herself not to blink. "Would you have told me what happened when I opened his book?"

"We might have done," Dread said, thoughtfully. "But how many wizards has curiosity killed over the years?"

"I almost got killed for nothing more than doing my job," Elaine pointed out, wondering where she'd found the nerve to verbally spar with an Inquisitor. "I want to know what happened to me before it happens to someone else."

"An admirable motive," the Inquisitor agreed. She couldn't tell if he believed her, or if he accepted what she was saying seemed reasonable. "It is clear that your...experience changed you in some ways. Magic, particularly unrefined magic, can have some unfortunate effects."

He looked up and waved at the waitress, who had been giving their table a wide berth. "Order whatever you like," he said. "The Inquisition can afford a large breakfast from time to time."

Elaine hesitated. She wanted to ask him questions, but if there was one thing she'd learned from being a librarian, it was that the questions a person asked often taught the hearer more about that person than they might realise. If magical accidents did change a person in ways more subtle than compulsion spells or even outright transfigurations, it was something almost unknown to her...

...Except that it wasn't, not after the Black Vault had been decanted into her head. Magic had *never* been as well understood as the Peerless School claimed, and there were all kinds of magical traditions that never quite fit into the high magic defined by the Grand Sorcerers. It was possible for a magician to accidentally boost his own power, or be caught up in an accident where his power was suddenly blasted into levels he couldn't even have imagined, but the results had rarely been good. Madness often followed a sudden growth in one's magical power, as if the human mind couldn't cope with suddenly inheriting a vastly increased level of magic. It was strange to realise that the Grand Sorcerer had spent decades training and flexing his magic before even being considered one of the senior wizards, let alone competing with his peers for the ultimate prize.

And if Dread suspected that her powers had been boosted,

he *would* be keeping an eye on her. Not out of suspicion that she'd hidden something, or that she'd lied to him about what had happened when she opened the book, but because she might go completely mad and at the same time develop levels of magic beyond her grasp before the accident. The thought of a maddened magician storming through the streets blasting buildings apart in revenge for slights, real or imagined, had to be the Inquisition's worst nightmare. Despite herself, she wondered just how hard it had been for them to take the risk of allowing her to wake up. They could have cut her throat while she was helpless, long before she'd realised what had happened to her.

She ordered breakfast thoughtfully, looking at the menu to try to determine what were the local specialities. The Darlington had charged far more for far less, she was amused to discover; the locals seemed to like plates of meat and eggs for their breakfasts, as well as long rolls of brown bread and butter. She hesitated and then decided to order as much as she could eat. There was no way of knowing when she would be able to eat again.

"A good choice," Inquisitor Dread observed. Elaine wondered if he was mocking her, but his face seemed curiously composed. "Your friend Daria would approve of the meat, if not the eggs..."

Did he know...of course he knew. Rumour claimed that Inquisitors had remarkable powers to divine curses and enchantments, even the complex and subtle charms that turned a normal man into a werewolf. He'd probably interviewed Daria while Elaine had been fighting for her life – Daria had used the Inquisition as an excuse to escape work for a few days – and discovered that she was a werewolf at the same time. The Inquisition probably wouldn't bother with her unless she turned into a criminal, which far too many werewolves did. It wasn't as if they had any hope of gainful employment when their true natures were exposed.

"Daria always enjoys eating meat and never puts on an ounce of weight," Elaine agreed, trying to sound resentful. A werewolf had a far faster metabolism than a normal human and burned food at a far quicker rate. It probably explained why Daria spent so much of her life chasing boys when she wasn't working. She hesitated. Asking the Inquisitor about her family had been one thing, but asking a more sensitive question would have been risky. And yet who else could answer her questions? "Sir...what kind of effects can magical accidents have?"

Dread studied her for a long moment, as if he were wondering why she'd asked that particular question. "It can depend on precisely what happened in the accident," he said. "One particularly insane wizard once poured every one of his potions into the same pot to see what would happen. Nothing did...until his maid tried to sweep it all up and the mess decided to fight back. Somehow they merged into one being, a vaguely humanoid form made out of gel – and with a surprisingly sweet smell."

Elaine shivered. She'd heard rumours about that particular incident. "And then there was the werewolf who became a...pureblood were," Dread continued. "Every time he sees the moon, he becomes a copy of the closest living thing to himself; a rat, a snake, his wife...I believe that he accidentally bit her and now they make sure to share the same bed so they can swap forms every night. They find it quite interesting to exchange gender roles every so often.

"And then there was the poor girl who transformed randomly into an object whenever she became stressed, or the boy who shifted between human and horse forms whenever he saw a mare, or the twins who swap bodies on an hourly basis..."

Elaine felt a flush of irritation. He was toying with her. "None of those would concern the Inquisition," she said. If they didn't care about someone like Millicent playing games with people who didn't have her power or connections, why would they care about people who were accidentally cursed? Even werewolves were targeted more by the city guards than the Inquisition. "What did you think had happened to me when you came to check up on my...accident?"

Dread met her gaze evenly. "Some magical accidents give magicians an unexpected boost in power," he said, calmly. "Your...treatment of your former tormentor suggests that you suddenly gained powers that you might not be able to control. And the fact that you are visiting this strange little state suggests that you *know* that something has happened to you, doesn't it?"

His voice suddenly became heavy with compulsion. "What happened to you when you picked up that book?"

Elaine swallowed. It took every ounce of strength she had to keep her voice from trembling, or babbling out secrets she knew would get her killed. "I don't know," she said, somehow. It wasn't quite the truth...his words seemed to be humming into her head, forcing her to talk. "I just wanted to come here and find out what had happened to Duke Gama."

"An interesting choice," Dread observed. His voice was back to normal, but Elaine refused to react. It was certain that he could start trying to compel her again at any moment...and if he kept working away at her, eventually she'd break. His magic required stronger magic to resist and Elaine wasn't up to the challenge. The shielding spells floating in her mind required time and patience to set up, or power that she simply didn't have. "And were you interested in Duke Gama before your accident?"

"No, sir," Elaine said, honestly. "I never even knew he existed until I opened those boxes and read the attached details."

"But that leaves us with an interesting problem," Dread observed. "Did you come here because you were curious, or because one of the effects of the curse was to plant a compulsion in your mind to come here? It is quite easy to place a subtle command into a person's mind without them ever realising that they'd been influenced. The more...emotional a person, the easier it is to command them while they're convinced that they're acting according to their own will. And how emotional are you, I wonder?"

Elaine hesitated. The possibility that someone had placed a compulsion in the spell to go to Ida hadn't occurred to her, which could itself be an effect of the spell. Her bindings tutor had made several things clear, including the fact that the human mind was remarkably good at inventing justifications for its actions that always made sense – as long as they weren't examined in the cold light of day. But then, he'd added with his famous sneer, alcohol was just as good at influencing a person as magical spells – and that didn't have any magic in it, nothing more than natural chemistry.

"I like to think that I am not emotional," she said, finally. It wasn't entirely true, she had to admit. Her early life – and Millicent's torments – had burned some of her emotions out of her, at least in her own mind. There was no point in ranting and raving about the universe's unfair treatment of her when nothing would happen to make her life worth living. And the aching sense of loss she'd felt when she'd finally worked out the difference between an orphan and a normal child had faded away years ago. "Whatever happened to me could happen to others."

"Of course it could," Dread agreed, as the waitress returned and put a large plate down in front of her. Dread, it seemed, had ordered fried meat and chopped potatoes. Daria would have loved the spicy food, but it made Elaine's stomach turn over in futile rebellion. "But what happened to you also *did* happen to others."

Elaine stared. "Oh, I'm not talking about the book being charmed; that's unique, as far as I can tell. But you're hardly the first child to grow up without a real family, or face bullies at your school. The results can sometimes be very unfortunate as long-buried emotions start boiling through the mental blocks the mind erects to protect itself. Do you know that most abusers of children were people who were abused themselves?"

"That makes no sense," Elaine said, with the private reflection that the entire conversation made no sense. "If they knew how horrible it was to be abused, surely they wouldn't abuse others."

"But the human mind is a complex thing," Dread said. "Some abused children convince themselves that they actually *enjoy* being abused, a conviction so powerful that they carry it over into adulthood. Others come to believe that they *deserve* the abuse because it is the only way they can draw a line between their caring parents and the way they're being treated. And because these...values are so ingrained in their minds, they never actually question any of them when they become adults. They might as well try to convince themselves that water is dry."

He shrugged. "And it can become worse when one is being

bullied at school," he continued. "A person may believe that they deserve it, that they truly are all the horrible things they get called by their peers, or they may become convinced that no one else cares about them and bury it all away in their minds. And some of them, coming into magic, lose all sense of proportion and retaliate massively against their tormentors. They are so convinced of their own helplessness that when they discover they are no longer helpless, they just lash out with overwhelming force."

Dread took a bite of his meat and then smiled at her. "Would you still claim to be a stable person?"

"Yes," Elaine said, crossly.

"Self-delusion," Dread said. "No child growing up into adulthood is stable; male or female. Some are just better at convincing themselves that they're stable and they don't have anything to worry about. And what happens when they discover that all the things they once took for certainties no longer are? I think your friend Millicent found out just what happens when her victim suddenly became more powerful than she could imagine."

Elaine stared at him. It made sense – and it was completely wrong. Elaine hadn't had her power boosted – but she could, part of her mind whispered, if she was prepared to pay the price. Instead, she'd been crammed with forbidden knowledge that gave her insights into magic that no other living magician shared. Even the Grand Sorcerer would have had problems. He would have had to read the books one by one and so he might not have grasped how they interlinked together.

"I didn't mean for that to happen," Elaine confessed. And yet part of her had felt nothing less than exultation when she'd seen the fear on Millicent's face. "Why do you *let* it happen?"

Dread lifted a single eyebrow. "I beg your pardon?"

"You and your Inquisition swan around controlling magic, the final sanction against evil magicians, and yet you don't intervene to stop powerful magicians picking on their inferiors," Elaine snapped. She felt tears rising to her eyes and blinked hard to suppress them. "Where were you when I was at the Peerless School?"

"I never claimed that we were perfect," Dread said, seriously. "And you know as well as I do that people have to develop their own controls, their own self-discipline, to understand and master magic. A certain amount of unpleasant behaviour is acceptable."

"Not to the person on the receiving end," Elaine snapped. She was almost shouting at him. "Don't you care about them?"

"I care more than you can imagine," Dread said, flatly. There was something in his voice that warned her not to press the question any further. "But I also know that we need to breed strong magicians and we cannot do that by coddling people who may be far more powerful – potentially – than their tormentors." He put down his fork and looked at her. "Are you still prepared to claim that you are stable?"

"I think I know how to control myself," Elaine said, sharply.

"You would be astonished – and depressed – by how many magicians have believed the same thing, only to end up convinced that the right thing to do is to lay waste to the countryside and enslave entire populations," Dread said. "I was...I was involved in the liberation of a city-state that had been taken over by a single extremely powerful magician. And *he* thought that he was making everything better for his people. I think that he really *believed* every word he said about how killing and torturing dissidents made the world a better place."

He shook his head. "But in the end, we had to kill three quarters of the population to save the rest," he added. "Those choices are never easy, I am afraid. But someone has to make them."

"I thought that that was the Grand Sorcerer," Elaine said, waspishly.

"Who do you think gave the order?" Dread asked. "We didn't decide to slaughter upwards of fifty thousand people on a whim."

He smiled as he started to drink his hot coffee. "Eat up before it starts to go cold," he ordered. "We have a long walk ahead of us."

Elaine blinked. "We?"

"I think I'd be happier keeping you where I can see you," Dread said. He leaned forward and looked directly into her eyes. "I don't like the fact that you turned up here – I think you were...influenced to come here by the charm that hit you. And the choice is between taking you with me or leaving you in my room, shackled to the bed. And because I don't know just how powerful you really are..."

"All right," Elaine said, as grandly as she could. Without a clear idea of how powerful she was, he would have to knock her out to make sure she couldn't escape. "You may come with me."

Dread didn't bother to respond to the sally. "Drink up," he said, instead. "We have an appointment with the Court Wizard at Eleven Bells."

Elaine looked at him. "Does the Court Wizard *know* that we have an appointment with him?"

"Of course not," Dread said, crossly. "It would spoil the surprise if I announced myself ahead of time. And it would give him time to think up some lies."

He grinned, picking up a pipe and sticking it in his mouth. "Something is very strange in this kingdom," he added. "The game's afoot."

Chapter Fifteen

One thing about walking with an Inquisitor, Elaine rapidly noticed, was that everyone seemed to assume that she was under arrest. A handful of elder people looked at her as if they expected her to suddenly pull out her wand and start transforming people into frogs at random, while others hid their possessions and made signs to ward off evil gods when they thought the Inquisitor wasn't looking. Some children catcalled in her general direction until Dread drew his wand and waved it towards them, knocking them down to the ground with irresistible force. Elaine wondered if this was how most of the werewolves felt when they entered a normal town. They'd be aware of the hatred and fear directed at them, even by people who prided themselves on control of their faces.

"I'm sorry about the rabble," Dread said. Elaine was surprised; she'd never heard of an Inquisitor apologising for anything before. "They do seem to take one look at us and assume that you should be in handcuffs."

"I thought you and your fellows tried to keep the world safe," Elaine said, after a moment. "Why do they hate you so much?"

"Because we could turn on them at any moment and tear their lives apart, looking for even a hint that a magic threat has crossed their minds," Dread said. "People don't like power without responsibility and accountability – and right now, who do we report to? There's no Grand Sorcerer living in the Watchtower."

He shrugged and made a show of checking his clockwork watch. The remaining onlookers swiftly remembered urgent business elsewhere and scattered, leaving them standing alone in front of a large grey building. It seemed to blur into the rocks that ringed the city, probably linked into tunnels that went all the way up to the king's castle. Some of the knowledge in Elaine's mind pointed out that the city would be almost impregnable to an army, unless that army was supported by powerful magic. Even getting a few hundred troops up the tiny roads – with the enemy hurling rocks from high above – would be difficult.

"I thought we might visit the Crypt first," he added, "and then we can go visit the Court Wizard."

The stone doors were solidly locked, but Dread lifted his staff and tapped firmly on the stone, undoing the charms that bound them together. Elaine watched as the stone slid apart, revealing a long line of steps descending down into the base of the earth, illuminated only by burning torches. Someone clearly visited regularly to replace the torches, binding them with careful charms to allow them to light up whenever the main doors were open. Elaine remembered charms that would produce light for her upon demand as she realised that someone could slam the door closed and leave them trapped in the caves. But then, who would be foolish enough to do that to an Inquisitor?

Dread led the way down the long flight of stairs, pointing out natural caves hollowed out by water erosion over the centuries. Some of the caves appeared to have been inhabited, probably where most of the population hid when an invading army threatened their walls. Elaine found herself sensing misdirection charms bound into the caves, making it harder for anyone to find their way in or out of the maze. It was easy to imagine that the caves reached down all the way to the legendary dragon who inhabited the centre of the world...

She yelped as she stepped through another darkened stairwell and came face to face with a real dragon. It was dead, centuries old, all of the skin torn away by sorcerers intent on using it for their potions, leaving only its skeleton as a warning to anyone who dared trespass in the Crypt. There was something almost...obscene about leaving such a noble creature in such a state; part of Elaine wanted to suggest that they took it out and buried it properly. She doubted that Inquisitor Dread would agree, not when the mere attempt at moving the creature might remind magicians of what the necromancers had summoned from alternate worlds to wreak havoc on their planet. Better to leave it buried under Ida and long forgotten.

"The noble family who rule this state would prefer that you kept all of this to yourself," Dread said, as he picked up an object from a stone table. It was a clenched human fist, lying beside a stone knife and wand. The wand caught Elaine's eye at once, for everyone *knew* that the only material that could channel magic properly was wood. Had it been petrified as thoroughly as Millicent herself, or was it something more remarkable?

"Don't touch," Dread added, as Elaine reached for the wand. "You don't want to awaken anything that might have been left to sleep here."

He held up the clenched fist and spoke a word Elaine had never learned at the Peerless School. Words of Power were dangerous and often unpredictable, unless used by the strongest of wizards. The knowledge in her head spoke of the kind of self-discipline needed to use Words of Power without one's mind wandering, allowing mischievous entities to slip into the spell and misdirect it so that one didn't quite get exactly what one wanted. There was a ghostly roar from the dragon and its skeletal mouth began to slip open, revealing a spinning gateway into a pocket dimension. Dread caught her hand – his touch was cold, very unlike Bee's – and pulled her inside. The world went black...

...And she was standing in the centre of a long stone tunnel, illuminated by magical lights that hovered above hundreds of tables. Each one held a stone coffin, decorated with the picture of the man who had been buried under the mountains. Elaine stepped closer, prompted by a flicker of memory from the books dumped into her head, and saw a strong-faced man with a beard and two black eyes that seemed to stare at her out of the ages.

"The Warlord Elian," Dread said. "He served under the First Emperor in his advance towards the northern seas, eventually bringing a dozen small states into the empire. In exchange for his services, the First Emperor agreed to leave Ida completely alone, a promise that was kept until the first necromancers waged war on the state during their advance on the Golden City. Some of them openly swore to desecrate

Elian's tomb, claiming that he'd sold them out to the Empire in exchange for his people remaining free. But Ida never fell and his memory is still honoured, at least here. The Golden City prefers to forget that there was a time before the Empire."

But it hadn't been as simple as that, Elaine knew; the knowledge in her head told a different story. The first necromancers had claimed to be fighting for the freedom of the northern continents – as Dread had said earlier, perhaps they'd even believed their claims – and nationalism had provided the fuel for a war that shouldn't have taken more than a year or two to end. But the Empire had gone through a series of weak Emperors – including a madman who had been intent on stamping his face over the entire world – and they hadn't been able to stop the necromancers without resorting to the same tactics the necromancers had pioneered. And that had started the process that had turned a hero into the Witch-King...

She looked around, feeling the pocket's odd dimensional nature tearing at her eyes. Nothing seemed to be quite right, as if the dimension hadn't been secured properly. "How big is this place?" she found herself asking. It seemed to stretch for miles. "How many people are buried here?"

"All of the population has a right to be buried under the mountains," Dread said. There was an odd note in his voice. It took Elaine a moment to realise that he was worried. Dead bodies weren't dangerous in and of themselves, but dark sorcerers could strip them for supplies and necromancers could bring them back to a shambling parody of life. "After the Second Necromantic War, the Grand Sorcerer struck a deal with the Kings of Ida – they'd be allowed to keep burying their dead, provided they buried them all inside a pocket dimension, a dimension that could be collapsed into nothingness if necessary. They weren't happy – their religions believe that the souls of the dead become part of the mountains, which protect their state – but there was no other alternative. After the horrors the Witch-King unleashed, we would have done anything to prevent a graveyard being turned into a source of undead soldiers."

Elaine shivered. Even without the knowledge in her head,

she would have known how deadly the undead were, particularly to those who didn't know how to stop them. They could be beheaded, or chopped apart, and yet they would keep going. The only way to stop them was to reduce them to ashes, which consumed vast amounts of fuel and magic. It said something about the sheer scale of the war that the necromancers hadn't just concentrated on bringing every last graveyard back to life, but also summoning other creatures from the darkness and sending them against the Golden City. The Peerless School, the Regency Council and the Inquisition would do *anything* to prevent it from happening again. She was surprised that the first Grand Sorcerer had been prepared to compromise as far as he had.

Dread pointed towards a particular coffin. "That one was prepared for Duke Gama while he was alive," he said. He nodded at the writing someone had scrawled along the bottom of the stone case. "It claims that he was a great and wise man who never had an enemy worthy of the name. They always write that sort of nonsense on coffins and it is very rarely true. Better to forget it and assume the worst of everything."

Elaine blinked. "How would you know?"

The Inquisitor gave her the kind of look a long-suffering tutor would bestow on a particularly stupid student. "Who do you think investigates when someone in a royal or noble family dies unexpectedly?"

"You," Elaine said. It should have occurred to her that there had to be a reason – beyond filial piety – why people like Millicent didn't try to remove their elderly relatives to try and claim their inheritances ahead of time. Some of their seniors – like Lady Light Spinner – would be powerful enough to be nearly impossible to kill, but others would be vulnerable...of course the Inquisition would investigate. They'd probably start by interrogating everyone who could have benefited from the death with their compulsive voices and making sure that they didn't have anything to do with the murder of their relative. And then they'd start work on the staff. Even enslavement charms had their limits – and someone who was cleverer than the slave masters realised could outwit the spells binding them to servitude. "I should have thought of that."

"Yes, you should," Dread said, mercilessly. She couldn't tell if he was irritated with her or just as uncomfortable in the midst of so many dead and decomposing bodies as she was. "There was once a widow who refused to marry again, or start writing a proper sealed will so as to keep her hold on all of the people sucking up to her in the hopes that she would leave them her money, who died suddenly. Too suddenly. And yet I couldn't work out means and opportunity until I realised that someone had been very clever, ordering one slave to take out a bottle of poison, another to put it in the milk without being aware that it *was* poison, and a third to give the poisoned glass to her mistress. It turned out that if she died without a proper will, the money would be spread out among the family, including to the person who plotted her murder. He would have got less than he would have expected if he'd actually been in the will, but he did have gambling debts to pay."

Elaine shivered. Perhaps there was something to be said for being an orphan after all. "What happened to him?"

"Dead," Dread said, flatly. "I believe that the rest of her money was shared out among her relatives and her household – and her slaves were freed. The Grand Sorcerer insisted on it."

"Good for him," Elaine said. She walked forward and studied Duke Gama's face. He'd been fat, if the picture was anything near accurate, with a faintly unhealthy cast to his eyes. It had to be accurate, if only because a statue intended to be flattering would have probably been thinner and made him look more dignified. "Was there anything suspicious about Duke Gama's death?"

"Nothing that demanded the attention of an Inquisitor," Dread admitted. "Gama wasn't the kind of man to keep his desires under control. He had the reputation as a great trencherman and loved going to parties where he could eat all he wanted, even though the hosts became very inventive when they came up with excuses as to why he shouldn't attend. His life was largely dictated by wine, women and song...mostly the women, according to the Court Wizard. His singing was apparently appallingly bad. When he died, it was evidently only a surprise that it had taken so long.

"But that isn't uncommon among the younger heirs," he added. "They're the ones who have no chance of inheriting something significant – and Gama went off on his gorging lifestyle after his brother's heir and spare were born. The Court Wizard concluded that Gama literally ate and drank himself to death. And as you know, his books ended up in the Great Library."

Elaine frowned. "You talked about compulsions," she said. She wasn't sure how much she dared say, but maybe Dread could sort out the shadow she felt hanging over her and she could retreat into obscurity. *Someone* would have to take Miss Prim's place at the Great Library. "Could someone have hit him with a compulsion to just keep eating and drinking until he was dead?"

"It's a possibility," Dread said, after a moment. "But such a compulsion would be...not particularly easy to miss. It would have him literally eating and eating until he threw up; surely *someone* would notice such odd behaviour. He was still the heir to the throne if something happened to his nephew..."

"Maybe it was the prince who did it to him," Elaine said. How much could she say? "He thinks he can become the Grand Sorcerer. Perhaps he cast a very subtle spell over his uncle..."

"It would have to have avoided attention from the Court Wizard," Dread said. He sounded rather more troubled than she would have expected. "A spell like that would probably be noticeable – and one of the reasons we have Court Wizards is so that they can notice if something is badly wrong with their charges. And yet the prince thinks he can climb to the highest position in the world."

He looked over at her. "Have you ever *met* the prince?"

"Not really," Elaine said. "I saw him at a distance at the Darlington when Bee..."

A thought struck her. "Is Bee one of your people?"

Dread blinked. "Who...ah, the romantic patroniser," he said. "I'm afraid that young Master Bee is nothing to do with us, apart from having a brief contract with the Inquisition five years ago when he started his career in the south. He doesn't work for us now and we didn't steer him towards you...that was what you were asking, wasn't it?"

Elaine flushed. She was used to Daria's light teasing – and she tried to give as good as she got – but being teased by an Inquisitor was surreal. And yet part of her had wondered if Bee had been...encouraged to show an interest in her to see what she would do, if anything. Finding out that he wasn't, if that was the truth, was reassuring. And yet...

Inquisitors weren't supposed to be able to lie, but it was fairly easy to bend the truth creatively without breaking their oaths and vows they swore when they took office. What if Bee wasn't working directly for them, yet had been pushed towards her by someone other than Daria, or if one of his old contacts had suggested that he should show an interest. Dread could presumably tell what he thought was the truth, but one of the other Inquisitors knew perfectly well was a lie. Just how well did Inquisitors work together anyway? She'd never heard of more than two of them involved in anything, apart from policing the streets during festivals and the Grand Sorcerer's funeral. Their reputation was normally terrifying enough to keep even the rowdiest of street thugs under control.

"You might want to ask him who he's actually working for," Dread added, as he bent over the coffin and started to work a complicated series of incantations over the stone lid. "He works for someone who wants more patronage in the city, someone who has an interest in who comes out ahead in the coming contest. And if he had reason to believe that your talent could swing the contest in someone's favour..."

Elaine's eyes narrowed. "Who...?"

"Ask him," Dread said. He stepped back from the coffin and shook his head. "There's nothing here, not any longer. I was a fool to think I would find anything here. If he was cursed, or charmed into killing himself, all of the traces are long gone."

He straightened up. "It's time to go meet the Wizard Trebuchet, Court Wizard to King Hildebrand," he added. "Do you think his staff will try to delay us while he starts climbing out the window?"

Elaine stared at him. "Does that happen very often?"

"You'll be surprised what a guilty conscience can make someone do," Dread assured her. "And how stupid they can be if they realise that they don't have any way to escape justice..."

He shrugged. "At least the smart ones can be entertaining," he added. "We spent months rounding up all the fetches one particularly dangerous wizard had created."

Chapter Sixteen

"I'm afraid that the Wizard Trebuchet is busy," his assistant said. She was young, barely three years younger than Elaine herself, wearing the robes of someone who had graduated with honours from the Peerless School. Elaine disliked her on sight, although she couldn't have said whether it was because the girl was beautiful – with long red hair and bright green eyes – or because she had an air of irritating competence. "He does not have time to see anyone..."

Dread held out his skull ring and glared at the assistant. "I am afraid that we are here on a rather more vital matter than anything that could possibly prevent him from seeing us," he said. "Now, unless you wish to bar the path of an Inquisitor, which will have dire consequences for the rest of your career..."

The girl started to mutter a charm, power building up in the surrounding air. Dread gave it a hard look and the half-completed spell fragmented into nothingness. "You may want to learn to cast spells without advertising your intentions to your opponent," he said, with surprising mildness. "Although it remains to be seen if your future career will include magic."

He made no motion, but the girl's form flashed blue and then froze below the neck. "You are under arrest for attempting to impede the path of an Inquisitor," he said, in the same mild voice. "Your case will be decided by the next Grand Sorcerer, when one is finally appointed. Until then, I suggest that you wait here until we emerge and can take you away to a holding cell."

The girl stared at him frantically, all of her arrogance gone. "But what should I tell anyone who comes to visit the Court Wizard...?"

"You can tell him that the Court Wizard is very busy," Dread informed her. He smiled, rather coldly. "It will actually have the benefit of being true, now. Won't it?"

Shaking his head, he motioned for Elaine to follow him as he walked around the girl's desk and through a pair of wooden doors. Elaine took one last look at the helpless girl – perhaps she could free herself, although it was difficult to cast such charms while one's hands were unable to move – but where could she go if she did escape? Every Inquisitor, military soldier and city guardsman would be looking for her. The Inquisition had a long reach and it never forgot a slight, or a culprit. And just what had been going through the girl's mind when she'd tried to block Dread's path?

"She may have grown an overstated view of her own position," Dread observed, when Elaine finally risked asking the question. "Or maybe she has orders from her superior to bar anyone's path when he's...*busy*. The problem with sending out Court Wizards is that some of them decide that they can get away with taking money to look the other way from time to time. We already know that Trebuchet is taking money from the King."

Elaine stared at him. "How do we know that?"

Dread smiled. "You should have spent more time outside the Golden City," he said, pointing one long finger at the door. "There, a wooden door is common; even the poorest families can afford wood for their furniture or even to burn in their fires. But here, wood is sparse and rarely used for anything if there's a substitute. A wooden door is the height of luxury."

"But someone could kick it down," Elaine pointed out. "Or simply steal it..."

"There are charms woven through it to make that an...unpleasant experience," Dread said. "Trebuchet may be corrupt – the evidence suggests that he's certainly used his position to enrich himself – but I don't think he's stupid."

Elaine kept her opinion to herself as Dread pulled out his staff and used the iron-tipped wood to push the door open slowly. She could hear a kind of grunting sound, accompanied by gasps that didn't sound as if they came from a male throat. Dread stepped into the room, pulling his cloak around his body, and snickered coldly. Elaine followed him in and stopped, dead. An immensely fat man was sitting in a comfortable chair, wearing nothing at all, while a naked young woman knelt between his legs, taking his penis in and out of her mouth. The girl stopped and stared in horror, before letting out a yelp and running as if all the demons in recorded history were after her. Dread watched her go, and then turned his attention squarely on Trebuchet. The magician, who was trying frantically to cover himself, seemed just as horrified as Elaine felt.

"I would suggest that you simply use a charm to conceal your...delicate parts from us," Dread said, dryly. "It would probably save time."

He sat down and faced Trebuchet squarely, motioning for Elaine to stand behind him. "I see why your assistant was so intent on telling us that you were busy," he added. "How much of your time do you spend attending to your orders from the Regency Council and how much of your time do you spend indulging yourself? I see that that girl wasn't exactly a slave..."

"Her mother wants an introduction at court when the next season comes around," Trebuchet said, sullenly. "I..."

"Was merely using her to push her daughter into satisfying your urges," Dread injected, sharply. "And besides, unless that girl's mother gave birth when she was a little baby herself, she would be too old for the next social season."

"Her family came into money," Trebuchet admitted. "There's nothing quite like a middle-aged woman who thinks that she should have been a social queen and is intent on making up for lost time."

"Did you think to remind her that keeping up appearances in the Golden City can be extremely costly?" Dread asked, coolly. "Or do you not care what happens when she gets there and discovers that a single dress can cost more money than there is in this entire Kingdom?"

"That isn't any of my concern," Trebuchet said, quickly. "I provide a service..."

Dread used his staff to hit the floor, hard enough to make a sharp noise. "You are put out here to serve the interests of the Regency Council, not to have your knob sucked by girls pimped to you by their own mothers," he said, sharply. "We are here to investigate the affairs of the late Duke Gama, brother to your master and uncle to his heir. What happened on the day that he died?"

Trebuchet swallowed, hard. "I made a full report to the Grand Sorcerer," he said, quickly. Elaine had to smile. The Grand Sorcerer's death would have been sensed by every magician in the world. "I assume that you have access to it."

"Let us assume, for the sake of argument, that I haven't bothered to read it," Dread said, very patiently. "What happened on the day that he died?"

"I...I was woken up in the morning by my maid, who said that there was an urgent message from the castle," Trebuchet said, finally. He didn't seem to remember very clearly, something that puzzled Elaine. Come to think of it, surely Dread *should* have been able to read the report he'd sent back to the Grand Sorcerer. "I put all of that in my report..."

Dread's patience seemed to come to an abrupt end. "I read your report very carefully," he said, with an icy tone in his voice. "I read it very carefully and noted all the questions that you left unanswered. And *they* started with a very obvious question. What happened to cause his death?"

Trebuchet glared at him, trying to maintain what was left of his dignity. "I attended upon the corpse at once," he said, finally. "The doctors were already there, trying frantically to resurrect him. They wanted me to try spells that might give him a chance to live, but of course I refused..."

Elaine winced. Of course he had refused. If someone was that far gone, a spell intended to heal him might bring back an unsound mind in a healthy body – or bring back one of the undead, intent on eating its way through the living population. Even without a guiding mind, the slaughter would have been terrifying. And Trebuchet would have been accused of necromancy and unceremoniously burnt at the stake. It was a punishment intended to ensure that the necromancer had no hope of surviving past his own death.

"Of course," Dread agreed. "And what did the message actually say?"

"That Duke Gama was dying and that my presence was needed," Trebuchet said. "I went to the bed, checked the body, and watched him die. The light went out of his eyes and that was the end of a once-proud man..."

Dread leaned forward. "Did he try to say anything to you before he died?"

"Just gasps and moans," Trebuchet said. "I couldn't make out a single word."

Elaine blinked in surprise. "The official report said that he commended his elder brother and wished his nephew the best of reigns," she said. "Was that a lie?"

"They always put crap like that in the official reports," Dread said, dryly. If he was irritated at her interruption, he didn't show it. "You'd be surprised to discover how many famous last words were actually written by their surviving heirs and inserted into the history books."

"Sir," Trebuchet said, "I really must protest. This...personage" – he waved at Elaine – "is clearly not an Inquisitor, nor an Advocate..."

Dread smirked. "Is there a reason you feel you need an Advocate?"

"I do not have to submit to questioning by someone without official standing," Trebuchet insisted, firmly. "I have the right to appeal to the Grand Sorcerer..."

"Who happens to be dead," Dread said, sharply. "I am sure that the next Grand Sorcerer will punish me for overstepping my bounds, but the task of hunting down rogue magicians doesn't actually stop between Grand Sorcerers." His eyes narrowed. "And I do *not* have to allow you an Advocate if I feel that it would place a barrier between me and the truth. Your rights do not exist during an official Inquisition. I suggest you remember that."

He leaned forward. "As it happens, this young woman is a potential candidate for the Inquisition," he added. "She has every right to be here, although I may banish her outside to talk to your assistant if I feel it necessary."

But an Inquisitor couldn't lie... Elaine realised, a moment later, that he hadn't exactly lied. Everyone who'd been through a magical accident that might have enhanced their power would be a potential candidate for the Inquisition, particularly if their power *had* actually been enhanced sharply. It would be one way to keep someone with rogue talents firmly under control. But Elaine, with a head stuffed full of knowledge she could barely use...what would they make of her when they found out the truth? She doubted they'd let her run free in a world where powerful sorcerers could use what she knew to turn themselves into necromancers.

"I hope she is as...accommodating," Trebuchet said, finally. There was a tone in his voice that made Elaine flush. How could *anyone* think that of her? But Millicent hadn't hesitated to use her body to get whatever she wanted and the girl Dread had frozen was clearly in the same mould. "I was unaware that Inquisitors were allowed to have...assistants."

Dread ignored the jab. "You were there when Duke Gama died," he said, returning to the original topic. "Who was there with you?"

"The King was there, holding his brother's hand," Trebuchet said. "The Prince wanted to attend, but his father sent him out and ordered his two stalwart companions to make sure that the Prince stayed away from the body. They did as they were told, even though their friend tried to fight them. The King's wrath would have been painful to see."

Elaine felt an odd flicker of sympathy for the Prince. She wouldn't have wanted to see any of her family members slipping away into the next world, but at least the Prince *had* family members. Perhaps not having any made her more inclined to be sympathetic to a young man's desire to say goodbye to his uncle, even though it would be a terrible thing to watch. There were stories of those who watched Death come for their families, trying to fight the personification of Death herself, or trying to bargain with her, offering their lives in exchange for the dying man. Some of the stories did imply that Death *would* bargain if she were offered something worthy of her attention.

But they were just stories, weren't they? Except the knowledge in her mind suggested ways and means of summoning the seven cosmic abstracts, the personifications of the endless attributes of the universe. They were powerful beyond belief, but they could be controlled...if the sorcerer who had tried to summon them was very lucky. Some magicians were even supposed to be able to *see* Death when she finally came for them.

Dread's words brought her out of her trance. "Once the

Duke was confirmed dead," he said coldly, "what did you do?"

"I ordered the druids and clerics out of the room and sealed it with a binding ward," Trebuchet said. "I put out the fire and worked a standard preserving charm over the body, and then ran through the basic tests for poison, dark enchantments and other issues that might have shortened his life. As I wrote in my report" – he shot Dread a defiant look – "I found nothing that might have suggested that the Duke was...encouraged to meet an early end. I took samples of his blood, urine and shit, which I sent to the Golden City along with my report."

"And I'm sure that the Grand Sorcerer was pleased to receive a crate of shit," Dread muttered.

"The druids found nothing, I am sure," Trebuchet said, nastily. "I would have heard if they *had* found something to alarm us..."

"They said nothing to me about it," Dread said. Elaine wondered if that was another half-truth, something said to distract attention from a greater truth. There was no reason that the druids *had* to report to Dread. "What did you do after you had checked for poison and curses?"

"I called the King back in, along with his chief druid, and formally pronounced the Duke dead," Trebuchet said. He sounded as if he were on surer ground now. "The King took his signet ring and placed it in the castle vault for the next second son, once the Prince has a couple of children of his own, and then prayed over the body. Bells were rung to signify the departure of the Duke's soul, after which we attended a big service where we commended his soul to the mountains. I had the body transferred to the vault" – he pretended not to see Elaine's flinch – "and then wrote my first report to the Grand Sorcerer. It was sent down to the iron dragon, taken to Pendle and then teleported to the Golden City."

"You appear to have followed procedure," Dread observed, calmly. "What happened to the Duke's possessions?"

"I had certified that the Duke had died of natural causes – or at least as natural as one can get when a person seemed intent on eating himself to death," Trebuchet said. "That meant that his will could be read and the first bequests distributed in line with the provisions in the document. The Prince received most of his uncle's possessions, although some thousand crowns were put aside for the Duke's illegitimate son. I'm afraid that his wife was barren."

"You mean her husband's brother saw to it that she could never have children," Dread said. Elaine looked at him sharply. Why would *anyone* refuse to allow their sister-in-law to have children? But from an aristocratic point of view, it limited the number of potential heirs or ambitious relatives who might have tried to claim the throne. The last thing a kingdom as small as Ida needed was a civil war. "What happened to his bastard son?"

"Oh, the Duke was most generous to him," Trebuchet assured the Inquisitor. "He played with the King's son and daughter, became one of their knights...there was no reason to think that his lowly birth stood in his way to becoming a great man in his own right...

"...but then he left."

Dread's eyes narrowed. "Left? Left where?"

"He just left Ida and vanished into the surrounding countryside," Trebuchet admitted. "There was no reason for it as far as anyone could see. The Duke treated him as a natural son, he wouldn't have inherited the kingdom even if he *had* been a natural son...the gods know what happened to him."

Elaine leaned forward. "Did his father know where he had gone?"

"I don't think so," Trebuchet said, after a moment. "I did offer to try and use sorcery to track him down, but the Duke refused. I liked to think that he'd decided that his son would be better off joining the Imperial Army or maybe even sailing out to the islands and setting up a life far from home. The gods know that bastards aren't always popular as they grow up into strapping young men."

"Yes, they do," Dread mused. He shrugged. "You were the one who performed the first examination of the Duke's private library. Did you notice anything special about the books...?"

The change was remarkable. Trebuchet opened his mouth,

and then froze horribly. His entire body started to shake, blood dripping from his mouth and nose. Dread jumped forward, casting a countering charm that Elaine had never learned in the Peerless School, but it was already too late. Trebuchet's body exploded, scattering blood and guts everywhere. Elaine swore out loud as blood drenched her hair and clothes. Dread seemed just as shocked.

"What..." she managed to say. "What was that?"

"A lethal curse," Dread said. The Inquisitor had remained calm, somehow. "Someone didn't want him talking about those books."

Chapter Seventeen

"Are you all right, Milady?"

Elaine shook her head. It was rare for her to have time to enjoy a proper bath; the apartment she shared with Daria didn't have more than a washbasin and she was too shy to visit the public baths, even the ones reserved for women alone. But Ida's King had been willing to have the Inquisitor and his 'assistant' move into his castle and get cleaned up properly. The three maids assigned to Elaine had helped her to undress, climb into the bath and wash all the blood away from her body. Her clothes, they'd warned, would have to be thrown out. They were just too stained to be washed and reused.

Her mind kept returning to the horrible moment when she'd seen Trebuchet explode. She'd never seen anything like it before; she'd never seen *anyone* die in front of her in her entire life. Even the sickliest of the orphanage children had been taken away before their illnesses had killed them, although she'd known that they would never be returning. But she had never been too close to anyone at the orphanage. They were either adopted and taken away, or eventually sold to slave traders and taken away. Elaine had been unusual in that she'd been left in the orphanage until she was old enough to make her own way in the world.

The knowledge at the back of her head had identified the curse that had killed the Court Wizard. According to the text of a book on banned curses crafted for use in warfare, the curse was intended to prevent someone from revealing secrets; it bonded with the victim's magical field, rendering it almost undetectable, until it sensed that they were on the verge of confessing to their interrogators. And then it struck, inflicting so much damage that the victim's body literally shattered in front of the watchers. It was almost impossible to make someone who had been cursed in such a manner talk.

They couldn't talk freely, even if they didn't know that the curse was there, while truth spells and torture would simply trigger the curse once the interrogation reached the right spot. It was a chilling thought and she felt a moment of sympathy for the Inquisition. Who knew how many others, perhaps unknowingly, were walking through the Golden City with such powerful curses attached to their soul?

She closed her eyes as the maids came up behind her and pushed her head down lightly into the water. Warm water lapped around her body, washing away the dirt and blood, before they helped her out and started to dry her with a white towel. Elaine would normally have pushed them away – she didn't have a maid in the apartment; the very thought was laughable and somewhat creepy – but she didn't resist as they dried her off and produced a green dress for her to wear. It didn't match her eyes, yet at least she could wear it. The thought of having to send someone to the inn to pick up her spare outfit was humiliating.

"You don't need to worry about my hair," she said, quickly, as one of the maids started to brush it carefully. It looked as if she intended to spend longer than Daria had making Elaine look pretty, which wasn't necessary. If royal princesses were treated in this manner every day, unable to even wash themselves without help, it was a miracle that more of them weren't completely spoilt brats. But then, they were also breeding cows for their families. There was definitely something to be said for not being born into the aristocracy. "Just brush it and then let it hang free."

"But Milady, you have such nice hair," the maid said, insistently. She wore a collar that Elaine found depressingly familiar. "I was ordered to ensure that you were suitable for your presentation to the King."

Elaine blinked. "My presentation to the King?"

"The King wishes to see you and your master at High Table," the maid said. She would have been ordered to prepare Elaine for the meeting even if Elaine argued against it. "You have to be properly prepared for him."

Elaine rolled her eyes and settled back onto the table as her hair was washed again, brushed, and then braided into two ponytails that reminded her of her childhood. The orphanage had been severe about how its children should look, providing uniforms and insisting that all the girls had the same hairstyle. Elaine had been glad to leave and grow her hair out a little once she'd gone to the Peerless School; she'd certainly never been allowed to experiment with perfumes until she'd left the orphanage. And then she'd never really used them until Daria had started pushing her into going on a date with Bee.

But the maids didn't seem to care. Elaine felt frankly useless as they poked and prodded at her, applying light makeup and dabs of ointment until she felt like an ornament, rather than a living person. Daria had given her makeup that had felt naturally part of her face. The maids had given her makeup that felt like a facemask, one that might crinkle away from her if she tried to smile. How could *anyone* endure living as a human doll? Perhaps they were influenced from birth to believe that that was their due. There were tribes on the Western Islands that bound their women's feet to make them small and dainty, even though it caused them great pain. One of their gods had ordered it as an act of worship, apparently. Elaine suspected that he had been a demon in disguise.

They finally helped her to her feet and pointed her at the mirror. Her face was pale, patted with white makeup that made her look like the doll one of the kinder matrons had given her, years ago. The green dress seemed to offset her pale face naturally, while a golden necklace called attention towards the shape of her breasts. She felt herself flushing and then sighed as one of the maids hastily reapplied makeup to hide the flush. They seemed intent on turning her into a doll. Spells danced through her mind to drive the maids away, or break the collars that ensured that they would always be loyal and obedient to their monarch, but she ignored them as best she could. The gods alone knew what the King wanted with them.

Outside the warm room, Castle Adamant was cold, illuminated by torchlight rather than magic or the gas lights used in some parts of the world. The small army of servants seemed accustomed to the cold, wearing furs to keep themselves warm or simply ignoring it with the dedication of the magically enslaved; the handful of guards wore suits of armour that probably included spells that kept them warm and alert. Battle spells she'd never learned at the Peerless School – she hadn't had the talent to go into combat magic – shimmered through her mind. A handful of carefully-charmed garments could make their wearers invincible, as long as they didn't encounter an enemy with stronger magic.

Castle Adamant didn't seem to be partly built into a pocket dimension, unlike most of the houses belonging to the wealthy in the Golden City. Elaine suspected that it made sense, from their point of view; Ida had never had a strong magical tradition and they'd probably worried about the danger of a cunning enemy collapsing the pocket dimension and crushing the interior of the castle. What would be a nuisance in the Crypt would be a disaster in the living breathing heart of the kingdom. The Crypt...

A thought struck her. It was a mad thought, one that would have been dangerous even without an Inquisitor nearby, but it refused to fade from her mind. Death broke all enchantments, everyone agreed; even the darkest of enslavement charms would be shattered if the victim were bound to only one person, who happened to die before the charm was passed on to a younger master. And Trebuchet was very definitely dead. Even a necromancer would have had problems raising his corpse and sending it out to prey on the living.

She caught one of the maid's hands and halted her. "I want you to have my clothes, the ones that were splattered with blood, brought to my rooms," she ordered. She had a feeling that the King would have organised rooms for her and Dread, if only to ensure that they were where he could see them. No King would be happy with an Inquisitor sniffing around, perhaps digging up secrets that should remain buried. "Have them bagged and left for my inspection."

"Yes, Milady," the maid said, with a bow. Elaine allowed herself a moment of relief – and regret. It had been quite possible that the maid would have been forced to check with her master before she did anything he hadn't already cleared her to do. Enslavement charms were rarely subtle, but then they didn't need to be subtle to do their job. It was a chilling reminder of what could have happened to her if she'd been sold to the slave traders from the orphanage.

The King's Great Hall was enormous, larger than Elaine had expected. It was also cold, warmed only by a massive fire at one end of the room. A dozen heavy wooden tables – Elaine remembered what Dread had said about wood being expensive in Ida – were lined up along the hall, with a single raised table at the far end. Inquisitor Dread stood at one end of the high table, speaking with one of the King's servants. He turned and nodded to Elaine as the maids brought her up to the table. Elaine was oddly piqued that he didn't show any sign of noticing her outfit, although she didn't want an Inquisitor lusting after her. Some of the knowledge in her head suggested that Inquisitors were sworn to lives of chastity. Daria would have made a joke about that explaining why they were always in such foul moods.

"They insisted on giving us the royal treatment," Dread said. Elaine looked at him sharply. He didn't seem to have changed at all, merely swapped his black robes for another set of identical black robes. Or maybe his robes had been charmed to prevent blood from sticking to them and becoming impossible to remove. Inquisitors were meant to walk into danger on a daily basis. "The King wants us to join him for dinner before we continue our investigation."

Elaine wasn't sure what to say. She wasn't even sure why Dread had brought her along, let alone tell everyone that she was his partner in the investigation. But they were working on the same puzzle, weren't they? Whatever had happened to her had to be connected with what had happened to Trebuchet. And anyone that could curse a fully-qualified Court Wizard had to make the Inquisitors nervous. No Court Wizard was appointed unless he was fully trained in all branches of magic, and powerful as all hell to boot. Trebuchet could have turned her into a toad simply by snapping his fingers.

"Thank you," she said, finally. Maybe Dread just wanted to keep an eye on her. If he thought that her powers had been boosted, he had to consider her a potential danger to the entire world. Maddened magicians could tap into levels of power that were normally far beyond them, at a price of abandoning all hope of returning to sanity. And then there were the demons that fed on such fools. "They took hours to wash me..."

A trumpet blew before she could finish her sentence. "Kneel for His Majesty, the King of Ida," a voice thundered from nowhere. "Give him great honour, as he deserves."

Elaine went down on one knee, as did the handful of other guests. Inquisitor Dread didn't move, but then an Inquisitor wouldn't bow the knee to anyone below the Grand Sorcerer himself. The King marched into the room and nodded in return, allowing his guests to return to their feet. At least Ida had never developed the elaborate royal protocol of the southern continent. The Empress of the South was supposed to remain concealed from her subjects at all times, hidden behind a screen whenever she held audience. Maybe that was where Lady Light Spinner had picked up the habit of concealing her face. And yet the Empress had a reputation for also seducing everything on two legs. Perhaps being locked up in a gilded cage, powerful enough to have half the continent executed but not powerful enough to change her apartments, was enough to turn her into a man-eater.

King Hildebrand, father of Prince Hilarion, was a tall middle-aged man with russet hair and beard hanging down to his chest. He was powerfully built, but his gait gave evidence of too much good living over the past couple of decades; he wore a pair of spectacles rather than have a simple corrective spell used to fix his eyesight. Elaine could have understood that for someone like her, without the money to hire a druid to craft and implement the spell, but even the poorest monarch shouldn't have had any problems convincing a druid to heal his eyes. His Court Wizard could probably have crafted the spell himself.

He wore a suit of golden armour decorated with purple strips of cloth that she recognised as signifying a monarch. Only monarchs were allowed to wear purple and gold, although the Grand Sorcerer's formal robes were *also* purple and gold, a reminder to the monarchs that he was very definitely their superior. Elaine knew from some of the history books that had been jammed into her mind – history as she *hadn't* been taught it at school – that some of the monarchs had feared that the Grand Sorcerer would eventually become a tyrant. Anyone with unquestioned authority could become corrupt, but none of the Grand Sorcerers had fallen prey to the temptation to abuse their power. They probably swore mighty oaths that kept them from crossing that line.

"I welcome you to my kingdom," he said, holding out a hand to Elaine. It took her a moment to realise that she was supposed to kiss it. "I am sorry that your first mission for the Inquisition ended so badly."

He didn't sound concerned, not for a monarch whose Court Wizard had been cursed and then killed in his own castle. And he believed that Elaine was training to join the Inquisition...but very little was known, publicly, of how Inquisitors were trained. It was quite possible that the Inquisitors threw prospective candidates in at the deep end to see how they coped.

"The matter has not yet ended," Dread said. "Someone deliberately cursed your Court Wizard; that person remains unknown. We will have to continue our investigation until we determine what actually happened to him."

"He was always fond of his own experiments," one of the guests said. He wore dark clothes and a bright silver medallion that reassembled a large Crown. The Treasurer, Elaine guessed. "Instead of attending hunting or fishing expeditions, he would continue his own experiments in his quarters. Is it not possible that he could have cursed himself by accident?"

"Only a very foolish or untrained magician would have cursed himself accidentally," Dread said, in his very even voice. Elaine suspected that he didn't like the thought of wasting time talking and eating when they should be searching the wizard's chambers. "The rawest of magicians would know to set wards to prevent that from happening..."

"But Hilarion wouldn't have known, would he?" A new voice demanded. Elaine turned to see a girl, barely old enough to be of marriageable age, emerging from a side door. She had long red hair and wore a black dress, her face a strange blend of ethnic traits. The King had married a woman from the other side of the world, according to the history books Elaine had read while travelling to Ida, and had two children with her. "You should never have encouraged his ambitions."

"That will do," the King snapped. "I told you to remain in your quarters, young lady."

"And I said that I wasn't going to remain a pampered princess," Princess Sacharissa said, with a determination that Elaine could only admire. *She* wouldn't have backed down in front of Millicent, even if she didn't have enough magic in her to light a candle flame. "My brother has gone off to the Golden City, where they are going to eat him alive, while you expect me to remain in my chambers and keep myself pretty for the first inbred moron who wants to marry me."

She sat down at the table and waved to one of the maids. "You may as well serve the food now," she ordered. "There won't be any useful discussion until after they've eaten."

Dread smiled thinly at Elaine, and then turned to the guests. "What kind of experiments was the Court Wizard running?"

Princess Sacharissa answered before anyone else could speak. "He had an obsession with turning lead into gold," she said. "And an obsession with ways to extend his life. You'd think that a magician would be wise enough to know when his time was running out, but not our one! He kept looking and looking for secrets that would keep him alive...and then my brother became interested in magic. I tried to tell him that he was being a fool."

"That will do," the King said, again. "You will eat and then we will...discuss this matter very thoroughly."

"I think I would wish to talk with you later," Dread said, to the Princess. "Do not leave the castle."

"As if I would be allowed to leave without a pack of werewolves around me," the Princess snorted. She seemed to be brave enough to be sarcastic to an Inquisitor. Elaine felt a hot flash of envy, which she quickly suppressed. "Don't worry. I'll be here when you want me."

Chapter Eighteen

Daria would have enjoyed the meal, Elaine thought, as she dug her way through a plate that was far too large for her. Undercooked meat, a handful of unidentified vegetables and a thick gravy that actually had to be spooned out of the jug wasn't what she wanted in a dinner. Dread didn't seem to care what he was fed, while the King and Princess ignored each other in stony silence and the courtiers took their cue from their master. Elaine would have liked to ask Princess Sacharissa what had happened to make her brother so interested in magic, but it was impossible to speak to her in front of her father. It was almost a relief when the final course – a pudding so sweet that it made Elaine's teeth hurt – was over and a pair of maids were ordered to show them to Trebuchet's chambers.

"That Princess is smarter than her father and brother put together," Dread observed, as soon as they were out of the main hall. "I'd expect someone like her to be more...interested in marriage than in running the Kingdom. But seeing her father doesn't have a second male heir..."

Elaine blinked. "What would happen to her if Prince Hilarion is killed during the contest?"

"Her husband would become the next King, I think," Dread said. "Ida doesn't seem to like the idea of a female ruler, even if she *is* as smart as anyone else they could hope to get. Prince Hilarion's wild dreams might just be the only thing saving his sister from an arranged marriage and permanent exile to another kingdom. I wonder if he knows it."

"You mean he could be doing it deliberately?" Elaine asked. "But he's risking his life..."

"I know," Dread said. "It would be smarter for him to pressure his father into keeping his sister at Ida, at least until he assumes the Throne." He shrugged. "Anyway, put it aside for the moment. Walls have ears."

Elaine didn't understand until she looked at the maids. They were charmed, of course. They'd take whatever they heard straight back to their master. Dread might have commented on the Princess *knowing* that they'd take what he said back to the King, although Elaine couldn't even begin to guess at his motivations. Did he like the idea of having the princess more involved in governing the state, or did he want her under control? There was no point in trying to guess.

No one in their right mind would go into a magician's chambers without his permission, or without the absolute certainty that they had the power to overwhelm any defensive wards backed up by hidden spells. Dread stopped outside Trebuchet's chambers and gingerly poked the wooden door with his staff. There was a long pause, and then Elaine felt a number of spells slowly shimmering into existence. Some were designed to deter intruders, pushing them away by inducing fear into their hearts; others were far nastier, intended to stop strong-willed intruders in their tracks. Dread stepped forward, muttering under his breath, matching his magic directly against the dead magician's magic. Trebuchet had created a cunning network of spells to keep unwanted intruders out of his quarters. It was work on a level Elaine knew that she would never be able to match.

"Stand away from the door," Dread ordered, stepping to one side. "I think I dealt with all of the dangerous spells, but..."

He tapped once on the door with his staff. It exploded outwards and slammed into the stone wall with terrifying force. It would have killed either of them if it had caught them in its headlong flight. Dread poked at it suspiciously and then stepped into the chamber, holding his staff ahead of him like a weapon. Elaine realised that he'd woven so many spells into the staff that it was almost another wand. A very simple weapon, one that would be almost impossible to recognise without luck or inside knowledge. How many other weapons did Dread have up his sleeve?

"He was clearly very paranoid about someone entering his quarters," Dread observed, mildly. "I can still see spells hanging in the air, watching for targets. Don't touch anything until I check it first, understand?"

"Yes, sir," Elaine said, softly. This was something she'd never trained to do. "What should I be looking for?"

"Anything out of place," Dread said. He hesitated. "Most magicians key their wards so that they come apart after they die, or switch their obedience to his designated heir. Trebuchet clearly wanted to make sure that no one ever entered his quarters while he was alive, or dead. If I hadn't been here, it might have been months before someone with the right qualifications came to Ida to unpick the spells and make it safe for the next incumbent. Interesting, really. I wonder what he was trying to hide?"

Elaine looked around as she stepped into the chambers. The first room was warm and comfortable, with a fireplace and a stack of coal on one wall. It was crammed with books, each of the bookshelves bursting with volumes and countless others piled on the floor as if Trebuchet had simply put them down and left them there in the absence of any space on his bookshelves. Part of her found it charming, remembering the piles of books in the Great Library; part of her was outraged that anyone could treat books like that. She leaned closer and read some of the titles. Most of them were common spellbooks, but a handful were rare and quite valuable. And a couple were definitely on the banned list.

"That's the problem with the printing press," Dread said, when Elaine called his attention to the volumes. "The printers don't really know what's banned, so they copy books without realising that they're setting themselves up for execution or a life in the salt mines; the rogues then take the copies and distribute them everywhere. It's dangerous to risk it in the Golden City, but here, without any other trained wizard for miles around, Trebuchet could have kept an entire library of forbidden knowledge and no one would have been any the wiser."

He frowned as he studied the books. "Interesting choice of reading matter," he added. "Why would he want to learn about fetches when he was studying life extension? Or about mental seed magic?"

Elaine shivered as the horrifying possibilities started to slip into her mind. A fetch – a magical double of a person – could be used, given enough magic, as a secondary body.

She couldn't imagine how one person could live in two bodies at once, but Trebuchet had been through the Peerless School and had had years of experience in doing several things simultaneously. Maybe he could have created a fetch to house his soul when the Inquisitors started asking questions he didn't want to answer. But fetches simply didn't *last* very long, not if they had to be convincing. Most homunculi were easy to spot, even for the untrained. They just looked less human than the undead hordes.

But mental seed magic was worse. A magician with enough power – and a complete lack of scruples – could create a seed of his entire soul, all of his knowledge and experience, and implant it in an unsuspecting victim's mind. The seed would slowly grow until it had taken over the person's body, absorbing their magic into itself and allowing the creator to live again in a new body. And no one would know until it was too late. Elaine shuddered at the thought, picking up the volume and glancing at the first page, which bore a demonic sign. A sorcerer had traded his soul for knowledge he'd hoped would allow him to avoid the fires of hell. There was no way to know if he'd succeeded.

"Put that down," Dread said, sharply. Elaine obeyed at once. "This entire room will have to be sealed until a team of experts can be dispatched from the Great Library and..."

Elaine smiled. "I do have that experience..."

"Yes, you do," Dread said. He hesitated. "But you might be exposed to risks you're not ready to handle. I think you'd better leave it for the Inquisition to handle."

Elaine flushed. How dare he dismiss her like that? And then she realised that he might be right. Anyone who looked at those books ran the risk of being corrupted, even though she already had all of their knowledge in her head. But he didn't know that, did he?

"Yes, sir," she said, shaking her head. "Do you want me to do anything with these books for now?"

"Just leave them," Dread said. He shook his head. "I think you'd be better off talking to the Princess. She probably won't want to talk to me."

"But I won't know what questions to ask," Elaine protested. "Shouldn't you be there...?"

"I'll tell you what to ask, but the main thing is to find out just what Trebuchet was teaching his royal pupil," Dread said. "Trebuchet was a powerful wizard, but I don't think that he could have taught him enough to make him a competitor for the Grand Sorcerer's position. And any Court Wizard should have known better than to try. It would only upset the political balance in the Empire."

He hesitated. "And I would have to be escorted if I spoke to her," he added. "It might be easier to learn from her if there wasn't anyone in the room who might take her words to her father."

"I see," Elaine said. "So...what do you want me to ask her?"

* * *

Princess Sacharissa was lying on her front when Elaine entered her quarters, performing a standard spell she'd learned in the Peerless School to discover the presence of eavesdroppers, if any. The Princess had clearly been crying, one hand rubbing her rear where her father had evidently taken his belt to her. Elaine felt a hot flash of sympathy, remembering her own experience with corporal punishment. The Princess wasn't immune to her father's hand, or perhaps to her husband, when she finally got married. It wasn't uncommon, but it still sickened her. How could anyone treat their daughter like that?

"You're a very lucky girl," Princess Sacharissa said, between gasps of pain. "Does your master treat you like that?"

"No," Elaine said, quickly. Dread wasn't really her master at all. "I need to talk to you..."

"About my brother, or about the fat-arse who got himself killed?" Princess Sacharissa asked, tightly. "I'll tell you whatever you want to hear about Trebuchet. He hated me and didn't bother to hide it. Do you know what he offered my father?"

Elaine could guess, but shook her head. "He said that he could make a slave collar for me that would turn me into the ideal princess," Princess Sacharissa said. "Thank all of the gods that my father rejected the idea. Slave collars are very difficult to remove and their influence lingers on for years afterwards...I would have been at everyone's mercy. Princess Ella used to have a collar and she always did what she was told..."

"Poor girl," Elaine said, sincerely. "Why did your brother start to learn magic from Trebuchet?"

Princess Sacharissa shrugged. "Our mother died when he was seven years old," she said. "I was barely two years old at the time. She had the Dark Cough, you see; I think she must have brought it from her homeland and was never properly treated before it was too late. And then she died and my brother was devastated."

Elaine nodded. The Dark Cough was a magical illness, one created when wild magic festered into an unsuspecting individual with enough of a magical talent to power the disease. Anyone unlucky enough to catch it without knowing the dangers would find themselves weakening slowly until they finally died, no matter what the druids did to try to save their lives. The Dark Cough fed on magic and magical cures would simply speed up the process of the disease. There was no known cure, even in the medical knowledge that Elaine now possessed.

"He always wanted to be a magician, but after my mother died he was *driven*," the Princess continued. "He always talked about raising the dead, claiming that he could find a way to unite our mother's corpse with her soul and bring her back to life. Trebuchet...offered to try to teach him to use his talent properly, rather than do something that would inevitably cross over into necromancy. And our father encouraged him because he wanted his son to be powerful."

Elaine shivered. What Princess Sacharissa was describing – what Prince Hilarion had hoped to do – was impossible. There was no spell that could summon a person's soul back from the land of the gods and permanently bind them to a dead body. The best that would happen was that the body would become a lich, a near-undead corpse with independence; it was far more likely that she'd become one of the undead and accidentally unleash a new plague upon the world.

And yet she could understand a person being so desperate

to have their mother back that they would consider almost anything. She remembered long dark nights in the orphanage, crying into her pillow because she was so alone; what would she have said if someone had offered her the chance to go to her parents? Elaine was honest enough to admit that she would have taken the chance as soon as it was offered, even if it came at a very steep price. She would have done *anything* to have her parents returned to her. How could she hate Prince Hilarion for what he'd done, for what he was trying to do, when she understood him so well?

"He just kept studying and studying," Princess Sacharissa said. "I think he actually outpaced his tutor fairly early on, for Trebuchet would call some other wizards to the castle and have them spend a few weeks adding to the boy's knowledge. And sometimes my brother would leave the castle and go off to study somewhere, returning weeks later tired, but happy. I used to think that he would use his powers to replace Trebuchet and send the strange old man away from the castle. Instead..."

She shook her head. "Instead, he decided to become the Grand Sorcerer," she said. "And my father *encouraged* him!"

Elaine could understand her shock and dismay. Prince Hilarion was the only heir to the throne his father had, at least as long as he was unwilling to admit that girls could rule just as well as men. Allowing him to take part in a contest that could easily kill him was unwise, to say the least. And Trebuchet should have known that the Grand Sorcerer wasn't likely to come from aristocratic stock, no matter how talented. It would twist the balance of power between sorcerers, traders and aristocrats too far.

She rubbed her forehead in irritation. Nothing about this made sense to her. Had Trebuchet taught the Prince magic that he shouldn't have been allowed to know existed? Or had someone else used Trebuchet to teach the Prince? Or had Duke Gama been a far more powerful sorcerer than anyone had guessed...? Most sorcerers were intensely competitive, eager to prove themselves more powerful than anyone else, but there was no law that stipulated that a powerful magician had to be registered. He might have kept a very low profile as he urged Trebuchet to train up his nephew and send him out to join the competition.

"Tell me about your uncle," she said, instead. "How did you get on with him?"

"I think we shared a special bond," Princess Sacharissa said. "He was like me, you see; he was a useless spare to the throne. I think he was the one who urged my father to ensure that I did get an education – and that I didn't get turned into a slave. And then he died a few months ago and they wouldn't even let me keep his books!"

Elaine could understand *that*, all right. "Why don't you just leave the castle?"

"I tried to run away when I was twelve," Princess Sacharissa admitted. "My father's huntsmen caught me before I managed to get more than a few miles away from the castle and my father...my father was not happy about it at all." She rubbed her rear unconsciously. "Where were you born, anyway? How did you get into the Inquisition?"

"I don't know," Elaine admitted. The orphanage had been in the Golden City, but she could have been born anywhere. The thought continued to gall her. "I never knew my parents."

"Lucky you," Princess Sacharissa said. "Dad isn't too bad when he's just dad, but when he's King Hildebrand...well, I have to shut up, look pretty and do exactly as I'm told. And ever since mother died, I've seen more of King Hildebrand than I have of my father."

She looked up at Elaine. "You really don't know where you were born?"

"No," Elaine said. "I could have been born anywhere."

"Really?" Princess Sacharissa asked. "With colour like yours, I would have thought that you were born here. You certainly have the right colour of hair for a child of the mountains."

She grinned. "Do you think we could be sisters?"

Elaine stared at her. She hadn't noticed, but the Princess was right. The maids *did* have the same colour of hair as she had, and Princess Sacharissa's face could have passed for a slightly slanted version of her own. And yet...even if her family *had* come from Ida, why had they seen fit to abandon her in the Golden City? Who had they been and why had they abandoned her?

"Don't cry," Princess Sacharissa said. "Whatever else happens, you can always talk to me."

She shrugged. "An Inquisitor," she added. "Father couldn't stop me from talking to you, could he?"

Chapter Nineteen

"I suppose it is possible that you do come from here," Dread said, an hour later. "You do have the right hair colour for it, but I wouldn't place too much faith in it."

He sounded rather disturbed, as if Princess Sacharissa's casual remark had confirmed a nasty thought of his own. "These aren't the days when regions had their own looks and there were few children of mixed blood," he added. "Your parents might have come from the other side of the world, or been a couple that produced a child that *looked* like someone from Ida. There's no way to know for sure."

Elaine nodded, reluctantly. "Besides, you were given to the orphanage immediately after birth, according to their records," Dread mused. "Someone paid for you to remain there until you were old enough to live on your own, but who? Some aristocrat with a guilty conscience or maybe a trader family unwilling to admit a bastard into their ranks? No one bothered to record it back then."

"I know," Elaine said. "But...is that unusual?"

"It depends on the exact circumstances," Dread said. He gave her an odd look. "Someone from an aristocratic family, pushed into a loveless match, might have managed to get a serving maid pregnant and give the child away for adoption rather than have her hanging around the home. Sometimes they pay a poorer couple to take in the child and raise her as their own, but it can lead to scandal..."

He shrugged. "Anyway, I suggest that you get some rest," he said. "Tomorrow morning we'll have to go down the hill and catch the iron dragon back to the Golden City."

Elaine blinked. "We're not staying here?"

"Something is definitely wrong here," Dread admitted. He didn't sound nervous, but Elaine suspected that he was more worried than he wanted to admit. "The King insisted that we sleep in Castle Adamant tonight, but tomorrow we will go home and await the assignment of a proper investigative team to Ida. And you can go back to the Great Library."

"Yes, sir," Elaine said, softly. She hadn't realised how much she'd enjoyed working with him until it was about to come to an end. And the Inquisitors would probably ask her questions and keep asking her questions until they worked out what Duke Gama's cursed book had actually done to her. "Ah...did they give us separate rooms?"

Dread laughed, humourlessly. "They're not connected," he assured her. "Sleep tight – we'll leave as early as we can tomorrow morning."

Elaine walked into her chambers and shut the door. It was the most luxurious suite of rooms she'd ever had, complete with a bed large enough for five people, a bathtub with working hot and cold running water and a mirror that allowed her to see her entire reflection at once. A small bag just inside the room smelt funny, but it wasn't until she looked at it that she realised that they were the blood-stained clothes from the curtailed meeting with Trebuchet. She locked and bolted the door, and then spent twenty minutes setting up wards that would prevent anyone from breaking it without strong magic. Inquisitor Dread would probably be able to break in, but no one else in the castle should have the type of magic needed to break through the wards. Or so she hoped. Princess Sacharissa had said that she didn't have magic of her own, but if her brother was a powerful magician it was quite likely that she had the talent as well.

She walked over to the bathtub, poured in enough warm water to flood the interior, and then knelt down and started to wash off the makeup the maid had placed on her face. It felt good to have her skin breathing properly again; it was easy to see why Princess Sacharissa had turned out the way she had. Elaine would have been driven to rebel by less constraining circumstances. Washing off the last traces of makeup, she walked over to the mirror and studied her reflection. Princess Sacharissa had been right. She *did* look as though she had come from Ida.

There was a new glint of determination in her eye as she walked over to the bag of blood-stained clothes and pulled them out, one by one. Blood was linked to magic in ways no one fully understood, even the handful of Blood Magicians trained by the druids and sworn to secrecy about their art. The knowledge in her head seemed to suggest that blood – which kept the body going – was symbolically tied to a person's magic, and to a person's soul. It was easy to use a blood sample to track someone down, unless they were powerful enough to ward themselves against discovery. And, according to some of the forbidden rites in the back of her head, it could be used to summon someone's soul back from the dead.

No one really understood the nature of the gods, or what happened after a human soul separated from the body. What *was* understood was that a soul continued to have an affinity for the husk that had housed it for so long, even though they might have gone onwards to a better place or drifted into the fires of hell. Even considering using the rites to call a soul back from the next world was a dangerous step towards necromancy, but she had to *know* what had happened to Trebuchet. And what he knew, if anything, about the spell that had crammed her head with forbidden knowledge. Whatever curses had been used to prevent him from talking while he was alive wouldn't hold true after he was dead.

She hesitated for a long moment, before picking up her shirt and using the blood to draw out a protective circle on the floor. The books seemed to disagree about the precise rituals for summoning demons, but they all agreed that a dead soul needed a circle of blood to exist in the mortal world. They also warned of the dangers in increasingly elaborate terms, noting that the lost souls sometimes turned aggressive and attacked the foolish mortals who dared to recall them to the mortal realm, or tried to possess the living and live again. Aided by the knowledge crammed into her head, she drew out the next set of protective sigils. Even if the lost soul intended to be hostile, she would be ready.

Pouring a jug of water as a final precaution – the dead couldn't cross running water, for no reason that any mortal understood – she stripped and stood in front of the circle, feeling magic swirling around her nude body. There were rituals for subtle magic – female magic, some of the books claimed – that didn't seem to jibe with the more controlled magic developed by the Peerless School. She now knew subtle curses that she could have used against Millicent, without Millicent ever realising what had happened to her. The most frightening part of what she'd become was that she truly didn't understand the limits of her knowledge. New ideas and concepts seemed to pop into her head every day.

She crossed her arms over her bare breasts and mouthed a single word. "Trebuchet," she said, shaping the thought as best she could. She didn't know enough about him to really *know* him, but she recalled her first sight of him and what she'd been told by everyone in the royal court. Carefully, feeling the magic flaring to live, she sank to her knees and whispered his name again. "Trebuchet..."

And something answered. Elaine flinched back, feeling...*something* crawling over her skin, as it started to manifest inside the circle. There was nothing visible, but she could sense it, something starting to take on a vaguely humanoid form. She closed her eyes and concentrated on the memories she had of the Court Wizard. The dead often tried to play tricks on the living...and they didn't quite follow the same rules as the living did. It was quite likely that Trebuchet had already spent years, as he understood the term, in the land of the dead. Who knew what happened to a soul once it was separated from its body?

"You have called me," a voice said. She felt it in her mind rather than her ears. "You wish to ask questions of me?"

It didn't sound familiar, but most of the knowledge had warned that it wouldn't be even remotely familiar. "I called you," Elaine confirmed. The sense of something lurking just outside her closed eyes grew stronger. She was in no danger as long as she didn't break the circle ahead of time, but it didn't feel that way. The magic seemed to have taken on a distinctly alien tone. "I want to know why you died."

The sound of laboured breathing grew louder. "I died because I was a pawn in a game I didn't understand I was playing until it was far too late and I died and I died and I died and I died and..."

"I know," Elaine said, softly. The dead couldn't be trusted completely, according to what she'd read. And they no longer had the same priorities as the living. "I know you died. And I am sorry that you died. And if you tell me what I want to know, I may be able to bring the person who cursed you to justice."

"He will never be brought to justice," Trebuchet's voice said. Elaine pressed her eyes tightly closed as she felt someone looming right on top of her. It was an illusion, a trick of the dead, but it felt alarmingly real. "He waited for hundreds of years to start the pebbles rolling towards disaster. A mere bookworm such as yourself could not stop him. Even the Inquisitors could not stop him."

There was a ghostly chuckle, right on her ear. "But you know how much has been forgotten over the years," Trebuchet said. "You know that better than anyone else, don't you?"

His voice hardened. "And yet you are pathetic," he added, mockingly. "You fear the touch of a man even as you want it. You spy on your friend and now you fear her because of her curse. You want to know the truth even when it will do you no good."

Ghostly lips pressed against hers, a mocking parody of a kiss. "Make me live again and you will have all your answers," Trebuchet whispered. "Give me your living blood to drink, allow me to swarm within your body..."

"No," Elaine said, flatly. The books had warned of this danger. "I cannot help you to come back to life. You would do better to ask the gods."

"The gods do not care," Trebuchet's voice said. He laughed, humourlessly. "As private parts to the gods are we; they play with us for their sport. I can see them watching us, betting on us, throwing down visions and thunderbolts so that we may amuse them as we scurry around and praise them in desperate fear. The gods are not our friends. They are nothing better than demons."

Elaine shivered at the absolute confidence in his voice. She had never been particularly religious, not when the gods had done so little to help her in her troubled life. And she was far from the only one. It had been centuries, perhaps thousands of years, since the gods had sent anything but visions to their believers. And their visions were often misleading, or difficult to understand before it was too late.

"They watch us because we amuse them," Trebuchet added, softly. "They do not care about us."

Elaine cleared her throat. "I want to know who cursed you and why," she said. The books had insisted that some souls needed a firm hand. Trebuchet was clearly one of them. "Do I have to compel you?"

"But that isn't want you really want to know," Trebuchet said. His ghostly presence seemed to press against her body, ghostly fingers running up towards her neck. "You want to know who brought you into this world and why. I could tell you, in exchange for some of your life."

"I cannot make that bargain," Elaine said. There was no such thing as 'some' of a person's life. Trebuchet would drain her and leave her body an empty husk. It was possible that she might even become one of the undead. Inquisitor Dread would open the door to discover her rotting corpse lunging at him, desperate for blood. "Who was it who cursed you and why...?"

"Your mother was a whore, a willing servant for He Who Will Come," Trebuchet said, before she could start using Words of Power to compel him to answer her questions. "Your father carried a bloodline that had been perfectly preserved for hundreds of years, ready for He to use it again. And again. And again. And again."

Elaine was shaken, but somehow she managed to keep her eyes closed. "What bloodline does he carry?" she asked. "Who was he?"

"Ah, his true name has never been spoken," Trebuchet said, craftily. "But I could find it for you, if you gave me your life."

Temptation warred in Elaine's breast. He was right. She *did* want to know, and somehow her life seemed a small price to pay for that knowledge. And yet she knew that it would bring her no happiness. If her mother had truly been a whore...

...But if her mother had been a whore, how had she found the money to pay for Elaine's upbringing, even in the orphanage? With that sort of background, she would have been lucky not to go into the brothels that catered for the truly perverse, the handful of establishments that were talked about in whispers – when they were mentioned at all. They wouldn't have minded taking in a whore's child. She would have taken the money and left Elaine behind to their tender mercies.

The dead couldn't lie, she'd been told, but they would have even fewer inhibitions than an Inquisitor about warping the truth, or deliberately misdirecting their victims. And Trebuchet had been an asshole even when he'd been alive. The gods were probably tormenting him right now for his sins and he was trying to get back at them by misdirecting Elaine...

"I don't want to know about my father," she lied. She *did* want to know, but she would find out another way, somehow. "I *command* you, by Rod and Book and Candle; who was it who cursed you and destroyed your life..."

Her eyes snapped open as *something* intruded into the room. Where Trebuchet's ghost should have been floating inside the chamber, there was...something else, something far greater than Elaine's merely human mind could grasp. It surged forward, trying to force its way into the mortal reality, the sheer presence holding her frozen as it started to imprint itself on the human world. Trebuchet was long gone, his soul shredded in a moment by the creature as it materialised, long fingers of mental force reaching down into Elaine's soul. She opened her mouth to scream...

...And lashed out, knocking over the jug of water. It washed over the floor and broke the circle. The presence was instantly gone, leaving behind nothing more than a wave of magical force that picked her up and threw her backwards into the wall, before the blood washed away completely into a liquid mess. Elaine fell to the ground, yelped in pain as her buttocks hit the stone floor, and then closed her eyes in relief. Something from one of the higher dimensions, perhaps a god, perhaps something far darker, had tried to hijack the summoning, despite all of her precautions. It should have been impossible. Dread was right. Something was definitely rotten in the state of Ida.

She lost track of how long she sat there before she finally pulled herself to her feet and staggered over towards the mess on the floor. Raw magic was crackling around the water, only to disperse into nothingness at her touch. Elaine looked down at the remains of the circle and sigils she'd drawn before starting the summoning and then started to clean it up. If Dread, or someone else, had seen them, they would have been able to guess what she'd done. The maids couldn't be trusted to clean up *this* mess. They would certainly have reported it to the King, even if Elaine tried to claim that it was the result of feminine troubles. If he knew anything about magic, he might have guessed the truth.

The mirror seemed to glow faintly as she caught sight of her own body. She looked a terrifying mess, with bruises everywhere and blood staining her legs. Shaking her head, she started to wash herself thoroughly, just before she caught sight of the mirror again. It *was* glowing, and not with the reflection of her own power. Something was definitely wrong...she stared at her own image and saw her face and hands move, even when she *wasn't* moving herself...

And then her reflection's face twisted into an absolute look of revulsion and slapped her across the cheek.

Elaine stumbled back, more in shock than in pain, just in time to see two dark-suited figures stepping out of the mirror. There was a dimensional gate there, just as she'd seen in the Great Library, and none of her wards had been configured to block it. She hadn't even realised that it was there! Dread would have noticed, she told herself as she grasped frantically for her wand...but it was where she had left it, in what remained of the dress she'd been given by the maids. She hadn't needed it to summon Trebuchet's ghost.

She lifted a hand, preparing to cast a spell, when one of the figures pointed a strange-looking wand at her. There was a brilliant flash of light, a moment of absolute paralysis...and then she blacked out completely.

Chapter Twenty

Someone was whispering at the back of her mind. Elaine could *hear* him, even though she couldn't make out the words. The voice didn't sound pleasant; it sounded annoyed, almost petulant. She tried to listen, her mind only dimly understanding what had happened to her, before there was a tidal wave of pain and she screamed, opening her eyes wide. Her body refused to move...

...Her hands were tied. Worse, her hands were tied to the ceiling and her feet were chained to the floor. Her mind swam in disbelief, before she remembered what had happened just after the summoning. Someone had stepped into her room through a mirrored door and stunned her. And then...she had to have been kept under while she was dragged through the tunnels on the other side of the looking glass. A sense of despondency overcame her as she realised that she could be miles from Inquisitor Dread. She should never have come to Ida. It had all been a terrible mistake.

"She's awake," a voice said. He didn't sound familiar. "It shouldn't take her longer than a few minutes to recover from the curse that stunned her. Perhaps less, if she *is* the one you seek."

"I seek the bookworm," a voice boomed. Elaine looked around, finally sighting a hooded man bending over a crystal ball. The Peerless School had tried to teach Elaine and her classmates how to infuse a crystal ball with magic to allow long-range communications between cities, towns and military formations, but only a handful of her peers had mastered the art. They'd been assured of good positions and better salaries as soon as they graduated. There were never enough crystal balls to go around. "She has to be the one we seek."

The hooded man stood up and advanced on Elaine, who tried to flinch back. Above her, the chains tightened, pulling her hands upright as far as they would go. The dungeon – she was sure that she was in a dungeon – was spelled to prevent the imprisoned convicts from escaping, of course. There was no point in putting criminals in a locked room without having some form of security entity on guard. Elaine might have been able to banish it, if she'd had access to her wand, but it was nowhere in sight. And no human could hope to *outthink* a security entity. She wouldn't be halfway to the door before it slammed shut in her face.

"You are our prisoner," the hooded man informed her. His eyes travelled up and down her naked body, watching with cold amusement as Elaine flushed bright red. "There is absolutely no hope of escaping our grasp. Your cooperation now will encourage us not to harm you more than strictly necessary."

One of the witches from the books Daria was always reading would probably have spat in his face, but they had the ultimate power – the writer – on their side. Elaine stared at him, trying hard not to show her fear. Without her wand, it would be much harder to cast any spells...and even if she did have her wand, the security entity would probably take it from her before she could escape. It wasn't as if she could perform a teleport under her own power. And the dungeon would be surrounded by wards to prevent criminals from simply vanishing in a flash of light.

"So, one simple question," the man said. "Are you the bookworm?"

Elaine winced, knowing that her expression had probably answered his question. She'd always been a bookworm – why not, when she'd had few friends at the Peerless School – but he wasn't asking about her reading habits. The curse on the book from Duke Gama had dumped the contents of millions of books into her head. Of course she was a bookworm. What better name for someone like her?

"Then we have found you," the man said. He laughed, with a kind of grim amusement. "We send teams of hunters to your city to try and identify you and you walk right into our hands."

"I told you that she had been charmed to come to Ida – and to think that it was all her own idea," the voice from the crystal ball said. It sounded vastly amused by the whole concept, even as Elaine shuddered in horror. Inquisitor Dread had pointed out that she might not be acting of her own volition, but she'd dismissed the thought as laughable...and that too might have been part of the spell. "You always had your doubts about the power of magic."

"This kingdom has been kept safe by sword and archery, not magic," the hooded man rebutted, sharply. "Sorcery always threatens sorcerers with corruption, doesn't it?"

"An argument for another time," the voice said. "I suggest that you prepare her for her role in the plan. And make sure that that Inquisitor is dead. The last thing we need is an Inquisitor poking around."

The crystal ball darkened as the spell linking it to another faded and died. Elaine braced herself as the hooded man studied her, one hand holding a strangely thin wand. His eyes, the only part of his face she could see, were bright, almost feverish. Whatever he wanted, it wouldn't be something good. And if they'd killed Dread...

Everyone *knew* that Inquisitors were untouchable. Kill one, or even take him prisoner, and the Inquisition would tear the world apart looking for the people responsible – and then kill them with gleeful abandon. Even the darkest of dark sorcerers preferred to remain hidden rather than provoke a fight with the Inquisition, for backing them was the power of the Grand Sorcerer himself – and all the knowledge stored in the Black Vault. Elaine shivered as she finally drew the lines between her new status as the bookworm and the enemy plan. They wanted the knowledge to even the odds between themselves and the Inquisition.

All of the spells and rituals that could be used to enhance one's magical power worked – at the cost of one's sanity. No wonder Dread had been so concerned about her mental state – and no wonder that the dark sorcerers wanted to get their hands on the knowledge in the Black Vault. Dark sorcerers wouldn't care about madness; they were probably already pushing the limits of sanity as far as they would go. They would use the knowledge to boost their power and then strike before the Inquisition was ready for them. And it would all be her fault. Her fault. Her fault...

The words drummed away in her head as the hooded man placed the wand against her left breast, drew it back...and then struck her with considerable force. Elaine couldn't help herself. She screamed as the pain lanced through her body, as if she'd been raped by a red-hot poker. Pain seared across her breast; he drew back his hand and lashed her right breast, and then her buttocks. Elaine screamed again, reaching into her head for the mental disciplines she'd learned at the Peerless School, but the magic refused to form in her mind. The cold iron chains wrapped around her hands had to be dampening the magic somehow. It was a prison. Of course they would be dampening the magic.

She cringed back as the hooded man – the torturer, she now realised – prepared another stroke...and then stopped, watching her. It wasn't uncommon for people to be tortured, provided that they weren't important; truth spells cost more than torture equipment, after all. And besides, truth spells were finicky. It was far more economical to torture someone, breaking them down piece by piece until they broke and confessed to all their sins. Rumour had it that every nobleman retained his own personal torturer.

The torturer held the cane against her mouth, and then jabbed it sharply into her neck. Elaine yelped in pain, feeling the pressure growing against her throat. He was about to crush it...the pressure grew stronger and her breathing started to falter, just before he stepped back and walked around to her rear. A moment later, she felt him jab the cane into the small of her back...and there was another flare of excruciating pain. And again, and again...

He wasn't doing it to ask her questions, part of her mind insisted; he hadn't even bothered to ask her *any* questions. It struck her that he was torturing her for the sheer hell of it, enjoying himself as he watched her screaming in agony...maybe it aroused him. Some of Daria's more perverse boyfriends, according to her, enjoyed slapping girls or being slapped themselves. Elaine hadn't believed either until now. How could anyone enjoy inflicting, or receiving, pain?

"Let me explain to you how this is going to work," the man said, underlining his words with another sharp lash of the cane. "I have worked as a torturer for the king for the past ten years, during which time I have gained experience in breaking hundreds of people, shattering their wills until they become helplessly compliant and obedient. I can read you like a book."

He chuckled, as one does at a joke that isn't particularly funny. "I know that you're not strong, that you haven't been trained in pain resistance," he added. "And I know that, right now, you don't have enough magic to even call for help. I can keep working on you for days, or weeks, or even months until you are completely broken. Do you understand me?"

Elaine said nothing. He reached out and squeezed one breast tightly. "Do you understand me?"

"Yes," Elaine said, finally. Her entire body felt as if it were on fire. Part of her even found his touch, as repulsive as it was, far more comfortable than the cane lashing her body. Some of the knowledge in her mind hinted that that was the point, that pain would eventually tame her to the point where she would be grateful for every small mercy. She did try to find some advice on escaping torture, but most of the information seemed to assume that she had her hands free. None of the information on picking locks or bare-handed combat seemed useful to her. "I understand."

"You have been here for a week," the man said. "Your dreadful friend" – he chuckled, again – "is dead. There is no one who knows where you are, or what you're doing here – apart from us, of course. If you cooperate, the pain will go away and you can even live a normal life here. It is a shame to waste such a fine specimen of womanhood."

Elaine tasted blood in her mouth. Oddly, she found his claim that Dread had been killed to be reassuring. The voice from the crystal ball had ordered the torturer to make certain that he was dead, rather than simply informing him that it was done. She couldn't have been a prisoner for more than a few hours at most, surely. And if he considered her a fine specimen of womanhood...

She swallowed hard, trying to speak. "What...what do you want?"

"We want the knowledge in your mind," the man said. He prodded her with his cane. "I am going to break you, here and now, so that the knowledge can be extracted. After that, assuming you behave, we will do our best to take care of you. If you don't behave, we'll be forced to throw you to the men. I suggest that you behave."

He was lying, Elaine realised. The knowledge in her head had identified the spell that had cursed her in the Great Library, the spell that had turned her into the bookworm. It *was* possible to transfer the knowledge from one person to another, but except in very specific circumstances the transfer would result in the death of one of the people involved. It was almost certain that Elaine would be killed during the transfer. And even if she survived, her mind would be permanently damaged. It was a terrifying thought.

"No," she said, finally. Maybe she could get him to talk. "Why are you doing this?"

"Why, for the Cause," he said, in surprise. "Don't you even *know* why you're here?"

Elaine gathered herself. "You could tell me," she said. "I might decide to help you willingly."

"You will help us when I break you," the man said. He lashed out with his cane, slicing across her chest just under her breasts. "Do you think that we would trust you to give us the knowledge we want without suspecting a trick? Or that you might use the knowledge against us later?"

Elaine stared at him. "What Cause?" she said. "Why are you doing this?"

The man smiled. "The greatest reason of all," he said. "The quest for independence."

She saw it, as clearly as if he'd drawn a picture for her in front of her eyes. The monarchies resented their subordination to the Grand Sorcerer, even though it was the price they paid for peace along their borders. Ida had better cause to resent it than most; the state had been impregnable, even during the worst of the Necromantic Wars. They didn't want to pay fealty, let alone taxes, to the Grand Sorcerer and the Golden City. Was that why the Heir to Ida's Throne had gone to the Golden City and announced his intention to join the competition for the Grand Sorcerer's position? If he won, would he grant the monarchies their independence once again?

And with the knowledge in her head, his victory would be assured.

It would be disastrous. The Empire had had hundreds of years of peace and prosperity after the end of the Second Necromantic War. Successive Grand Sorcerers and Regency Councils had fostered trade and economic development, building roads and iron dragons that linked states together into a single whole. A war, even without necromancers being involved, would be war on a scale unimaginable to most people. The entire Empire would convulse as state after state tried to secure its independence, destroying all that bound the Empire together in their struggle. And that wouldn't displease the monarchs. How many of them resented the increasing demands from the traders for political representation in exchange for taxes?

Prince Hilarion and his father had to be mad. Couldn't they see that such a war would be utterly devastating...or perhaps they *intended* it to be devastating. Ida would survive a war largely unscathed, particularly if Prince Hilarion was as powerful as he claimed and he had a small force of sorcerers backing him up. And when the dust had settled, maybe they would ride down from the mountains and impose their own order upon the ruins of the Empire.

"Listen to me," she said, urgently. "This is madness..."

She broke off as he lashed her back, again. "I don't care about your opinion of what you think we're trying to do," the man sneered. "I want to break you. Tell me – how do you turn a man inside out?"

He struck her again, and again, firing questions at her one after the other. "How do you make the dead speak? How do you turn the seas to wine? How do you summon demons and bargain with them for power and immortality? How do you..."

"I won't tell you anything," Elaine said. She could barely think against the pain, but one thought stayed in her mind. The knowledge in her head could not be allowed to fall into Prince Hilarion's hands. Even Deferens would be a better Grand Sorcerer than a man who intended to tear the system down. At least he'd sworn the Mage's Oath. "Do you understand me? I won't tell you anything."

"They all say that," the torturer said. He leered at her as he reached down to stroke between her thighs. "They all say that they won't talk, that pain itself won't break them – but everyone breaks in the end. You *will* break and then you will be collared and then you will have the knowledge ripped from your mind."

Elaine shivered in horror. Collars – slave collars – weren't completely perfect, as long as they were forced on an unwilling victim. It was possible to break them, although not easy even for the strongest of souls. But if he broke her down to the point where she would willingly consent to be enslaved, there would be no hope of resistance. She would be someone's property for the rest of her life. Why had she never realised, in all of her life, that slavery was such a great evil? Even the slaves who had the chance to buy their way out of bondage lived lives of unrelenting toil and drudgery. How could *anyone* tolerate such a system?

Of course you tolerated it, a voice in the back of her head whispered. *It suited you to pretend that the slaves were less than human. Even as a poor woman without a husband, you were superior to the slaves – and you never forgot it. How could you realise that they were your equals without admitting that you were just as hopeless as them?*

"No," she said. "I will not talk."

Pain seared her body, again and again. She couldn't tell if he was just whipping her, or if he was using curses and charms to break her resistance. Elaine tried desperately to cling onto some memory, some happy thought that would give her strength, but nothing seemed to work. Hands grasped at her body, humiliating her by pulling her legs apart and touching her most private parts. She was going to break...even the thought weakened her. She would break...

"Step away from her," a sharp voice ordered. It was familiar, so familiar that it cut through the pain tearing away at her resistance. She heard a yelp from the torturer as a pulse of magic threw him across the room. "Now!"

Elaine opened her eyes and saw a face she'd feared she would never see again.

Inquisitor Dread.

Chapter Twenty-One

Dread stood there, his black cloak swirling around him.

Elaine thought, as pain trickled away from her body, that she'd never seen anything more magnificent. Dread held his staff upright in front of him, staring directly at the torturer and his assistants. Just as he was, he was the most dangerous person in the room and they all knew it. Behind him, peeking through the door, her eyes opening wide with horror as she saw the marks on Elaine's body, was Princess Sacharissa. Elaine couldn't even begin to imagine what she was doing there.

Dread lifted a finger and tossed a wave of force at the torturer, knocking him back into the wall. As if it had been a signal, the first of the assistants charged directly at Dread, fists whirling as if he thought he could beat an Inquisitor in a fistfight. Dread didn't give him a chance to find out; he eyed his opponent, who slowly came to a halt and froze in place. Dread stepped forward as soon as ice had covered the assistant and kicked him in the groin. Chunks of frozen flesh crashed down everywhere.

The second assistant had some magic. He made a series of gestures with his hand and needles – hot needles of inquiry, according to the knowledge in Elaine's head – shot off the table and lunged towards Dread. The Inquisitor held up his staff and the needles froze in mid-air, before turning and racing back towards the second assistant. He turned to run, too late; the needles slammed into his back and burned through his body. Hexed to produce incredible pain in their victims, they tore through him and blew him screaming into the next world.

Dread ran forward as the chains suddenly tightened around Elaine's hands, threatening to crush her wrists. He cast a complex spell that shattered the iron chains, showering Elaine with dust as she collapsed in a heap. Her entire body hurt, pain surging through every last part of her mind. Dread caught her before she hit the ground and cast a second spell on her. This one started to push the pain into a corner of her mind. It still hurt, but at least she could think clearly.

She caught Dread in her arms and gave him a kiss, driven by relief and a strange emotion she couldn't quite identify. He gently pushed her away and held out a black robe, looking away as Elaine donned it and stumbled to her feet. Princess Sacharissa held out a hand and Elaine took it gratefully as Dread walked over to the torturer.

"Dead," he said. "It looks to be another curse and..."

The crystal ball exploded with a shattering crash. "They'll be coming after us," Princess Sacharissa said, quickly. "My father's huntsmen will be seeking us..."

"Then we'd better get out of here," Dread said. He pulled Elaine's wand out of his robe and passed it to her. "Elaine; can you walk?"

"I think so," Elaine stammered. After everything – the summoning, the stunning, the torture – she felt faint and wanted to collapse. But the enemy ruled Ida and probably had other sorcerers to call upon. Even an Inquisitor would have problems defeating more than two or three fully-trained combat sorcerers. "What...what happened to you?"

"They sent me a gift of food at night, claiming that it was an old custom from Ida," Dread said, as he examined the doors leading out of the torture chamber. "I knew that there was no such custom, so I checked each and every piece of food...and finally discovered a very cunning attempt to poison me. There were two components, both harmless in themselves, but together they would have been lethal. Luckily, my spells recognised them and I was careful not to touch any of the food."

He shrugged. "I went to check up on you and discovered that you'd been taken from your room," he added. "Princess Sacharissa was good enough to admit that her father had been up to something...and that you'd probably been taken to his dungeons. So I came down and found you."

"After fighting his way through an entire squad of guardsmen," Princess Sacharissa said. She was staring at Dread in a manner that Elaine found disturbing. "Weren't you going to mention that part?"

"They weren't ready for me," Dread said. "I'm afraid that the next set of guardsmen will be ready – and they'll probably be backed up by magicians. I think we need to get out of the castle now, quickly."

"I know the secret passageways out of the castle," Princess Sacharissa said. "As long as you take me with you, I'll show you how to escape."

"I wouldn't dream of leaving you here," Dread assured her. "Now...shall we go?"

Outside the torture chamber, the air was deathly still. A handful of bodies lay on the ground near the stairwell, covered in boils and blisters that marked a very nasty curse. Elaine shuddered at the sight and then concentrated on walking down a second set of steps that led even further under the castle. The walls closed in rapidly, leaving her feeling as if the entire building was going to come crashing down on her head. Finally, they stopped outside a blank wall and waited until Princess Sacharissa placed her hand against the stone. A block of stone moved to one side and allowed them into a second tunnel.

"We can't go to the city," Princess Sacharissa said. She *had* tried to escape her father and his plans for her before, Elaine remembered. "They'll have watchers stationed on the walls, looking for us. I think we will have to leg it down the mountain."

"Not much choice," Dread agreed. They reached the bottom of the steps and opened a second hidden door. This one opened out into a gully, with a stream heading down towards the bottom of the mountain. It was hard to be sure, but Elaine suspected that they were on the other side of the castle from the city. "How well do you know these mountains?"

"I used to ride through them when I was a child," Princess Sacharissa said. She hesitated, staring around the darkened landscape. In the distance, Elaine could see the first glimmer of dawn starting to illuminate the sky. "I don't think that much will have changed since then."

"Let's hope so," Dread said. "We need to get down to the plains before the next nightfall, or we will have to find a place to hide on the mountainside."

Elaine shivered as she heard the sound of a wolf in the distance, remembering Daria's true nature. A werewolf would have no difficulty tracking them across the broken mountainsides, perhaps leading a squad of guardsmen down their trail. Or perhaps summoning a flock of wolves to aid in the hunt. Some werewolves had an almost familial relationship with their beastly cousins.

"Thank you for coming to save me," she said, before they started on their way. "I...I thought I was dead."

"I thought that my father had finally gone insane," Princess Sacharissa admitted. "What the hell was he thinking?"

"Assuming it was him doing the thinking," Dread said, slowly. "The books we found in your wizard's room...they could be used to influence a person's mind."

Princess Sacharissa looked over at him. "You mean that my father is under my brother's control?"

"It's possible," Dread admitted. "I won't know for sure until I have a chance to examine your father personally." He changed the subject quickly. "That secret passage didn't look very well guarded."

"There are guard posts inside the castle," Princess Sacharissa explained, "and the passageway only opens for members of the royal family. Even my mother couldn't have used it without my father's help. He once told me that he and mother used to walk out before he became King and enjoy a picnic on the mountainside. I miss the man he used to be."

"Power changes people," Dread said, as they started to scramble down the gully. "Some people become better when they take on power, others allow it to corrupt them and drive them mad. Someone born to the purple has a higher chance of going mad than someone born without power."

"That isn't quite what you said earlier," Elaine remarked, waspishly. "You implied that giving the powerless power could be very dangerous."

"In a different way," Dread said. "People born to power...they never question the rightness of their position. They just accept what they have..."

He shook his head. "I suggest that we concentrate on the walk for now," he added. "We have a long way to go."

The walk rapidly turned into a nightmare as the sun rose, warming the gully and threatening to burn all three of them. Elaine felt sweat trickling down her face as she scrambled down the path, wishing that she could take a break, but knowing that they didn't dare stop for a rest. Behind them, she was sure that she could hear the sound of dogs barking and wolves howling. One of the few jobs available to openly-infected werewolves was that of hunting master, using a werewolf's powerful sense of smell to track game through the forests and mountains so beloved of the aristocracy. One of them could be on their tail right now.

"It was easier when I was a child," Princess Sacharissa muttered. "I should have worn proper clothes instead of this...nightdress."

Dread ignored her. "I think..."

He swore. "Get down and into the stream," he added. "Hurry!"

The sound of baying dogs grew closer as the stream flowed towards a waterfall. Elaine couldn't swim and almost fell over the edge before she caught hold of the rock and started scrambling down. She finally lost her grip on the slippery rock and plummeted into the deep pool, gasping for breath as she struggled to keep her head above the water. Dread caught her arm and pushed her towards the waterfall, into a cave just behind the falling sheet of water. Elaine could barely hear anything over the thunder of the falling water, but Dread seemed to be almost impossibly aware. Something was very definitely hunting them.

Elaine squeezed as much water as she could out of her robe, looking over at the Princess. They shared a faint chuckle; no one, even Daria, would have considered them a decent couple. Their outfits were clinging to their wet skin, revealing every curve of their bodies. No one would need to imagine anything...

"Quiet," Dread hissed. "They're coming."

"I can't hear anything," Princess Sacharissa said. Elaine couldn't make out anything either, but Dread held up one hand. "What's coming..."

"A werewolf, I think," Dread muttered back. Elaine winced. Dread was so aware...could *he* be a werewolf? The

Inquisition would probably overlook a little thing like lycanthropy if they thought that a werewolf would make a good Inquisitor. But he didn't have the faintly canine features that most werewolves possessed. Daria's eyes were alarmingly like a dog's pair of eyes. "I don't know if they can track us here."

Princess Sacharissa reached out and took Elaine's hand as they waited. What seemed like hours passed slowly before Dread finally ducked under the waterfall and peeked outside. "Nothing," he said. "Either they lost the scent or they're lying in ambush. But we have to move."

The sun was higher in the sky as they kept heading downwards, drying their clothes even as it threatened to burn their skin. Elaine kept glancing around, looking for possible threats, even though she suspected she wouldn't see anything until the enemy actually attacked. The books on warfare she'd absorbed into her mind extolled the virtues of surprise attacks and ambushes, although most of them did note that surprise was often far more difficult to achieve than many of the history books suggested. Elaine found herself wishing, not for the first time, that she'd learned more background material at the Peerless School. Or maybe she should have gone hunting, if she'd been able to afford it. Millicent's family certainly *had* been able to afford it for their children.

A low growl caught them all by surprise. Dread spun around, raising his staff to confront the oversized wolf standing on the rock above them. The wolf was easily twice the size of a normal wolf, its dark eyes intimidating as hell. It opened its jaws, revealing teeth that could crush a man's head in a single bite, and leered at them. Elaine had no difficulty reading its expression. It wanted to kill and eat them – and it would, if they showed any signs of resisting.

"Keep your hands where I can see them," the werewolf growled. "And you, put down that staff."

Dread muttered a curse under his breath and the rock exploded, but the werewolf was already leaping into the air and was unharmed. Of course, part of Elaine's mind noted; the werewolf would have known from Dread's scent what he was planning, probably before the idea had gelled properly in Dread's mind. It landed neatly in front of the Inquisitor and lashed out with a single paw, knocking Dread to his knees with effortless ease. Princess Sacharissa started forward, only to freeze when the werewolf turned his head and looked at her.

"Do not move," he said, "or a whipping from your father will be the least of your troubles."

Elaine felt her wand in her hand, thinking fast. A death-curse would work, surely, but it might catch Dread in the blast as well...and it would reveal what had happened to her. There had to be another idea. She hesitated and then gambled, pushing all the power she could muster into raising an illusion right in front of the werewolf. A plate of meat, larger than the werewolf itself, seemed to materialise in the air. The animal part of the werewolf's mind reacted and jumped forward, abandoning Dread. It jumped right through the illusion and then turned around, snarling in rage. Elaine felt herself drop to her knees from sheer terror as the werewolf met her eyes. Whatever the werewolf's masters had ordered, it no longer wanted to take her alive. Wolves had their pride; it was just about all they had left.

The werewolf lunged at Dread again, but he cast a spell that raised a shield and deflected its leap, before he threw a fireball into the beast's fur. It howled in pain and leapt twenty meters into the lake and then jumped up again, coming right at the Inquisitor. Dread began a death-curse that shattered when the werewolf struck his shield, the force of the impact knocking the Inquisitor back to the ground. And then it leapt up and came right at Elaine.

She screamed as the beast knocked her down and placed one paw firmly on her chest. Blood welled up where its claws pieced her flesh, leaving her worrying about the dangers of infection – could it turn her into a werewolf too? But it had a collar around its neck...the demand for bloody revenge on the bitch who had tricked it was struggling with orders to return the unwilling bookworm to the prince – unharmed.

The beast won and it leaned forward, its jaws opening wide. Elaine saw Dread stumbling to his feet, but there was nothing the Inquisitor could do. The words for a hundred death-curses rose into her mind and she shaped a single thought, knowing that it would save her life only to risk losing everything to the Inquisitors. But there was no choice. The death-curse lanced upwards and blasted the werewolf away from her, leaving the body crashing down near the lake. A moment later, it slowly returned to human form, revealing a dark-skinned man covered in hair. Most werewolves shaved to hide their true nature; Elaine knew that Daria did, even though female werewolves had less body hair.

Dread caught her arm. "Where did you learn that spell?"

Surprisingly, Princess Sacharissa came to her aid. "Don't you dare yell at her," she snapped, with all the arrogance of a royal upbringing. "Elaine just saved our lives."

"Yes, she did," Dread agreed. He looked over at Elaine, his eyes burning into her soul. "When we get down to the plains, we are going to have to have a long talk. Understand?"

"Yes, sir," Elaine said. If nothing else, perhaps Dread would help her to find a compromise that would help her stay alive. She hadn't asked to be turned into a bookworm. "For now...can we get down before the end of the day?"

"I think so," Dread said. He grinned, suddenly. "If nothing else, the dead werewolf should give other hunters a touch of reluctance to advance further."

He gave her one last worried look and then started off back down the trail. Princess Sacharissa followed him and, after a moment, Elaine followed him as well. The maps she'd looked at hadn't gone into many details, but from what she remembered there was an independent city-state at the base of the mountains, along the shores of Silver Lake. It was closely allied with Ida, yet its ruler was elected and it wouldn't be quick to jump when Ida called the tune. Or so Elaine hoped. Being tracked down by werewolves was bad enough, but if they were detected in Lakeside, they would face guardsmen and combat magicians.

And she knew that they were in no state for a fight.

Chapter Twenty-Two

Lakeside seemed much more laid back than Ida, as far as Elaine could tell. The population wore more colourful clothes and no one seemed to bat an eyelid when they saw three strangers walking off the mountain. Dread had cast an illusion spell to appear as a father with his two daughters, neither one of whom bore any resemblance to wanted fugitives. Elaine couldn't see any sign that any of Lakeside's population was even looking for them, but there was no way to be sure. Lakeside *was* a pretty obvious destination for them.

"I had to book tickets on a coach tomorrow to Garston," Dread said, after they'd waited for him in the inn. "I don't want to go back to the iron dragon – it's too obvious a place for them to look for us."

Elaine nodded, exhausted. They'd booked an inn with two rooms, although Dread had warned them that they needed to set up proper wards – and remove all the mirrors – before they went to sleep. Elaine had been relieved to discover that he hadn't realised that Castle Adamant had had a secret network of gateways into a mirrored dimension, even though it wasn't very reassuring. If an Inquisitor could miss that, what else could he miss?

"Good thinking," Princess Sacharissa said. *She* didn't seem to have given any thought as to what she would do once she fled her father's kingdom. Was she even qualified to do anything? "Have you called the Inquisition and warned them about my father?"

"There are...political problems," Dread admitted, reluctantly. "I told my superiors, but...they can't act at once."

Elaine stared at him. "There's a rogue sorcerer – probably more than one – and a royal family with a mad plan to bring down the Empire and you can't do *anything*?"

"There are political problems," Dread repeated. "Right now, there isn't a single unifying source of authority – and there won't be until the next Grand Sorcerer is selected. Without his orders, we do not have the legal authority to take over Ida and hunt down her royal family – we can't even arrest his foolish prince. There would be a terrific outcry over it."

"Madness," Princess Sacharissa said. "My Kingdom's subjects are at the mercy of my father and whoever is controlling his brain and you can't do anything about it!"

"I agree," Dread said. "I have suggested most strongly that we put together a force anyway and keep Ida under close watch, but the others may not agree to go along with my suggestion. Everything is a little crazy between Grand Sorcerers; the last thing we need is rumours that the Inquisitors are plotting to remove candidates they don't like."

"I thought you were sworn to serve the state faithfully – magically binding oaths," Elaine said. "Why...?"

"You ought to know that any oath, even one sworn on a person's name, can be circumvented with a little ingenuity," Dread said, ruefully. "If I sincerely believed that assassinating all of the candidates was the right course of action, I could do it without losing my powers. And even if you haven't thought of that" – he smiled, dryly – "I assure you that the candidates themselves will have thought of it. What could someone do with a carefully-tuned memory charm?"

He shrugged, thoughtfully. "The Inquisition has never been popular," he added. "We do our job too well."

Elaine nodded. "And so they fear you, even as they battle to control you."

"Oh yes," Dread said. "Fear keeps the world going round."

He straightened up. "Which leads neatly to the next question," he said. "What happened to you when you were hit with Duke Gama's spell?"

Elaine took a breath and started to explain, watching Dread carefully as she spoke. Whatever else happened, he would be angry – and horrified – that she hadn't told him at once. Maybe that too had been a command included in the spell – she hadn't told anyone about her new knowledge – but it no longer seemed to have any effect. Or maybe she'd just been paranoid.

"Let me see if I understand you," Dread said, finally. He looked over at Princess Sacharissa, and then looked back at Elaine. "The spell gave you all of the knowledge in the Black Vault?"

"All of the knowledge in the entire Library," Elaine said. It was beyond her comprehension – and she'd been the target of the spell. There were hundreds of thousands of volumes – no one had a precise count – within the Great Library. "I can tell you details from history books covering the Inquisition..."

"Most of those books are untruthful," Dread muttered. He looked up at her, sharply. "You had all this knowledge and it never occurred to you to tell *anyone*?"

"No, sir," Elaine admitted. "I didn't even tell Daria."

"You must have been out of your mind," Dread snapped. "Didn't you think about what someone could do with that kind of knowledge before you decided to head off to Ida?"

Princess Sacharissa came to Elaine's rescue. "You skulls have a reputation for...extreme solutions to problems," she said, her voice calm and very reasonable. "What do you think she expected from you if she told you the truth?"

Dread nodded, slowly. "Very true," he admitted, "although we wouldn't have killed you. You didn't *ask* to become a bookworm..."

He hesitated. "Were you tempted to use the knowledge in any way?"

"I did something to Millicent," Elaine admitted, in a small voice. He had every right to be angry about that, even though he and his fellows had never called Millicent to account for her crimes. "And...and I spied on Daria."

The whole story slowly tumbled out. Her curiosity about the secret Millicent had mentioned, finding the chest...and finding the magical supplies inside. She didn't know exactly why she had confessed so openly, but in some ways it was a relief. At least they'd hold her to account for something she'd actually done deliberately.

"I just assumed that you did know that you were sharing your apartment with a werewolf," Dread said, shaking his head. "How did you manage to miss the clues?"

Elaine looked down at the ground. "I just...I guess I am as stupid as Millicent says I am," she admitted. "I never thought that Daria might be a werewolf...and I never thought twice about coming to Ida."

"*That* wasn't completely your fault, I think," Dread said, reassuringly. "Your past history doesn't suggest a person likely to drop everything and go on a trip five hundred miles from the Golden City on a whim. But...they clearly knew what had happened to you. If I hadn't shown up, they would probably have waited for you to visit the Court Wizard and grabbed you there and then."

Elaine felt...violated. Someone had placed commands in her mind and she had followed them without even *thinking* it through. Millicent had been kind to her by comparison; she'd *known* that she was being compelled to act, even though resistance was futile. Even the cold knowledge that few people were logical enough to notice that they were being subtly influenced didn't help.

He stood up and started to pace the room. "Let's see...Duke Gama dies – the only person who can assure us that it was a natural death does so. But we know that he was involved because he was cursed, and he died when he started to tell us the truth. The king tries to kill an Inquisitor and has his men torture you...his son wants to become Grand Sorcerer and may be trying to get his hands on you to boost his powers."

Princess Sacharissa frowned. "Would that work?"

"Of course it would work," Dread said. "The price, however, is very high."

The Princess lifted her eyebrows. "Sanity," Dread explained, reluctantly. "And that's just for starters. Madness brings with it the ability to call on magic powers rarely mastered by mankind, powers that eat away at the flesh of their victim even as he believes he is their master. They say that that is what happened to the Witch-King."

Elaine shivered. She knew the truth behind the Witch-King, but did Dread? She wanted to tell him, and yet...she didn't really want to talk about it. If he believed in Valiant, and looked up to him as a possible role model, why should she ruin his ideals by telling him the truth? What possible good could it do?

"Never mind him," Elaine said. "What are we going to do about the problems in Ida?"

"First, we're going to get you back to the Golden City, where we can keep you under guard until we have a new Grand Sorcerer to judge your case," Dread said. Elaine had to fight to repress a snort. What if the new Grand Sorcerer was Prince Hilarion? Or Deferens? *They* wouldn't be inclined to view her sudden acquisition of forbidden knowledge very lightly. And she doubted that any of the others would take a better view of it. "And then..."

He shook his head. "I don't even know where to begin sorting this mess out..."

"Maybe you should forget convention and just move against my brother," Princess Sacharissa said. "Surely, if you can stop him, everything else won't matter."

"You're missing the point," Dread explained, patiently. "The Inquisition exists to prevent the misuse of magic and magical artefacts. It does not exist to vet candidates for the post of Grand Sorcerer, at least without direct orders from the reigning Grand Sorcerer. We depend upon a degree of consent from the rest of the population to carry out our duties. If they start thinking that we're picking and choosing the Grand Sorcerer..."

He shrugged. "The results could be outright civil war," he admitted. "I suspect that my superiors will find some way of dealing with the problem, but not immediately. I don't think your brother can win without the help of this young lady."

He nodded to Elaine. "So we should be fine as long as we keep you well away from him," he added. "You won't try to run off again?"

"Not as long as you don't try to kill me," Elaine said, seriously.

Dread didn't smile. "I hope it doesn't come down to that," he said, flatly. "I'll do my best to keep it from becoming a problem for us."

Elaine was still thinking about possible solutions. "Couldn't you put it to a vote?"

Dread blinked in surprise. "A vote?"

"You have six possible candidates for the position – five, if we exclude Prince Hilarion," Elaine pointed out. "What if you told them what was going on and then asked them to commit their support to investigating the Prince and flushing him out – you'd just need three votes in favour and then you could reasonably claim that you had the support of the next Grand Sorcerer, whoever he might be."

"Assuming that the investigation turned up enough dirt to prove that he was up to something dangerous – and illegal," Dread said. He stroked his chin thoughtfully. "And it would be very embarrassing if one of the dissenters became the next Grand Sorcerer. And we'd need proof..."

"I thought that you had the powers you needed to investigate anyone on suspicion of necromancy," Elaine said, in surprise. "Couldn't you just tell them what we know."

"We don't have absolute proof that Prince Hilarion is involved in this crazy plan," Dread said. He smiled sourly at her expression. "Think about it. We know that his father was involved, as was his former Court Wizard, but we don't have anything on Prince Hilarion himself. And we don't even know if his father is a willing conspirator or under the control of person or persons unknown."

Elaine remembered the voice speaking out of the crystal ball and shivered. But if pressed she would have to admit that she didn't know who had been on the other end.

"And Prince Hilarion is very well connected through his father and grandfather's complex network of marriage alliances," he added. "And most of the aristocracy will rally around him without absolutely watertight proof that he is controlling his father and experimenting with banned magic. It might even be hard to prove that the spell he used on you, through that cursed book, was illegal. He could merely smile and deny all knowledge, or claim that he hadn't thought that anyone would be stupid enough to open the volume without checking first..."

Elaine scowled at him, but she had to admit that he had a point. The druids spent most of their time dealing with the fallout from magical disasters, which were mainly caused by some idiot walking into a set of wards or accidentally triggering a spell they didn't know how to control. Every magician worthy of the name used wards and booby traps to safeguard his possessions. There was no law against doing it, if only because it would be widely ignored. And anyone stupid enough to try to burgle a magician deserved everything he got.

And Dread was right. The aristocracy were determined to retain what few rights and privileges they had left. They would definitely rally around Prince Hilarion unless there was watertight proof...proof that they might never be able to acquire. Once there was a new Grand Sorcerer...but what if Prince Hilarion *became* the new Grand Sorcerer?

She hesitated. "What if we killed him?"

"He's my brother," Princess Sacharissa objected. "I know he can be an asshole at times, but..."

"Killing a potential Grand Sorcerer is a serious crime," Dread pointed out. "I don't think we would be able to convince everyone that we'd done the right thing." He shrugged. "Are you always this bloodthirsty?"

Elaine stared at him. She *hadn't* been bloodthirsty before the accident, any more than she'd have stood up to Millicent – and her aunt – or talked to an Inquisitor like he was a friend. And now she'd seen four men die in front of her – five if they counted the werewolf as human – and was coldly talking about killing another man. It wasn't what she wanted to be...

...But was there any choice? What if Prince Hilarion became the new Grand Sorcerer?

The thought kept spinning around in her mind. What if...what if...there had to be a way to stop him, but...what?

A thought struck her. "Where is he staying at the moment?"

"With the Duke of Randor," Dread said. "At least he was last time I heard – I suppose he could have decided to desert the Golden City by now if he thinks we have proof of his misdeeds."

"I wouldn't count on it," Princess Sacharissa muttered. "He was...always a stubborn bastard."

"Why don't we burgle the house and see what he has in his secret chests?" Elaine asked. She would *never* have dared think of *that* before the accident. "Or what if we..."

"That would be technically illegal," Dread said, deadpan.

"I would not be able to accompany you."

Of course, Elaine realised. He'd taken his oaths. "But I can't think of anything better," she said. "Unless we just keep our heads down and hope for the best."

"You should be kept under firm guard until the new Grand Sorcerer is selected," Dread said. "But let me give the matter some thought. I should be able to come up with a possible solution that will suit both of us."

"I want to go out with Bee again," Elaine said, firmly. For once, she was going to chase a man – by following Daria's advice and running away very slowly. "You can have me escorted if you like, but I am going."

Princess Sacharissa gave her an odd look. "You have a boyfriend?"

"Sort of," Elaine said, reluctantly. Princess Sacharissa was beautiful. She could have any boy she wanted, just like Daria. There was no way she was going to allow her anywhere near Bee until she'd decided just what she wanted to do with him. "And no, you can't have him."

Dread laughed. "Get some rest," he said. "We catch the coach to the Golden City at dawn – hopefully we should be well away before they catch up with us. If they do..."

Elaine frowned. "Do you think they'll come after us?"

"They must," Dread reminded her. "They're committed – they were committed the moment they tried to kill me. They have no choice but to play it out to the end."

He doffed his hood to them and left the room, carefully creating the wards that should keep them both safe overnight. Elaine watched him go and then looked over at Princess Sacharissa, who looked back at her as if she didn't quite believe what was happening. Elaine felt the same way. Had it really only been a week ago when she'd had nothing more important on her mind than working for Miss Prim?

"Tell me something," Princess Sacharissa said. "He may be your master, but he isn't your lover?"

Elaine flushed. "No, he isn't my lover," she said. And he wasn't really her master either, although part of Elaine was tempted to work with the Inquisition in future – if they ever agreed to allow her out of their sight. "Are you interested in him?"

Princess Sacharissa didn't flush. "What if I was?"

Elaine felt an odd pang of sympathy for Daria. Had her friend felt the same way when trying to talk her into entering the wonderful world of boys?

"He's an Inquisitor, married to his job," Elaine said, simply. "Just remember that he won't put you first – he can't. They want single-minded ruthlessness and they get it."

She shook her head as she climbed into bed and waved her hand at the candle flame, using a tiny charm to dampen its glare. Sleep shouldn't have come easily, but she was exhausted and – for once – her sleep was dreamless. She only awoke once to the sound of quiet sobbing. The Princess had finally realised that everything was real.

Elaine did the one thing she could for the prideful girl. She pretended she hadn't heard anything.

Chapter Twenty-Three

The Inquisition was housed in the Watchtower itself, a blocky structure that provided an excellent vantage point over the surrounding territory – and the Golden City. Elaine had visited it while she was in the Peerless School, but had never visited it afterwards – and certainly never as a possible candidate for the Inquisition's attentions. The looks some of the guards tossed at her suggested that *they* thought that she should be going into the building wearing handcuffs...and they didn't even know why she was there.

Inquisitor Dread led her through the public part of the building, walking through the waiting room. A handful of junior Inquisitors were attempting to cope with a backlog of magical complaints, ranging from tricks played by junior magicians to more serious incidences of dark magic being used against helpless civilians. The death of the Grand Sorcerer had left a power vacuum in the heart of the Empire and it wouldn't be filled until a new Grand Sorcerer was selected to fill his shoes. And then the more rowdy elements would be brought under control, or crushed. Elaine knew enough now, from Dread or from the forbidden knowledge in her heart, to know that part of the price of becoming Grand Sorcerer was to keep magic and magicians under control. The new Grand Sorcerer would establish his authority by stamping on the rowdy elements, just incidentally reminding the non-magicians why they needed a Grand Sorcerer in the first place. Someone had to keep magicians firmly in line.

She blinked in surprise as she heard a girl babbling drunkenly. "She did this to me," the girl said, loudly enough to be heard halfway across the room. "Where's my owner? This floor hasn't been swept in weeks. I should be going to work...I'm human! I'm not a..."

Elaine stared until Dread nudged her. "Her housemate transfigured her into a broom when she refused to do any housework around the apartment," he said, by way of explanation. "But the housemate wasn't a very skilled witch and caused a mental transformation as well as a physical one. Even now she has been returned to flesh and blood, part of her still thinks she's a broom – and that she has *always* been a broom."

"But..." Elaine began, before shaking her head. Transforming a person into an inanimate object was easy, but it was almost impossible to do the reverse and transform an inanimate object into a person. But someone whose mind had been warped into thinking that she was a broom wouldn't notice that what she thought had happened to her was impossible. No amount of calm reasoning from the Inquisitors would change her mind. "What are you going to do with her?"

"That's up to the Inquisitors on duty," Dread said. "It depends; maybe we'd use a simple spell to adjust her mind, or maybe we'd see to it that her friend got a taste of her own medicine. Or maybe we'd just have to wait and let the girl get better on her own."

He shook his head as Elaine looked around the massive chamber. There were people who had been tricked into drinking love potions, whose relatives had brought them to the Watchtower to complain to the Inquisitors. Some love potions were little more than practical jokes, the effects wearing off within days, but others were permanent, rewriting a person's mind around pleasing the object of their affections. They were banned, by edict of one of the previous Grand Sorcerers, yet it was easy enough to produce one of the more powerful recipes. The Great Library had never managed to round up the majority of the copies of books describing love potions.

The knowledge buzzing through her head told her that it might be impossible to save the people who'd drunk the love potions, or at least stop them becoming fixated on *something*. Given time, the druids could probably refocus the spell on something harmless, leaving the victim capable of living a fairly normal life. If not...she wondered, absently, what would be the best thing to do for the victim. They'd pine away and die if they weren't allowed to unite with the person they thought they loved.

Love potions are no joke, she thought, as she looked away from a young man with wide hopeless eyes. Even Millicent hadn't tried to spike a person's drink with a love potion. It was one of the few acts that would get someone – anyone – expelled from the Peerless School, their wands snapped, before they were sold into slavery. The ones that wore off within hours would still leave scars that might last for a lifetime.

She wanted to look away from the crowd of victims, but she couldn't. A young woman was screaming about how she should have had a tail rather than bare legs; Elaine realised, after a moment, that she was a mermaid who had been the victim of a cruel practical joke. She'd be a fish out of water in the Golden City, even if she could survive without water. Two young men had been fused together by magic, stumbling around as if their conjoined body hadn't quite figured out how to coordinate itself. A number of waitresses had been hit with a charm that convinced them that they couldn't wear clothes, even in public. Their parents were shielding them as best they could from the gaze of the young men in the crowd. Elaine suspected that only the presence of a handful of scowling Inquisitors had kept the young men from trying their luck.

Dread shook his head as they reached a heavy stone door. "Let us hope that this will all be over once a responsible authority takes his place as Grand Sorcerer," he said. "The Inquisition is being pushed to the limit by the sudden upsurge in magical crime."

"And yet you came all the way to Ida to check up on me," Elaine said. She hadn't realised, not really, just how hard it would be for the Inquisition to cope with magical crime between Grand Sorcerers. Normally, when the Inquisition showed up, anyone with any sense would head for the exit as quickly as possible. But there weren't enough Inquisitors in one place to patrol the entire city. "Why was I so important?"

"Are you not glad I did?" Dread asked, ducking her question. She'd learned from their three days in various coaches – the iron dragons would have been direct, but their enemies would have been watching all the direct routes – that Dread tended to be sardonic when answering questions to which he felt the person should already know the answers. "And besides, I had unsolved mysteries."

Elaine felt the repulsion spell on the door pushing at her, just before Dread pressed his hand against the stone and the spell snapped off. "This is the part of the Watchtower that is rarely shown to outsiders," Dread said, softly. "You must not speak of what you see or hear inside this part of the building."

The door opened, allowing them entry before it closed with an audible *thud*. Silence fell, almost like a physical blow. There were so many muffling spells in the air that even Elaine's rudimentary magical senses felt blinded, as if her head were suddenly full of cotton wool. Dread seemed to be speaking – she could definitely see his mouth moving – but she couldn't hear a word. And then her ears popped and she could hear normally again.

"We don't want people spying on us," Dread said. His voice sounded funny inside the Watchtower, slightly dampened by the active spells all around them. "There are more wards around this part of the building than there are anywhere else outside the Golden Palace."

He led her down the corridor, Elaine struggling to keep up with his long strides. The interior of the Watchtower was another pocket dimension, although one that didn't quite make sense to Elaine's mind. Unlike the Great Library, it didn't appear to be larger on the inside than on the outside; it was almost as if the interior was rapidly shuffling itself around to accommodate permitted guests and confuse unwelcome intruders. The thought made her shudder; given enough time and power, the Inquisitors could have infused a personality into the Watchtower, or perhaps summoned a demon and used it as a source of power. She hoped it wasn't the latter. All the knowledge in her head insisted that only a fool would trust a demon to keep a promise. They were older than mankind and very – very – devious. And they delighted in watching humans suffer and die.

There seemed to be no other Inquisitors in the private part of the building, but she was unable to escape the sense of being permanently watched. The corridors seemed to be shifting all around them – at one point, she was sure she saw doors flickering in and out of existence – before they finally reached a large hall. A set of demonic statues awaited them, braced for the command to spring to life and attack the intruders. What did it say about the Inquisition, Elaine wondered, when they were so careful to take precautions even inside their stronghold? It seemed to take paranoia to ridiculous levels.

A young woman, her features blunt and plain, looked up at them as they entered. She wore a white set of robes, which surprised Elaine until she realised that the Inquisitors probably intended for her to serve as a druid as well as a secretary. Only druids wore white robes, unlike the black favoured by the Inquisition – and almost every other sorcerer of great power.

"Welcome home," she said, to Dread. She barely even glanced in Elaine's direction. "The Circle received your message yesterday and they are waiting to speak with you."

Elaine blinked in surprise. When had Dread sent a message? But it was a silly question. Dread was a powerful sorcerer with access to spells used only by the Inquisitors. He could have sent them a message without allowing Elaine to see it at all.

"Wait here," Dread said. "You'll be called in to face the Circle once I have finished briefing them. I shouldn't be anything more than ten minutes."

Elaine watched him passing through another pair of stone doors and then settled down to wait. The secretary ignored her, at least on the surface, although the feeling of being watched by unknown eyes seemed to grow stronger by the minute. She could almost *feel* the spells crawling throughout the building, watching for intruders; there were so many spells that it was hard to see why they weren't interfering with one another. But the Inquisitors would be able to recruit the best talent from the Peerless School; they'd probably selected the students with the greatest aptitude for charms and programming wards and offered them advanced training in exchange for servitude. No one really knew how a person became an Inquisitor, but with their connections to the

Peerless School they could probably identify promising talent early.

It was more like forty minutes until the door opened of its own accord and Elaine felt a compulsion pushing at her, urging her to walk through the door. The sensation was thoroughly unpleasant as she found herself moving almost against her will. Shivers ran down her spine as she walked into the heart of the Inquisition, the legendary Star Chamber itself. It was illuminated by a glowing silver star hanging over the table, casting an eerie flickering light over the room. The five people in the room – the Circle, Elaine assumed – wore black robes, but nothing else. None of them were familiar, apart from a middle-aged woman Elaine was sure she'd seen somewhere before. They didn't seem to wear the skull rings that marked them out as Inquisitors.

And there was no sign of Dread...

"Please be seated," one of the men said. He was approaching old age, with wrinkled skin and a horrifically scarred face that bore mute testament to a magical duel against a dark sorcerer in his youth. Elaine was surprised that she didn't know him, even by reputation. Someone who had been so badly scarred should be instantly recognisable. Maybe it was just an illusion shadowing his real face. There would be little hope of a normal life if his friends knew him to be an Inquisitor. "Thank you for coming."

Elaine nodded, slowly. Dread hadn't given her the impression that she had had much of a choice. "We understand that this must be an unpleasant experience for you," the man continued. One of the other men, a dark-skinned man with bright red eyes, snorted. His eyes had to be an illusion, Elaine told herself. Someone like that should have been even more recognisable than the scarred man. "Please would you tell us, in your own words, exactly what happened to you since you opened Duke Gama's legacy?"

She felt the compulsion pushing at her the moment he phased the question and started to babble. The Inquisitors merely listened, without bothering to comment on her description of her dinner with Bee or her discovery that Daria was a full-blooded werewolf. They'd told her to tell them everything, after all. No one interrupted as she explained how she'd decided to go to Ida, how she'd encountered Dread and finally been kidnapped, only to be saved by the Inquisitor and the Princess of Ida. Princess Sacharissa had been left with one of Dread's friends, for the moment. She had had no idea what – if anything – he intended to do with her.

Once she'd finished explaining her story, they started to ask questions. Each of them was asked pleasantly enough, but there was enough compulsion floating through the air to make a mockery of free will. She found herself answering the same question, asked in several different ways, over and over again. How could they expect her to lie to them when the entire chamber was crawling with charms to make her talkative, and truthful. It took her some time to realise that they were trying to extract all the detail they could, not trying to catch her out in a lie. A handful of questions even related to the contents of the Black Vault, considering what knowledge might be stored inside the Great Library – and now Elaine's head. She felt her blood run cold as she realised the implications. Countless spells in her head were useless to her, but a more powerful magician would be able to use them as he pleased. It wasn't just Prince Hilarion who would want to get his hands on her.

"One final question," the old man said. "Why did you not bring yourself to us when you discovered what had happened?"

At least they seemed to accept that she hadn't lied to Dread when they'd first met. "I was scared," Elaine admitted. "I thought that you would kill me."

"We should," one of the other Inquisitors said. His face was so bland that Elaine wouldn't have given it a second thought if they'd met on the streets. It was a definite advantage for an Inquisitor to remain unnoticed. "We cannot remove spells from your mind, nor can we prevent you from remaining silent in the face of mental probes and torture."

"Trying would break your mind," the fourth male Inquisitor said. Unlike his companion, he was handsome, too handsome to be real. Either he was using a glamour to hide his real appearance or he'd had his features redesigned into something that was obviously unnatural. In its own way, it could be as much a disguise as the bland man. "It would be kinder to kill you outright."

"But we are sworn to protect the innocent," the woman said. "You did not choose to become a bookworm. We should not kill you for something that wasn't your fault."

"And yet you did try to summon a ghost back to the mortal world," the bland man said. "It is clear that the knowledge in your head has had an effect on your personality. We cannot afford to trust you in public society."

"Even if we did," the handsome man added, "you would become a prize for each and every sorcerer who wishes to boost his power. You are not bound by the oaths sworn by the Grand Sorcerer on the day he takes on the duties of his post."

"It has been suggested that we destroy the Black Vault and its knowledge," the woman said. Elaine was starting to suspect that they were communicating between one another without her hearing them. "And yet the knowledge might be needed one day."

"By whom?" The bland man demanded. "Would you trust yourself with that power?"

Elaine hesitated, and then spoke up. "You already have all the power you could possibly need."

The elderly man chuckled, not unkindly. "There is no such thing as too much power for a sorcerer," he said. At his age, he had to be as powerful as anyone else in the Golden City. "The problems arise when one of them seeks to become far more powerful unnaturally, trying to boost his power because he is in a hurry. Even we are not immune to temptation."

"That's why we should kill you," the bland man said. "You are simply too dangerous to be left running around, even if all the compulsions in your head have been removed."

"And there's no way we can be sure," the woman said. "Anyone who peeks inside your head will be able to drain the knowledge crammed into your skull."

Elaine stared at her, desperately. Had she come home merely to die at the hands of the Inquisition?

"But there is another problem," the elderly man said. "You and our friend Dread have raised a very serious concern. Prince Hilarion may have long-term plans that threaten the

Empire."

"More than threaten, if they gained access to the Black Vault's knowledge," the woman pointed out. "They could bring us down."

"We cannot act openly," the elderly man admitted. "You and Dread – and your allies – may act without our blessing. We will decide your fate later."

Elaine nodded. At least they'd be able to do something about Prince Hilarion before she faced them again. And if they failed...

She shook her head. If they failed, chances were that she wouldn't be alive to worry about it.

Chapter Twenty-Four

Dread met her outside the Star Chamber.

"They wanted to kill me," Elaine said. Part of her didn't want to believe it. "I...they wanted to *kill* me!"

"They are charged with defending the establishment," Dread mused, as he drew her into a private room. It might have been his office. "And *you* are a threat to the establishment."

"*I didn't ask to be a threat to the establishment*," Elaine snapped. All the stress of the past week was finally breaking through. She started to shake, feeling hot tears prickling at the corner of her mind. "I didn't ask to become a bookworm!"

"A plague doesn't ask to kill and cripple thousands of innocent humans," Dread said, softly, but with great force. "A tidal wave doesn't act out of malice. Tornadoes don't throw houses through magical dimensions because they think it would be a huge joke. Wild magic doesn't warp the very structure of reality for fun and games."

He placed one hand on her shoulder. "I'm sorry about what happened to you," he said, gently. "It represents a failing on our part, one of imagination. No one ever expected someone to manage to slip all of the books in the Great Library out past the wards, but that is precisely what happened and we have to deal with it. You should never have been caught up in this, yet no magic known to us can go back in time and change it. It isn't fair; you did nothing to deserve it. But that doesn't change the fact that we have to deal with the situation as we find it."

Elaine sagged against his arm. "But...what now? Even if we stop Prince Hilarion and his plan, whatever it is, what happens to me afterwards? I didn't ask to become a source of all the forbidden knowledge in the universe..."

"Repository, I think you mean," Dread said. Elaine

thought he was laughing at her until she realised that he was deadly serious. "Or are you actually going to start inventing new spells based on what you know?"

"I...I don't know," Elaine admitted. Now that the truth was out...she could drain the Blight, or tap its magic for her own use. But *that* would probably start a panic once the Inquisition realised the truth. Knowledge was useless without power; the Blight had enough power to reshape the entire world, if it were used properly. "Why me?"

"The world isn't fair," Dread said. "You were in the wrong place at the wrong time and were caught up in the middle of a power struggle that has raged since the Second Necromantic War. Now, I *suggest*" – it was unmistakably an order – "that you dry your eyes and start thinking about what we're going to do next."

"I have to go talk to Daria," Elaine said. If nothing else, she owed her friend a hug...and a confession. And if Daria turned into a wolf and tried to eat her? Maybe it was exactly what she deserved. "Prince Hilarion can wait for a day."

She paused as a thought struck her. "Is he even still in the city?"

"He's still here," Dread confirmed. "I'm surprised he hasn't fled, but he has to know that time isn't exactly on his side. It's possible that he thinks he can still become Grand Sorcerer and simply order us to forget the matter."

"Or he has something *really* nasty up his sleeve for when we push the issue," Elaine said, darkly. "What did they plan to do about Ida?"

Dread frowned. "They're going to take it to the Regency Council and try to convince them to order troops moved towards Ida," he said. "It really needs a Grand Sorcerer's imprint before we move, but we should be able to get some spies into the mountains and prepare for an invasion without his permission. But doing that will be risky – and costly, if it does come down to a fight. Ida has never fallen to an outside force."

"But surely you can assemble more magicians," Elaine protested. "You could call upon every graduate from the Peerless School if necessary."

"Not all of them are combat magicians," Dread said. "And

someone on the other side has been teaching magic to the Prince. How many others do you think he might have turned out over the years?"

"But surely he couldn't outnumber the Peerless School..."

"The trick would be concentrating our forces in one area," Dread admitted. "Even with the authority of the Grand Sorcerer, it would take weeks – perhaps months – to gather every combat magician we have...and they probably wouldn't give us the time. Prince Hilarion might already have plans to ally with other kingdoms against us; we could find ourselves having to put down several separate rebellions at the same time, with our resources desperately overstretched."

He snorted. "We will make what preparations we can, but Prince Hilarion has timed his little plan perfectly," he added. "No doubt he already has contingency plans..."

Elaine blinked in surprise as an idea occurred to her. "Why don't we assassinate his *father*?"

"You've definitely become bloodthirsty," Dread observed. "I have considered the possibility, but right now the King of Ida is safe and sound inside a castle that it would be impossible to break into quietly..."

"But we managed to escape through the secret passages..."

"All of which will be blocked up by now, or heavily guarded," Dread said, overriding her. "And I'd bet a thousand Crowns that the Princess's signature has been removed from all of the access points."

"I won't take that bet," Elaine said. She shook her head. "So...do we try to burgle Prince Hilarion's current residence or not?"

"It's the only plan we have," Dread said, reluctantly. "I need to start making some preparations. You have been assigned quarters here..."

"I have to go to Daria," Elaine said, flatly. Two weeks ago, she would never even have *dreamed* of arguing with an Inquisitor. The prospect of impending death really *did* concentrate the mind. "You can send someone along to look after me, if you like, but I *am* going to see her. And I *am* going to have another date with Bee."

Dread studied her for a long moment. "I can see that your father must have been stubborn," he said. She'd told him what the ghost had said when she'd summoned Trebuchet back to the land of the living. Dread had been rather more worried by the force that had driven Trebuchet back to the next world. It implied that someone had access to a great deal of magic – or direct assistance from the next world. "But you do realise that they have to be watching for you? Going on a date – or even back to your apartment – might be just what they want you to do."

"I know," Elaine admitted, "but I am not going to cower inside until the new Grand Sorcerer is selected. And if the Star Chamber decides that I am too dangerous to let live, I can at least enjoy life a little before I die." She looked up at him, and then down at her feet. "I have never really lived at all. First there was the orphanage and a staff who refused to let me do anything, then there was the Peerless School and Millicent...and then there was a boring life in the Library. I want to *live*!"

"You've definitely changed," Dread observed. He smiled, as if the issue wasn't really worth fighting over. "You can go, on the condition that you have at least two of us with you. They won't *look* like Inquisitors, but they *will* look after you."

Elaine looked into his grey eyes, saw that he wouldn't budge any further, and nodded. "I will," she said, softly. Was this was it was like to have a father? Someone who cared and worked to protect his daughter? Or was she merely dreaming it was, because her own father had always been a mystery to her. If her mother had been a whore, what had her father been? Her client, her pimp...or something else altogether? "Thank you."

Dread looked mildly surprised. "For what?"

"For caring," Elaine said. She felt tears stinging her eyes again and wiped them away with a flash of irritation. "No real father could have done better."

Dread smiled, a smile that touched his eyes and made him look almost human. "Would you like to know," he enquired dryly, "just how many fathers have used magic on the boys who came courting their daughters? I have seen fathers turn boyfriends into toads, or use compulsion spells to drive them away, or insist that they swear formal oaths before even inviting the girls out to dinner. And I have seen parents who use magic to substitute for raising their kids. Instead of teaching boys and girls to be careful, they use magic to enforce proper behaviour from their children. Every time, it explodes in their faces – badly. But no one ever seems to learn."

He shook his head. "Magic isn't a substitute for everything and it certainly doesn't solve all problems," he added. "If everyone realised that, instead of looking for quick fixes, the world would be a much happier place."

***

Every Inquisitor that Elaine had heard of – she'd only met one formally – wore black robes and carried skull rings. But it seemed that a great deal of what she'd known about the Inquisition either wasn't true, or was incomplete. Inquisitor Cass was a blonde and bubbly girl wearing a long green dress that set off her hair nicely; Inquisitor Karan was short, dumpy and had unkempt red hair that Daria would have enjoyed fixing over an hour or two. But there was no mistaking the skill they showed in working magic, or the sheer power flaring around them when they entered the room. Millicent would not have dared to pick on either of them.

"Hi," Cass said, with a wink. Her voice was light and airy, so airy that Elaine realised at once that she was overacting. But maybe a male wizard, unable to take his eyes off her chest, wouldn't realise that he was babbling out all his secrets to a chit of a girl. "I understand that we have to look after you?"

"Yes," Elaine said, flatly. Cass managed to make her feel dowdy, even unintentionally. It wouldn't have bothered her before Daria had finally kicked her into trying to start a proper romance. She was certainly *not* going to allow Cass to escort her on the next date. "How much has he told you?"

"Only that we're not to allow you to be taken by anyone," Karan informed her. She was subdued, almost submissive. Elaine started to look for a collar before realising that it was just as much an act as Cass's blonde bimbo pretence. "And that we should be careful about where we let you go."

It was possible, Elaine decided, that Dread had *also* told

them that Elaine was not to be taken alive, even if they had to kill her themselves. It wouldn't be difficult; even without wands, either of them was more than a match for Elaine herself. The spell which had surprised Millicent probably wouldn't work on a sorceress who had spent most of her adult life matching herself against the best in the business. She wanted to be angry at the Inquisitor for his action, if he *had* issued such orders, but it was hard to blame him. Anyone who had a clear idea of the horrors unleashed by the necromancers would do anything to prevent them from being unleashed again. The last war had nearly destroyed the entire world.

"Sounds about right," she said, mildly. She wondered if she should confirm that they should follow Dread's orders, if there were such orders, but she couldn't bring herself to say it out loud. "Shall we go?"

Seen from the North Peak, the Golden City seemed to glow with light. Where Ida had been drab and grey, and Castle Adamant a brooding monstrosity on the hill, the Golden City was alive. She had never really understood it before, but the Golden City was the best and worst of the Empire gathered in one place. The styles and techniques developed by thousands of different civilisations had been fused into one, while people from all over the world travelled to see the Golden City, each one adding a little more diversity to the most diverse city in the world. There were even people who believed that the streets were paved with gold.

But not all of it was kind, she knew. Some came to the city, fell into poverty and never managed to climb out. Different cultures rubbed each other the wrong way; different priests used their daily sermons to call down hellfire on their rivals. From High Tory to Low Town – and the Blight – the city was the empire in miniature. Powerful men and women, some aristocratic and some magical, ruling over thousands of small states. And the Blight, perhaps, serving as a counterpart to the necromantic wars...or the dead lands where the Witch-King had made his final bid for power. Nothing would grow there for thousands of years, unless some of the undead mutated into forms that could survive the waves of wild magic washing across the continent. It wasn't a comforting thought. The one thing everyone knew about wild magic was that it couldn't be controlled – and that its effects were effectively random.

She allowed Cass to precede her down the road leading into the city. Unlike Ida, the Golden City didn't bother with a road that was part of its defence line, although if a hostile power gained control of the mountains the Golden City would be forced to surrender anyway. But who would dare attack the Grand Sorcerer? Just for a moment, she wondered just how far the Prince's plans actually went. Had he forged links with the states closer to the Golden City, convincing them to send their armies to attack? It didn't seem likely, if only because the preparations would be noticed...wouldn't they? But if there had already been one catastrophic intelligence failure, why couldn't there have been a second? Or a third...?

The sights and sounds of the Golden City were music to her ears after the dour city of Ida. Street vendors competed savagely with each other in advertising their food, drink and souvenirs of the city. A pair of candidates for the City Council were engaged in a political debate, egged on by the crowd who had brought rotten vegetables to throw at candidates they didn't like. Half the city didn't have the property, money or magical qualifications to vote, which didn't stop them enjoying the debates and the chance to throw stuff at their social superiors. The City Guard knew better than to intervene unless people started throwing objects – or magic – that could cause real harm.

A witch operating a stall was offering curses, potions and charms for anyone's requirement. Selling curses wasn't technically illegal, but it did tend to draw the Inquisition's attention on the grounds that it represented a misuse of magic. Elaine suspected, even without drawing on the knowledge in her head, that the witch wasn't really offering anything more than placebos. A person without proper magical training was unlikely to realise that the curses didn't work, or only worked briefly; the witch probably claimed that they caused ill-luck rather than something specific. The love potions might be real, or they might be something intended to push someone into growing the confidence to ask their intended victim out. They didn't *not* work, one of her tutors had once explained, but they weren't really magic. The distinction was lost on the uninitiated.

"And I tell you that the proper place for a woman is on her knees," a voice boomed. There was magic in it, not compulsion spells but magic intended to convince the listener to keep listening. No one threw rotten fruit or eggs at the speaker. "She should remain silent, forever faithful and obedient to her man, silently serving him as is her natural role..."

Elaine rolled her eyes, noting without surprise just how much of the crowd was male. Vlad Deferens was in his late thirties, with unkempt black hair and a scruffy long beard. He wore a bright red tunic and kilt – the nasty part of Elaine's mind wondered what, if anything, he wore under his kilt – and carried a faintly disturbing staff in one hand. The tip of the staff looked alarmingly like a very important male organ. It was clear that Deferens used it to do all of his thinking.

"And as Grand Sorcerer, I will see to it that women return to their natural place," Deferens thundered. "I will make collars freely available to every man who wishes to control his wife, to encourage her to be submissive and obedient..."

Elaine stared at him, feeling outrage growing in her breast. She had never been a wife, but she'd seen enough of married life to know that men were just as responsible for marital problems as women. And women invariably got the worst of it, even in the most cosmopolitan cities. They could be beaten by their husbands, forced to obey his every whim...magic provided some freedom, for sorceresses, but not for those who were only mundane.

"He's been doing this all week," Cass muttered. The female Inquisitor sounded just as disgusted as Elaine felt. *She* was one of the most powerful magicians, male or female, in the world. Deferens would have her abandon all that to become little more than chattel. "I don't even know how seriously he takes the contest to become Grand Sorcerer if this is the sort of shit he excretes at every opportunity."

A spell danced through Elaine's mind and she triggered it before she had a chance to reflect on what it actually did.

There was a brief pause when she thought it did nothing, before a gust of wind blew across the stage and flicked Deferens' kilt up, exposing him to the world. The crowd burst into laughter; Deferens looked to be very small, although Elaine had nothing to compare it to. Grand Sorcerer candidate or not, Deferens would find it very hard to live that down.

Cass gripped her wrist and dragged her away before she could do anything else. Behind her, she heard the sound of rotten fruit being thrown at a target. Who knew what would happen now? Maybe Deferens would do something so stupid that he'd be put out of the running.

And if *that* happened, she realised, Prince Hilarion's chances of victory became that much higher.

Chapter Twenty-Five

Her apartment almost felt unfamiliar to her as she entered, after trying to convince her bodyguards to wait outside. They refused to listen to her and insisted on searching the apartment before allowing her to go inside. Elaine heard enough of the *discussion* between Cass and Daria to know that her friend wasn't happy about the sudden intrusion – and completely mystified. It was another thing for Elaine to regret, she realised, and to feel guilty over. Daria's life had been turned upside down just because she had been friendly to an almost-friendless girl.

Daria didn't look different physically, but she seemed younger to Elaine's eyes. Or maybe Elaine had grown up. Had she ever been a mature adult since she'd left the Peerless School, or had she merely been marking time and pretending that she was still a teenager? But then her teenage years hadn't been anything interesting, really. She'd sometimes believed that she'd been born old.

"Well," Daria said, finally. "Who was that...blonde *person* in our apartment?"

"It's a long story," Elaine admitted. She couldn't blame Daria for being a little irritated. Her friend had always been a deeply private person, despite the number of boys she had invited to enter her. As a werewolf, she'd known what it was like to be hunted; the Peerless School would have expelled her if enough of the important parents had complained. Werewolves were not trusted in human society. "I...I want to tell you, but it could put you in very real danger."

"You've been with the Inquisitor," Daria said. At one point, her deduction would have surprised Elaine. Now, she knew that the werewolf had smelled Dread's scent on her. And everyone else's, for that matter. "I assume that your trip to Ida didn't go precisely as planned?"

Elaine flushed. It hadn't really been planned at all,

something that – in hindsight – should have warned her that she wasn't entirely acting under her own volition. She'd been luckier than she wanted to admit. If she hadn't encountered Dread, she would have been broken and then killed in the torture chamber below Castle Adamant. And as it was, she'd managed to meet her own obligations under the Mage's Oath. The Inquisition now knew about a dreadful threat to the entire Empire.

"It didn't," she said. "Daria...I love you, but this could put you in danger. If you want to leave, I will understand..."

Daria shook her head, tossing her long mane of hair. "I think you know me better than that," she said. She *knew* that Elaine wasn't exaggerating. It was easy to control one's voice to lie, but a great deal harder to control one's scent. "When have I ever backed down from a fight?"

"Never," Elaine agreed. "Just listen, please."

She started with the entire story, running through it from beginning to end, and then detailed what they'd discovered in Ida. Daria listened silently, her nose flaring slightly; in hindsight, it was easy to see a distinctly canine aspect to her features. Her big eyes were remarkably like a dog's eyes. No wonder Millicent had laughed so much when she'd hinted at Daria's secret. Elaine had missed something right under her own nose.

"Sounds like you're in trouble," Daria said. She shrugged as she picked up the latest collection of pamphlets from the touts – and supporters of the various candidates. "I can see why the Prince would want to cheat. He has exactly *five* supporters – and one of them is Lord Melchett, so he doesn't count."

Elaine snorted. Lord Melchett had been the heir to a distinguished family...until he'd been caught engaging in a practice that made incest and necrophilia look forgivable. His family had disowned him, his friends had melted away and he'd started drinking himself to death. What he'd done wasn't exactly *illegal*, but High Society had passed judgement on him and treated him as a pariah. Elaine had little patience for Millicent and the rest of the aristocrats, yet for once it was easy to take their side. Lord Melchett was a disgrace to the entire society of inbred morons.

She took one of the sheets of paper and skimmed through it. Prince Hilarion's allies were few and far between; an aristocrat who was known for dabbling in magic, a pair of tradesmen who wanted a powerful political patron – and no one was higher than the Grand Sorcerer – and an aristocrat who had lost a suit against his peers that had been judged by the previous Grand Sorcerer personally. Elaine guessed that *he* hoped that the new Grand Sorcerer would reverse the ruling. But all of them had good reason for gambling on a long shot.

But Prince Hilarion also seemed to have a great deal of money. She doubted that it had all come from Ida; the cost of a successful political campaign, let alone one by a candidate to become Grand Sorcerer, was staggering. Prince Hilarion had to have other backers, but the touts hadn't succeeded in tracing them. They'd probably handed over bags of Crowns, knowing that even the Inquisition would be unable to track them back to their source. He was buying influence in various places, influence that would be all the more effective for being underestimated...

...And yet...what was he *doing*?

There were only vague hints in the knowledge she'd absorbed about just what happened in the process of selecting a new Grand Sorcerer. Almost nothing was known publicly, although it was assumed that it was a test of a candidate's magical power and their political support within the Empire. It was almost as if whoever had devised the contest – the first Grand Sorcerer, perhaps – hadn't wanted to write *anything* down. Maybe the knowledge was in her mind, still locked up until she asked the right question, or maybe the details were passed on by word of mouth. But if that were the case, who was in charge of masterminding the contest?

"It could be a repeat of the Jury Law," Daria said, when Elaine outlined her thoughts. "I had to study that for work, back when they were offering me the chance to become a manager and even open my own shop."

Elaine felt her mind click as new knowledge seemed to blossom open in front of her. The first century after the Second Necromantic War had seen corruption spreading throughout the Empire, particularly within the Golden City.

It was simple for the rich to bribe juries into taking their side, using their power to ensure that no laws were passed limiting the practice. The early Reform Party had had real problems making any kind of changes. Finally, the Grand Sorcerer of that era had died and been replaced by a man with different ideas about how a city should be run. He'd expanded each of the juries until there were no less than five hundred prospective candidates for each jury, forcing anyone who wanted to bribe them to bribe them all, even though only thirteen of the five hundred would actually serve on the jury itself. The cost of bribing promptly skyrocketed. It wasn't a perfect solution, but even the richest of citizens would have problems bribing every possible member.

"See who gets the most bribes?" Elaine said. It sounded possible, but it seemed a little unlikely. "Maybe they just throw magic at one another until all but one of them are dead."

"Could be," Daria agreed. "But I was thinking that the victor would be the one who managed to galvanise enough support from the city's power blocks. Power is one thing, but they all have power. Actually ruling the state needs more than just raw power. Maybe the tests force them to cope with a crisis and see how they handle it."

Elaine nodded. There were thousands of books on the history of government in the Great Library...and they were now all in her head. Some states had eaten their – metaphorical – seed corn and suffered economic crashes due to bad leadership. Others had lasted for centuries before the dictates of aristocratic supremacy put an idiot or a madman in power. Hell, the reason why the Southern Continent was governed by an Empress – and never an Emperor – was that their last Emperor had been a madman who slaughtered his way through most of the upper classes before one of the widowed women, forced to share his bed, cut his throat as he slept.

"You should ask your friend the Inquisitor," Daria added. "I bet they'd know, if anyone does..."

"It doesn't matter for the moment," Elaine said. "I have something else to tell you."

Daria paused, pretending to consider. "You're getting

married to Bee? You dumped Bee for Dread? That Princess you brought here convinced you that girls are more fun than boys?"

Elaine laughed, despite herself. Daria always took such an irreverent view of the universe. "It's worse than that," she admitted. "I have a confession to make."

"You stole my latest boyfriend?" Daria asked. "Bah – how terrible. And he was terrible in bed too..."

"This is serious," Elaine snapped, angrily. "I'm trying to make a confession here..."

"I try not to take life too seriously," Daria admitted. "Not having anywhere permanent to call my home does tend to ensure that I remain flippant at all times."

Elaine shook her head. After spending so long nerving herself to confess to Daria, it was weird to see the confession being waved away so flippantly. But Daria still didn't know what she was talking about. How could she?

"I discovered that you were a werewolf," Elaine said, in a rush. "I'm sorry, it was wrong of me..."

Daria gaped at her and then started to laugh. "We have known each other for seven years," she said, between laughs, "and you only *just* found out that I am a werewolf?"

Her chuckles grew louder. "I always assumed that you *knew!*"

"I never even considered the possibility," Elaine admitted, ruefully. Of *course* Millicent had laughed. She'd realised Daria's secret long ago. "I..."

Her friend held up her palm in front of Elaine's eyes. It was covered with fine, almost invisible hairs. "I have more hair on my body than you do," she said, dryly. "You never bothered to take a peek when you were helping me to dress?"

"I always hated it at the orphanage," Elaine said. Communal living there had been embarrassing, particularly when dealing with children who had actually grown up in a family before being sent to the orphanage. They'd peeked on the girls as they tried to wash, despite their complaints. No one in the orphanage had really cared if the children started to pick on each other. "And then Millicent sent me streaking naked through the corridors..."

"I wouldn't have minded," Daria said, gently. "It's not as

if you are particularly attracted to women..."

Elaine stared at her friend and braced herself to say the words that might destroy their friendship forever. "I peeked inside your chest," she admitted. "I was curious and it was just there..."

"And you saw the amulet that keep my lycanthropy under control," Daria said, emotionlessly. Elaine would have given her soul to have the same sense of smell as her friend, to know just what she was really feeling. "I never wanted to be a beast again."

The words came tumbling out, as if she'd wanted to talk about it for a long time. "Some of us are born werewolves, others are turned into werewolves by accident or when they marry one of the folk," she said. "My parents were both werewolves, but they were both turned werewolves instead of born werewolves. I never actually turned wolf until I was thirteen..."

Elaine frowned. "I thought that born werewolves could change almost as soon as they were born," she objected.

"Sometimes the magic throws up a few weird things," Daria admitted. "I grew up believing that I was the only one of the folk who couldn't change into a wolf. They even tried to bite me so that I would be infected by the curse, but nothing happened. The best they could conclude was that I was naturally immune to lycanthropy. No one realised that I *did* have some of the werewolf senses, even as a child."

She shook her head. "I think my parents were a little relieved," she added. "They hadn't enjoyed being werewolves, or having to join the Travelling Folk."

"The druids couldn't help?" Elaine asked. "Surely they could have..."

"The Travelling Folk wouldn't go to a stinker druid, even if he was on fire and needed someone to piss on him," Daria said. "You don't really know what it's like to be one of the Folk. The best that happens is that the stinkers think that you're a thief. If you're unlucky, they chase you out with magic and gunfire."

Elaine frowned. "The stinkers?"

"*We* are clean," Daria said, with some dignity. "You people don't know how to wash properly. I can smell you from halfway across the city."

She shook her head. "There are few secrets among the Traveller Folk," she continued, quietly. "I was astonished by how shocked so many of you..."

Elaine smiled. "Stinkers?"

"I was going to say *civilised* folk," Daria said, with great dignity. "I remember seeing girls terrified when they first saw blood coming out of their crotches, convinced that there was something seriously wrong with them. My family had taught me better; hell, my first cycle was the event that would change me from a girl to a woman. I could get married, or move away from my parents, or even leave the Travelling Folk. Instead...

"The first time, I found myself naked in the forest with no clear idea of what had happened to me. I was convinced that one of the boys had played a prank on me. A couple of them were magicians and they definitely could have mesmerised a young girl into running away naked. But I was too ashamed to tell my parents or anyone else. The next time...

"I'd blocked it out of my mind because it hurt so much," she continued. "The pain started, as did the animal impulses. My clothes suddenly itched so badly that I had to tear them off and run through the forest naked. I could *feel* my body twisting and breaking, aching as if it was trying to use a muscle I'd neglected over the last thirteen years. And then I saw my hand change into a paw and I lost all rationality. I ran through the woods howling as a wolf, so lost in the animal urges that I ate raw meat and indulged myself. Then...

"And then I ran into one of the magicians. In my delirium, I believed that he was responsible for what had happened to me and I went for his throat. I almost killed him when he managed to knock me back with a blast of raw power, stunning me. He could have killed me then, before I reverted to human form. Instead I woke up with my parents and the wise woman looking down at me. For whatever reason, my cycles had brought the change with them. It took years for me to get used to the change."

She shook her head. "Born werewolves change so often that they become more...flexible than turned werewolves," she said. "Every time I changed, I hurt so badly and then I had to be supervised at all times. It wasn't my fault, everyone said, but I always had two bigger werewolves with me to make sure I didn't lose control completely. I had to take years of this treatment before I learned enough control to be trusted out on my own. And then they discovered my talent and allowed me to go to the Peerless School. There, they gave me an amulet to control the change. I have only changed once in the last year..."

"To find me when I fled," Elaine said. "I don't deserve you."

"You have changed over the past few days," Daria said. She leaned closer and made a loud sniffing noise. "Your scent has changed too, a little; more confident, more interested in boys..."

Elaine flushed. "Shame about the flush," Daria teased, "but I'm sure you will beat that quickly enough."

She reached out and placed her hand on Elaine's shoulder. "I understand what it means to go through a change, although I'm not *quite* sure that you were as helpless to stop yourself as I was," she said. "Your change is unprecedented in my experience and I don't think anyone could have helped you. But..."

Elaine felt another stab of guilt as Daria's voice hardened. "...I don't think you should go peeking in my room again. One thing you should know from the orphanage – and I know from the Travelling Folk – is that what little privacy one can get is important. Do that again and I will do unto you what my father did when he discovered that I'd transformed once before without telling anyone."

"And what was that?" Elaine asked. The Travelling Folk were strange. Who knew what they considered acceptable punishment for a young girl? "Did he beat you?"

"I'll leave it to your imagination," Daria said, darkly, and then laughed. "It's bound to be more terrifying that way."

She patted Elaine's shoulder and then let go of her. "Now," she said, "how can I help with dealing with Prince Handsome? Want me to date him and then bite him?"

"That isn't funny," Elaine protested. "It would lead to another werewolf pogrom and..."

"I know," Daria said. "It was a terrible joke."

She shook her head. "On a completely different matter, Bee came around again and offered to cook you dinner in his apartment," she said, changing the subject. "Do you want to go see him tonight?"

Elaine hesitated. Going to a boy's apartment could mean getting more than she bargained for – but perhaps it was time to live a little.

"Yes," she said. "You can set it up for me?"

"Of course," Daria said. "What are friends for?"

Chapter Twenty-Six

"I'm glad to see you again," Bee said, as he opened the door. "How was your trip?"

Elaine hesitated, unsure what to say. "It was...educational," she said, finally. "It's strange how people live away from the Golden City."

Bee grinned, welcoming her into his apartment. "The more isolated a community, the easier it is to maintain its own society even though it is technically part of the Empire," he said. He'd seen dozens of states, Elaine knew. Her own experience was still limited to the Golden City and Ida. Once the whole affair was settled she intended to travel again, if Dread and the Inquisitors let her. "There are places that make the Golden City look chaotic and places that make it look orderly."

He chatted away as he waved her to a sofa and started to take a steaming pot off the stove. "I don't get to cook very often," he admitted. "I hope you enjoy my food."

"I've never had a boy cook for me before," Elaine said. Daria had once commented that boys who knew how to cook, and made sure that the girls knew it, had greater success with romance than boys who expected women to do all the cooking. "Is it something from the South?"

"One of our regional specialities," Bee said, cheerfully. "I grew up with my mother making this – and she insisted that we all learn to cook."

He put the pot down on the table and grinned as he waved her over to the seat. "Traditionally," he said as he took the lid off the pot, "we would put raw meat inside and let the soup cook the meat." Elaine followed his pointing hand and saw boiling liquid, smelling faintly of chicken, inside the pot. "You can put in spices or vegetables to match your taste, as each person has a different idea of what they enjoy eating. Some of us put in so many chillies that we burn ourselves when we try to eat them. I've cooked the meat inside the soup for your first time."

Elaine had to smile as he started to ladle out the soup. Each spoonful held pieces of cooked chicken, beef or fish. She wasn't particularly fond of fish – the Golden City was a long way from the nearest coast, making fish expensive – but the soup smelt lovely and the freshly-baked bread neatly complimented the taste. Each piece of meat, she realised, would have added a little extra something to the flavour.

"Eat up," Bee urged. "I can't maintain the cooking spell on the pot."

Maybe he was lucky, having no magic. Elaine considered it as she took her first sip of the soup and then started to eat rapidly. It was a faintly sharp taste, with hints of lime and several spices she didn't recognise; it flavoured the chunks of meat nicely. Bee passed her a small set of spice pots and she experimented by adding them to each different spoonful. The flavours changed each time, some edible and some too hot to touch.

"We normally experiment with the first bowl and then make a second one once we know what we like," Bee explained. "Every meal is a little different because the meat may be of lesser quality or the spices may be from different places. It makes life interesting when we go visiting each other at home."

"You should open a restaurant," Elaine said, honestly. "You'd make a fortune selling food in the Golden City."

"There already are some places that serve Southern food," Bee said. His face twitched, as if it were caught between a grimace and a smile. "None of the ones I've tasted have been very good. I've had to cook myself if I wanted food from home. When I don't cook, I prefer exploring foods from other parts of the world."

"You have lived a fuller life than me," Elaine admitted. It was a rueful thought, but she'd never realised just how...bland her life had been before she'd been hit by Duke Gama's spell. The part of her that wanted something more exciting had been drowned out by the part of her that knew that she didn't want excitement, and considered adventure to be someone else in trouble far away from civilisation.

Now...she was a target for everyone who sought forbidden knowledge, even though she wasn't seeking it herself. What would they do to her if they kidnapped her again? "You know, I never asked. Why did you come to the Golden City?"

"I told you," Bee said, innocently. "My superiors want more influence in the Golden City and they dispatched me to make sure that they got it. The Golden City makes decisions that touch upon the entire world. Any influence we can win here would be very valuable for us."

"I see," Elaine said. He *had* mentioned it before, but she'd been too shy to follow up on it. "If you don't mind me asking, who are you working for?"

"The Empress of the South," Bee said. Elaine gaped at him, too surprised to speak. "She wants influence in the Golden City..."

"I thought that she didn't like men," Elaine said, recovering from her surprise. "Why are you serving as her agent?"

"Men aren't supposed to rule back home," Bee reminded her. "There's no reason why a man can't serve as the Empress's agent – and some of the societies in the Golden City find it easier to deal with a man. It never seemed particularly understandable to me, but...I rather like my job, even if I do have to deal with filthy politicians all the time."

He hesitated, just long enough for Elaine to realise that he was worried. "I thought you knew, to be honest," he added. "Does that bother you?"

"No," Elaine said, although she wasn't sure if she was being truthful. Coincidence or not, there was a link between the Empress of the South and Lady Light Spinner...and Lady Light Spinner had good reason to want to keep an eye on Elaine. But Elaine had met Bee *before* Millicent had been turned into a tiny statue and it seemed unlikely that Lady Light Spinner had had any advance warning. Unless one of the gods had granted her a vision... "It just struck me that I didn't know."

The evening wore on as they finished their soup and shared fruit juice, chatting about nothing in particular. Elaine found herself relaxing completely in his company, studying the way the firelight reflected off his face and clothes, wondering if she really *did* have the nerve to try to kiss him. But he'd already kissed her in the Park. They should have had no trouble kissing again. And yet...

"I've never been anyone's agent," she said, returning to the original question. "How do you serve your Empress?"

"By speaking with her voice," Bee said. He seemed happy to talk. "Before I left, she and her advisors gave me a detailed briefing on what I had to offer people – and what lines I couldn't cross, even if we were offered everything we wanted in exchange. I came here with a duplicate of her Great Seal, charmed to convince the others that I spoke with her name, and then started bargaining. Some of the factions in the city were happy to bargain. Others were reluctant to talk to us unless they were offered hefty cash bribes."

Elaine giggled. "Is it a little like seducing a woman?"

Bee blushed bright red, causing Elaine to flush too. "I wouldn't have put it *precisely* that way," he said, with stiff dignity. And then he broke down into giggles himself. "But it *is* the same basic idea, just using different tools."

"The thought of one country trying to seduce another..." Elaine said, between giggles. "And what happens when they start to separate?"

"You have marriage vows and marriage rows," Bee punned, badly. "Diplomacy is the art of getting what you want without offending anyone too badly. When it goes wrong..."

He shrugged. "Some countries have no reason to talk to us and don't even consider an alliance," he added. "Some countries fear us and will try to form alliances against us. And some think that we'd betray them if it suited our interests. Even the Grand Sorcerer had problems keeping various nations from lashing out at their neighbours."

"The Grand Sorcerer brought peace," Elaine said. They'd had that hammered into their heads at the Peerless School. The system was intended to prevent another major war, even one that didn't include necromancers. "I always believed that to be true."

"Oh, it is true," Bee said. His face darkened. "But he couldn't bury all the differences between countries completely. Countless issues haven't been settled because the Grand Sorcerer prohibited actual fighting between states, so they continue to fester. Some states bear grudges for things that took place hundreds of years before the First Necromantic War."

He stood up in one fluid motion. "I looked up Ida after you left," he said. Elaine looked up, sharply. "There's very little to interest the Empress there. Ida only trades with its neighbours – not very much at that – and has no apparent interest in converting its impregnable defensive position into an offensive stand against the states down on the plains."

Elaine frowned, worried. "Did you speak to their representatives here?"

"There's nothing to talk about," Bee said. "One rule of diplomacy is that you should never show interest unless it is in your interests to show interest. If Ida wants something from the South, they have to open the dialogue themselves. And so far they have largely ignored us."

Elaine relaxed, slightly. The thought of Prince Hilarion using Bee as a way to get at her was terrifying. He could have offered money and power – and influence, for the Empress of the South – in exchange for Bee helping him to catch Elaine. But no one should have been able to draw a line between Bee and Elaine, or so she hoped. No wonder the Inquisitors were so worried about her safety. Rumours spread through the Golden City faster than an iron dragon.

She held up a hand and pulled Bee towards the sofa, suddenly feeling her heartbeat pounding away inside her ears. Part of her wanted to run...and the rest of her wanted to live a little, to enjoy life while she could. Prince Hilarion might kill her, or kidnap her if he got his hands on her, and she knew better than to think that she could resist him indefinitely. The Inquisitors were sworn to obey the Grand Sorcerer. If Prince Hilarion became the victor, they would have no choice but to follow his orders. She would have to run, to flee the city, if *that* happened, yet there was nowhere to go. Except, perhaps, the South...

Bee's arms enfolded her and his lips met hers, a kiss that seemed to set her entire body burning with an unfamiliar flame. She'd never been with a boy before, nor had she experimented with another girl, and only rarely with herself.

Suddenly, she wanted to pull off her clothes before it was too late. Bee's kisses were becoming more passionate, his hands stroking her back as he pulled her closer and then pushed her down on the sofa. For a moment, she felt trapped and helpless as his weight pushed down on her, before he took himself on his elbows and kept kissing her. She kissed him back, realising that Bee wasn't going to hurt her, at least not intentionally. Daria's advice had been very specific, both about what potions she should drink beforehand – and about what she should let him do to her the first time. And about how boys could be remarkably insensitive at times.

She gasped as she felt his hands working at the straps of her dress, before they came loose and it started to be pushed back towards her chest. Her breasts were exposed as Bee slipped back, his bright eyes meeting hers as he lowered his mouth to her nipple and started to lick it slowly, but steadily. Elaine felt a wave of pleasure running through her, even though part of her mind was disgusted at what he was doing. And yet she'd had dreams where she'd taken him in her mouth and licked and sucked him until...well, she wasn't quite clear on that point. Her dreams had never been too focused on specifics...

Bee sat back and started to undress, pulling off his shirt to reveal a hairy chest and arms that were faintly muscled. Elaine reached up and stroked his chest, so different from her own hairless body. Daria *would* have hairs on her chest, even if they were difficult to see with the naked eye. Her boyfriends might have realised the truth and then fled in horror, terrified of the thought of being close to a werewolf who might assume wolf form at any moment. Daria had better control than that!

"I..." she started to say, and then stopped. "I..."

"Hush," Bee said, as he pulled away the rest of her dress. She was naked, apart from a sheer pair of silken panties Daria had given her; naked and exposed to his gaze. Elaine found herself flushing again, suddenly realising why so many girls in the Peerless School had used magic potions and glamours to enhance their appearance. A single negative comment when she was exposed would have been far more crushing than any barbed comment from Millicent. "It's going to be fine."

He removed his own trousers, revealing his manhood. Elaine stared, finally understanding some of the private conversations between girls at school. Bee's penis was massive to her eyes, something that helplessly drew her towards it. And yet the thought of that thing trying to go inside her was different to accept. One of the books she'd absorbed noted that the male sexual equipment was never as varied as it seemed when erect and ready for action, and yes – it *could* go inside her without problems. Some of the other books contained detailed instructions that made Elaine blush when she realised that the knowledge was there, ready for her to use. And a handful contained information that even *she* recognised was inaccurate.

Elaine reached out towards Bee, feeling a strange mixture of emotions as she took his manhood in her hand. It was huge, and yet it squirmed in her hand, seeming to leap forward of its own will towards her thighs. Touching it felt almost natural and yet it was almost *also* like touching a spider, or something else that triggered the deeper fears in the human mind. Some of the books seemed to speculate endlessly on the precise nature of sexual desire, but they never seemed to agree with each other. Women could not both be sexless creatures, knowing nothing of sexual desire, and also carnal beings whose lusts were so powerful that they had to be kept under control. The two statements were contradictory. Both had probably also been written by men.

Bee's hand slipped between her legs and touched her gently, before he started to stroke around her. Elaine gasped, feeling an unearthly tingling running through her body, even though he felt clumsy compared to the times when she had played with herself. He didn't know precisely where to touch her for greatest effect, she realised, as more knowledge poured through her mind. Boys believed a great deal of nonsense about girls; girls believed just as much nonsense about boys. The two sexes, it seemed, had never bothered to just *talk* to one another. They just made assumptions based on their own bodies, or beliefs that had never been properly challenged.

Elaine felt her legs open as Bee positioned himself for

entry. She reached forward, as the books advised, and took control, guiding him into her virgin vagina. He seemed to surge forward and there was an odd moment of discomfort, discomfort that would have been worse if she hadn't listened to Daria and taken the Modest Maiden potion before coming to Bee's apartment. It felt so strange, at once both exciting and terrifying, to feel something slipping inside her. Bee's breathing was growing faster as he seemed to pause, just for a long moment, and then started to thrust inside her. There was another sensation of discomfort, followed by a burst of pleasure that surprised her...and then led to a second burst of pleasure as Bee moved faster and faster. He'd lost control, if some of the books were accurate; he could no longer stop even if Elaine wanted him to pull out. She felt a tidal wave of pleasure, perhaps boosted by the potion, as he thrust faster and faster...and then she felt something hot and warm bursting inside her. There was a final wave of pleasure and she found herself pulling her to him, trying to keep him inside her. It no longer felt like a terrifying intrusion, not even slightly.

Daria had told her, time and time again, that having a boyfriend was the greatest thing in a woman's life – and that boys felt the same way about women. Elaine hadn't believed her, not until now, not until she'd realised that sex could be for more that procreation. Some of the books hinted at what happened when virgins discovered sex for the first time, others seemed to vie to outdo one another in emotional descriptions of their first times with a person of the other sex, or even the same sex. Elaine wanted him to have sex with her again and again and again...

...And yet, it wasn't really like her, was it?

The thought bothered her as she looked up and saw Bee smiling back at her. He seemed to be glowing with light, no longer even remotely a stranger. Of course he wasn't, Elaine told herself; he'd just been inside her. There was no point in moving to conceal the gap between her legs, not any longer. Or in getting dressed...

But did he really love her? And did she love him?

Chapter Twenty-Seven

"But I'm a virgin!"

Daria broke down into giggles. "I hate to break it to you," she said, "but you're not, not any longer. I can *smell* him on you."

Elaine flushed. She hurt, just a little, between her legs. The knowledge within her mind suggested that the first time was supposed to hurt a little for women...and the Modest Maiden had merely ensured that she didn't feel the pain while Bee entered her for the first time. Some of the authors, the ones who acknowledged that women could have sexual feelings, had noted that it was easier to have sex if the woman was wet, her own body producing the lubricant to make it easier for the man to thrust inside her. But it took time for the man to learn how to encourage her body to generate the lubricant and the potion hadn't been a perfect substitute.

She tried to change the subject, quickly. "How *much* of him can you smell on me?"

"Let's see," Daria said, taking a deep sniff. "Lust, admiration, desire, fear..."

Elaine blinked. "Fear?"

"Guys are just as scared on their first time as girls," Daria said, with a wink. "Even after they become more experienced, they are still sometimes scared when they meet a new woman. The mere act of having sex, either by entering or being entered, renders a person vulnerable to colossal emotional harm. If you'd told him that he was too small..."

"He wasn't," Elaine protested, and then flushed again. "I..."

"You can tell me all about it," Daria said, with a leer. "Did you have a good time or what?"

"A very good time," Elaine admitted. "And yet...did I do the right thing?"

Daria leaned over and patted her head. "What makes you think that there *is* a right thing? You had sex with a guy you like and who likes you, instead of a guy who has pushed you into going to bed with him or a guy your parents selected for you and you only met on your wedding day. There's no prospect of him having given you a child – you took the potion to prevent that – and you're hardly of aristocratic blood. You don't even need to worry about the prospect of giving your hubby an illegitimate child."

She shrugged. "Welcome to the wonderful world of men," she added. "Look on the bright side. No one can use you as a virgin sacrifice any longer."

Elaine shivered as Daria's words unlocked more books within her mind. There were spells that involved virgins – and children – being murdered to feed the darker gods, or summon demons, or merely boost the sorcerer's power. Each spell lay within her mind in precise detail, some of them presenting a dreadful temptation. She could jump right up through the different levels of magicians if she offered her firstborn son to the demons...

She pushed the thought away, angrily. "I suppose you're right," she said. "Does he love me?"

"A word of advice," Daria said, with brutal frankness. "Young men confuse lust and love quite badly. He may want to build a relationship with you that results in you both being sealed after you develop true love for each other. Or he may only *think* that he does and in reality he hasn't quite fallen for you. Guys are...S-T-U-P-I-D."

"I have never had any problems with *that* type of spelling," Elaine said, remembering one particular trader couple who had come to the orphanage to find someone to adopt. The woman had said that Elaine wasn't very P-R-I-T-Y. Maybe that was true, but she *did* know how to spell *pretty*. "So...what do you think I should do?"

"Have fun," Daria advised. "What do *you* want from all of this? Sex? I'd say that you had it – I'm sure he'd be happy to keep having sex with you for as long as you wanted. Love – in that case, work on seeing him outside his apartment, with his clothes on. Get him to take you around the city and see all the monuments. Have a swim with him in the public baths, or go watch a stage show...I think they're still playing *The Artful Apprentice* at the Odeon."

Elaine had to smile. *The Artful Apprentice* had been written shortly after the First Necromantic War and told the story of a young magician who had never listened to his master. Eventually, after a long series of humiliating mishaps, he'd managed to turn himself and his wife into snakes, whereupon his master had banished him to the forests outside the city. The play was deliberately written to be amusing, but also educational. Magic could be very dangerous when the sorcerers didn't bother to think through what they were doing first.

"Or there's the *Perverted Pant*," Daria added. "Maybe not the kind of play to take someone to see unless you know them very well. It...isn't exactly clean."

"I've heard of it," Elaine said, tightly. Even now, after discovering that sex could be fun, there were limits. What sort of person would have themselves transformed into female clothing so they could be worn, without the wearer knowing that they were carrying a voyeur around with them? And what sort of fool would rely on someone else to get him out of his perverted idea of fun when it stopped being funny? "I don't think Bee would like that one."

"Ask him," Daria said. She grinned. "And while you're at it, you might want to see if he has any skeletons in his closets. A wife back home, another girlfriend, a set of particularly nasty fetishes...men like to think that they have secrets and they're harmless. Most of the time they're wrong."

She shrugged and changed the subject. "There are some advantages to being a werewolf," she admitted. "You can generally tell what someone likes – or doesn't through their scent and involuntary reactions. I knew a guy who was...rather brash, although a fairly decent chap. He didn't know that I was a werewolf, but he never liked putting his cock in my mouth – and it took me weeks to realise that the whole prospect of it terrified him. I might have bitten down hard and removed his cock."

Elaine winced at the thought. If women were penetrated, it opened them up to the man's penetration, but the men were vulnerable to losing their most important organ. There were spells – not exactly forbidden, but frowned upon – that placed *teeth* within a female vagina, one of the nastier tricks in the darker tomes. Someone like Millicent would probably have considered it a huge joke.

"So," she said, finally. "What did you do?"

"I just had sex with him instead," Daria said, with a wink. "He was a good guy, even though we were hardly soul mates. But if he'd known that I was a werewolf..."

She shook her head. "I don't think it would have mattered to him that much," she admitted. "He would have had the same reaction to any set of really sharp teeth."

Elaine nodded.

"I suggest that you go wash, *thoroughly*," Daria ordered. "Trust me; your stench wouldn't just be obvious to werewolves right now. There are magicians who will know *exactly* what you did last night."

"Understood," Elaine said. In truth, she was still confused. Did Bee love her? Did she love Bee? Or were they both just driven together by hormones? Was this sort of confusion *natural* when sex was involved? "And after that..."

"I think that we will have visitors," Daria said, sniffing the air. "I suggest you hurry."

***

Elaine had never spent long in the shower, a habit that had been hammered into her at the orphanage. Each child was given five minutes of water to wash, after which they were expected to be clean, having washed away all the soap. The matrons had punished any of the children who took longer than five minutes, or emerged still dirty. Even now, even with water relatively cheap in the Golden City, Elaine still needed less than ten minutes to wash herself – and study her body in the mirror.

She looked...*older* somehow, even though there was no single change that she could identify. There were a handful of marks on her skin where Bee's hands had torn at her, and a whole series of bruises from where the torturer had lashed out at her skin. Dread had provided some basic medical care – stripping off in front of him had been embarrassing – and the damage was well on its way to healing, but it was still visible. She was mildly surprised that Bee hadn't commented on the bruise. Perhaps he'd thought that they were natural...

...Or perhaps he'd thought that they'd come from her master. It wasn't unknown for apprentices to be beaten by their masters, even though Miss Prim had never lifted a hand to Elaine or to any of the other girls in the Library. Maybe Bee was beaten by the Empress of the South...she giggled at the absurd thought, although she suspected that Bee hadn't been a virgin when he'd met her. Perhaps the Empress's reputation was genuine and she'd seduced him before sending him out on her service.

There was a faint bloodstain on her legs, all that remained of her maidenhead. She washed it away with warm water and then scrubbed her legs clean, feeling a whirlwind of conflicting emotions. She'd enjoyed herself and yet there was a feeling that she hadn't quite done the right thing. Perhaps it was a form of sexual buyer's remorse. There would never be a second time that she lost her virginity. Some spells offered her the chance to restore her maidenhead, but it wouldn't be the same. She'd lost something – innocence, perhaps – when she'd opened her legs and invited Bee to enter her body.

She finished washing and dried herself with a simple spell, pulling on her bathrobe as she left the washroom. Outside, a small party seemed to have gathered around the table, led by a man it took her a long moment to recognise. Inquisitor Dread had put his robes aside and settled for donning the brown and yellow robes of a part-time worker. Cass and Karan wore the same civilian clothes they'd worn before, but there was something about them that made them seem even *less* like Inquisitors. Princess Sacharissa looked utterly unlike a princess in a light green dancing dress, but it wasn't her that caught Elaine's attention.

There was a small dark-skinned man, wearing a grey uniform, who seemed uncomfortable so close to the Inquisitors and Daria...Daria's face was caught between human and wolf forms, covered in fur and bristling with sharp teeth. Elaine stared; some werewolves could hold themselves in the midst of the transformation, gaining skills that combined both those of human and wolf, but she'd never seen it before. A wolf-man would be a very dangerous enemy.

Daria relaxed and her face slid back to normal, the fur slowly fading into her skin until it became almost invisible. "Your friend here wanted to know if I could be a Limbo," she said, as she smiled at Elaine. "I can...if not for very long."

"I understand that you had a good evening," Dread said, to Elaine. The two bodyguards grinned at her behind Dread's back. They'd probably been watching...strange how that had never occurred to her, even as they'd been undressing. "I trust you didn't tell him anything *too* important?"

"I believe you already know," Elaine said, tightly. The bodyguards were there to spy on her as much as protect her from whoever wanted the knowledge in her head. "Or didn't you bother to watch me last night."

"You were very good," Cass assured her, her bright eyes wide with innocence. "If that really was your first time..."

Elaine flushed, feeling magic flickering around her. But Cass would have little trouble beating her in a fight, even with the technique that had caught Millicent by surprise. It was quite possible that dozens of sorcerers had already reinvented it...or that the Inquisition used the technique themselves to deal with dark sorcerers. They might well have kept it to themselves, using the story about Inquisitors being the most powerful magicians in the world to hide its existence.

"That will do," Dread said, as Daria started to hand out glasses of juice. She took a special pleasure, it seemed, in giving the most childish container to Dread, who seemed not to notice the implied sneer. "We have work to do."

He tapped the table, effortlessly taking charge of the meeting. "You already know most of the people here," he said, to Elaine. "This" – he nodded to the dark-skinned man – "is Cat. He does have a real name..."

"But using it would be a dangerous weakness in my line of work," Cat said, in a whispery voice that had to be partly an act. Elaine saw the pale skin around his neck and realised, with horror, that he'd once worn a slave collar. "I prefer to be known as Cat."

"Cat was once one of the most masterful sneak thieves in the city," Dread said, remorselessly. "He burgled thousands of houses, stealing thousands of Crowns over a period of three years before he was caught in a sorcerer's booby trap. The Sorcerer Balthazar had never bothered to construct the standard wards around his house; instead, he set traps throughout the building, waiting to see who would blunder inside. He was in the middle of a long-running dispute with the Sorceress Morgana at the time."

Elaine smiled, remembering the two magicians. They seemed to spend half of their lives as lovers and the other half fighting savagely against each other. Miss Prim had once complained that they'd even had fights within the Great Library, despite all the wards designed to prevent violence inside the building. Everyone knew their story – and everyone feared getting caught up between them.

"So he was caught," Dread continued. "The Sorcerer handed him over to the City Guard, who had him pushed in front of a judge, sentenced to enslavement and then collared. Once all his loot was recovered, he was sent to work as a menial slave..."

"Which is where you found me," Cat said, in the same voice. "And you have sworn to make my freedom permanent if I do one task for you."

Dread nodded and unfurled a map. "Count Lucas, the illegitimate son of the Duke of Randor and also one of the possible candidates to become Grand Sorcerer, owns a large mansion at the edge of High Tory," he said. "Rather unimaginatively, it is called Randor Mansion."

He chuckled, humourlessly. "For reasons unknown, he and Prince Hilarion have become friends and the Prince is currently living within the mansion. It is heavily guarded, with a small private army, and hundreds of wards interwoven within the walls."

"Which may not be a bad thing," Cass pointed out. "So many wards would likely start to interfere with each other."

"But he has a small army to back him up," Cat said, softly. "I thought that private armies weren't allowed within the city."

"There's no Grand Sorcerer to order them out," Dread said, crossly. Elaine could see why he was worried. Every candidate for the Grand Sorcerer's position had a sizeable retinue and their allies had offered more, including soldiers and even lesser magicians. The Garrison possessed better-trained soldiers than the private armies, but they would be badly outnumbered if the private armies decided to go to war within the city. One false move and there would be blood in the streets. "I believe that...certain authorities are working on bringing other troops near the city, but that will take time."

He tapped the map firmly. "All of the candidates have been kept under discreet observation, even before we discovered that one of them might be cheating..."

"Or at least cheating outside the rules governing cheating," Karan added. "Every time we have a magical contest, cheating becomes epidemic. No magician likes to lose."

Dread ignored her. "We know that Prince Hilarion and Count Lucas spend the day visiting people who might be able to assist them and the nights enjoying themselves in the Golden City. Prince Hilarion may have set a new record for spending his father's money at terrifying speed, enjoying the services of high-class whores and drinking parlours. He's actually pulled a great many lesser noblemen – and magicians with aristocratic blood – into his faction, although it doesn't seem that this has yet translated into political power..."

"Of course not," Daria commented, acidly. "The ones who are backing him are the ones who have the most to gain from a massive shift in the balance of power."

"Correct," the Princess agreed. "Doesn't drinking and wenching invalidate him for the post?"

"No," Dread said. "The only outright quality that would ban him would be lacking magical powers – and he very definitely does have magic. Any trace of necromancy or certain other forbidden acts would force the Inquisition to crush him, setting a whole range of dangerous precedents."

He snorted. "I'll say one thing for him," he added. "He's got nerve. His plan has been exposed and he's still trying to make it work. But if he won, he would win it all."

"So it would seem," Cass agreed.

"Our mission – or rather Elaine, Daria and Cat's mission – is to break into the mansion and find proof we can use to convince the Star Chamber to act. Evidence of necromancy; evidence of spells that could produce a bookworm...whatever it is, we need it. Find it, get it to the Watchtower...and then we can strike. Once Prince Hilarion is removed, we can wait for the next Grand Sorcerer to be confirmed before we move against Ida."

"I have a question," the Princess said, into the silence. "Is Lucas really involved in my brother's plot?"

"I don't believe so," Dread said, after a long moment. "I'm not even sure how they *know* each other."

"The Duke of Randor was an old friend of my grandfather's," the Princess said. "Lucas...is his son, from the wrong side of the blankets. But he was always a good guy to me."

"Then we'd better hope that he remains a good guy," Dread said. "But maybe he was the one who taught Prince Hilarion."

Chapter Twenty-Eight

"That's them on their way to the party," Cat muttered, from where he was lying on the roof of Anchor Mansion. "And they've got one hell of a following today."

Elaine followed his gaze. She didn't know what sort of agreement Dread had cut with the Anchor Family, but they'd agreed to allow the Inquisition to establish an observation post on their roof that allowed the team to look down into High Tory. The outskirts of the richest part of the city were bustling with life, yet somehow less active than the poorer parts of the city. Prince Hilarion was visible for a brief moment as he walked down the driveway and climbed into a coach, a girl clinging to his arm as if he were incredibly attractive. He *was* handsome, Elaine would happily admit, but he was also a prince and a powerful sorcerer. Far too many girls would be drawn to him in the hope that some of his glory would reflect on them.

She rolled her eyes as the long parade of admirers and supplicants sorted themselves out into carriages and headed down the road towards the seedier parts of town. Like many young aristocrats – and trader children – they had a positive taste for slumming it in the poorer parts of the city, although only those who were tired of living would go into the Rookery after dark. The criminal element might have been quieter with additional patrols of City Guardsmen, Garrison soldiers and private armies, but they wouldn't hesitate to attempt to steal from a particularly dumb aristocrat who'd been separated from his party. But Prince Hilarion and Count Lucas were sorcerers. Only a fool would try to pick on them openly.

"It costs more money each day to keep those people happy than I stole in three years," Cat said, crossly. Elaine kept glancing at the sneak thief – and at the pale skin around his neck, where the collar had once been. She knew that collars could be removed, but it was very rare for *anyone* to be offered their freedom by their master. Why should the masters bargain when the collars kept the slaves nice and obedient? "And I'm the one who was punished for stealing."

Elaine ignored him and concentrated on Randor Mansion. Like most of the mansions in High Tory, it had nothing more than a small courtyard at the front and a solid wall surrounding the mansion itself. The real defences were unseen; the guards, the wards and probably a number of entity-powered surprises. And it was huge; having nowhere to go but up had forced the builders to keep pushing the mansion ever higher. Elaine had never realised until she'd absorbed the knowledge of the Great Library just how much magic went into buildings in the Golden City, even the ones without interiors larger than their exteriors. If something were to happen to drain away the magic infused into the mansion's walls...the entire building would probably collapse.

Maybe Ida had had a point when it had shunned magic as much as possible. Its buildings might be constructed from ugly grey stone, but they were solid. A sudden drain on local magic wouldn't bring them tumbling down into dust. And if magic were to be drained over the entire city, much of the Golden City would be destroyed. She looked away from the mansion and towards the faint haze that marked the presence of the Blight. Perhaps the real reason no one had tried to drain the wild magic was because the spell could easily get out of control and start draining magic from across the city, destroying it in an afternoon.

"That's interesting," Cat said, suddenly. "Look who's come to pay them a call."

"Wizard Kane," Daria said, looking up from where she sat beside them. Cat had been nervous until Elaine had assured him that the spells surrounding their hiding place would make it impossible for anyone to see them. "I wonder why he's here."

Elaine frowned. Four of the candidates were known quantities; Prince Hilarion was a largely-unknown figure...and then there was the Wizard Kane. Little was known about him, even after the broadsheet editors had sent their best writers to track down dirt on the enigmatic sorcerer. He was older than Dread, from what Elaine had been able to deduce, and classically trained, but little else. Maybe he was gambling everything on becoming the Grand Sorcerer. At least he wouldn't be as bad as Deferens...

There was a brief discussion between Kane and one of the servants, and then Kane just walked away from the building. Maybe he'd hoped to speak to Prince Hilarion or Count Lucas, or maybe he'd been intending to admit that he couldn't win and bow out of the contest. There was no way to know. Darkness fell over the city rapidly as the lights started to go out, parts of the city still glowing as the night life began in earnest. Prince Hilarion and his cronies would be partying for hours to come.

"Remember what I said," Cat hissed. "You do exactly as I tell you down there, or I'll just leave you. I will *not* be a slave again."

"I understand," Daria said, impatiently. "Shall we go?"

They walked down the stairs and out into the mansion's courtyard, heading towards the wall that separated it from Randor Mansion. Dread had told them that he expected that the inner defences would be weaker than the ones on the gates, if only because warding spells were expensive and not always completely reliable if the builder hadn't been a sorcerer. Up close, Elaine could feel the wards buzzing through the air, partly anchored into the bricks that formed the wall. Dread had been right, although she could tell that some of the wards were new, probably created by Prince Hilarion and his friend. But she, using the knowledge in her head, could have done a better job. There was something very crude about the spells surrounding Randor Mansion.

Cat looked over at her as Elaine produced her wand. "Are you sure that you can break through the wards?"

"Yes," Elaine said, flatly. There were entire libraries of books on making – and breaking – wards...and they were all in her head. "Daria..."

"Get on with it," her friend urged. She had already shifted to the halfway form between human and wolf, a veiled threat to Cat. A werewolf could track him down from across half the city – and would be a great deal less kind than the

Inquisition. "Hurry."

Elaine closed her eyes and reached out with her second sight. It was astonishing how few wizards ever bothered to really develop their senses, even though magic gifted them things that mundane humans could never match. Guided by the information in her mind, she located and identified seventeen separate wards, each one spinning through the air surrounding the mansion. Some of them were nothing more than repelling charms, convincing anyone who touched them that they really – really – wanted to walk away; the remainder grew steadily nastier. Two of them would inflict pain on someone stubborn enough to ignore the repelling charms; the remainder were a combination of change spells and freeze spells, apart from a single compulsion spell that carried a powerful command to commit suicide. Someone had put a great deal of effort into protecting the mansion without really knowing what they were doing. There were so many wards that they were *definitely* interfering with one another.

Carefully, she reached out towards them mentally, shaping countering spells in her mind. A cunning wizard wouldn't just rely on brute force. There would be wards in place that monitored the other wards, watching for a break or even a bulge where no bulge should be. And they would be shielded by the main wards, protected from direct interference. But no one could have expected to meet a bookworm. Slowly, she aligned the magical field surrounding her with the ward, and then reached *through* the ward towards the secondary set of detectors. They weren't very complex, but they were easy to mislead. Whatever happened to the rest of the wards, the secondary set would keep cheerfully reporting that everything was fine.

A sorcerer would normally live alone, allowing him to link the wards directly to his own mind and making them much harder to crack. But these wards were anchored within stone and brick rather than a human mind; carefully, Elaine disabled them one by one, creating an open space in the wards. And, with a little help from Daria, she scrambled onto the wall and peered ahead of her. There seemed to be no other surprises until they reached the mansion's walls.

Daria shifted completely to wolf and leapt over the wall in a single bound, Cat clinging desperately to her neck. Elaine smiled as the thief scrambled off the wolf, allowing Daria to return to the halfway form. Her fur would hide her body from prying eyes; she'd had to leave her clothes behind when she'd shifted into a wolf. Elaine stepped up to the mansion walls and reached out, again, with her mind. The builders had, unsurprisingly, woven another set of wards within the bricks and mortar. They would be more finicky, much harder to remove or disable. But perhaps she didn't *need* to disable them.

She felt out the wards as she stepped along the wall, heading towards a heavy stone door. It was so heavily warded that it would be impossible to break, at least not without setting off alarms all over the building. Cat let out a moan of dismay as he sensed the wards – his magical talent was only good enough for sensing magic – but Elaine ignored him. The wards would keep out an army of combat magicians if they used brute force, yet the designers had overlooked a single terrifying weakness. There was nothing stopping light from passing through the windows.

"Take my hand and close your eyes," she ordered. There were some nasty spells curling outside the glass, preventing someone from simply breaking it to get inside, but there were no protections on the glass itself. "Hang on..."

She shaped the spell in her mind – a subtle combination of thoughts that produced a shockingly powerful effect – and closed her eyes, triggering the spell. When she opened her eyes they were standing inside the mansion, having briefly become light and passed through the transparent glass. She smiled, before feeling a cold shiver as she looked up at the wards. From the inside, they looked more dangerous than she'd realised...and whoever had designed them should have at least left a warning spell on the glass. But there was none.

"Come on," she hissed, as Cat produced a popular tool for burglars from his bag. It cast light that was only visible to the would-be thieves. The designers had put a lot of hard work into creating something that wouldn't trigger alarms, or so they'd claimed. Dread had been less sanguine, but he'd accepted that there was no other choice. "Prince Hilarion's rooms are on the higher levels of the house."

The interior of Randor Mansion reminded her of Howarth Hall, complete with tacky artwork and absurdly expensive paintings on the wall. None of them looked familiar, but she kept her senses sharp and swept her mental focus over everything before stepping past it. There were plenty of charms that could turn a seemingly-innocent looking item into a trap, just like the one that had caught Cat. He'd been incredibly lucky. A thief caught by a sorcerer could be legally killed, or enslaved, and no one would give a damn. Anyone who broke into a sorcerer's home, the Grand Sorcerer had said, deserved whatever they got. Even the Guardsmen tended to walk quietly – and quickly – around buildings belonging to sorcerers and whistle for the Inquisition if there were any crimes that involved magic.

They slipped back into the shadows as a small group of chattering maids walked past, wearing uniforms that had clearly been devised by a young man, revealing almost everything without the subtle hints that went into so many of the dresses Daria had shown Elaine before her world had gone completely crazy. The maids were all collared – and they would be ruthless in defence of their master's house. Some thieves believed that collared slaves were completely incapable of resistance. Few of them survived to make the same mistake twice.

Daria leaned closer to her and whispered in Elaine's ear. "What language are they speaking?"

Elaine hesitated. She'd only spoken Imperial – and a handful of magical words – before Duke Gama's spell had struck her. Now...she had a rough comprehension of all other known languages, but it was confusing, as if she really needed a tutor to show her the difference between how words were written and how they were pronounced. But it wasn't Imperial, all right; it struck her that they were speaking Ida's native language. They could have come with Prince Hilarion, or they might have been living in the city before he arrived. Or he could have sent them ahead of him...it wouldn't take great magic to know that the Grand Sorcerer was dying. The entire city had known about it weeks before Death finally claimed him for her own.

"I think it comes from Ida," she said. "But I can't understand it properly."

"Probably charmed with the collars," Cat said, as he slunk further down the corridor and up a long pair of staircases. Elaine followed him, watching for traps, but she found nothing apart from a watching ward that was easy to disarm. The Inquisition had provided plans of the building, including details on where Prince Hilarion and his men were sleeping. Elaine couldn't understand why they had collected so much data, or how, but they probably wanted to keep an eye on all of the possible candidates. "I..."

Daria slipped past him. "People ahead," she hissed. "Get back..."

Too late. A pair of maids rounded the corner and stopped, staring at them. Elaine reacted with a speed she hadn't known she possessed, snapping off a binding spell that caught them both before they could open their mouths and start screaming for help. Daria caught them before they hit the ground and dragged them into an unoccupied room, snarling at Cat when he tried to take advantage of the maids' helplessness. Maybe he *had* spent five years as a slave, forbidden to touch women or indulge himself in any way, but that didn't excuse molesting a helpless slave.

"We'd better move quickly," Daria snapped. "Those girls will be missed soon."

Elaine nodded as she led the way up the next flight of stairs. Collared slaves were nothing if not obedient – and dedicated. No collared slave would take a break, or deliberately work slowly to annoy a master he couldn't rebel against in any other way; they'd be missed sooner rather than later. And then their supervisors would find them and know that there were intruders in the house.

Prince Hilarion's suite was guarded by a sentinel who looked to be a human cross-bred with a troll, a semi-humanoid race that was barely intelligent and existed only in isolated areas, well away from humanity. Cross-breeds were rare – although the knowledge in Elaine's head pointed out that the werewolves were the result of a curse and trolls might have come from the same place – and this one looked to have been shaped in a kiln and baked alive. And there were supposed to be troll civilisations in the mountains near Ida...

Daria shifted back to human form and walked forward, swinging her naked hips invitingly. The half-troll stared at her for just a second too long, giving her a chance to wrap her arms around him and jab him with a charged wand, sending him stumbling to the floor. Elaine followed Daria as she positioned the guard neatly against the wall, rolling her eyes at how Daria was checking out the man's warped body. The door had a handful of other charms worked into it to discourage would-be intruders, but disarming them was simple. They didn't even have the flair one would expect from a sorcerer defending his territory, something that puzzled her. Whatever his power, it seemed as if Prince Hilarion had only learned by rote, rather than understanding what he was doing at a very basic level. The Peerless School would have cured him of that bad habit if he'd ever attended.

The door opened easily and Daria led the way into the most luxurious suite Elaine had ever seen. A series of rooms, each one just as luxurious as the next; three of them bedrooms for the Prince and his two companions. Daria kept sniffing, her half-formed snout twitching as it scented the Prince's activities ever since he had come to the city.

"Oddly familiar stench," Daria said, puzzled. "But someone has used a scattering charm. I wouldn't even have realised it was there if it hadn't been interfering with the other scents."

"Maybe the Prince is just paranoid about his scent," Elaine said. She knew exactly how he must have felt. "Or maybe..."

"But I can smell him," Daria said. She made a face. "And I really wish I couldn't."

Cat led the way forward, searching for points of interest and watching for traps, leaving Elaine to stare at the Prince's colossal bed. He'd brought a considerable number of slaves and assistants with him to the city and the bed looked as if it could have housed more than ten of them at a time. The thought made her smile as Cat whispered for her to come and check out the final door. It was locked – and clearly sealed with magic. There was something surprisingly ham-fisted about the spell, as if the caster had been in a tearing hurry. Elaine bent down, carefully unpicked it and opened the door...

...And reacted barely in time to counter the freeze charm that was hurled at her from the inside. She heard Daria snort in disbelief as a figure ran out and then froze, staring at Elaine with the same horror that Elaine felt. The figure couldn't be here, unless her aunt had turned her into a thief. And *that* suggested that the whole situation had already worsened beyond repair.

"*Millicent?*"

Chapter Twenty-Nine

Millicent seemed equally shocked to see her. "*Frogeye*? What are *you* doing here?"

"Never mind her," Daria snapped. Millicent's eyes went wide as she took in the sight of Daria's partly-transformed body. She would have known that Daria was a werewolf – she'd clearly come prepared for werewolves, or Daria would have scented her long before they entered the chambers – but she might never have seen one frozen in the midst of a transformation. "We have other problems."

Cat pushed past Elaine and stepped into the sealed chamber, shining his light around to illuminate books and a handful of scrolls that looked to date from the time before the printing press. A couple of titles were familiar to Elaine; the others were completely unknown to her. Did that mean that they were unknown to the Great Library as well? Or were they merely books of so little significance that they'd never been included in the Library's collection?

"This one I recognise," Cat said, picking up a bound volume. "I..."

Elaine felt the flash of magic just a second too late. Cat dropped to the ground, his features twisted in agony, the book falling on the floor beside him. There was no need to touch him to confirm his death. The spell had been as insidious as the one that had turned Elaine into a bookworm – and far deadlier. There was no way to touch or open the book directly without the right code words; unpicking the spell would take experts from the Inquisition. Elaine suspected that she *did* know how to do it, at least in theory, but unpicking the spell might be beyond her skill. And there might be a second spell hidden under the first to destroy the book if the spell were removed by the wrong person.

But she didn't need to touch the book to feel the shimmering pattern of dark magic under the covers. Elaine might never have been a powerful magician, even before the spell that had turned her into a bookworm, but Miss Prim had taught her how to hone her senses and develop disciplines that had served her well in the Great Library. The book had a sense of evil surrounding it that was far darker than any other book she'd seen, a sense that even *touching* the book would result in a foul taint touching her soul. If the Inquisition had been worried by the spell that had turned Elaine into a living repository for the Great Library's knowledge, they'd panic when they realised what had been drifting around the world for hundreds of years, just waiting for a dark magician to find it.

"He's dead," Daria said, in shock. Elaine wondered, vaguely, if she'd thought the entire mission was a lark, rather than a deadly serious mission. There were *no* legal penalties for a magician who killed intruders in his house. "Elaine, I..."

"You fools," Millicent snapped. "Don't you know better than to touch something that may be charmed to punish interlopers? What in all the names of all the gods are you doing here?"

Elaine began to chuckle. One way or another, she would never be intimidated by Millicent again. "You're one to talk," she said. "I bet you weren't invited to the mansion, were you?"

Millicent flushed, the first sign of embarrassment that Elaine had ever seen on her. Clearly, *something* had been going on that had attracted Millicent – or, more likely, her formidable aunt. What did it mean when Lady Light Spinner had sent Millicent to rob Prince Hilarion's mansion? Or had the real target of her interest been Count Lucas?

Her head snapped up as she felt the alarm echoing through the magical protections around the mansion. Small magic spells wouldn't have triggered any alarms, not when half of the household used magic for daily tasks, but the death spell would definitely have alerted the guards. Elaine found herself thinking fast, trying to determine how to escape. The knowledge in her head was more of a hindrance than a help. She knew too little to risk choosing a plan and then sticking to it. At least one question was answered. Millicent's own entry had probably been conducted in the same way as Elaine, with Millicent leaving the wards disabled to permit her to leave as quietly as she had come.

"They're coming," Daria said. She shifted almost all the way to wolf-form, assuming a disturbing posture that suggested trouble. Very few people would want to tangle with a werewolf at close quarters. "At least twelve of them, all men."

Millicent looked over at her. "You can *smell* them?"

"I can smell *you*," Daria growled, her voice far less than human. "You *stink* of fear and terror."

Millicent started to speak, but Elaine ignored her. Picking up a cloth from the room's small table – after a quick check for nasty surprises – she used it to pick up the poisonous book and wrap it up so it could be carried. Daria's packsack had been designed for use in werewolf form as well as human form; she'd have to carry it out of the building. The plan had come together in Elaine's mind without her being quite aware of it. Dread needed to see the book to have the proof he needed to move openly against Prince Hilarion. They *had* to get it out to him.

"Here," she said, as she shoved the book into Daria's packsack. "Slip completely into wolf form and race out of here before they think to adjust the wards to prevent anyone leaving."

Daria looked up at her, her dog-like eyes bright with worry. "But what about you...?"

"Never mind about us," Elaine said. Millicent was staring at her with an odd expression of respect on her face. Had her brief transformation taught her a lesson, or was she merely scared that Elaine would do it again? Being trapped in an immobile form was every magician's worst nightmare. "You get the book out of here and to Dread. Go."

Daria took one last look at her and then shifted completely into wolf form. Elaine watched, unable to suppress a tinge of horror, as her face became that of a wolf, her body somehow growing larger and stronger. Werewolves were larger than ordinary wolves, even the half-intelligent breeds created by magicians with a great deal of power and few scruples about experimenting on living creatures. But Daria would scent her fear.

The wolf cocked its head at her and then turned and slunk down the corridor, away from the oncoming guards. Elaine could hear them now; it sounded as if a small army was on its way to their position. She took one look at Millicent, saw the fear written clearly on her old enemy's face...and knew that Millicent had never really grown up. Despite everything she'd done over the years, it was no longer easy to hate her. Elaine smiled at the thought, gathered some of her magic into a concentration in her hand, and then took up a position just outside the chamber. Somewhat to her surprise, Millicent followed her, gathering her own power.

"We hit them and then we start running," Elaine muttered. It was possible that Millicent would start running in the wrong direction, away from Elaine, but there was nothing she could do about it. Millicent might not take orders from her if she started issuing them. "Here they come..."

The guards charged up the stairs and came right at them, brandishing staves and spears. There were no rifles, part of Elaine's mind noted; not even swords and knives. It seemed to make no sense until she realised that the guards probably had strict orders to take any intruders alive. None of them appeared to be combat magicians, but if Cass and Karan could take off their robes and pass as normal girls, there was no reason why Prince Hilarion's combat magicians couldn't do the same.

Elaine lifted her hand, shaped a thought, and blew a roaring column of flame down the corridor. The guards wore charmed armour, but there was nothing protecting their faces from the heat of the blaze and the lead guards staggered back, screaming in pain. Elaine felt the house's magical protections starting to concentrate on the blaze – all houses in High Tory had magical fire protection to prevent a holocaust that might consume the entire district – and tossed a second spell. All of the lighting flickered and died instantly.

A brilliant flash of light flared out as Millicent tossed a spell of her own towards the guards. It wasn't one typically taught at the Peerless School, even though it wasn't forbidden; Elaine only knew it through the knowledge dumped into her head. Millicent had probably learned it from her aunt. Many other well-born children had had private lessons from their families in magic before they ever attended the Peerless School. Two of the guards started to scream, their faces burning with a terrible white light; Elaine grabbed Millicent's arm and pulled her backwards, tossing a third spell behind her as she fled. The Night Terrors wasn't a particularly powerful spell, but it would take a trained sorcerer to dispel – and mundane humans would have real problems pushing through illusions of their worst nightmares coming to life.

They ran through a series of corridors, almost crashing into a trio of maids. The girls were advancing on them, carrying a handful of knives and brooms that they intended to use as makeshift weapons. They wouldn't have a choice, Elaine knew; the collars they wore would push them into intercepting the intruders even if the odds were badly against them. Millicent cast a spell that sent the maids falling limply to the ground, rather than killing them outright. Elaine was surprised, and impressed. She had never thought that Millicent had any concept of restraint.

She could feel the wards flickering around her as they sought to counter her spells and lead the guards directly after them. Another group of guards appeared in front of them and Elaine knocked them down, just before allowing Millicent to pull her down a thin corridor that was used by the servants to stay away from the upper-class guests. Elaine was surprised that Millicent even knew about it, before remembering that Millicent's family probably spied on everyone else in High Tory with as much interest as the Inquisition. Knowledge was power in the Golden City and whoever got to it first had an advantage over everyone else. How long would it be, Elaine wondered, before they altered the wards to bar their exit? A normal sorcerer would have had to do the work himself – and Prince Hilarion and Count Lucas were still out on the town – but there was nothing normal about either of them. What if they'd given one of their subordinate magicians the key to unlocking and reshaping the wards?

They stumbled down a flight of stairs and emerged into a dining hall large enough to seat half of the nobility comfortably. It looked as if the maids were cleaning up after an orgy – a type of party that even Daria considered disgusting – but the moment they saw the girls they turned and advanced on them, throwing leftovers and cutlery with deadly intent. Elaine felt tiredness grabbing at her – she'd used too much of her power already – and stumbled; Millicent cast a spell that knocked away most of the incoming missiles and smashed the tables for good measure. A door burst open at the far end, revealing a line of guards who ran forward, carrying deadly weapons. Whatever plans they'd had to take the intruders alive had been cancelled.

Elaine felt a very complicated spell pushing at her mind and cast it before she could think better of it. For a long moment, nothing happened...and then the swords the guards were carrying came to life. Millicent stared at her in disbelief as the guards screamed and dropped their swords, unable to keep them from slicing away at their arms with their charmed blades. Some of them were from Caitiff, Elaine realised; a line of alchemists who boasted that their charmed swords could cut through anything. It looked as though that included the sword arms of anyone unlucky enough to be carrying them when the swords were hit with an animation spell.

Millicent came to her senses and pushed Elaine towards the other exit as the spell – feeding on the loose magic in the room – started to get out of control. Smashed tables came to life, lashing out at the maids and knocking into the guards. Knives and forks started to move, almost as if they were running, towards their targets. Some of the maids dropped to the ground, their hands clutching at their collars. The spells keeping them loyal and faithful – making them property, their lives completely out of their control – had been drained away and failed, freeing them. Elaine hoped that some of them would be able to escape before Prince Hilarion and his friend came home from their midnight revels. Slavery might be legal, but it sure as hell wasn't moral.

"How..." Millicent began, and then caught herself. "How long will that spell last?"

The words of a very ancient warlock, who had written a single volume before vanishing under mysterious circumstances, echoed in her mind: *Take a simple kinetic spell and shape it so that it keeps going as long as there is magic in the area,* the warlock had said. *Eventually it will suck up all the magic and fall apart, but first it will neutralise all the other magic within reach. And what happens if the magic doesn't come back?*

"I don't know," Elaine admitted. It would take vast amounts of power to animate the entire room for more than a few seconds; no wonder her uncontrolled spell had started to drain all the sources of magic it could. But draining a ward was such an obvious trick that almost all wards had protections built in to stop someone trying, which suggested that there would be very definite limits to what she'd unleashed. She pushed the thought aside as they turned the corner and looked towards the main doors. Nine guards – and a man wearing the black and red robes of a combat magician – stood there, waiting for them.

She nodded to Millicent and they ran back up the stairs, sharply. It might give them some more time, particularly if the guards hadn't realised that Daria had gone her own way. They'd concentrate on sealing off the exits first, and then search the rest of the mansion floor by floor. How many men did they have in their private armies? Dread had implied several hundred at the very least. Prince Hilarion could probably call upon the entire Ida Royal Guard if he'd felt that he needed them.

Millicent shaped a spell and tossed it back down the stairs as a band of guards started to give chase. Elaine felt a flicker of envy for the obvious power reserves at Millicent's disposal, even though there was nothing particularly subtle about her spell-casting. Another pair of half-trolls appeared in front of them and Millicent knocked them down, while Elaine concentrated on casting diversion spells that would confuse the defenders and make it much harder for the wards to track them. But their eventual capture seemed inevitable.

"This way," Millicent said, leading her up to the third floor. Elaine glanced at her sharply, wondering what Millicent knew that made her so confident – and yet so reluctant. The third floor housed the more trusted servants, the butlers and particularly elite servants who were paid in gold rather than forced to serve through compulsion spells. Millicent walked ahead as though she knew precisely where to go and opened a door that led into a small smoking room. It was empty, yet surprisingly comfortable, without the gaudy luxury that marked so much of High Tory. "Follow me."

She opened up a large cupboard, revealing a solid wall. Before Elaine could say anything, she pressed her hand against the stone and it clicked open, revealing a secret passageway. Elaine stared at her as she stepped inside, urgently beckoning for Elaine to follow her into a tiny flight of steps that led down towards the basement. The secret passageway hadn't been on the plans Elaine had memorised; the Inquisition clearly didn't know about them...and yet Millicent *did*?

"We should be able to get down into the tunnels from here," Millicent muttered, as they kept walking down the stairs. The only light came from a globe Millicent summoned into existence and held in front of her. "I don't know if Prince Hilarion knows about this or not – we tried to keep it a secret from just about everyone."

Elaine nodded, remembering some of the legends she'd heard. The Golden City was *old*, with more than two *thousand* years of history – and buildings piled upon buildings as building techniques improved over the years. It was supposed to be riddled with secret passages, some under the mountains and leading outside the city, others linking various mansions together and allowing for secret deals to be struck. Officially, they didn't exist; people who ventured in without invitations tended to vanish in the darkened catacombs. No one had ever *considered* the possibility that one might lead to Randor Mansion. Or maybe Dread had felt unable to tell her that the tunnels existed.

"There's so much stray magic around here that it's very hard to be sure that the tunnels remain the same," Millicent said, more to herself than to Elaine. "But this should be the right way home. My Aunt will want to talk to you, again."

She hesitated. "I have also been ordered to apologise to you," she added, bluntly. "My aunt feels that I acted badly in...teasing you over the years."

Elaine looked at her, sharply. All the old bitterness was still there, even if she had...matured.

"You did," she agreed, finally. "And I really think that you need to grow up."

Chapter Thirty

"I must confess that I am surprised to see you," Lady Light Spinner said. "I would not have expected you to raid Prince Hilarion's mansion."

"And I didn't expect to see Millicent there, either," Elaine snapped. Lack of sleep and a growing awareness of her own abilities gave her confidence. "Do you have any idea how much you ruined?"

"No," Lady Light Spinner said. With her face hidden behind the veil, it was difficult to tell if she was telling the truth. "Millicent was acting on instructions from me."

"I'm sure that would have saved her if Prince Hilarion had caught her in the act," Elaine pointed out. She was tired and weak and she didn't have time for games. "Wasn't there a case only a few months ago when a sorcerer turned a burglar into a chicken and had him for dinner?"

She shrugged. "Enough games," she continued, angrily. "What was Millicent doing in Prince Hilarion's mansion?"

Millicent snorted, even though her eyes looked fearful. "What were *you* doing in Prince Hilarion's mansion?"

"Presumably the same thing," Lady Light Spinner said, coolly. "We were looking for evidence to prove that Prince Hilarion is unsuited to becoming Grand Sorcerer."

"Cheating has always being part of the contest," Elaine commented. Lady Light Spinner seemed to nod behind her veil. "And did you find anything of interest?"

"I was studying his books when you arrived," Millicent said, after exchanging glances with her aunt. One way or another, a reputation for stealing into houses owned by sorcerers wouldn't help her social standing. "If I'd touched one of them..."

Elaine nodded, remembering the look on Cat's dead body. He'd frozen in an expression of agony as every cell in his body died an awful death. The pain would have been so bad that death would have been a relief. Even Millicent didn't deserve to go the same way.

"It would have been the end of you," Elaine said. She stood up, ignoring the glass of water offered to her by one of the maids. "I need to go back to..."

"To the Inquisition," Lady Light Spinner said. Elaine stared at her, wondering how she knew...before dismissing it as a silly question. The Inquisition had assumed that her powers had been boosted beyond their natural levels; why couldn't Lady Light Spinner have assumed the same? And she'd already tried to convince Elaine to join her once. "They seem to have...quite an interest in you."

"They do," Elaine agreed, tonelessly.

"And they have a habit of...terminating people who push at the edges of what is permissible," Lady Light Spinner said. Her eyes lifted and looked directly at Elaine. "I could protect you from them."

Elaine had to smile. "Protect me from the Inquisition?"

"The Inquisitors are not all-powerful," Lady Light Spinner said. Her head cocked to one side, but her eyes never left Elaine's face. "And I may become the next Grand Sorceress. I will be able to order the Inquisitors to leave you alone."

"You might," Elaine agreed.

"I will," Lady Light Spinner countered. "Prince Hilarion is likely to...face justice for his actions." She'd already heard about the dark spellbook, rigged to kill anyone who touched it without permission. "Count Lucas may withdraw if there are suspicions around his role in the whole affair. Deferens has left the city after accidentally exposing himself to the watching crowds; he hasn't bothered to announce his withdrawal, but leaving the city is practically an admission of defeat. That leaves me, Administrator Mentor and Wizard Kane. Kane is not a serious contender..."

Elaine smiled. "Are you sure of that?"

"And that leaves me and Mentor," Lady Light Spinner said. "He has a great deal of support from magicians he has mentored over the years, but I have political support and deals with various magical families. And I have a great deal of magic at my command. It should be an even fight."

"Assuming you're right," Elaine agreed. "You seem to be

counting Kane and Count Lucas out right from the start."

"Lucas will be tainted, like it or not," Lady Light Spinner said. "And Kane is a nobody. He has very little support, even from the radicals who believe that changing the government is the best way to move forward – which means moving power into their hands. No one takes him seriously."

No one took me seriously before I became a bookworm, Elaine thought.

"Consider it," Lady Light Spinner said. "I would be happy to have you working for me – and I would keep the Inquisition from taking you away. Freaks like you are *always* dangerous to their beloved status quo."

Elaine nodded, remembering how the Star Council had reacted to her...and they'd *known* that her magical talents hadn't been enhanced. They'd merely known that she possessed enough magical knowledge to make whoever gained possession of her the most powerful – and dangerous – wizard in the world. It was quite possible that the next Grand Sorcerer would order her killed – and the Inquisition would have no choice but to carry out the order. She might be better served finding a place to hide well away from the Golden City.

"I will certainly consider it," Elaine said. The clock on the wall said that it wouldn't be long until dawn. "I have a question. How did you know a way out of Prince Hilarion's mansion?"

Lady Light Spinner laughed. "The Duke of Randor hired a sorcerer to design a series of pocket dimensions that would merge with the loose magic running through the catacombs and allow him access to the tunnels, without allowing anyone else to get into his house. But the sorcerer he hired to construct the network had a prior claim on his loyalty. He could tell me everything, even though he was oath-sworn to secrecy, and he did. I just kept it in reserve until I needed it."

Elaine nodded, thoughtfully. Millicent had sneaked in, rather than use the catacombs, because the secret entrance was a secret without price. If it got out that Lady Light Spinner had managed to gain access to a sealed mansion, there would be political upheaval throughout the Golden City. Sorcerers and aristocrats had several things in common, but the most important one was that they both enjoyed their privacy. Lady Light Spinner would instantly become the most hated person in the city as the families struggled to check all of their wards and links to the underground catacombs.

"I trust I can rely on your discretion," Lady Light Spinner said. "The Inquisition is not supposed to know about this little trick."

"Of course not," Elaine agreed. The Inquisition tried to enforce fair play, rather than try to keep the various aristocratic houses from fighting each other. Their fighting had to be conducted covertly, acknowledging the Grand Sorcerer's dominance...and preventing it from spilling out into the rest of the city. That would draw the wrath of the Grand Sorcerer like nothing else. "Why do you wear a veil?"

Lady Light Spinner looked at her for a long moment...and then drew the veil away from her face, exposing her to Elaine's gaze. Elaine couldn't help recoiling as she took in the scorched and damaged features, the scars running over the woman's face. The only thing normal about her was her eyes, the only part of her body she showed off to the world. Her hair was gone, revealing a scalp that should have belonged to an elderly woman.

"I was like her once," Lady Light Spinner said. There was a catch in her voice, something that caught Elaine's attention. She kept her voice normal through strict discipline. "But there is always a price for power."

Knowledge tumbled through Elaine's mind. There were ways to enhance a person's power, but they could go horrifically wrong. In Lady Light Spinner's case, it was clear that she *hadn't* managed to boost her own power; there was no sign that she was actually insane. She'd attempted a forbidden act and ended up badly scared and mutilated, with nothing to show for the pain she'd inflicted on herself.

She caught herself looking at Lady Light Spinner's body. It was hidden beneath the shapeless robe, but...what had happened to it? Might it be warped and misshapen, or twisted and blackened by the raw magic she'd unleashed...or perhaps it would be normal, a cruel joke from the magic she'd attempted to bend to her will. The spell hadn't dredged out new channels for conducting magic in her mind. It had torn her body apart instead. Elaine wasn't sure that she could have continued to live like that, not knowing that any hint of what had happened to her leaking out would mean her doom. Misshapen freaks were banished from the cities, if they were lucky. It would have been legal for anyone to kill Lady Light Spinner on sight.

"I'm sorry," she said, and meant it. Too many students at the Peerless School were tempted to try to force open their magic channels too early. A brief meeting with someone like Lady Light Spinner might have convinced them that it was a bad idea. "I..."

"I don't need your pity," Lady Light Spinner said, harshly. "Millicent, show her to the door. Now!"

"Yes, Aunt," Millicent said. She was terrifyingly pale. Could it be that she'd never seen her Aunt's face in her entire life? And what would it mean when she realised that the auntie she'd practically worshipped was one of the freaks everyone hated? "Come on...Elaine."

Elaine would have smiled at Millicent's brief inability to remember her name, but she was too tired. All she really wanted to do was go home and sleep.

***

Cass and Karan met her at the door of her apartment as she stumbled inside, having clearly already met Daria when she came home. Daria was sleeping on the floor, still in werewolf form; burned marks covered part of her fur and there were bloodstains around her muzzle. But she'd made it home, presumably giving the book to Dread before going to sleep. Elaine exchanged brief greetings with the two Inquisitors, staggered into her bedroom and fell asleep without even bothering to get undressed. She was so tired that the nightmares that had tormented her since becoming a bookworm failed to make any headway into her mind.

When she awoke, the entire experience seemed like a dream. Had she really burgled a house with Daria and a man called Cat? Had they really encountered Millicent and escaped by the skin of their teeth? And had she really seen a face that was carefully hidden from prying eyes?

Bookworm

Remembering Cat made her shiver. She'd seen too many people die in the last few days, ever since she'd woken up to discover what she'd become, but Cat's death had made a terrifying impression on her. It would have been easy for Elaine to die the same way, by picking up a book with a deadly curse and opening it before checking for unpleasant surprises. She'd known, intellectually, that many of the forbidden texts were guarded by spells that would keep their contents safe from prying eyes, but it was hard to believe it at an emotional level. Books had always been her friends, there for her when she'd had no real human friends of her own. How could they become dangerous?

It was a silly question, she knew. A little knowledge could be a very dangerous thing; mundane books might not be directly harmful, but they contained knowledge that could become lethal very quickly in the wrong hands. Back when the printing press had been invented, there had been various factions insisting that it should be banned, pointing out that allowing people to read might give them unpleasant ideas. An educated lower class was one that knew enough to realise that it was being exploited by its elders and betters. And yet education could turn a person with talent and no training into someone who could change the world.

She was still thinking about it as she washed and dried herself, before pulling on her work clothes. No more dresses for her, at least until she saw Bee again. The thought of him made her stop in her tracks, just for a moment. What would he have said if he'd seen her breaking into a house and stealing a book that killed people who touched it with their bare hands? Or...had he hidden links with Lady Light Spinner? The Lady was a close friend of the Empress of the South. Or...

There was no way to know, she thought firmly as she glanced at herself in the mirror. She looked strictly functional, thankfully. Outside, she could hear voices; Daria, Dread and a couple of others she didn't recognise. Bracing herself, she opened the door and stepped into the living room. The book they'd stolen lay on the table, polluting the air with its mere presence, and Dread was flicking his way through it page by page.

"I am...pleased to see that you survived," Dread said, without looking up. Elaine wondered just how truthful that actually was, even though Inquisitors weren't supposed to be able to lie. Her death would have solved a great many problems for the Inquisition. "You recovered a very rare book. In fact, I was led to believe that this book was destroyed centuries ago."

Elaine shrugged as she sat down facing him, gratefully accepting a cup of hot chocolate from Daria. "I didn't recognise it," she said. It hadn't occurred to her during their meeting with Millicent and then their run to safety that that was unusual. The Great Library was supposed to stock a copy of every forbidden tome in the world, every book that even glancing at the cover could earn a reader the death sentence. "What is it?"

There was a long pause. "I may have contaminated myself," Dread admitted. "The Star Council will not be happy."

Of course not, Elaine thought, sourly. Dread would have absorbed knowledge that had been buried for a very good reason. And, unlike her, he might have been tainted by the residues of power and intent burned into the volume, his very soul threatened with the ultimate corruption. Madness might already be tugging away at his mind.

"Never mind that," Daria said, impatiently. In human form, she seemed to have a scar on her arm and the visible part of her chest, a remember of how badly she'd been hurt during the frantic escape from the building. "What exactly *is* it?"

Dread hesitated. "This is not a standard grimoire," he said, finally. "Most forbidden volumes were copied by dark sorcerers and their slaves, the knowledge being passed down from masters to apprentices...often subject to being lost when the apprentice finally killed the master before he'd learned everything he could. Some of the dark sorcerers wrote down their own spells and charmed the books to remain hidden until they died, whereupon other sorcerers would be able to make use of the knowledge. Dark sorcerers simply don't work together very well."

"Which didn't stop the Witch-King and the necromancers

from nearly destroying us," Daria pointed out, crossing her arms under her chest. "Don't we have an evil prince to stop?"

"It is in the nature of dark sorcerers always to struggle for supremacy," Dread said. "The necromancers might have won if they'd managed to stay united until we were defeated. Instead, they constantly bickered with each other and sometimes turned their legions of undead on their fellow necromancers. It gave us time to regroup and prepare a counter-offensive that eventually destroyed the necromancers.

"The Witch-King knew that the necromancers couldn't win unless they were united," he continued. "We never fully understood how he managed to keep them all in line – until now. This book details the precise procedure for seeding a section of a person's mind inside an unsuspecting victim. The seed eventually takes over completely, creating a whole new person who is almost an exact copy of the magician who created the seed. I believe that the Witch-King, during the years before he declared himself, was finding necromancers and seeding them with his own personality. There was never a second Necromancer's Council; instead, there was just one mind in many bodies."

He grimaced. "The spells here are much more powerful than any we've seen elsewhere," he added. "Powerful enough to overwhelm almost anyone, even a powerful magician. We should be grateful that they were lost for so long."

"I've heard of something like that," Elaine said, slowly. The knowledge from the Great Library hinted at it, although the writers had clearly not known the specifics – or had been too frightened to put pen to paper. "But surely the necromancers would have refused..."

Daria had a more practical objection. "I thought that a person who'd been enslaved would be unable to practice magic," she said. "Wouldn't the new...well, the new Witch-Kings have no power to draw upon?"

"The Witch-King didn't collar them," Dread said, patiently. "His seeds infiltrated their minds and they eventually *became* him, with access to all of his powers and whatever was natural to the bodies they possessed. He may have eventually become one mind with many bodies. And he almost won the war."

Elaine nodded, remembering the descriptions of the final days of the Second Necromantic War. An entire continent had been laid to waste to destroy the Witch-King and his followers.

"This book was written by the Witch-King himself," Dread said. "There were always rumours that he had created a grimoire of his own, but nothing ever surfaced...until now."

He stared down at the blank cover. "Anyone with even the rudimentary magical abilities possessed by the lowest student would eventually be able to use the principles in this book to construct his own spells," he added. "The spell that killed Cat came out of this book. So did the spell that Duke Gama used to charm his private volumes – and the spell that killed him. There is enough in here to take someone from very basic abilities to the very highest levels of magic, all the while turning him into a monster."

Princess Sacharissa gulped. "And it was hidden in Ida for hundreds of years?"

"Almost certainly," Dread said. "And it leads to one final point. This is the proof we need to stop him. The Inquisition will arrest him today."

"I need to be there," Elaine said, before she could stop herself.

"And me," Daria said, firmly. "We both need to be there."

Chapter Thirty-One

"Absolutely out of the question," Dread said, firmly. "Do you have any idea how dangerous it could be?"

A thousand images of maddened or desperate sorcerers fighting their inevitable destruction washed through Elaine's mind. "Yes," she said, "but I should be there anyway. I know more about dark magic than any dark sorcerer."

"That is not a good thing to put on your résumé," Dread said. His eyes met hers and held her gaze. "He's going to be desperate; merely possessing that book is grounds for immediate execution. You will be his target if he realises that you led us to him."

"I need to be there," Elaine insisted. In truth, she suspected that she would never believe that the threat was over until she'd seen Prince Hilarion die. The Inquisition would probably prefer him to die resisting arrest than to surrender, knowing that his knowledge would make him a target for every other sorcerer who wanted to boost his powers. "Please..."

Dread looked at her for a long moment, and then nodded. "Meet us at the Spearpoint in two hours," he ordered, finally. "And you are going to have to obey orders. A duel with a magician powerful enough to become the Grand Sorcerer is never easy – and he could have boosted his powers greatly over the last few years. The Inquisitors won't have time to protect you if Prince Hilarion decides it's time to fight."

"And he will," the Princess said. "He was never at his best when he was backed into a corner."

"I will do as I'm told," Elaine promised. Daria, beside her, nodded shortly. "How many Inquisitors are you going to bring with you?"

"A small army," Dread said. "I've already sent out one set of messages, declaring an alert. The remainder of the force will meet up at the Spearpoint, assuming that Prince Hilarion doesn't decide to run."

Daria leaned forward. "And what if he does?"

"Then we have to improvise," Dread said. "There are really too many people in the Golden City to risk fighting a pitched battle here."

Elaine nodded. The population was high even without the hundreds of thousands of visitors who had flocked to the Golden City in the wake of the Grand Sorcerer's death. An all-out battle between different magical factions was likely to leave half the city in ruins.

"Meet us at the Spearpoint if you don't change your mind," Dread added. "And don't be late. We won't have time to wait."

***

By long convention, dating back to the era before the empire first stumbled into existence, the Spearpoint was technically enemy territory. Upon declaring war, the Emperor would stand in the patch of ground that comprised the Spearpoint and plunge a spear into the ground, symbolically striking the enemy country. The Spearpoint had become a temple to the gods of war after the empire had claimed the entire world, one decorated with statues and medals representing the campaigns that had been fought by the army. One statue was curiously out of place to Elaine's eyes; Valiant, hero of the First Necromantic War – and villain of the Second War. Dread had skimmed through a book written by his greatest hero and had never realised it.

One Inquisitor was terrifying to anyone who had something to feel guilty about – or just suspected that the Inquisitors believed them to be guilty. A small army of Inquisitors was far worse, although Elaine had expected more than twelve men in black robes. Behind them, there was a small platoon of combat magicians and a number of civil guardsmen. The guards would be there mainly to move civilians out of the combat zone, knowing that a single dark magician could overwhelm them within seconds. Elaine didn't feel reassured, even when Dread nodded to her and introduced her to the other Inquisitors. Not all of them looked happy to see a bookworm in the flesh.

Dread glanced around at his squad and then led them onto the street, heading up towards High Tory. None of them spoke out loud, although Elaine had the faint sense that they were communicating somehow on a level she couldn't understand or access. A couple of them even looked like werewolves, complete with the canine features that Millicent had noticed on Daria. Elaine hadn't realised that the Inquisition took werewolves, but it was starting to seem as though a great deal of what everyone *knew* about the Inquisition was false. How many Inquisitors *were* there in the entire world if twelve Inquisitors constituted an army?

"The target is still in his mansion," Dread said, briefing the other Inquisitors. Elaine, tagging along at the rear of the army, barely heard him. "The scouts say that he's clearly preparing for departure. We intend to intercept him before he can leave High Tory."

Elaine had to smile as the implications sunk in. High Tory was the wealthiest place in the city, but it was also the least densely populated. Dread was saving lives at the cost of making some very powerful political enemies. But then, waiting until Prince Hilarion managed to escape into the slums – or the countryside – might have been waiting too long. Who knew what other tricks Prince Hilarion might have picked up from other forbidden books?

The crowd scattered as the Inquisitors marched, even the soldiers and upper-class tourists giving them a wide berth. Interfering with the Inquisition carried stiff penalties, penalties that would break almost anyone. Elaine saw a mother snatching up a child who would otherwise have run out into the street and been trodden on by the Inquisitors. The fearful looks left her feeling bitter, almost jaded. Was this how it felt to be the Grand Sorcerer, knowing that the only thing keeping the city from collapsing into civil unrest was fear of the strongman in the Imperial Palace? Or what if she *had* been boosted into a terrifyingly powerful magician? Would people have stared at her in the streets if they'd seen her? The thought was a depressing one.

Dread issued orders calmly and precisely, ordering the guardsmen to evacuate the surrounding buildings while the Inquisitors prepared their operation. Some of them carried amulets and bracelets that provided specific magical tricks to call upon, ready to test the wards, while others produced long silver swords that seemed to gleam with light. All of them carried wands in holsters attached to their belts, but none of them seemed to need them. They would all be proficient at magic without wands.

She found herself glancing in the direction of Millicent's home and wondering what had happened to her, and her Aunt. Dread had listened to her when she'd told him about Millicent, leaving out the details about the secret passageways and Lady Light Spinner's accident, but he hadn't commented on Millicent's actions. Cheating *was* part of the tradition for the contest, after all, and Millicent *was* one of the nobility. He might have decided to let it pass, rather than start a second political catfight.

"Good," Dread said. His voice carried easily across the square. Elaine looked up from her musings and saw six Inquisitors standing in front of the gates, suggesting that the others had gone to cover the ways out of the mansion. "Set One; go."

Three Inquisitors ran forward, raising amulets charged with carefully prepared magic and pressed them into the wards. Elaine felt the wards suddenly spinning out of control as the Inquisitors started to hack into them, using a technique that she knew she couldn't have matched. But she'd been trying to slip through the wards; the Inquisitors were trying to break them. They didn't need to worry about anyone in the mansion being alerted. Chances were that Prince Hilarion's spies had already warned him about the Inquisitors on their way to High Tory. No doubt every magician who could afford it maintained their own watch on the Inquisition. No one became a powerful sorcerer without bending the rules, giving them all something to feel guilty about.

Elaine was surprised that they hadn't demanded the Prince's surrender, before realising that it would be pointless. There was no exception in the rules for anyone who learned dark magic deliberately. Prince Hilarion would either be executed after interrogation or killed when he tried to resist arrest. The real problem was Count Lucas – who might be innocent – and the slaves inside the building, who definitely were. There was a final flash of light and then the wards collapsed, allowing the second team of Inquisitors to advance forward, wands at the ready. A person appeared at the main doors to the mansion, holding his hands in the air. Count Lucas...

Dread was ready for him. "Count Lucas," he bellowed, using his wand to amplify his voice. "By order of the Star Chamber, you are to be taken into custody and interrogated relating to the learning and use of dark magic, both punishable under the Edict of Year One. If you surrender yourself into our custody, we will determine your guilt or innocence in an interrogation chamber. Refusal to surrender will result in a presumption of guilt and we will not try to take you alive. This is your only warning."

Count Lucas staggered towards Dread, keeping his hands in the air. "He's gone crazy," he said. Elaine's eyesight wasn't perfect, but a simple spell allowed her to study him closely – and see the burn marks on his face. Someone had used a spell to torture him into submission. "You have to stop him."

Dread produced a pair of charmed handcuffs. "I have to take you into custody," he said. "Turn around and place your hands behind your back."

Elaine could see the Count's reluctance before he finally complied. The Inquisitors laced their handcuffs with magic, ensuring that they did more than make it difficult for a person to escape. Any attempt to use magic, even the smallest spell, would result in immediate pain, flooding the mind and making it impossible for the captive to concentrate. No magician would be happy if he was deprived of the ability to work magic, even if it was the only way to guarantee his survival. But if he was guilty...

She shook her head. Count Lucas would have had nothing to lose if he was guilty.

The door swung open again and a string of half-naked women ran out, carrying whatever weapons they could. There was no sign of the soldiers who served in the Prince's private army, but the slaves would be a serious problem. Or maybe not; the third set of Inquisitors stepped forward and started casting stunning spells towards the girls. They were defenceless, urged on only by their collars, and easy to take down. The guardsmen removed them at once, taking them to a hospital where the druids would remove their collars and take care of them. Once freed, they would definitely provide valuable intelligence; Elaine hoped that they could tell her what had happened to the slaves who had been freed earlier.

And then Prince Hilarion himself walked out into the courtyard.

Elaine knew something was badly wrong with him even before she met his eyes. His form was shifting rapidly, as if his body were warping and he was trying to use glamours to maintain a normal appearance. Lady Light Spinner had a stable, if mutilated form; she could tailor her spells to hide it. But the Prince was still trying to stabilise his body. She shivered as he started to twitch, as if hundreds of tiny spiders were running around him at the very edges of reality. Every time she tried to look directly at them, they seemed to slip back into the corner of her eye.

"I am the Grand Sorcerer," Prince Hilarion boomed. Beside her, Daria let out a suppressed snicker. Elaine elbowed her hard, realising that Prince Hilarion was completely mad. "I am your lord and master. Bow before me and I will let you live!"

The waves of power surrounding him were terrifying. He might not have had the sheer presence of the late Grand Sorcerer, but the combination of raw power and mental compulsion was almost too strong to resist. Elaine felt her knees tremble; behind her, she heard several of the guardsmen falling to their knees. The remainder were backing away as quickly as possible, unwilling to face a maddened sorcerer. Even the Inquisitors seemed stunned, although Elaine could sense several of them weaving complex spells. There *were* ways to take down a sorcerer who was, in theory, more powerful than the rest of the world.

"You have been infected by dark magic," Dread said. Elaine understood, finally, why the Princess admired Dread, even felt a little attraction to him. Nothing really seemed to faze him, even the dangers of facing a mad sorcerer who could probably break through his wards and kill him with raw force. "Your Highness, try to think rationally. Is this really what you want?"

Prince Hilarion seemed to stumble, as if the pressure pushing down on his fragile body was growing too powerful to endure. Dread's voice stayed calm and reasonable as he spoke, trying to talk Prince Hilarion out of fighting the Inquisitors. The Prince was powerful, but maddened by the currents of magic flowing through his brain. Who knew *what* would make sense to someone who couldn't think straight? Drunken men did crazy things...and this drunkard was as powerful as a minor god.

Dread repeated his question as the Prince started to advance forward again, showing no fear at the monstrous sight. "Is this really what you want?"

"Yes," the Prince snarled, and blasted out a blinding white sheet of energy. Elaine thought for a horrified moment that Dread was dead, before realising that the Inquisitor had jumped to one side at the last moment. Her magical sensitivity almost drove her to her knees; Prince Hilarion had just unleashed enough power to wreck half the city and create a whole new Blight. Maybe she could beat him if she drew on the wild magic in the Blight...but there was no time. The Prince lashed out again and reality started to flicker, the Inquisitors shielding themselves as best they could. "I am the Grand Sorcerer!"

Dread tossed a charm at the Prince's back. It was a simple tickling charm, one that might be used by a trainee wizard teasing his best friend, one she wouldn't have expected anyone to use against a maddened wizard. But Prince Hilarion spun around and unleashed another blast of light towards Dread, striking the mansion and blowing right through the magic infused into the stone. The front of the mansion started to collapse as Dread vanished in a flash of light, reappearing perched on top of the wall. Prince Hilarion pointed one twisted finger at him and threw another blast of magic, only to see Dread fall down behind the wall and the magic fly harmlessly off into the air.

Another Inquisitor ran forward, zapped Prince Hilarion with a hex that older students learned and used to torment the lesser students. Prince Hilarion spun around, but before he could crush the Inquisitor like a bug another appeared out of nowhere. Elaine watched, barely able to comprehend the levels of magic Prince Hilarion was unleashing, but finally understanding what the Inquisitors were doing. That level of power should be enough to allow Prince Hilarion to win easily, if he had time to stop and think about what he was doing. They were keeping him off balance, forcing him to react emotionally rather than rationally. He was too maddened to even think through a way to use his vastly greater power to become Grand Sorcerer.

An Inquisitor fell, knocked back by a wave of magic, but the others kept leaping in, striking out at him and then jumping back. Prince Hilarion's hand flew off when one of the Inquisitors cut it with his sword, causing a mass of tainted magic to spill out of the wound. Someone who had been to the Peerless School would have known basic charms to prevent wounds from growing any worse, if not directly healing them, but Prince Hilarion had never had a classical education. His magic was spewing out of control and harming him more than healing him.

"You," Prince Hilarion bellowed. He strode towards Elaine, brushing aside the Inquisitor who tried to distract him. His form seemed to be wavering now, as if...*something* from another dimension was trying to force itself into his body. Elaine could feel reality screaming in pain as the maddened Prince exerted his will. Some of the books in her head warned that there were entities out there, scratching at the walls of reality and trying to force their way into the human realm. "You did this to me."

Elaine stared, transfixed by fear, as Prince Hilarion reached out towards her. There was no longer anything remotely human about his body. The warps seemed to be reshaping him into a giant insect, almost a spider. She felt a hot trickle around her legs as the blood seemed to boil in her body, just before a dark-clad form caught her and hurled her away to safety. The shock of the impact jarred her back to reality, just in time to see the Inquisitor who had saved her being burned alive by Prince Hilarion. He seemed to be screaming in pain as fires tore through his head, yet somehow he remained alive, caught eternally on the very brink of death. Prince Hilarion was warping time around him, keeping him in mortal stasis...

She reached into her knowledge for a spell, but nothing came to mind. He had to be drained...

And then Dread rammed a sword through his neck, severing his head from his body. Prince Hilarion seemed to stop, stumbling to his knees...and then, horrifically, he seemed to reform into a single being of darkened light. Elaine cried out in horror as the ground started to shatter beneath her feet, just before the other Inquisitors joined in. They hacked the Prince to pieces faster than he could repair himself.

The light faded and died. A single body, seemingly unmarked, hit the ground.

Dread checked it, carefully, and then looked up at his men. "He's dead," he said, simply. "It's over."

Chapter Thirty-Two

"I was so scared."

Elaine couldn't stop shaking, even though she was in the Watchtower and surrounded by Inquisitors. Her stained clothes had been replaced and she'd washed, but she still felt dirty – and ashamed. When the maddened Prince had come for her, her mind kept reminding her, she'd frozen rather than fled. She hadn't even been able to save her life. An *Inquisitor* had saved her at the cost of his own.

"Everyone is scared from time to time," Cass said. The female Inquisitor had showered alongside her and changed into another set of black robes. She managed to make them look almost appealing on her. "I was scared when I saw my first demon, or the monster someone had shaped from shadow and turned into a personal guard dog. Fear isn't the worst thing in the world; it's how you react to fear that proves what you are."

"I froze," Elaine reminded her. "What does that say about me?"

"That you need more training and experience," Cass said. She checked her wand and a small array of magical tools in her belt and then headed for the door. Inquisitors seemed to take even less time washing than Elaine did. "I think you did fine, all things considered. Come on."

The interior of the Watchtower was buzzing with Inquisitors and City Guardsmen, some of whom looked at Elaine as if they didn't understand what she was doing there. It was a busy day for them, Elaine realised, as she saw a line of people in handcuffs being escorted down to the cells buried under the mountain. All of Prince Hilarion's private army – and his staff – had to be picked up and held until the exact nature of their service was revealed. They might have known what he had in mind, or they might have been innocent dupes. The Inquisitors couldn't afford to let them remain in the city until the truth came out.

"We don't normally allow strangers into the interrogation zone," Cass commented, as they passed through a set of the most complex wards Elaine had ever seen. She felt magic pressing down around her, suppressing any urge she might have felt to use magic herself. A sense that someone – or something – was watching her nagged at her mind as Cass led her through a pair of stone doors. The Inquisitors knew that magicians made dangerous criminals and did whatever it took to keep them under control. "Do *not* try to enter any of the cells without permission."

They walked down a long corridor, passing doors that led into small cells, each one barely large enough to swing a cat. Some of them were occupied by criminals who looked up at her as she passed, others seemed empty to her eyes until she realised that they were occupied by the gang of thieves who had discovered a way to turn themselves invisible permanently. The Inquisitors had caught up with them anyway, probably using werewolves to track them down and throw them into jail. They'd be working on ways to get the spell off them before fitting them with collars and sending them to the salt mines.

Two guards, both wearing full Inquisitor robes, stopped them as they reached another set of doors and questioned Cass briefly before allowing them into the room. It was dark, so dark that Elaine found it hard to see at first until the light came up suddenly, revealing a handful of dark figures surrounding a chair. Count Lucas sat in the chair, pinned down by a beam of light that seemed to come from miles overhead, his eyes staring wildly around him as he tried to see his tormentors. A spider's net of wards surrounded him, slowly wearing down his resistance to the point where he wouldn't even be able to *think* of lying to the Inquisition. Elaine felt a flash of sympathy that she wasn't quite able to suppress. Even if he were found innocent and released, Count Lucas would always have the memory of having his mind ground down to the point where he couldn't hide anything from his interrogators. The knowledge in her mind confirmed that the spells the Inquisitors were using could cause permanent damage to a person's mind.

"I knew nothing about his plans," Count Lucas protested. He certainly *seemed* to be telling the truth, but the Inquisitors didn't appear to be convinced. They fired questions at him, sometimes asking the same question over and over again, a technique that would make it hard for the Count to stick to anything but the truth. "He zapped me as soon as we got home from the party, turned me into a helpless witness...I swear it before all the gods!"

"But he was staying in your house," Dread's voice said. "How could you, a candidate for the position of Grand Sorcerer, not sense what he had brought *into* your house?"

"I didn't sense anything," Count Lucas screamed. Sweat was visible on his forehead as he started to struggle against the light. "I don't *know* what happened!"

"Your house contained no less than five books on the proscribed list," another Inquisitor said. Elaine knew that the true answer was more like six, although the Witch-King's personal volume hadn't been on the list because everyone who had known about its existence had believed that it had been destroyed a long time ago. "Even *possessing* those books is an automatic death sentence. You would certainly never be accepted as Grand Sorcerer...why didn't you keep a close eye on what your friend was doing?"

"Because he was my friend," Count Lucas said. "Don't you care about your friends? Or don't you skulls have any friends?"

The Inquisitors ignored the insult. "Prince Hilarion thought he could become Grand Sorcerer," he said. "Why did you believe that he had a chance?"

"I didn't believe that he had a chance," Count Lucas said. "I thought he would lose, that perhaps he would back out and support me in exchange for later considerations. And I thought if I kept him close..."

Dread nodded to Cass and led the way out of the room into a smaller, well-lit chamber. "They think Count Lucas was a honest dupe," he said, shortly. The interrogation had clearly been going on ever since the Count had arrived at the Watchtower. "There is no way he should be able to conceal the truth from us now...unless there is something in the forbidden texts?"

Elaine started at the question. "I don't think that anything I know about would help him to resist for very long," she said. "If he was an immensely powerful wizard he might be able to brush off the spells, but that would be noticeable – wouldn't it?"

"It certainly should be," Dread agreed, dryly. "But someone bringing one of the darkest texts in the world into your mansion should *also* be noticeable."

"I don't think that Count Lucas set up the wards," Elaine said, slowly. "If they weren't directly linked to his mind, he wouldn't be able to use them with as much...skill as the original builder. They might have missed the book altogether."

"Possibly," Dread said. He shook his head. "We'll keep working on him. If we clear him as innocent...we will have to convince him to withdraw from the contest anyway. At the very least, he has been incredibly careless and we cannot risk that in a Grand Sorcerer."

Elaine scowled as a thought occurred to her. "Couldn't he have been...programmed somehow by Prince Hilarion? Like Duke Gama programmed me?"

"I wouldn't have said so," Dread said. "Subtle commands work better when they're vague; you were given an urge to go to Ida and allowed to come up with your own *justification* for *why* you wanted to visit Ida. Someone more powerful than yourself, someone with more self-control, might have started to ask *why* you wanted to visit Ida. At that point, the subtle spell would probably have lost its grip on your mind.

"But programming someone to ignore something so dangerous is a great deal harder," he continued. "A single textbook of dark magic would be so dangerous that the controller would have to resort to more powerful spells to keep it from the target's awareness. Those spells tend to have unfortunate effects on a person's intelligence – and somebody *would* notice."

He led her through a series of guarded doors until they reached a larger room. The chill in the air struck her the moment they walked through the door; the cold light blazing down from high overhead revealed a body lying on an examination table. Prince Hilarion looked as handsome in death as he had been in life, although she could sense the aroma of rotting magic surrounding his corpse. The warped body he'd possessed at the end of his life was gone.

"Reverted to normal," Dread said, seriously. "Luckily for his father, he didn't have the power to shift his body permanently into a higher plane – or we would never have been able to stop him without scorching half the city as well. His brain shows all the signs of dark arts dementia, insanity caused by using the dark arts to boost one's powers. The druids think that he was dying even as he made his desperate bid to escape us."

Elaine wasn't surprised, somehow, to recognise the druid who had examined Prince Hilarion. It was the same person who had examined her after she'd been hit by Duke Gama's spell.

"His brain has been completely destroyed," the druid said. He shook his head sadly. "I'm surprised he managed to last as long as he did, even though his thoughts were extending into other dimensions. I don't think he would have had the discipline to trap his soul permanently in a lifeless body."

"And his body is here," Dread said. "Are we sure that it *is* Prince Hilarion?"

"The body matches the signature of the blood taken from him when he was a baby," the druid said, briskly. "He was confirmed as a legitimate child and registered as a lawful heir to the throne of Ida. This is not a fetch or some other form of magical duplicate. This is what remains of Prince Hilarion."

Elaine closed her eyes. It had been just over a week since she'd become the bookworm and there was so much that she didn't understand. Why had Prince Hilarion wanted her in the first place if he already had the Witch-King's book? Had he wanted the rest of the knowledge in the Great Library? Or was there some aspect to his plan that they hadn't understood before he died?

"He may have already been insane," Dread said, when she raised the issue. "Insane people never make sense at the best of times – and insane sorcerers are prone to do almost anything without having a rational justification."

"I do wonder about that," the druid said. "There was nothing particularly *subtle* in the way he attempted to enhance his magic potential. If he'd been doing it for years before he came to the Golden City, he would already have been mentally crippled. Even the most intensely disciplined mind would have trouble coping when the very fabric of their reality was crumbling around them."

"The Princess did say that her brother didn't seem to be insane," Dread mused. "Are you suggesting that he used the spells to give himself vast power when he knew that he'd been found out and we were breathing down his neck?"

"It certainly looks that way," the Druid said.

"But that makes little sense," a voice said, from behind them. Daria strode into the chamber, escorted by Karan and another Inquisitor. Now she knew what signs to look for, Elaine had no trouble in recognising the Inquisitor as a werewolf. "If he knew he'd been detected, why not flee the city?"

"He may have thought that he could have won," the druid said. "People who use magic to enhance their powers are never rational. He wouldn't be the first magician to doom himself by opening his mind, firmly convinced that he could handle the sudden shock when the new channels in his mind started to flow. If he'd been rational when he confronted the Inquisition..."

Elaine remembered the waves of power rolling off Prince Hilarion and shivered. The Peerless School taught that magic was nothing without control. Even the merest magician, someone so weak that they would never be offered a chance to study at the Peerless School, could kill himself if he failed to develop proper control. There were plenty of cautionary tales about children who accidentally set fire to their bedding, or older teenagers, driven by teenage hormones, who wreaked havoc in a person's mind. Control, her tutors had told her time and time again, was the key to becoming an effective magician. A magician without control would probably destroy himself before he could become a threat to anyone else.

And Prince Hilarion hadn't been formally trained at the Peerless School. It seemed a neat answer to the questions they hadn't even been able to form. The Prince hadn't known what he was doing, had lost control very quickly and had been unable to pull himself back together in time to fight the Inquisitors. And yet...where did *she* fit in? Come to think of it, where did Prince Hilarion's father and his kingdom fit into the entire puzzle? Someone had worked hard to ensure that Elaine – or someone – became a bookworm, providing a way to pull knowledge out of the Great Library without triggering any alarms. Where did Elaine herself fit into the puzzle?

She looked down at the Prince's body and wondered. "Is...is he my father?"

"I would have said that he was too young to be your father," Dread said. "He's only thirty, according to the records. He would have had to have fathered you when he was seven years old if he was your father."

"Unless the orphanage records were tampered with," Elaine said. It was an uncomfortable thought, but it *was* possible. "I might be fourteen now instead of twenty-three..."

The druid laughed, not unkindly. "I think you will discover that orphanage records are better than that," he said. "We were charged with studying them all after your little...accident and you have definitely been around for twenty-three years."

"There's an easy way to check," Daria said, impatiently. She leaned forward and sniffed at the body, drawing back in shock. "Most of the body's original scent has been obliterated, but there's enough left for me to get a sense of what he was. He wasn't your father, Elaine."

Elaine shook her head, sadly.

"You should be relieved," Dread said. "Did you really want him to be your father?"

"You might be better off not knowing," the druid agreed. "There was a really upper-class lady who paid a thousand Crowns to have her family tree worked out...and then she had to pay another *three* thousand Crowns to have it hushed up."

"The matter isn't quite over," Dread said, as they returned to the more comfortable parts of the Watchtower. "Once we have a new Grand Sorcerer, we will move in on Ida and find out what was going on in that mountainous state. It seems to me as if Prince Hilarion had his father completely under his control; it is possible that the old man has collapsed with his son's death, depending on just what spells were used to take control of him. In any case, we can afford to wait a few more days. The contest is set for three days from now."

Elaine nodded. Lady Light Spinner had been right about at least one thing; there were only three competitors left in the contest. Maybe two, if Kane had decided to bow out gracefully and leave the more powerful sorcerers to face one another in combat. Or whatever they had to do to prove themselves worthy of the title.

"The new Grand Sorcerer will also be the one who decides what is to become of you," Dread said. The way he said it sent shivers running down the back of her spine. "The Star Chamber isn't ungrateful to you for what you did, but you do represent a considerable danger to the status quo. You don't seem to have been...contaminated by the darker spells that were dumped into your mind, yet anyone with enough power could capture you and drain you of all the knowledge you possess. Prince Hilarion might have targeted you because his appetite for dark magic grew stronger after he read the Witch-King's book."

"Elaine saved you all," Daria said, sharply. Her face seemed to become more wolfish for a long chilling moment. "How can you threaten to kill her?"

"We know what she did for us," Dread said. For a moment, he looked old; old enough to be Elaine's father. "But we also know that her mere existence presents a powerful risk to the empire. Someone could capture her and make her talk. And then we would have another Prince Hilarion on our hands, perhaps more than one."

Elaine understood, even though the concept of the Inquisitors arguing over her eventual fate was terrifying. Dread was right, perhaps righter than he knew. If she could be tempted into violating Daria's privacy, what else could she be tempted into doing?

"I understand," she said. "I won't leave the city until after you decide what to do with me."

Dread nodded. "Go home, get some rest...I'll leave Cass and Karan with you until after the contest," he said. As bodyguards and watchdogs, Elaine knew. They'd never been anything else. "And I suggest that you light a candle in your favourite temple as a sign of thanks. The situation could have become a great deal worse."

He shrugged. "But we nipped it in the bud," he added. "If nothing else, you played a vital role in saving the entire city. We will never forget what you did for us."

"If it's really over," Daria said, pensively. "I seem to recall that gratitude never lasts very long."

Chapter Thirty-Three

"I'm surprised that you have never been here before," Bee said. "This place is famous around the entire world."

Elaine shrugged, thoughtfully. The Great Museum, unlike the Great Library, was open to everyone, allowing them to view artefacts from a thousand years of empire and magical development. It had always been in the Golden City, but Elaine had never visited before realising that she might not have that long to live. She had privately resolved to cram as much as she could into her last two weeks of life before the Inquisitors decided to kill her. It would have been nice to believe that they would spare her life, but she knew, better than they did, just how dangerous her mere existence was to the established order. She honestly couldn't see anything else they could do.

"I never came here before," she admitted. Bee gave her an odd look, as if even he could tell that she was acting strangely. She'd gone to his apartment the previous evening, practically dragged him into bed and spent the night curled up beside him. It no longer mattered to her what Bee really wanted, if he wanted a girl to marry or a girl in every city. All that mattered was living a little before the Inquisitors killed her. "It was just..."

She shrugged. "I just kept putting it off," she said. But the orphanage tutors had never taken the homeless children on field trips. They'd been more concerned with teaching the skills that would make the orphans capable of holding basic jobs. The only part of her pre-Peerless School schooling she remembered with any enthusiasm had been the tutor who'd taught her to read. "Thank you for coming with me."

Bee smiled, holding her hand. It was funny how comforting she found that gesture, even though she knew that he could do nothing to help her once the new Grand Sorcerer was enthroned and made a decision about her future. At least

Lady Light Spinner owed her some gratitude. Kane didn't know her and Administrator Mentor knew her as a girl who had been sent to him for punishment, if he remembered her at all. But then, Lady Light Spinner knew – already – that Elaine knew secrets that should never be spoken out loud. That alone comprised a good reason to kill her.

"You're welcome," Bee said, looking over at one of the cabinets. "Do you think that that is actually the sword of the Witch-King?"

Elaine followed his gaze. The greatest of heroes – and villains – carried swords that were far more than just swords. Some had carried an entrapped demon within their metal, turning them into unstoppable weapons, while others were infused with magic that gave them a certain kind of intelligence. The sword in front of them certainly *looked* impressive – it was dark, so dark that it gave the impression of absorbing all light into its darkness – but she knew better than to assume that it was real. An artefact created by the Witch-King would be targeted by every would-be dark sorcerer with delusions of grandeur. If the Grand Sorcerer hadn't been able to destroy it, he would have tossed it into a volcano or sent it spinning through the dimensions to somewhere far beyond the reach of mankind. The dark sword in front of them was nothing more than a duplicate, warded just enough to prevent anyone from discovering its true nature.

"Perhaps," she said, finally. Why spoil Bee's illusions? "Its true name has been lost long ago."

Bee shrugged and moved onto the next cabinet, housing potion gourds from a tribe of warriors who had resisted the empire for nearly a hundred years, thanks to potions – brewed by their druids – that gave their men superhuman strength. Eventually, the empire had come to terms with them, after developing counters that neutralised the effects of their magic potion. Two nearby cabinets showed two warriors from the tribe – a short thin man and a tall fat man, both smiling pleasantly at the crowds – in full tribal outfits. Had anyone really shown off half of their chest when fighting? The short one carried a sword, but it didn't look like he had ever really needed it. Below them, a small black-

and-white dog pretended to cock its leg against the side of the cage.

Bee seemed more interested in mundane artefacts recovered from the era before the First Necromantic War. Elaine smiled as she considered a blackened piece of metal, recognising it – from the knowledge in her head – as a kind of iron dragon. The pre-war empire had been supposed to be a wonderful place, although wonderful was always determined by the people writing the history books. They'd had magic and technology that her own era was just starting to redevelop. And then the undead had risen from the grave and set out to slaughter the entire world. By the time the fighting had finally come to an end, the empire had been devastated...

And then the Witch-King had come within moments of final victory.

"They don't tell us much about the wars in the South," Bee said, as they studied drawings and paintings of battles between the living breathing humans and the undead hordes. One of the undead was easy to stop – their limbs could be chopped off, or their bodies incinerated by magic – but an entire army was a far tougher proposition. The undead grew smarter as they grew in numbers, yet even without brains four of them could hack a living soldier to death while he was trying to destroy one of their comrades. And a single bite would be fatal to their victim. "We never really believed that they were as horrific as you claim."

"Even when the refugees fled to you?" Elaine asked, mildly. "And your own soldiers saw the undead walking out of the water and advancing on your shores?"

Bee nodded, pointing towards one of the other paintings. The Battle of the Silver Desolation had been the first major battle between the Witch-King's forces and the Southern Continent, which had largely believed itself isolated from the necromancers and their war. But the Witch-King had known just how vitally important the South had been in the First Necromantic War and he had taken steps to destroy it in the Second War. An army of undead didn't need to breathe, or to rest, so there was nothing stopping them from marching under water until they reached the South and then walking up onto the beach. The South had suddenly found the war developing a new front located within their territory.

"All we had were the undead," Bee reminded her. "They were nasty, true, but the Witch-King never turned the fullness of his wrath on us. The rest of the tales..."

Elaine nodded. The Battle of the Bottles, where both sides had been forced to unleash demons against the other. Thankfully, even the Witch-King had realised that unleashing demons would eventually destroy the entire world and refrained from unleashing any more until the very last days of the war. It had been too late to save his base from being scorched by the first Grand Sorcerer. And the Battle of the Rift, where a sorcerer had opened a canyon below the ranks of the undead, watched them fall into thin air and then closed the canyon again, crushing them to bloody pulp. It was said that nothing grew on the land tainted by the undead. And the Battle of Long Beach, where a handful of soldiers and a single combat magician had held off the undead just long enough for reinforcements to arrive. They had all died, but they'd saved two whole cities from a fate worse than death.

Memories that weren't hers flickered through her head. They hadn't all been victories, not by a long chalk. The Storming of Helgoland, when the undead had marched up to the walls, building a pile of their bodies large enough to let them climb over and run down into the city, killing everyone inside. And they'd all risen as undead and joined the colossal army. If anyone had survived, no records had been taken of their existence. There was the Sack of Kamet, a small town that happened to be in the path of a demonic army; rumour had it that anyone who visited the remains of the city heard the screams of the damned as they promised their captors everything, if only they would let them go free. And not all of the atrocities had been committed by monsters. One city had been sacked by an army of humans, humans who had been under no magical compulsion at all, and the population had been systematically robbed, raped and killed. It said something about the final years of the war that no one had raised a voice in complaint when the state that had provided the army was wiped out completely by the Grand Sorcerer, without a single child being spared. In a war that had had far too many atrocities committed by all sides, the Sack of Kamet still stood out as a monument to human barbarity. The demons had been demons; the Witch-King had been mad. What excuse was there for humans who turned on their fellows so savagely?

Bee caught her arm. "Are you all right?"

"Just tired," Elaine said. She managed a wink. They hadn't managed to get much sleep last night and that had mainly been her fault. Not that Bee had been complaining, of course. He'd been a willing participant in their shared pleasure. "Maybe we should move on to the next section."

The next chamber paid homage to all the Grand Sorcerers, from the very first one to the man who had died only two weeks ago, leaving a power vacuum in the heart of the Golden City. They hadn't stated his date of death yet, Elaine noted; they wouldn't do that until the next Grand Sorcerer was in place, with the city swearing loyalty to him. She couldn't remember if there had been a reason for the tradition or if it had been someone's whim that had become tradition when everyone had forgotten why it had been started in the first place.

She smiled at the thought that they'd tried to cover up his death. Every magician in the world would have felt the Grand Sorcerer die. Maybe it could have been hidden from the rest of the population, but Elaine doubted that it would have lasted more than a few days. Even up to his death, the Grand Sorcerer had been very busy hearing petitions and standing in judgement of magical crimes. A few days absence would have started tongues wagging all over the city.

"I never understood why you all swear loyalty to the Grand Sorcerer," Bee said, as they looked at the last painting. The Grand Sorcerer seemed to be scowling disapprovingly at them. He'd never been fond of the perks of power and had been known to sack his assistants for enriching themselves or using their positions to surround themselves with luxury. It had been a policy that had found favour with most of the city, who wanted their taxes spent on important issues rather than enriching politicians. "Why do you swear to serve him?"

They didn't, Elaine knew. Few magicians would willingly

swear an oath that would place them so firmly under someone's control. They'd sworn to uphold the system instead, to ensure that the next Grand Sorcerer was chosen properly rather than hundreds of wizards and magicians fighting it out for supremacy. Civil war within the Golden City would have wiped out most of the population and brought the empire crashing down in ruins. It crossed her mind that that might have been what the mad Prince had had in mind, but even that didn't explain everything about his plan. She wondered briefly if he'd prepared something that would have allowed him to rise from the dead, yet the Inquisitors would have thought to check for that. They might have decided to destroy the body rather than returning it to Ida for burial. No one who bore witness to the battle that had nearly destroyed High Tory would have spoken out against such a decision.

"Because that's how the system works," she said, finally. It wasn't something she felt comfortable with, even with Bee. The first Grand Sorcerer had devised a structure to prevent his comrades from fighting...and dressed it up neatly to prevent them from rebelling against it. "We don't question it."

She turned...and stopped dead as she saw a hulking figure standing in the doorway. Judd was standing there, his immense form blocking the light. Elaine was astonished to see him – as far as she knew, he was never allowed to leave Lord Howarth's mansion – and why was Lord Howarth showing any interest in her now? What had changed that he actually knew about?

"You are summoned to face your Guardian," Judd said, in his grating voice. "You will accompany me to Howarth Hall."

"Now wait a minute," Bee said, quickly. "We're on a date..."

"I have to go," Elaine said, wearily. She'd never actually formally claimed emancipation from Lord Howarth, if only because he'd shown no interest in trying to actually serve as her Guardian. An oversight, she realised; an oversight that she should have corrected while she had a chance. Lord Howarth might believe that he could push her into working openly for him. "Can you go back to Daria and let her know what happened?"

Bee stared at her for a long moment, and then nodded. "Good luck," he said, and gave her a kiss. Elaine returned it, wondering if watching them kissing would irritate Judd. But his expressionless face was still blank when Elaine broke the kiss and stepped up to the butler. Bee looked after her. "Do you want me to come meet you...?"

"Lord Howarth will summon you when he wishes to meet with you," Judd informed him. He looked back at Elaine. "You will accompany me now."

He spun around and marched out of the building, moving almost like a parody of a soldier. People saw him coming and scattered out of his way, even the ones who couldn't sense his true nature. Judd seemed like an unstoppable iron dragon as he ploughed through the streets. Elaine followed him, trying to resist the temptation to try to pump him for information. Judd had never been a great conversationalist and much of his conversations to her over the years had been thoroughly unpleasant. No wonder people were scared of him.

The walk to Howarth Hall took less time than she had expected, but she was panting because of the effort involved in keeping up with Judd. She saw the gates open to admit them as they approached, before closing behind them with an ominous thud. This time, the gardeners had introduced a collection of wild birds from the far islands into the garden, clearly trying to maintain the appearance of wealth and power. She wondered, absently, how long it would be before Lord Howarth ran out of time and had to admit that he was broke?

She walked through the interior of the house, looking around. One side effect of Duke Gama's spell had been to enhance her memory, even the parts of her mind that didn't deal directly with magic. Some of the tacky but expensive artworks and trinkets were gone, suggesting that they had been sold on to produce money for their owner. Others seemed to have been moved to one side, earmarked for disposal. A painting that had been charmed to hold an impression of a long-dead woman's personality – she had screamed abuse at anyone who came into the house without the proper level of aristocratic blood, including Elaine – had been removed from the wall and placed against it, blocking the woman's sight. Elaine guessed that she'd seen Lord Howarth selling off the family trinkets one by one and hadn't been shy about making her opinion known.

Judd opened the door to Lord Howarth's study and allowed her to walk inside. Lord Howarth was nowhere to be seen, but as Elaine sat down she realised that a number of the books on the bookshelves had been removed. She felt a brief pang of pity for them – they'd been published in the days before the printing press – before hearing Lord Howarth coming down the other corridor towards her. The door crashed open and Lord Howarth stepped inside.

He looked ghastly. His clothes were a mess – he'd always prided himself on being a dandy – and his face was blotched with the effects of too much alcohol. Elaine guessed that he hadn't been able to pay the druids for rejuvenation spells and treatments that would have helped mitigate the worst effects of whatever he was drinking.

"Lost everything," he said, as he slumped into a chair. "Will lose the home soon; will lose everything soon. Will have to leave the city and go die out in the countryside. But house there no longer exists..."

Elaine frowned. He sounded drunk too, she realised. His words were slurring together as he spoke, almost as if he couldn't quite focus on whatever he was trying to say. If he was broke, if he was running out of things he could sell without tipping off the rest of his creditors, his social standing was about to drop to rock bottom. Elaine felt a flicker of pity, even though he'd ignored her for most of her life. She doubted that *that* was about to change.

"Had only one thing left," Howarth muttered. "Someone came to me; offered to pay my debts. Gave me enough Crowns to go to the club and get lucky on the tables and..."

He gasped, almost as if he couldn't speak the words out loud. "Only thing I have left is you," he said. Elaine realised what he meant in an awful moment, just before she felt strong hands grabbing her neck. How the hell hadn't she sensed someone behind her? "I sold you. I gave you to someone who wanted you and..."

Elaine started to struggle, trying to draw on her magic, but there was a brilliant flash of light and she plunged down into darkness.

Chapter Thirty-Four

"I know you're awake," a calm voice said. "You may as well open your eyes and join me for a drink."

Elaine cursed inwardly. She'd come back to awareness only ten minutes ago, but she'd kept her eyes closed in the hope of not alerting them to her listening ears. Instead, whoever was in the room had somehow sensed her awakening and waited, patiently, for her to open her eyes. All she'd been able to feel was that she had been placed in a chair and metal bracelets had been wrapped around her hands and ankles, as well as making it harder for her to work magic. Escape would be almost impossible.

She sighed and opened her eyes, trying to shield them against the light. A man was looking down at her, studying her thoughtfully. She recognised him – and then wondered why she was so surprised. Wizard Kane *also* wanted to become Grand Sorcerer and Elaine was *still* the quickest way to gaining the knowledge that would make someone the most powerful person in the world. And very little was known of his background....

Something clicked in her mind as she realised who he resembled. The colouring wasn't entirely correct, and the eyes certainly weren't, but the cheek structure was unmistakeable. Kane looked like a younger version of Duke Gama. Elaine had only seen graven images of the Duke, or she would have recognised him earlier. And yet he didn't *look* as though he had come from Ida.

She smiled. "You're the Duke's son, aren't you?" she asked. "His illegitimate son."

Kane didn't bother to try to deny it. "My father seduced a woman who was part of a visiting mission to Ida," he said, without bitterness. "She got pregnant; her family were furious and threatened to kill her for having a child with a man she hadn't married. And my father couldn't marry her because he was already married." He shrugged. "Not that I blame him for cheating. His *legitimate* wife is so cold that no one would dare put their manhood inside her, for fear of it freezing solid and then breaking off."

He chuckled. "The bitch made my life hell for the first few years," he added. "It wasn't until Hilarion came along that she lightened up a little, partly because I got on well with the little Prince. We were close friends for quite some time. Oh, there were times when I felt bitter because any son the bitch had would inherit everything my father owned, but...well, Hilarion was being groomed as the Crown Prince and he *hated* the protocol lessons. And my father was decent enough to ensure that I got a good education too."

Elaine stared at him, trying to reconcile everything she'd learned in Ida with what Kane was telling her. "But I am forgetting my manners," Kane said. He picked up a cup and passed it to her. "You can move enough to drink, but not enough to get out of the chair."

He was right, Elaine realised, but she hesitated to drink. "I shouldn't worry about poison," Kane added, almost as if he had read her mind. "Right now, I can drug you or poison you or do *anything* to you. Why would I bother to trick you into drinking poison?"

Elaine took a sip of the water, taking the opportunity to look around the small room. It was depressingly familiar; a magician's workroom. A large wooden table provided space for the magician to work on his magic, a shelf held a small pile of reference texts and a number of jars contained various ingredients for magic potions. A couple – eye of newt, skin of frog – were familiar, but the rest meant nothing to her. She looked up as her eyes caught a motion and saw a small birdcage, holding a diminutive winged humanoid. The fairy looked back at her, her tiny porcelain-like face disturbingly human. Fairies were not intelligent, everyone knew, but few humans could bring themselves to harm one directly. And yet crushed fairy wings were a vital ingredient for several potions.

Reluctantly, she looked up at Kane. "You do realise that my Guardian has no legal right to sell me?"

"I think that that hardly matters," Kane said, dryly. "The

important issue is that you have been taken from the city, without leaving any trail for your Inquisitor friends to follow. They're going to see the remains of Howarth Hall and conclude that you and your Guardian – and his staff – were all killed when the demon he used to power his butler got loose. I left behind just enough of your blood to fool even a werewolf. The Inquisitors will breathe a sigh of relief that the problem you represent has been solved and go back to preparing for the selection of the next Grand Sorcerer."

"Right," Elaine said, trying to fight down despair. He was right. The Inquisition would probably be relieved if they concluded that she was dead and all the knowledge in her head was gone. Daria and Bee – she hoped – would look harder, but Kane had known that he would have to hide his trail from a werewolf. By now, he could have taken her halfway around the planet and they would never find her. "What do you want with me?"

"All in good time," Kane said, mildly. "Where was I? Ah, yes; my father was kind enough to insist that the Court Wizard, a venal and ambitious man, school me in magic. I had something of a talent for it, you see. The Prince couldn't study magic as much as he wanted, but I had all the time in the world. It was easy to master enough of it to go to the Peerless School, my father helping me to conceal my origins for fear that I might be rejected. By the time I arrived, I knew more charms, hexes and curses than some of the tutors."

Elaine remembered Professor Whitby, a kind and harmless old man, and suspected that he was right. Not everyone had liked the elderly tutor, but he'd been careful to ensure that the students with the right aptitudes for planting and raising specific crops were offered their chance to learn how to do it properly. Elaine had spent a happy month trying to raise Crawling Fungus before the tutor had reluctantly told her that her magic didn't seem suited for the task.

"But I still thirsted for knowledge," he continued. "I would inherit nothing from my birth, even if my blood mingled the blood of two of the noblest families in the world. The Prince and I agreed that he would help me with my obsession in exchange for me tutoring him in magic. It was not long before we had both surpassed the tutors the Court Wizard hired for us and kept experimenting. Eventually, we found..."

His voice broke off, just for a moment. "We found..."

Elaine studied him, puzzled. Someone had spelled the Court Wizard's body to prevent him from talking; could someone have done the same to Kane? But why would Kane curse himself? What had they found? The small collection of forbidden manuscripts, or something much more dangerous? Something was nagging at the back of her mind, something that she should have recognised.

"We found...we found the key to knowledge and power," Kane said, finally. He looked shaken, almost as if something had been trying to keep him from speaking, but his voice rapidly returned to its confident tone. "I discovered that *I* could become powerful, so powerful that I could bend the world to my will. The Witch-King spoke through me and I realised just how his knowledge could best be applied. And when I realised what I knew – what I'd known all along – I determined to become the most powerful person in the world."

His eyes grew brighter. "I didn't ask to be born, did I? I didn't ask for my mother to die in childbirth and my father to have to refuse to recognise me as his child! Do you understand how lucky I was that I wasn't committed to an orphanage like you, or sold into slavery? I had noble blood, but no power. The bitch could have convinced my father to discard me if she'd managed to have a child of her own."

Elaine looked at him and wondered, grimly, just how much talent he'd had as a child. "I think you stopped her from becoming pregnant," she said. There *were* spells to do that, some of them common enough not to really count as curses. "Why did you do that?"

"I didn't," Kane said. "I think. It's so hard to look back at my life and wonder what was the first real sign of my magic coming to the surface. But she was such a cold woman that my father would probably have been unable to perform if she'd dragged him into bed. No love or lust or warmth in her heart."

He shrugged. "But I was powerless," he added. "I could

lose what little I had at any time. But if I became powerful in magic, I could bend the world to my will. And when I looked up from the Witch-King's book, I knew how it could be done. Hilarion would *suffer* for all the humiliations of my childhood."

"But you said Hilarion was your friend," Elaine said, alarmed. Kane sounded mad, but a more focused madness than that which had consumed his former friend. "What did you do to him?"

Something else clicked in her mind. "You seeded him with a little of your personality," she said. Kane bowed his head in acknowledgement. "Hilarion practically *was* you – or is it the other way around. Are you Hilarion?"

Kane snorted. "Do I sound like Hilarion?"

"I barely knew him," Elaine said. "What did he sound like?"

"Conceited, arrogant, convinced that he ruled the world..." Kane said. "He was legitimate so he was secure, even if he went on rampages in inns and beat up countless whores in an endless quest for pleasure. His father never provided him with real discipline, nor did he punish him for his many transgressions. He and that effeminate fool Count Lucas painted the town red while I studied magic and wondered which day would end my noble life. You would have hated him when you heard him speak."

"But he was once your friend," Elaine pressed. She saw the whole ghastly plot and understood just what Kane had done. "You seeded him with a little of your own personality and convinced him to join the competition to become the Grand Sorcerer. No one would pay any attention to you while – shock, horror – a noble-born prince was trying to compete. And when the Inquisition realised that something was rotten in the state of Ida, you drove him mad and sent him out to fight the Inquisitors."

Everything suddenly made a ghastly kind of sense. Hilarion should have fled the moment he realised that the plot had been uncovered, at least enough of it to justify the Inquisition attempting to capture him. Everything had been exposed when Elaine had found the Witch-King's book; surely, he should have known that the game was up and it was time to flee. And instead he'd terrorised his friend and tried to fight the Inquisition, boosting his own magic to the point where it would have killed him in short order even if the Inquisition hadn't managed to defeat him. What did it matter if half the Golden City were destroyed by the maddened sorcerer? Everyone would think the matter was over when the rubble had stopped crashing down.

"Indeed," Kane agreed. "And Count Lucas was never very enthusiastic about the whole idea of trying to become Grand Sorcerer. He only went along with it because Hilarion was so insistent on trying to gain power. The King had a dream of uniting enough aristocratic magicians together to dictate terms to the Golden City and actually having a Grand Sorcerer under his thumb..."

"He would have loved the idea," Elaine said, tonelessly. But the Grand Sorcerer would have been nothing more than an aspect of Kane's personality. He would have enough time to grow in power and start using the tools created by the first Grand Sorcerer to crush all resistance. Everyone was scared of the Inquisitors already, not without reason. What would happen when they were turned into a genuine secret service, keeping the common folk in line through fear of magic or violence. "He would never see you coming."

"The Grand Sorcerer makes a visit to every kingdom in the world over the first couple of years of his reign," Kane agreed. "I would go and speak with each of the kings privately, leaving a piece of myself in their minds. Over the next few years, they would all *become* me, joining one mind living in a hundred bodies. I would then take over the magicians, the traders, the civil servants who make the empire work...I would *become* the empire."

Elaine stared at him in horror. "You'd go mad," she said. But the Witch-King hadn't completely lost it, had he? He had been semi-rational right up to the last days of the war, smart enough to realise that indiscriminately releasing demons would tear the world apart and leave him with nothing to rule. How had he done it? The knowledge in her mind seemed to suggest one possible answer. He'd balanced his thoughts out over thousands of minds, providing a stability that one mind in one body lacked. Elaine wasn't sure if anyone could create such a hive mind deliberately, but the Witch-King had succeeded and Kane clearly believed he could succeed too. "What would be left of the world?"

Kane smiled. "Who cares about this world? Name me a single person in this world who is fair-minded, decent and willing to embrace difference. No one is..."

"Daria is," Elaine said, without thinking.

"And perhaps you should ask her," Kane sneered, "just how many people are scared of her because she's a werewolf."

He smiled. "And now I have you in my clutches and the plan is complete," he concluded. "I will enter the arena tomorrow" – Elaine flinched; she hadn't realised just how long she'd been unconscious – "armed with the knowledge in your head. It will be easy to allow Administrator Mentor and Lady Light Spinner to fight while I watch from the sidelines – and then I will destroy the victor, claiming the title of Grand Sorcerer for my own. And then my reign will begin."

"But you can't take my knowledge so quickly," Elaine said. Dread had given her a few tricks to help preserve her mental defences. Even without them, breaking her would take days even for a skilled interrogator. And then she realised the truth. It *was* possible to do it quickly, without violence, if the victim and violator shared biological traits. And *that* only happened if they were related.

The awful truth dawned on her. "You're my father, aren't you?"

Kane nodded. "I seeded you twenty-three years ago," he said. "I ensured that the whore I used as your mother had the child and gave her to an orphanage when she was finally born. I gave the orphanage staff enough money – and gentle mental pushes – to ensure that you wouldn't be sold into slavery or otherwise taken from the orphanage. Your magical talent was enough to get you into the Peerless School, but not enough to ensure that you could have your pick of jobs after you left. And then Miss Prim agreed to take you into the Library as a trainee librarian."

"I don't believe you," Elaine said. Not the bit about him being her father; they looked similar enough for that to be true. But she didn't believe that someone – anyone – could work on such a subtle plan, with so much to go wrong, over twenty-four years, perhaps longer. "Miss Prim was enslaved..."

"But not without some independence," Kane pointed out. "Who do you think hired her to steal from the Great Library in the first place?"

"You couldn't have planned so carefully and so well," Elaine said, flatly. The books on military and intelligence operations she'd absorbed insisted, flatly, that the more complex a plan the more likely it was to go badly wrong. And yet...who would have connected a parentless child with a sneak thief and the Kingdom of Ida? If a single strand of his plan failed, it wouldn't bring down the rest of the structure. "And how did you know I'd pick up the book..."

"It was charmed for you," Kane informed her. "And Miss Prim ordered you to be the one who dealt with it. You can work out the rest for yourself."

Elaine stared at him. For her entire life, she'd wondered who had given birth to her and why. Who had her father been, or her mother...and why had they refused to raise their child for themselves? She remembered, bitterly, what the druid had said. Sometimes it was better not to know. As a child, she'd wondered if she were the lost heir to a noble family, perhaps even to the Golden Throne itself. Foolish dreams, all of them. Dread had been right to suspect her, perhaps even to consider killing her. But now it was too late.

Kane smiled as he stood up and walked around behind her. "If you don't resist, the process won't be painful," he said, as he pushed his fingers against her skull. "And I will acknowledge you as my daughter when I am Grand Sorcerer. What could you do with a family tree that links you to the most powerful magician in the world?

"I am No-Kin," Elaine said, flatly. Bitterness threatened to overwhelm her. How Millicent would laugh if she knew the truth. "Right now, I have no father."

"No," Kane agreed. "I suppose you don't."

She felt his mind reaching out to touch hers, icy fingers probing through her thoughts and memories. The feeling was so...violating that she shrank back, but there was no escape. She tried to distract him, to misdirect him, yet he saw through all of her defences. Elaine tried to resist anyway as he started to read her thoughts, but it was futile. She could barely move as he took control of her mind. Resistance was futile...

And then she blacked out once again.

Chapter Thirty-Five

Elaine shivered as she struggled back to awareness, only to find that she was alone. Kane was gone, leaving her to try to recover from his violation of her mind. All of the knowledge she'd gained was still there, but it felt tainted, as if he'd raped her mind while copying the knowledge from her head. She felt filthy and helpless and very much alone.

Despair threatened to overwhelm her as she struggled against the chains holding her in the chair. She'd found out who her parents had been, only to discover that she would have preferred not to know. And her father had regarded her as nothing more than a pawn in a very long-term game. Elaine wasn't entirely sure that she believed everything he'd told her, but in the end it hardly mattered. Dread had been right about the danger she represented to the world, even though she hadn't intended to be malicious. He should have killed her the moment he realised what had actually happened to her.

Hot tears burned in her eyes as she started to struggle, only to discover that escape was impossible. The chains granted her limited freedom of movement, but she couldn't leave the chair and the magic infused into the metal absorbed any magic she tried to use before it could cut her free. Kane had been more than just any old magician, she realised dully; he'd had the power to win the contest honestly, without needing forbidden charms from the Great Library. But then, according to the knowledge in her mind, perhaps it wasn't too surprising. Mixing disparate bloodlines sometimes produced remarkable results. The last Grand Sorcerer had come from humble origins and risen to become the most powerful magician in the world.

Perhaps Daria or Dread would find her...but they wouldn't even know to look. If Kane had been telling the truth, all the evidence would suggest that her trail had ended in the ruins of Howarth Mansion, where she had apparently died alongside her Guardian. No one would quite understand what had happened, but it would be enough to keep anyone from tracking her down until it was far too late. And perhaps Kane had been right about the Inquisitors being privately relieved that she was dead. But they wouldn't find a body...

She fought down the urge to cry as she studied the chains, trying to find a weakness...but there was nothing. The knowledge in her head identified the entire system, a design used to imprison sorcerers far more powerful than Elaine had ever been. Escape was impossible, as was using magic to call for help. Her thoughts tormented her time and time again. By now, Kane could be in the Arena, using his magic to win the contest and become Grand Sorcerer. What would happen if the Inquisition worked out what had happened, too late to prevent him from taking power? There was no way to know. It had never happened before.

The door opened and she looked up, praying to all the gods that Daria or Dread or even Millicent had found her. But instead the person who stepped inside was a stranger, a woman wearing a slave collar and carrying a small tray of food. The smell mocked Elaine, reminding her that she'd been completely unconscious for days. Clearly Kane had decided to keep her fed, for the moment. But why? One possibility occurred to her and she shivered. He could easily have placed a seed of himself inside her mind and intended to leave her imprisoned until the seed had taken over and turned her into yet another body for a greater mind. Elaine flinched at the thought as the slave set the food down within reach and turned to leave. Maybe there was one chance to escape...

"Slave," she said, "unlock these chains."

The slave's voice was dull, utterly hopeless. "I may not do anything against the orders of my master," she said. Elaine wasn't too surprised. Slave collars made a slave completely obedient to their masters, but not to just anyone. They would be able to refuse orders from burglars and would-be spies. "You are to remain in this room until the master returns from his travels."

And how long, Elaine wondered, would that be? How did they intend to solve the toilet problem? The thought made her feel sick, before a thought occurred to her. Magic was useless against the chains holding her in the chair, but magic wasn't the only solution to the problem.

"I need something to pick my teeth," she said, as she took a bite of food. Kane hadn't decided to serve her anything better than sausages and bread. Her lips twitched in genuine amusement; it was almost like being in prison. "Can you find me something that I can use to remove pieces of food from my jaws?"

Someone who hadn't been enslaved might have wondered precisely why she needed a toothpick, but the slave didn't have any orders permitting her to think. Instead, she left the room and returned moments later carrying a pair of wooden toothpicks, putting them down on the table within reach. Elaine smiled gratefully at her as she finished the sausages and put the plate down, hoping that the slave would leave her alone with the toothpicks. The slave clearly didn't think that the toothpicks were any danger, for she left, leaving the plate with her as well. Someone hadn't given her specific orders about how Elaine should be treated, something that might have made perfect sense if they'd captured a powerful wizard, one so powerful that he never considered using something other than magic. Elaine had had to learn, a long time ago, that she just didn't have the power to use magic on a daily basis. It had always seemed a weakness, but right now it might prove her salvation.

She lifted up the handcuffs on her wrist and studied them carefully. One of the books she'd absorbed gave detailed instructions on how to pick locks, although it made it seem easier than Elaine had expected. If *she* had been holding someone prisoner, she would have charmed the handcuffs to make it impossible for someone to pick the lock, but that might have been difficult. The overwhelmingly powerful spell worked into the handcuffs absorbed magic indiscriminately, but there was nothing intended to stop someone using a more mundane tactic for breaking out.

It took nearly twenty minutes before she finally managed to unlock the first handcuff. It fell free from her wrist, allowing her to concentrate on freeing her other wrist and release her hands. The cuffs around her ankles were much easier to pick

– they seemed larger than the ones on her hands – and she stood up, taking a deep breath as she looked around Kane's research laboratory. Most of the items Kane had scattered around were useless, but a couple were forbidden outside the Inquisition – and one of the textbooks was very definitely on the forbidden list. She picked it up after carefully checking for unpleasant surprises and glanced at the first page. Someone had crafted a very old spell to keep away prying eyes and linked it to a deadly spell that would kill anyone who opened the book without proper precautions. She remembered Cat's death and shuddered, before picking up the book and a couple of oddly-designed wands. Kane had clearly been preparing them for his followers to use as weapons.

The thought puzzled her as she opened the door and peered out into a darkened corridor. Kane...seemed to be *too* powerful, *too* capable. Elaine had studied at the Peerless School and knew that there were magicians far more powerful than herself, but Kane seemed to be demonstrating too many skills to be quite real. An alchemist might be the most capable in the world, yet he wouldn't be a druid or a combat magician at the same time. She might have been wrong, but Kane seemed to have spent centuries studying magic. Maybe he'd been studying intensely ever since he'd left the Peerless School – the touts hadn't been able to find much evidence of achievement or the normal signs of a wizard building a power base – yet it still seemed unlikely. Elaine had cheated – Duke Gama's spell had crammed endless realms of knowledge into her head – and yet she couldn't use it all. She couldn't even *begin* to use it all...

And Kane seemed far too capable.

She considered it as she slipped down the corridor, eyes and ears alert for any suspicious movement. No one in the building would be her friend; they'd all be Kane's slaves or his allies, if he had allies. She couldn't even remember where Kane had been staying in the Golden City, if she'd ever learned. They'd been so focused on the Prince that they'd missed the real threat, the man they hadn't even realised was his cousin. Kane's plan had been brilliant, Elaine acknowledged grimly; her father had even managed to fool the Inquisition.

And yet...could it be that the plan was *too* complex to be believable?

She pushed the thought aside as she sensed powerful magic ahead of her. Kane had weaved a network of wards around his lair, each one capable of stopping anyone from breaking in – or leaving. Unlike Randor Mansion, *these* wards wouldn't need to be reprogrammed to prevent anyone from leaving without permission. Elaine slipped closer, drawing on the knowledge in her head to identify the wards. Nine of them were common, carefully designed to integrate with one another rather than cause interference; the tenth was unknown in the modern era. It dated all the way back to the Second Necromantic War. Perhaps the Witch-King himself had designed it, for it was directly linked to the magic generated by necromancy. Elaine shuddered the moment she saw it, knowing that it would be almost impossible to break or fool. It kept her prisoner as surely as the chains in Kane's lab had kept her prisoner. There was no way out.

The sound of footsteps echoed out from behind her and she slipped into the shadows, risking a minor charm to pull the darkness around her like a shroud. Two male slaves, both wearing collars and basic outfits that marked them as lower-class servants, walked past her and right through the wards. Elaine watched them go, realising in horror exactly what Kane had done to them once they'd become his slaves. The collars they wore allowed them passage through the wards, once the wards had determined that they were genuinely slaves. Anyone who hadn't been enslaved – or was trying to trick people into believing that they *were* slaves – would be detected and held for interrogation. There seemed to be no way out of the building – and even if she managed to get through the wards, there was no way to know exactly where she was in the city, assuming that she *was* in the city. Kane could have lied to her.

For a moment, she wondered if she should go back to the cell and chain herself up again before someone realised that she'd managed to escape, but she pushed the thought away angrily. There *was* one possibility, but it was dangerous, perhaps even insane...shaking her head, she headed back to the lab and looked around, hoping to find a spare collar. She found nothing, but the same slave who had brought her food entered moments later, carrying a small jug of water. Elaine's freeze spell caught her before she could sound the alarm.

The slave was young, barely older than Elaine had been when she'd entered the Peerless School. She felt an odd moment of sympathy for the girl – there was no way to know when or why she'd been enslaved – before she started to work on the slave collar. The charms that turned people into slaves were designed to be impossible for anyone, apart from the master, to remove, but Dread had managed it for Cat and Elaine suspected she knew how he'd done it. She recoiled as she sensed the enslavement charm inside the collar – it felt like looking at a poisonous snake, uncoiling as it prepared to strike at her – before bracing herself and starting to reprogram it. Dispelling the charm would have been simple; reprogramming it was a great deal harder. It pushed her right to the limits of her ability, but she was desperate. If she'd paid more attention in class...

She unhooked the collar from the girl's neck and, before she could think better of it, placed it around her own neck. Even lamed, the enslavement charm pressed against her mind, trying to turn her into a slave. It wasn't even remotely subtle, not like the suggestion that she should travel to Ida; it enforced the master's orders with such power that resistance was not even an option. Elaine shuddered, fighting to focus her mind, as she stood up and walked towards the wards blocking her escape. The spell kept pressing away at her, telling her that she should submit to her master, that she should be a good and proper slave. She called on all the mental disciplines she'd learned at the Peerless School to keep her mind free of its influence, hoping against hope that she could get through the wards in time. They shimmered into existence in front of her and Elaine stepped through. The wards didn't seem to bar anyone with the right enslavement spell, even one that didn't seem to be working properly. She passed through them without setting off an alarm.

On the other side, she found it almost impossible to remove

the collar. Certain basic commands were burned into the minds of every slave in the world; they could not remove the collar, they could not harm or kill themselves and they could not, directly or indirectly, harm their master or his interests. The commands threatened to overwhelm her; she stumbled to her knees as her hands twitched, trying to reach the collar. It was so hard to hold her thoughts together against the insistent commands trying to slide into her mind, so hard to be sure that she was really doing as she wanted to do...the collar came loose and fell to the floor, followed rapidly by Elaine herself. Her entire body was drenched in sweat, her head spinning out of control. Slaves were not meant to break free of their collars, even the ones who had been enslaved against their wills. And she'd put on the collar willingly.

It took all she had left to pick herself up and start stumbling away from the wards, heading towards the edge of the building. The collar was abandoned on the ground; she knew she should take it with her, but she couldn't even bring herself to pick it up. No wonder so many freed slaves remained servile, even after years of freedom. The commands were burned directly into their minds. There were some spells that would help, she knew, but she barely had the strength left to use them. Instead, she ducked into a side room as she heard footsteps, praying that the slaves wouldn't see the collar where she'd left it and realise what had happened. She was in no state for a fight.

It felt like hours before she was strong enough to start walking onwards towards the doors. Kane had taken over a building that had probably originally belonged to another sorcerer, judging from the misdirection charms that seemed to flicker through the entire building, but eventually she reached the doors. There were a handful of wards covering them, but they were simple, easy to remove. Elaine puzzled over that for a long moment, before deciding that Kane wouldn't have wanted anyone on the outside to sense the wards he'd constructed around his inner chambers. There wouldn't be anything for the Inquisition – or his rivals – to sense if they started to probe his home. But then, everyone had been focused on the Prince or the more powerful contestants. They wouldn't have spared much time for Kane.

Outside, it was dark, the moon rising slowly in the sky. She was at the very edge of the Golden City, looking up at the Watchtower and sensing the magical currents running through the entire city. A faint glow in the distance, towards the Parade of the Endless, revealed that powerful magic was being used and shaped by powerful magicians, those who believed that they could become Grand Sorcerer. The Arena was powerful enough to hold their magic from spinning out of control and ripping through the city. It was possible that the Inquisition would have kept the maddened Prince there if they had been able to take him alive. There were so many wards around the Arena that no one should have been able to break out, no matter how powerful they were...

She sensed a sudden surge of magic, just before the sky lit up with a brilliant white flash. The sound of thunder hit her ears a second later, almost driving her to her knees. Something had gone terribly wrong; the magic field surrounding the city was twisting, being violently pulled towards the Arena. Elaine stared, realising that the contestants had suddenly realised just how powerful – and knowledgeable – Kane had become. There would be Inquisitors there too, surely, and hundreds of other magicians. Elaine knew with a sickening certainty that it wouldn't be enough to stop Kane. Given time – and the knowledge he'd stolen from her – he would be able to absorb the power worked into the Arena. There were *gods* that would be less powerful than he'd become.

Bracing herself, trying to draw on the magic to give her energy, Elaine started to run. The Arena wasn't *that* far away, but she knew that she was tired and worn. And, despite herself she had the sickening feeling that it might be too late. Kane, by killing the other two contestants, would become Grand Sorcerer.

And then the world would be his.

Chapter Thirty-Six

The waves of magic grew stronger as Elaine ran towards the Arena, trying desperately to avoid the crowds of fleeing people trying to get *away* from the battle. Reality was bending and twisting right in front of her as the pocket dimension that enveloped the Arena, making it capable of seating the entire city in a tiny space, threatened to collapse, crushing everyone inside into nothingness. Elaine could sense Kane's mind working away at the spells that held the pocket dimension in place, taking control of it and draining the magic into himself. He'd go mad...

Or perhaps he was already mad. She could sense his mind spinning out like a spider's web, drawing on the collective stability of a dozen minds, perhaps a hundred minds. They could provide stability that other dark wizards lost when they tried to enhance their own magical power, or so Kane clearly hoped. But Elaine could feel the ragged edges of his thoughts and knew that he was being tainted by the sheer power he was channelling. Insanity was a very real threat.

She ducked to one side as hundreds of people fled past her, trying to use the magic woven into the Arena to see what had happened. Images flashed into her mind one by one, each one striking home with terrifying impact. Administrator Mentor and Lady Light Spinner had jousted, contesting their power directly, ignoring the threat from Kane until it was far too late. They hadn't realised what was happening until the Arena itself turned on them, twisting and reaching out for their souls. Elaine realised, with a frisson of horror, exactly how the next Grand Sorcerer was selected. They didn't just have to have raw power, but the discipline to take over the Arena and hold it steady. It represented the Grand Sorcerer's ability to juggle a thousand different problems at one time and still hold the Empire together. Those contestants who didn't realise the true nature of the contest were likely to die before realising that they'd lost. Kane had already been powerful; now he controlled the entire pocket dimension.

Dread and his fellows had realised, too late, what was happening to the Arena. They'd tried to collapse it, hoping to blink Kane out of existence along with his power. But Kane had already taken over most of the Arena and he'd been able to save himself from death. Mentor, the man who had once punished Elaine for Millicent's little joke, had tried to kill Kane directly, upholding the Mage's Oath. Kane had swatted him out of existence effortlessly, before turning his attention to Lady Light Spinner. But she was gone. Fled? Killed already? It didn't matter. All that mattered was the power flowing through him.

Elaine kept running, watching in dismay as the Arena slowly began to collapse in on itself. Kane seemed to be manipulating it deliberately, sporting with the thousands of helpless civilians who remained trapped inside the pocket dimension. Some made it out, fleeing in blind panic; others discovered that no matter how fast or how far they ran, they could never make it out of the dimension. Kane had altered part of the Arena so the distance between their seats and the exits became infinite. They were forever trapped on the brink of escape, completely at Kane's mercy.

The city's magical field kept twisting, almost as if the defences created by successive Grand Sorcerers were trying to stop Kane before he managed to take the entire city. Wards that dated back to the era before the First Necromantic War pressed in on him, trying to destroy him or starve him of the magic he was sucking into himself. But it was futile. Kane had already passed beyond anything they could stop. The wards were literally feeding him still more magic.

She turned the corner and ran towards the Parade of the Endless, only to see the Arena finally starting to collapse. The screams from those trapped inside grew louder as they finally died, while Kane's laughter echoed out over the entire city. Mad...or determined to ensure that no one fucked with him. Elaine skidded to a halt as the final crowd of escapees ran past her, their faces torn and twisted by blind panic, just before the Arena collapsed into nothingness. Kane stood where it had been, power twisting the very air around him.

Prince Hilarion had been a maddened animal, unable to concentrate or focus his power; it would have killed him even if Dread hadn't managed to slice off his head. But Kane had prepared properly for the sheer infusion of power that had overwhelmed his half-cousin. He might still be mad, but he would have control...and *that* would make him immensely more dangerous than a rampaging bull like Prince Hilarion.

Sheets of white lightning tore through the air as Kane flexed his supercharged muscles. Elaine could sense spells forming into existence, each one too powerful for anyone to stop. Some were basic, spells that every magician learned in their first year in the Peerless School, but boosted to a power level that made them powerful beyond nightmares. Others were older and far darker, unknown to anyone apart from Kane – and Elaine herself. Kane's power was spreading through the city, reaching out towards its intended victims. Elaine realised that he was powerful enough to compel the entire city, even the senior wizards. How long would it be before he started seeding their minds and turning them into copies of himself?

Maybe Kane hadn't realised just how far he could go. He could seed *everyone*, from the greatest of wizards to the lowliest of slaves. Kane would become the only life form left on the planet, each successive child becoming part of an intellect that would never die. Maybe he could even seed himself into animals, or creatures that combined humans and animal features like werewolves. There would never be any resistance because there would be no one else left alive. Kane would be alone forever in a billion bodies, each one a copy of himself.

He won't do that, Elaine told herself firmly, and prayed to the gods that she was right. *He wants to gloat over his supremacy. How can he do that if all of his old tormentors are dead?*

A pair of black-robed figures appeared out of nowhere, wands raised and ready. There were no games with harmless spells this time; the Inquisitors threw an entire series of death spells towards their target, spells that were almost impossible to stop. She'd been taught about one of them in the Peerless School, Elaine remembered, even though they hadn't been shown how to *cast* the spell unless they went into combat magic. The only certain defence, the tutor – a grumpy old man bearing the scars from fifty years of fighting dark magicians – had told them, was to be somewhere else when you were targeted. Kane, on the other hand, just seemed to absorb enough magic to kill a hundred men, before casually blinking both of the Inquisitors out of existence. They were gone completely, air rushing in to fill the space where they had been. Elaine didn't know of *any* spell that could do something like that. Kane had simply altered reality to the point where the Inquisitors no longer existed...

The ground shuddered under her feet as Kane exerted his will. A dozen mansions in High Tory, home to aristocrats with bloodlines so pure that they could trace their ancestry back for nearly a thousand years, collapsed into falling rubble. Elaine wasn't entirely sure how she knew what was going on, until she realised that Kane was using one of the semi-forbidden spells he'd probably learned from her mind. It allowed him to project images and thoughts across vast distances, into minds that were capable of comprehending what they were seeing. He was showing everyone – perhaps the entire world – what was happening to those who had ruled the world, only a scant two hours ago. The people who had been cowering in their mansions, hoping that their wards would save them, died before ever quite realising what had destroyed their lives. Great rents appeared in the ground as the catacombs opened up, disgorging creatures that had been warped and mutated by the wild magic under the city. Giant worms, semi-intelligent rats, even a colossal hamster...they rose up and started attacking the civilians. And everyone who fell...

...Rose up again. Kane knew how to summon the undead, how to infuse dead bodies with the dark infection that turned them into shambling parodies of man. He didn't even have to concentrate after the first handful had risen from the dead to feast upon the living. The dark magic that created the undead was powered by the souls of the living they killed. They could keep going until they ran out of victims, until the Golden City became a city of the dead, a necropolis. The original Necropolis had been burned to the ground when the

North Continent had been scorched; Kane would create a new one on the ruins of the Golden City. How far did his influence spread? Ida had kept the dead bodies of her royal family in a vault, where they could be animated again by a necromancer. Were there other illegal stashes of dead bodies in a world where the dead were supposed to be cremated, no exceptions? There was no way for Elaine to know, but Kane's senses had expanded so far that he could probably locate dead bodies on the other side of the world.

But he doesn't need to bother, Elaine thought, bitterly. *All he has to do is knock down a few more buildings and he'll have a massive army of undead slaves.*

She tried desperately to think of a spell that might stop him. Necromancers weren't immortal, but Kane was already more powerful than any historical necromancer, perhaps even more powerful than the Witch-King. There were legends about magical swords that might have stopped him in his tracks, yet she knew – now – that most of those stories were nonsense, comforting lies constructed to convince a nervous population that a necromancer could be stopped. The *real* necromancers had been overpowered by magicians, poisoned by spies or tricked into fighting each other. And the Witch-King hadn't been killed until the North Continent had been scorched.

And they'd never found a body...

No one was quite sure what the Witch-King had done to make himself so powerful – and pretty much beyond being killed. Kane might know the answer – he'd found the Witch-King's private notebook, after all – and he might even have improved upon what the Witch-King had done. If the first Grand Sorcerer had known, it had never been written down in the Great Library. Some stories suggested that the first Grand Sorcerer had been just as powerful as the Witch-King...and that all successive Grand Sorcerers, despite being extremely powerful in their own right, hadn't quite lived up to his power. Perhaps the original Grand Sorcerer had used necromancy too, only he'd had the mental discipline not to allow it to drive him mad. But then, he'd been the unquestioned ruler of most of the known world. He had already been supremely powerful.

A shape landed beside her and Elaine started, glancing over

to see a colossal wolf with long sharp teeth. A moment later, she recognised Daria's wolf form, despite the blood that stained her muzzle. Her friend started to shift back to human form, but held the transformation midway between human and wolf. She was naked, but almost covered in blood. Elaine reached for her friend and hugged her tightly, relieved to see her. Part of her had wondered if everyone she'd known was dead.

"The dead are coming back to life," Daria half-growled. Her fur felt surprisingly comforting, almost like cuddling a stuffed toy. "The entire city is coming apart and..."

She broke off as she saw movement, people crawling towards where the Arena had been on their hands and knees. Elaine followed her gaze and recognised a handful of the crawlers, upper-class aristocrats from High Tory. Some of them were naked, their skins showing the signs of recent beatings, while others tried to crawl with as much confidence as they could. But it wasn't easy to be defiant when crawling along the ground. Elaine felt a sudden chill as she recognised Millicent. Her old enemy was completely naked, her back whipped so badly that it was bleeding. She was crying, trying to hold herself together in the face of the awful compulsion dragging her onwards to face Kane...Elaine knew, now, that she would never hate Millicent again. What she'd done was nothing compared to the torment that Kane had already inflicted upon her – and what he would inflict on her in the future.

He wants to make them crawl, she realised. All the people who had been born legitimately, all the people who had mocked a bastard child who could so easily have been declared legitimate, all the people who had enjoyed wealth and status that Kane would never be able to enjoy...he wanted to make them crawl. There was no point in enslaving them, or turning them into copies of himself, when he could torment them by forcing them to crawl before him. He'd done worse, she realised dully. His power was enough to take over all of the slaves, to replace their enforced loyalty to their masters with enforced loyalty to himself...and to use them to punish those who had tormented him over the years. What else had happened to Millicent apart from a brutal whipping? There was no way to know, but Elaine could guess – and realised that she didn't want to know.

Kane's laughter echoed out over the city once again as the former masters of creation fell on their faces before him. He could do anything to them and they knew it, from simply destroying them to turning them into slaves themselves. Elaine watched Millicent as she fell on her belly and shuddered. Maybe Kane wasn't mad, not in the sense that Prince Hilarion was mad, but he'd gone too far. The temptation he'd offered his daughter had overwhelmed him and turned him into a monster.

She started to back away, heading away from the Arena. Direct attack would be worse than futile; it would reveal to him that she was still alive, still armed with the knowledge that he'd given her. But it wasn't enough to stop him. For all she knew, there was nothing that suggested how she could deal with him, even to hold him off for a few seconds. Prince Hilarion had been tricked into wasting most of his enhanced power, but Kane wasn't that maddened. He could blink her out of existence merely by snapping his fingers.

But there was another possibility. Kane had discovered the Witch-King's own book, the one that contained the darkest of his spells. Surely there had to be something there, something she could use to match him and stop him. She'd already resisted the temptation to abuse her power – and the knowledge that she'd had crammed into her head – and she could do it again. It didn't seem a very safe possibility, but it was all she could think of. If she could match his power, perhaps she could kill him before he destroyed the entire city – and the world.

Daria caught her arm as they slipped past a half-ruined building and nodded towards a figure lying in the darkness. Dread had been flung away from Kane when he'd first started to reveal his true nature, only to crash down outside the Arena and be trapped when the building had been knocked down by one of Kane's earthquakes. Elaine did her best to help Daria move the rubble, revealing Dread's damaged body. One of his legs had been broken beyond easy repair. His left arm ended in a bloody stump.

"I...I thought you were dead," Dread said. Elaine felt an

odd feeling in her chest as she realised that he'd *cared*. Was that what it was like to have a genuine father? "I should have realised that you wouldn't die so easily."

"Kane is my father," Elaine said, bitterly. The druid had been right. She'd been better off not knowing the truth. "What happened to the Witch-King's notebook?"

Dread looked at her sharply. "Why do you want to know?"

"I need to use it," Elaine said, and explained her plan. It was risky to say it out loud – it was impossible to tell just how far Kane's perception had spread – but there was no choice. "Where did you hide it?"

"You can't risk it," Dread said. He started to touch his leg with his good hand, grimacing against the pain. Elaine felt him work an odd spell, one so delicate that she could never have matched it herself, and his leg slowly repaired itself. "You'll go mad, just like him."

"I have to stop him," Elaine said. Surely there were words she could use to convince him, but nothing came to mind. "I..."

"...Will go mad," Dread said, firmly. He waved a hand towards where Kane was standing, his presence so firmly marked on reality that it could be sensed from miles away. "Don't you think that he's mad already?"

He was right, Elaine realised. Kane was mad, even if it was a different kind of madness to the one that had swallowed Prince Hilarion. The only thing that kept him even remotely balanced was the minds he'd seeded with his own personality...and those were likely to be overwhelmed if he kept absorbing more and more raw power. How long would it be before his bodies started to fail?

And then a thought struck her. There *was* one final possibility.

"I need you on your feet," she said, helping him up. The healing spell had drained him badly, suggesting that there was a very good reason the druids didn't use it unless there was no other choice. "I'm going to need your help."

Chapter Thirty-Seven

Kane's presence echoed in her mind as she led the way towards the one part of the city that very few people would enter willingly. The wild magic shimmering through the Blight was deadlier than anything else, except perhaps for Kane himself. Elaine had read hundreds of stories of what happened to people who blundered into the Blight and fell asleep, allowing the wild magic to transform them into monsters. The lucky ones had been allowed to leave the Golden City peacefully; the unlucky ones had been killed by their own families, or the Inquisitors. Wild magic was beyond control, even in the few areas where it pooled naturally; in the Blight, it was effectively poisoned. It would be difficult for anyone to drain it without risking their life, or integrity.

Elaine slowed as she reached the edge of the Blight, feeling its strange nature somehow countering the endless waves of power from Kane. Kane wanted everyone to respect him – and that demand for respect was slowly becoming a demand for worship. Elaine wondered, as she felt the Blight reaching out for her, if the gods had been necromancers who had become so powerful they'd been completely disconnected from the human world. No one was entirely sure where the gods came from, or what they saw in humanity. And some wizards had definitely believed that they could become all-powerful.

Tapping the Blight's power would be simple enough, she knew, provided that she no longer cared about her own survival. She'd worked out ways to drain it before she'd realised that doing so would be far too revealing. Now, she altered the spells she'd designed in her mind, angling them so that they would summon the Blight's power to her rather than dispel it harmlessly. It would probably kill her to try, but there was no choice. Kane had to be stopped. And if she was partly responsible for what he had become, her own life was a small price to pay to stop him.

"Stay here," she urged Daria. The werewolves had been created by wild magic. Daria would be vulnerable to the Blight in ways that wouldn't threaten a normal human, even a magician. Elaine had never realised just how brave Daria had been to track her down so close to the Blight, but then she hadn't realised that Daria had been a werewolf. "I need you two to lure him towards the Blight."

Dread looked at her, puzzled. "Are you sure you know what you are doing?"

The honest answer to that was *no*, but that would only have upset him. "I think so," Elaine said, carefully. And it was true enough. Whatever happened, she probably wouldn't last long enough to see what the wild magic did to her. "But you can't know what I'm doing, not when he might be able to read your mind."

"Understood," Dread said. Meeting someone so much more powerful than himself – and sane enough to be a long-term threat to the entire world – had to have been humbling. But he still took it in his stride. "How long do you need?"

Elaine hesitated. She honestly wasn't sure. "Give me ten minutes," she said, finally. Constructing the spells in her mind was one thing, but summoning them into reality was quite another. Controlling wild magic was difficult, to say the least. Many sorcerers had tried...and even those who had succeeded had escaped horrifically mutated. She remembered Lady Light Spinner's face and shuddered. Had she tried to tap wild magic to boost her own powers? "Good luck."

"And to you," Dread said, heavily. He took one last look at her, as if he was trying to remember her face, and then started to walk off. "I'll wait for Daria at the Shipper's Inn."

Elaine watched him go and then looked up at the werewolf girl. "I haven't been a very good friend, have I?"

"Well, you *could* have done more of the washing," Daria said, dryly. Elaine found herself giggling, despite the tears prickling against her eyes. "Listen to me; you're not a bad person, not really. And though I know you didn't want a life of importance, you have handled it well."

Elaine knew that she hadn't, but there was no point in arguing. "Thank you," she said, and gave her friend a hug. "If...if I don't come out of this alive...please will you tell Bee that I am grateful for everything?"

"Of course I will," Daria said. "And you *are* going to come out of this alive. And we *are* going to go trawling for men every night when this is over."

Elaine shrugged. "Maybe," she said. "Just...try not to forget me, all right?"

Daria's huge canine-like eyes met hers. "Don't you dare try to kill yourself out of some misplaced guilt," Daria said, flatly. "You didn't ask for any of this."

"I know," Elaine said. It didn't make her feel any better. "Good luck."

"May the gods be with us," Daria agreed. "I'll see you soon."

She shifted back into wolf form and padded after Dread. Elaine watched her go, feeling a sense of unimaginable desolation slowly overcoming her, urging her to call Daria back so that she wouldn't walk into the Blight alone. But she held her tongue, even when the werewolf looked back at her, and waved goodbye. Turning, fixing her spells firmly in her mind, Elaine turned and walked into the Blight.

***

At first there was nothing, apart from a sense that the air around her was sick and unwell. The wild magic had seeped into the buildings around where the magicians had conducted their experiments, warping everything into something that seemed increasingly unreal. Doorways seemed to gape open invitingly, suggesting that she could walk through them and into an unknown world; the road seemed to twist and turn through a series of increasingly unstable pocket dimensions. She could hear sounds in the distance, screams and laughter from those trapped within the Blight. They were long dead, she hoped, but their souls remained frozen, unable to proceed to the next world.

The wild magic seemed to shimmer around her as she approached the site of the old experiments. Buildings seemed to become odd, almost alien, covered with writing that was beyond her ability to understand. Great...*entities* seemed to brush the surface of mankind's reality, their thoughts taking on physical form in the midst of the Blight. A scuttling noise alerted her to a giant scorpion-like creature advancing on its prey, a mutated cross between a cat and a dog. Elaine shuddered, unable to tell if the creatures were real or just illusions thrown up by the Blight. The scorpion moved to sting, only to recoil as the cat-dog lunged forward, landed on top of the creature's shell and started to dig into the gaps with sharp teeth that seemed to have come from nowhere. Elaine watched the scorpion die and then hurried onwards, towards where the ghosts of the dead necromancers waited for her. She didn't dare go into any of the buildings, not knowing what could be waiting for her in the darkness.

She sucked in her breath as she came to the very heart of the Blight, a circle of ground that was absolutely dead and cold. Wild magic grew stronger as lightning began to flash overhead, each one illuminating a scene from the final moments before the Blight came into existence. The wizards cast their spells, pushing themselves to the limit, hoping to develop a form of necromancy that didn't include murder. A person could recover drained life force if cared for by competent druids. And if necromancy didn't include murder, was it really necromancy? They'd never had the chance to find out.

One by one, Elaine started to cast her spells. The wild magic started to slide towards her, a shifting wave as unstoppable as the tide. Magicians had once believed that they could hold back the incoming tide, but the pressure on their wards had eventually caused them to snap, drowning the magicians before they had a chance to escape. Now, Elaine realised as wild magic flickered around her, she was about to die in pursuit of her magic. The only consolation was knowing that Kane was about to die with her.

She closed down as much of her awareness as she could as the wild magic focused around her, slipping into the spells she'd designed to hold it. Higher magic could be controlled – once the first spells had been cast – by magic drawn from the wards; wild magic was just as likely to flicker out of existence for no obvious reason. Her own wards had been carefully designed, using theoretical models that had never been tried before they'd been added to the Black Vault's collection of banned volumes, using a series of twisting wards to try to contain the wild magic. Even *looking* at it too closely might be dangerous.

But she could still sense Kane. Her father's awareness would have encompassed the Blight, even if he'd chosen to try to ignore it. Even without Dread and Daria trying to lure him towards the contaminated part of the city, he would have sensed something of what she was doing. He'd *know* that she was drawing on wild magic and he would be coming for her. She could feel his presence start to move, great waves of power washing out as he slowly walked through the city. Buildings toppled and people died wherever he cast his gaze. His power thundered through the wards that had once protected the city, causing them to turn in on themselves. Anyone too close to him would be enslaved or have their minds blown out of existence. He'd become a mad god.

And yet, now she was more attuned to wild magic than anyone else had ever been, she could sense something else. Kane was Kane, but he...wasn't. Something far older and far darker had infested him, just like he'd infested his cousin. Elaine had wondered how any young mind – and Kane was young, barely old enough to be the father he'd become – could have worked on such a plan for so long. But the puppet-master had been a puppet himself, caught in a web so subtle that he'd never suspected its existence. It had whispered into his mind, fanning the sparks of resentment into a blaze that threatened to bring down the entire world, slowly turning him into a shadow of someone else. As if the awareness was suddenly enough to shatter a barrier she hadn't even known existed, she sensed an immensely old and powerful entity looking back at her...

No one had ever found the Witch-King's body...

She saw it all in that moment of horrified awareness. The lich – a dead body animated by a mind so powerful that it could never die – waiting for its chance to strike. Over the years, it had sown many seeds into fertile soil. Some had died, some had failed, some had alerted the Inquisition...but none had revealed that the Witch-King was still alive. His power not only kept him alive; it also hid him from all detection. The gods alone knew where he was hiding, his body animated by vast power and endless hate, laying his plans against the Golden City and the line of sorcerers that had defeated him. How far back had he been drawing up the plans to create Kane? Had he influenced Duke Gama into having an affair with Kane's mother? Or turned Gama's wife into an icy shrew, preventing him from having children who would have been legitimate? Or...there were too many possibilities. A mind that could plot over centuries, slowly feeding ideas and hints into the minds of its unknowing allies, might be beyond detection. How could anyone tell if a single event was part of a greater plan or nothing more than a coincidence?

The Witch-King's insane laughter seemed to echo in her mind. Each fragment of his plan was part of a greater whole, something that twisted events and provided new elements for him to pick up and manipulate. The orphanage had taught Elaine how to knit – it was seen as a valuable skill for a young woman with neither family nor money – and she realised just how well the Witch-King had knitted his plans. Even if pieces of his plan fell apart, he could keep going, knitting elements of his grand strategy back together or twisting it into something new. How could one fight a plan that was so all-encompassing...?

She started as Kane entered the Blight, his magical field flaring into blinding light as it encountered the wild magic. He was already trying to drain it, she realised, in the hopes of absorbing it into himself. And with the power he was creating...he could perform miracles, like restoring the Witch-King to a living body. There would no longer be any need for the Witch-King to use most of his power on keeping himself alive, keeping his soul firmly anchored in a rotting body. He would walk out upon the land and rebuild his empire, while whatever remained of the Golden City and the Regency Council struggled to recover from the damage Kane had inflicted on them. The Inquisition had been crippled, many of the aristocrats, traders and soldiers who made up the underpinnings of the empire had been killed...dear gods, King Hildebrand would lead Ida into rebellion and he wouldn't be the only one. The entire empire would come apart at the seams.

And behind it all, the Witch-King would build up his power once again, until he unleashed the third and final necromantic war.

The wild magic tore at her mind, threatening to absorb her into itself, but somehow she hung on grimly. There was no point in trying to talk Kane into surrendering, or even helping her to hunt down and destroy the Witch-King. By now, the Witch-King would have so thoroughly riddled his mind with his influence that Kane would literally be unable to comprehend what Elaine was trying to tell him. He'd automatically dismiss everything she said, as if she was merely trying to distract him...and distract him...and distract him...

She felt his influence reaching out for her and shielded her mind, using a technique that she'd learned from the knowledge crammed into her head. Kane knew it too, of course, but it would take him time to break her down enough to seed part of himself into her mind. And *that* would open her up to the Witch-King himself. The thought was terrifying, but she pushed it aside ruthlessly. Her entire body was quivering with wild magic as she sucked more and more of it into her cells, risking her entire life. Kane had already started the transformation towards a higher form of life, one composed completely of magic, but she was catching up with him...

...And they would both die when the magic ran out.

Elaine opened her eyes. She was surrounded by people, the ghosts of all of those who had died in the Blight. They were looking at her as if they expected her to save them; perhaps, once the wild magic was gone, they would be free to move on to the next world. Or maybe they'd just flicker out of existence and die. Elaine reached out for them, trying to use her magic to ask them to help her stabilise the power. Some of them, perhaps all of them, helped her to ground herself. She could hear their voices whispering in her mind, but she couldn't make out the words. They were trying to tell her something important...

Kane was standing at the edge of the blackened ground.

There was nothing remotely human about his form any longer. His entire body was glowing with light, magic flaring through the air only to fall back into a body that seemed to be constantly shifting into something else. Elaine could *hear* his thoughts pressing against reality, threatening her very life even as they recoiled from the wild magic that had consumed her. High magic, ordered magic, just didn't go well with wild magic. Any graduate of the Peerless School knew that trying to combine the two was very dangerous. But was Kane too far gone to care?

Elaine felt her body starting to come apart and knew that she could wait no longer. They were blood relations, even though she would have preferred to think otherwise. She reached out towards her father and their minds touched, just once. Kane's far stronger mind grasped the magic boiling through Elaine's body and soul and tried to take it for himself. Most magicians would have fought if they'd felt their magic being stolen, but it would have been the wrong response. Elaine took a breath and thrust all of her magic right at him, gambling that it would be enough to overwhelm him. He hadn't set up spells to tame and store wild magic...

Kane screamed as the two types of magic clashed together. Elaine heard – or felt – someone else scream in rage as Kane's mind shattered under the impact, the magic he'd stored demanding release. It poured through the network of influence that the Witch-King had constructed, bursting out into the minds of those who had listened to his whispers and tried to claim his power. Elaine had a sense – a very brief sense – that it might have killed the Witch-King himself, but he was a lich. A lich could be very hard to kill.

There was a brief moment of relief as Kane's magic field flickered and died, followed by a grim awareness that the wild magic was now free to burn through her mind. The ground came up to slam into her face and Elaine felt darkness enveloping her...

...And someone was whispering to her in the darkness. "We're free," the voice said. It was one voice that seemed to be hundreds of voices, all blended together. "And we thank you..."

And then there was nothing.

Chapter Thirty-Eight

Elaine slowly came back to herself, climbing out of a darkness that had threatened to overwhelm her mind. She had an odd sense of *déjà vu* as she opened her eyes, realising that she was in a hospital bed. A pair of druids were bending over her, one pulling a wand away from her forehead. The other passed her a thin tube and inserted it into her mouth. Elaine sipped it gratefully, and then tried to sit up. They held her down gently and held up a mirror in front of her face. Her brown eyes were gone, replaced by two fiery red orbs that seemed almost demonic. Elaine recoiled in shock. How could *anyone* look at her any longer?

"Wild magic always extracts a price," the druid said. It was no surprise that she recognised him. "Compared to some of the others, you were lucky. Very lucky."

Elaine sorted through her memories until she remembered what had happened. "The Blight?"

"Gone, it seems," the druid said. "You're going to be a very rich young lady, once the Council gets back together and pays you what they promised. And they probably owe you one hell of a reward for saving the Golden City, perhaps the entire world."

He smiled. "But rest for the moment," he said. "There are a great many people who want to talk to you, I'm afraid."

***

The next time Elaine opened her eyes, she saw Lady Light Spinner standing beside her bed, looking down at her from behind the veil. Elaine had lost track of what had happened to her after Kane had lashed out at both her and Mentor, but she'd clearly survived...and prospered. The robes she wore were those of the Grand Sorcerer, granted to her by default. She'd been the only one of the original contestants to remain in the contest and survive.

"You won," she said, through a mouth that felt as if she'd been slapped a dozen times. Her entire body felt numb. "Congratulations."

"Thanks to you," Lady Light Spinner said. She sounded oddly amused. "You saved my life."

We all make mistakes, Elaine thought, before realising that maybe it hadn't been a mistake. Even if Lady Light Spinner had been as bad as Millicent, she wouldn't have been *insane* – and besides, her warped body would keep her in check. And the Witch-King...it was impossible to tell if he was still alive, if one could call a lich alive in the first place. He might have been destroyed in the final backwash of wild magic.

"You're welcome," she said, finally. "How is the city?"

"Nine thousand dead, including many of the senior wizards," the Lady said, flatly. Elaine blanched. Apart from the Second Necromantic War, there had never been so many deaths among the magical community. The whole system for selecting and upholding a Grand Sorcerer was designed to prevent magical fratricide. "About a hundred Inquisitors were killed as well, most of them trying to stop Kane before it was too late."

She hesitated. "Your friend Dread survived, somehow," she added. "The druids finally managed to stun him and work on healing the damage he took while he was unconscious. I don't think he was too happy."

Elaine had to smile. That sounded like Dread.

"But overall it will take years to recover from what Kane did to us," Lady Light Spinner added, grimly. "We've already had to put off dealing with Ida until we've managed to sort out the wreckage Kane left in his wake. Far too many other monarchs are wondering if they can declare independence while the Empire is crippled."

She shook her head. "But that wasn't what I came in here to talk about," she said, changing the subject. "There have been a great many discussions recently."

"Concerning me," Elaine said. She'd expected as much. Her relationship to Kane might not have come out, although Daria or another werewolf might have realised the truth, but everyone had just had a harsh lesson in the dangers of forbidden knowledge being used. Those who didn't know that the Witch-King was still alive – which was almost everyone – would wonder if Elaine would go the same way. They would want to condemn her on the grounds that it would be better safe than sorry. "When will I be executed?"

"Some of the remaining senior wizards voted to kill you," Lady Light Spinner said, dryly. "But I am Grand Sorceress and I had the deciding vote. We...*agreed* to offer you a compromise, as we owed you our lives. Killing you might rebound upon us in some subtle way."

Elaine shrugged. Magic's laws were not – had never been – as well understood as the physical science that powered the iron dragons. Breaking an oath could be disastrous, as could striking down someone to whom you owed a debt. It was commonly believed that the gods arbitrated such actions, but no one knew for sure. The information on the gods that had been shifted into Elaine's head was more questions than answers. Even glancing at some of the titles was considered blasphemy by most of the major religions.

"The Great Library needs a Head Librarian," Lady Light Spinner said. "That person will have to be bound to the Library's service, someone who won't mind spending the rest of their life within the Library. Miss Prim, I'm told, was something of a special case."

She leaned forward. "Would you consider taking up the position?"

Elaine hesitated. It *was* what she had once wanted, a responsible position working with books, including ones that only existed in the Great Library itself. And no one could accuse her of secretly opening the Black Vault when all the knowledge inside the vault was already in her head. She could happily walk into the Great Library and let the rest of the world pass her by.

And yet her life had expanded after Duke Gama's spell had changed her. She wanted to spend time with Daria, chasing boys; she wanted to be involved with Dread and the other Inquisitors as they tried to track down and destroy the Witch-King. It was something she would have shied away from before the accident. Did she *really* want to accept the oaths and obligations that came with being the Great Librarian?

She rubbed her eyes. Was she imagining it, or were her eyes burning?

"The other option is probably having you restrained in some way," Lady Light Spinner admitted, carefully. "I don't want to have to turn on you, but..."

"I understand," Elaine said. It wasn't *her* fault. If she'd become Grand Sorcerer after so much destruction, Elaine would have wanted to clamp down on any other possible sources of disruption in the Golden City. Forbidden knowledge had been forbidden for a reason. "How long do I have to think about it?"

"Several days, at least," Lady Light Spinner said. "The Great Library didn't get destroyed in the battle, but there was enough damage to the surrounding buildings to make it difficult to get inside. After that..."

She smiled. "Take some time to think about it," she added, "but don't try to kill yourself. It is possible to live after being warped."

It took Elaine a moment to realise what she was talking about. Red eyes, even ones that looked like hot coals, were nothing compared to what had been inflicted on the veiled woman in front of her. Of *course* Lady Light Spinner would have considered suicide when she realised that no power in the universe could change her back into a normal person. Her bloodline was as illustrious as any other, but that wouldn't have saved her if High Society had realised what had happened to her body. Even a Grand Sorcerer might not be able to remain in office if everyone knew that she had been warped.

"Thank you," Elaine said. She hesitated before asking the next question. "How is Millicent?"

"Shocked," Lady Light Spinner said, shortly. No one would be able to face compulsion on such a scale and escape unscathed. A taste of what it felt like to be a slave would be good for Millicent, Elaine decided, even though she would probably blot most of it from her mind. The human memory didn't like to remember pain. "She'll be fine. She grew up a great deal in the last few days."

Elaine shrugged. Millicent didn't seem to matter anymore. Maybe she too had grown up over the past few days.

***

Elaine was amused to discover, when entering the private room that had been set aside for Inquisitor Dread, that Princess Sacharissa had taken over his care. She'd organised him into eating properly, relaxing as much as he could and trying to forget about what had happened to the city. The glamour that normally made Dread's face unrecognisable seemed to have faded slightly, revealing a face that was almost a frozen mask. Even when he smiled, he still seemed to have a face of stone.

"I understand that we owe you everything," Dread said, without preamble. Elaine took it in her stride. With so many Inquisitors dead, Dread had to feel that he should be out on the streets with the remainder of his fellows. How many Inquisitors were even left alive? "And that you're a hero."

"They should have made you Grand Sorceress," Princess Sacharissa said, from where she was sitting beside Dread. "You saved the entire world."

Elaine shook her head, numbly. Her magic seemed to have been...tainted somehow, perhaps by the moment wild magic had bypassed her defences and struck directly at her soul. Red eyes could be the merest sign of a corruption that had spread through her body. It still seemed to be ready for her to call upon when necessary, but now it rolled and seethed inside her mind. Who knew what would happen when she tried to work her next magic spell?

"I trust that you will assume the position the Grand Sorceress suggested," Dread said, gruffly. "You would be automatically considered one of the senior wizards, one of the people who could serve on the Regency Council. You'd do better at that position than many of the ones who died in the fighting."

"I think I will," Elaine said, "but there's something else we have to talk about."

She outlined, briefly, what she'd seen in the final moments before Kane had been torn apart by wild magic. The Witch-King was out there, unless he was dead...but there was no way to know for sure. His network had been crippled, yet he might have survived. A lich was very hard to kill.

"We were fooled," Dread said, when she had finished. "I

never even considered that there might be another person hiding behind the Prince."

"Two people," Elaine said, precisely. A long-dead sorcerer had lectured endlessly on the need for precision at all times. His words seemed to echo through her mind. Many sorcerers had written their own books and most of them were stored in the Great Library. And even the Witch-King, back when he'd been Valiant, had followed that tradition. "He might still be alive."

She felt despair as she considered the true scale of the problem. A lich could never die; a lich needed no food, no drink, nothing that humanity could provide. The Witch-King could simply withdraw back into his cave and wait for a hundred years, or a thousand, before he started to spread his influence once again. And there might be a hundred thousand people still out there who had been touched by him and didn't know it. The Witch-King was old enough to have more experience in subtle manipulation than anyone in the Empire.

He might be dead. She would have liked to believe that he *was* dead. But there was no way to *know*.

"He must have guided Kane to his books," Dread said, when she'd finished. "Or maybe he hid a shadow of himself in those books and waited for someone to come along and start reading them. I wonder how much of it Kane knew himself."

"Very little," Elaine said. Kane *hadn't* known that he'd just been a puppet. "But I think that the Witch-King was planning his return to power a long time before Kane was even born."

The sense of despair grew stronger. Even in hindsight, there was no easy way to trace cause and effect back to the Witch-King. No one could have linked a girl without a family to the Royal Family of Ida, let alone the Witch-King himself. But each piece had been carefully put into place and manipulated until all the actors followed a script the Witch-King had written. How did you fight someone so subtle that he could craft plans over a hundred years and wait for longer before they came to fruition? *Anything* could be part of his plan.

She looked over at Dread and shivered. If he hadn't come to Ida himself, she would have been taken by the Witch-King's servants and drained of all her knowledge. The Witch-King hadn't known *everything* about magic – no one did – but she knew almost everything that was known. Tapping her mind, through Kane, would have been enough to give him everything he lacked. He might know it all now, if Kane and he had been in close contact before Kane died.

And even without random chance – and Dread's paranoia – the Witch-King had come far too close to success.

"We have to find him," she said, and knew that Dread would agree. "I just don't know where to begin."

"Ida, perhaps," Dread said. Elaine glanced at him, surprised. "It was never overwhelmed by the necromancers in either of the great wars. Where better for the Witch-King to have a secret bolt-hole?"

Elaine nodded, thoughtfully. The lands once controlled by the necromancers had been left a thousand scars, including hundreds of tiny hiding places containing knowledge and magical artefacts created by the necromancers themselves. Various Grand Sorcerers had attempted to find them all before they fell into unfriendly hands, but no one had ever been sure that they'd all been found. The necromancers had been determined that their legacy would live on even after they died.

"But we'll find him," Dread assured her. He sounded confident, but then he'd always sounded as if he knew what he was doing. "And you can help us search for him. And maybe you can even find a way to destroy him."

***

Bee couldn't look her in the eye, Elaine realised. How could he? Her gaze was intimidating now, intimidating in a way that her magic had never been. Hundreds of books on psychology flashed through her mind – half of them seemed to disagree with the other half – and suggested that men would have problems with such a serious power imbalance. And *that* was strange. Elaine had never had the raw power of Millicent, let alone the senior wizards.

"My mistress is summoning me home," Bee said,

reluctantly. They'd kissed, but little else. The fire was gone. "After Lady Light Spinner became the Grand Sorceress, I completed the political deals the Empress wanted and she called me home."

And he hadn't fought it either, Elaine realised. She didn't need to read minds to understand that their relationship had been destroyed. The Witch-King had had the last laugh there, if nowhere else. Elaine's eyes showed her taint to anyone who cared to look. Perhaps she'd have to start copying Lady Light Spinner and hide her eyes behind a blindfold.

"Write to me from time to time, all right?" she asked. He wouldn't, she knew. "I can put in a good word for you at the Great Library."

Elaine kissed Bee one final time, and then walked out of his apartment.

She didn't let herself cry until she was safely back home.

***

"How do I look?"

"A very sexy librarian," Daria said, mischievously. "What does your new boyfriend think of it?"

Elaine snorted. The spells that bound the librarian to the Great Library were complex and almost unbreakable. Elaine now had a connection to the building that no one else could match, even if it did leave her wondering if she should be made of stone instead of living flesh from time to time. The Great Library was alive, almost intelligent – and it was now part of her.

"The Library is just glad to have a new librarian," Elaine said, honestly. It was difficult to say what, if anything, the Library thought of individuals. Miss Prim had also been bound, if unwillingly, to the Library – and *she* had tried to steal from it. "I think it was a little upset by what happened last week."

She kept her voice light, despite the odd feeling that she'd become a prisoner without quite realising it. The Great Library held her now, keeping her within the city; there would be no more trips to anywhere outside the Five Peaks. At least she wasn't trapped inside the building...but then, maybe there would come a time when she didn't want to leave.

"Good luck," Daria said, as they reached the main doors. The Great Library staff had already been told that Elaine would take Miss Prim's position. Irritatingly, half of the staff had already signalled their intention to leave the Library. With so many senior wizards dead, there were all kinds of opportunities opening up. "Want me to join you for dinner?"

Elaine smiled as she felt the Library's impatience. "And dancing afterwards?"

She waved goodbye to her friend and stepped through the door. The Great Library welcomed her, its presence reaching out to meet her mind. Where better for a bookworm to live than a library? It was happy to have her back within its walls and she felt the same way too.

Elaine smiled as she saw the staff and then tried to put a stern expression on her face. The Great Library was going to be very busy very soon, as thousands of sorcerers started studying for the new positions that were opening up, and they had to be ready. And the Witch-King might still be out there...

But for the moment, she was happy. And that was all that she had ever wanted.

The End

Elsewhen Press

a small independent publisher specialising in Speculative Fiction

Visit the Elsewhen Press website at elsewhen.co.uk for the latest information on all of our titles, authors and events; to read our blog; find out where to buy our books and ebooks; or to place an order.

Elsewhen Press

a small independent publisher specialising in Speculative Fiction

THE ROYAL SORCERESS
CHRISTOPHER NUTTALL

It's 1830, in an alternate Britain where the 'scientific' principles of magic were discovered sixty years previously, allowing the British to win the American War of Independence. Although Britain is now supreme among the Great Powers, the gulf between rich and poor in the Empire has widened and unrest is growing every day. Master Thomas, the King's Royal Sorcerer, is ageing and must find a successor to lead the Royal Sorcerers Corps. Most magicians can possess only one of the panoply of known magical powers, but Thomas needs to find a new Master of all the powers. There is only one candidate, one person who has displayed such a talent from an early age, but has been neither trained nor officially acknowledged. A perfect candidate to be Master Thomas' apprentice in all ways but one: the Royal College of Sorcerers has never admitted a girl before.

But even before Lady Gwendolyn Crichton can begin her training, London is plunged into chaos by a campaign of terrorist attacks co-ordinated by Jack, a powerful and rebellious magician.

The Royal Sorceress will certainly appeal to all fans of steampunk, alternate history, and fantasy. As well as the fun of the 'what-ifs' delivered by the rewriting of our past, it delights with an Empire empowered by magic – all the better for being one we can recognise. The scheming and intrigue of Jack and his rebels, the roof-top chases and the thrilling battles of magic are played out against the dark and unforgiving backdrop of life in the sordid slums and dangerous factories of London. Many of the rebels are drawn from a seedy and grimy underworld, while their Establishment targets prey on the weak and defenceless. The price for destroying the social imbalance and sexual inequality that underpin society may be more than anyone can imagine.

As an indie author, Christopher Nuttall has published a number of novels through Amazon Kindle Direct Publishing. *The Royal Sorceress* is his first novel to be published by Elsewhen Press. Chris is currently living in Borneo with his wife, muse, and critic Aisha.

ISBN: 9781908168184 (epub, kindle)
ISBN: 9781908168085 (400pp, paperback)

For more information visit bit.ly/TheRoyalSorceress

Visit the Elsewhen Press website at elsewhen.co.uk for the latest information on all of our titles, authors and events; to read our blog; find out where to buy our books and ebooks; or to place an order.

About the Author

Christopher Nuttall has been planning sci-fi books since he learned to read. Born and raised in Edinburgh, Chris created an alternate history website and eventually graduated to writing full-sized novels. Studying history independently allowed him to develop worlds that hung together and provided a base for storytelling. After graduating from university, Chris started writing full-time. As an indie author, he has published a number of novels through Amazon Kindle Direct Publishing. In 2012, Elsewhen Press published his alternate history / fantasy novel *The Royal Sorceress*. *Bookworm* is his second novel to be published by Elsewhen Press. Chris is currently living in Borneo with his wife, muse, and critic Aisha.